Jack McDevitt is a former naval officer, taxi driver, English teacher and motivational trainer, and is now a full-time writer. Twelve of his novels have been Nebula finalists. *Seeker* won the award for Best Novel in 2007. In 2015 Jack won the Robert A. Heinlein Award, given to an author of outstanding published works in science fiction and technical writings that inspire the human exploration of space. McDevitt was selected as the winner in recognition of his body of work, which includes over twenty-one novels and eighty-one short stories. Jack lives in Georgia with his wife Maureen.

Praise for Jack McDevitt:

'A fascinating story with exceptionally well written characters and extremely believable world building' myshelfconfessions.com

'Full of adventures, tension and some cliffhangers...classic hard science fiction' Jacksonville.com

'You're going to love it even if you think you don't like science fiction. You might even want to drop me a thank-you note for the tip before racing out to your local bookstore to pick up the Jack McDevitt backlist' Stephen King

'"Why read Jack McDevitt?" The question should be: "Who among us is such a slow pony that s/he isn't reading McDevitt?"' Harlan Ellison, Hugo and Nebula Award winner

'You should definitely read Jack McDevitt' Gregory Benford, Nebula and Campbell Award winner

Jack McDevitt

COMING HOME

headline

The right of Jack McDevitt to be identified as the Author of
the Work has been asserted by him in accordance with the
Copyright, Designs and Patents Act 1988.

First published in Great Britain in 2014 by
HEADLINE PUBLISHING GROUP

First published in paperback in Great Britain in 2015 by
HEADLINE PUBLISHING GROUP

1

Cataloguing in Publication Data is available from the British Library

ISBN 978 1 4722 0333 5

Typeset in Sabon LT Std by Palimpsest Book Production Ltd,
Falkirk, Stirlingshire

Printed and bound in Great Britain by
Clays Ltd, St Ives plc

HEADLINE PUBLISHING GROUP
An Hachette UK Company
Carmelite House
50 Victoria Embankment
London EC4Y 0DZ

www.headline.co.uk
www.hachette.co.uk

For Ginjer Buchanan,
longtime editor, inspiration, and friend

ACKNOWLEDGMENTS

I'm indebted to Michael Bishop for his advice and intuition; to Walter Cuirle and David DeGraff for technical guidance; to Sara Schwager, the copy editor; to my agent, Chris Lotts; to Mike Resnick; and especially to my wife, Maureen, who always has to read the second draft.

Dates not classified as Common Era (C. E.)
are based on the Rimway calendar.

PROLOGUE

When Alex Benedict graduated high school, his uncle Gabe, the only parent he'd ever known, provided the ultimate gift: a flight to Earth, the home world, the place where everything had started. It was a mixed blessing, though. Alex had a hard time adjusting to interstellar travel, though he didn't like to admit it. The jumps in and out of transdimensional space upset his stomach. And the constant changes in gravity levels never helped. But there was no way he would pass on the opportunity to see the oceans and mountains so prominent in his reading. And the great cities, Paris and Denver, Berlin and Shanghai. And the Alps and the Grand Canyon. The pyramids, the Great Wall, and the Arkon. And, for Gabe's sake, he pretended to be enthusiastic about touring the world capital in Winnipeg.

What most excited him was that Gabe had promised to include a visit to the Moon. That, of course, had been the stage for everything, where Neil Armstrong had climbed out of Apollo 11, stepped down onto the ground, and delivered his giant-leap statement.

But he was surprised to discover, on their arrival, that Armstrong's footprints were no longer there. "What happened to them?" he asked Gabe.

His uncle frowned. "Actually, nobody knows." Gabe was tall, with black hair beginning to gray, and sharp features that had been hardened by so many years digging into archeological sites under alien suns. "They were there for a while, but they disappeared during the Dark Age. Vandals, probably." Gabe shook his head. "Idiots." They were seated at a small round table in an observation lounge, drinking sodas and looking across the shops and hotels and cottages that covered the lunar surface at MoonWorld, the multiplex area reserved for tourists and shielded by a semitransparent dome. A few kilometers away, the cluster of walls and beams and platforms that had been the original Moonbase lay serenely in the vacuum, illuminated by the glow of the home world, which never moved from its position just over the horizon.

Alex leaned back in his seat. "Nine thousand years," he said. "It just doesn't look that old."

"Time tends to stand still in places like this, Alex. If you don't get wind and rain, nothing changes."

Alex picked up a change of expression, a darkening of mood. "What's wrong, Uncle Gabriel?" he said.

"I was just thinking how much I'd have enjoyed walking around and looking at the Apollo landers. The first manned spaceships."

"What happened to them?"

"They were here for over a thousand years. But when everything collapsed, they took all that stuff back to Earth. Too many people had access to the Moon by then, and they wanted to preserve as much as they could. So they put the landers in museums. Primarily in the Space Museum in Florida. Most of the rest of it went to the Huntsville Space Museum, where they were keeping other artifacts from the Golden Age. Eventually, though, they had to move it out of there, too, because they were losing control of the area. There'd been a worldwide economic collapse. Alabama just wasn't safe anymore. There was a lot of material from the first thousand years of off-world exploration. Helmets, personal gear belonging to the astronauts, electronic records from the early flights. Absolutely priceless stuff."

"So where'd they move it to?"

"Some of it was taken to Centralia. Which in those days was called the Dakotas. We don't know how much. Or what actually was saved." A look of weariness came into his eyes. "Whatever was left was put into a storage facility there. After that, we don't know what happened to it."

"It would be nice to find them," said Alex.

"Yes, it would. Some people have devoted their lives to trying to figure out what happened. Huntsville had artifacts from the very beginning of the space era. From the Florida Space Museum. From Moonbase. From Tyuratam. I'd give anything to have been able to look through all that."

"Florida was underwater by then, I guess?"

"Yes."

"What happened to the Apollo flight modules?"

"They were left at the Florida Space Museum and went under with the rest of the state."

"I bet you'd like to have one of those, Uncle Gabe."

Gabe took on a negative look. "I'm not sure what it would sell for. It's not exactly the kind of thing you could put on a bookshelf."

"You're kidding."

Gabe smiled. "Alex, I'd give anything just to have a chance to *touch* one of them." He sighed. "It's a pity."

"I don't think I'd have wanted to be around during a dark age. It's odd, though. They had interstellar flight. And data retrieval and everything."

Gabe nodded. "None of it matters if you have an unstable society and tin-pot dictators. They had several hundred years of economic collapse. Widespread poverty. A few people at the top had all the money and influence. They had terrible overpopulation, struggles over water and resources. Civil wars. And widespread illiteracy." The thirty-second to the thirty-ninth century. "It's a wonder we survived."

"But there were other worlds. Other places. How could they all have collapsed? I've read the books. I know what they say about greed and corruption. But I still don't understand how people let it happen."

"The colony worlds weren't self-sufficient at the time, Alex. So they just got taken over. People with money and influence gradually pushed everyone else out of the way. It was like a disease."

They sat quietly for a couple of minutes. Alex finished his soda and put the glass down. "Uncle Gabe, this would probably be a good place for a dig site. You ever think about coming here?"

"They don't allow it, son." He looked out at a crater rim. "I don't think there's much here anyway. The place has gotten a pretty thorough sweep."

They strolled over to the museum. There were about forty people inside, wandering among the showcases, buying souvenirs, looking at portraits of astronauts and pilots and ships ranging from the Apollo vehicles to modern interstellars. They went into the showroom, which offered a virtual tour of the original Moonbase. Posters informed them the tour would show the facility as it had been on the morning of March 2, 2057, when the first manned voyage to Jupiter was nearing its objective. "Sounds like fun," said Gabe. "Why don't we watch?"

"Jupiter's the big planet, right?" asked Alex.

"Yes. If it hadn't been for Jupiter, we probably wouldn't be here."

"Really? Why's that?"

"It acted as a sweeper. Cleared out a lot of the debris that would have rained down on Earth. Usually, if you don't have one of those in the planetary system, life stays pretty primitive. If it gets moving at all."

"The Jupiter flight was the first manned mission after Mars, right?"

"Yes. Mars was the first off-world settlement. Unless you count Moonbase, of course."

"I *know* that." Alex made no effort to hide his annoyance.

"Sorry," said Gabe.

"You know, Uncle Gabe, I can't imagine how they traveled around in those days without a star drive. It must have taken forever to get anywhere."

"It was fairly slow going, kid."

"I mean, they needed *three days* to get to the Moon."

Gabe laughed. "Yeah. They did. That's correct."

Alex looked out at the Earth. "You can almost *touch* it."

They sat down in a theater area with about a dozen other people and put on headphones. The lights dimmed, and soft music filtered in. *"Good morning, Alex,"* said an amiable female voice. *"Welcome to Moonbase."* The lights came back up, and Alex's chair seemed to be moving along a curving corridor. His uncle was beside him. The others were gone. *"My name is Leah,"* the voice continued. *"If you wish at any time to stop the tour, simply push the red button on the right arm of the chair. Push the yellow button to speak to your uncle."*

The corridor was cramped and gray. Not at all like the tasteful, spacious passageways of MoonWorld.

They turned left into an austere meeting room. Several people were seated on narrow chairs, and a young man in uniform was apparently checking off names and assigning quarters. Everybody wore odd clothing, the kind you saw in historical films. Hairstyles were strange. There was a pomposity in the way the women wore theirs. Girls looking like that would have been laughed out of Alex's old high school. And the men all had facial hair. As if they were trying to look like people who desperately needed to be taken seriously. Most striking, though, there were people of different colors. Racial variations had long since gone away in most areas of the Confederacy after thousands of years of intermarriage. *"Moonbase was established in 2041,"* said Leah, *"by a private corporation. Originally, the plan had been that it would be a government operation. Eventually, however, it became clear that wouldn't work. Moonbase, Inc. came into existence, made possible by an agreement among seventeen nations and eleven corporations."*

Their chairs navigated out of the meeting room. *"We are now in the living quarters,"* said Leah. *"Forty apartments are available for* staff. *Another thirty for visitors. The Galileo Hotel provides forty additional rooms.*" They passed through a doorway and found themselves in the lobby of the Galileo. A cube-shaped transparent pool was elevated overhead. There were probably twenty kids and a half dozen adults swimming and splashing around while others watched from the sides.

"Nice place," said Alex.

"*If you mean the pool,*" Leah said, "*it was so popular that they had to enlarge it on three different occasions.*" She took them to one of the apartments. "*As you can see, it's smaller than those available today.*" But it looked comfortable. The bed folded out of a wall. A display screen was mounted on the opposite side. Beneath the screen, on a table, was an electronic device. "*It's a computer,*" Leah explained. "*Note the keyboard. It's not unusual for the time. Data storage was still in a relatively primitive state.*"

"Did any of them survive?" asked Gabe. "I mean, any of the computers they had at Moonbase?"

"*There is one, which you can find at the Paris Deep Space Museum.*"

"What happened to the others?"

"*They disappeared, along with virtually everything else, during the Dark Age.*"

Gabe took a deep breath.

The Moonlight Restaurant was the most misnamed facility Alex had ever seen. It was cramped, with dull yellow walls and drab chairs and tables, overflowing with maybe thirty people. They drifted past a souvenir shop, whose shelves were filled with magazines and jigsaw puzzles and pullover shirts, some with images of the Moon and of Moonbase. There were models of a primitive-looking ship that Alex would not have trusted to take him anywhere. "*It's the* Isaac Newton," said Leah. "*It was one of the early vehicles carrying people to Mars.*"

Everything in the shop was sold in packages bearing pictures of other antiquated space vehicles and astronauts in clunky pressure suits. And, of course, a ringed planet. Saturn.

"Uncle Gabe," said Alex, "it's too bad they didn't leave some of the landers up here. Sitting on the Moon, they'd have lasted forever."

"If nobody ruined them."

"Think what one of them would sell for." Alex couldn't resist the comment because he knew how Gabe would react.

"That's not what matters, son."

The souvenir shop blinked off, and Leah took them outside. There was no multiplex in that era. The dome, of course, did not exist either. Several pieces of the automated equipment that had built the structure were scattered across the regolith. Three landing pads had been placed several kilometers away, near what appeared to be a cabin. *"It's actually a subway entrance,"* said Leah. *"It provides transport into the central complex."* They veered off again, toward an array of radio telescopes. *"Solar collectors, Alex. They supply power for Moonbase. If you'll look to your left, you will see that construction is getting started on a nuclear facility. At this time, it was still several years from completion."*

"As you are probably aware, Alex, March 2, 2057, is an historic date."

"Because of the Jupiter flight."

"Correct. Actually, they were going to Europa. They're getting ready inside, so if no one has an objection, we'll go to the command center and see what happens." The lights blinked, and Alex was seated in a wide room with seven or eight people, all watching displays and talking into microphones. The displays were mostly carrying lines of numbers, but one had an image of a gray globe, which had to be Jupiter, and another was showing the rugged, broken surface of a moon. *"Notice the giant red spot on the planet,"* said Leah. *"It's a storm. It was at least five hundred years old at this time, but didn't fade out of existence until the fifth millennium.*

"The person in charge of overseeing the Europa operation is Nazario Conti. He's over to your left." Conti was short but imposing, wearing a relaxed attitude that suggested historic projects were simply part of the normal routine.

"Is that an accurate representation of him?" asked Gabe.

"No. In fact we know he existed and that he was one of the senior

people on-site. But the records have been lost, so we don't really have any idea what he looked like or even that he was present during the operation at this moment."

Gabe did not reply, but his expression said it all. So much was gone.

"I should also add that the language has changed over nine thousand years. We'll have these people speaking Standard."

"What's the name of the ship?" asked Alex.

"The Athena. *It had a crew of seven or eight. Accounts vary. We know that the captain was Andrey Sidorov."*

"Have you a picture of him, Leah?"

"Regretfully, again, we do not."

Something was happening. Conti had been summoned by one of the operators. He pressed a button, and a voice came in over the radio: *"Moonbase, this is* Athena. *We have established orbit around Europa."*

The room filled with applause.

They had dinner in the hotel dining room. It was spacious and elegant, much in contrast with the mundane facilities that had been offered thousands of years earlier at the Moonlight. So far only the iced tea had arrived. Gabe tasted his. "You know," he said, "the difference between what the Moon is now and what it was like during the Golden Age isn't so much the nicer facilities."

"How do you mean?"

"When only Moonbase was here, there was a timelessness about everything. You looked out the window, and you were living in a place that hadn't changed in millions of years. Time probably didn't even seem to exist. MoonWorld, on the other hand, is temporary. Come back next year, and there'll be new shops. They'll have installed a different elevator somewhere." He closed his eyes and smiled sadly. "Imagine how complete the illusion would be if they'd left everything alone. If the landing modules were still out there. If you could still go see the Rover's tire tracks."

Alex nodded. "I guess so."

"Well, in any case, this is where it all began, son. This place marks the height of the Golden Age."

"Before they ran out of things to discover," said Alex.

"Well, I wouldn't put it exactly that way. But I guess you're right: by the middle of the third millennium, we'd exhausted most of the big issues. We knew the universe was governed by mathematics. We knew about evolution. Relativity. Quantum mechanics. Particle theory. Consciousness. We were aware there was no Grand Unified Theory." He shrugged. "Eventually, science became simply a matter of improving existing technologies."

The food arrived. Grilled cheese for Gabe, pork roll sandwich for Alex. "So you're saying there's nothing left to discover?"

"I don't know." Gabe picked up his sandwich. "They're talking about another breakthrough with life extension, but it may not be possible. And they're still trying to find a way to cross to one of the parallel universes. Or for that matter, even to demonstrate they exist. But I think that's about all that's left."

There were a couple of girls seated off to one side. One of them, a blonde, made eye contact with Alex. He tried a smile, but she looked away. "What?" asked Gabe, who noticed he'd been distracted.

"I was just thinking that when the opportunity shows up, you have to make your move."

Gabe started on his meal. "Absolutely," he said.

Alex smiled. His uncle thought his comment had something to do with MoonWorld. Well, maybe it did.

ONE

The Dark Age arrived like a thunderclap. The people of the world thought they were secure, that life would go on as it always had, and that they need not worry about details. So they did not pay sufficient attention to government and culture. They took their collective eye off what mattered. Science provided starships, but in the end the only thing the passengers cared about was a means of escape. Monetary systems collapsed, people quarreled endlessly over issues that could never be settled to everyone's satisfaction, political systems became hopelessly corrupted, and in the end, small armies of political, religious, and social fanatics delayed recovery across six centuries.

—Harold Watkins, *Road to Ruin*, 3711 C.E.

1435, RIMWAY CALENDAR. SEVENTEEN YEARS LATER.

It was a day that started slowly, like most days, then blew up. Twice. The first eruption came while I was tallying the monthly income for Rainbow Enterprises. A light snow was falling when our AI, Jacob, informed me we had a call. "It's from Dr. Earl."

Marissa Earl was an acquaintance of Alex's, a psychiatrist who belonged to his book club. I went back into my office and sat down. "Put her through, Jacob."

Marissa was fond of saying that psychiatry was the only scientific field that was still substantially unpredictable. I'd seen her only a couple of times, once at a fund-raising dinner, and again at a theater presentation. She was active in community arts and ran a few of the local events. When she blinked into my office, she was wearing a large smile while looking simultaneously troubled. But there was no missing the excitement. *"It's good to see you again, Chase,"* she said. *"Is Alex in the building?"*

"He's out of town, Marissa."

"Okay. When do you expect him back?"

"In two days. Can I help you?"

She frowned. *"Probably not. Could you get in touch with him for me?"*

Sure, I thought. If I don't mind having to make explanations later. Alex doesn't like to have his time away from the office interrupted by anything short of an emergency. "Why don't you tell me what's going on, and we can take it from there?"

Marissa was relaxed on a couch. A box rested on the seat beside her. She glanced down at it, leaned back, and took a deep breath. *"Does the name Garnett Baylee mean anything to you?"*

"It rings a bell, but I don't recall—"

"He was my grandfather. An archeologist." Her eyes softened. *"I never really saw much of him. He spent most of his time on Earth. Doing research. And, I guess, digging. He was especially interested in the Golden Age."*

"That's a period Alex has always been intrigued by, too, Marissa." It must have been a wild time. Nuclear weapons that could have ended the species overnight. The development of data processing and mass communications. People getting off-world for the first time. And, of course, it was when the big scientific discoveries were being made. Those who were around during those years saw incredible changes. New technologies constantly showing up. Diseases that had been fatal when you were a child were wiped out by the time you had kids of your own. Not like today, when stability rules. Or, as some physicists would say, boredom.

"He had a huge collection of books, fiction, from those years. My dad said he was always watching shows set in that period. And he was infuriated that so much had been lost."

"I'm not sure I know what you're referring to," I said. "We still have pretty good visual records of the third millennium. We know its history. There are a few holes, but by and large—"

"*I'm not talking about the history. What he cared about were the artifacts. Have you been to Earth, Chase?*"

"Yes. I've been there. Once."

"*There's not much left from the years when they were going to the Moon. It's all gone. Other than a few old buildings and some dams. My grandfather was always looking for stuff. Like maybe a pen that Marie Curie had used. Or a chair that belonged to Charles Darwin. Or maybe Winston Churchill's reading lamp.*" She shrugged. "*According to my father, it was his life. He spent years on Earth trying to track things down.*"

I wondered who Darwin and Curie were. "How'd he make out?"

"*He found a few things. An old radio. A few lost books. Nothing that was connected specifically to any historical figure, though——*"

"Books? Anything significant?"

"*Yes. One was* Tender Is the Night."

"Really? He was the guy who found that?"

"*That's correct.*"

"I think he and Alex would have gotten along pretty well."

"*He contributed most of what he found to the Brandenheim Museum. It's on display. You can take a look next time you're down there. They have a whole section dedicated to him.*"

"Sounds as if he had a decent career. You say you didn't see much of him?"

"*When I was about fourteen, he came back here to live with us. I'd only seen him once or twice before that, but I was so young, I can barely remember it. I was surprised to discover that our house belonged to him.*" She was looking past me, into another time. "*He apologized for not being around when I was younger. He was a nice guy. Did you know he found the only existing wristwatch? You know what that was?*"

"I've seen them in the old clips."

"*It didn't belong to anyone in particular, as far as we know. It was just a watch.*"

"Okay." The snow was coming down harder. "What actually can we do for you, Marissa?"

"*His room was on the second floor. He was with us for about seven years. But then he had a stroke, and we lost him. That was almost eleven years ago. Dad eventually took over the room and used it as his office. And I guess nobody ever really cleaned it out. Recently, we came across something on a shelf in one of the upstairs closets.*" She removed the lid from the box. My angle wouldn't let me see inside it, but I had a pretty good idea where this was leading.

"Well, Marissa," I said, "whatever it is, I'm sure we'll be able to get you a decent price for it."

"*Good. That's what I was hoping you'd say.*" She reached into the box and took out a black electronic device, wrapped in a cloth. She set it on the seat beside her.

"What is it?" I asked.

"*I took it to the Brandenheim. I thought the guy I was talking to would go crazy. He tells me it's a—*" She stopped and checked her link. "*It's a Corbett transmitter. It's for sending messages through hyperspace. This one is apparently an early version. They thought I was going to donate it, which I had originally intended. I just wanted to get rid of it. But I got the impression it's worth a lot. So I backed off. They got annoyed.*" She smiled. "*I guess I'm not much like my granddad.*"

"Okay," I said. "We'll take a look. When Alex gets back, he can check the record, and if he needs to see it, we'll have you bring it over."

"*Fine. I'd like to get an estimate of the value. You don't have any idea, do you?*"

"No, Marissa. I've never seen one of these things before."

"*Oh,*" she said. "*I thought you were a pilot.*"

"In my spare time, yes." I was running a quick check on my notebook. And got a jolt. "Holy cats," I said.

"*What? What is it, Chase?*"

"The Corbett is the breakthrough unit. It's the earliest model there was." The information I was getting indicated it dated from the twenty-sixth century. The early FTL flights had no reasonable way to talk to Earth. Until the Corbett came along. If the Brandenheim had it right, the thing was over eight thousand years old. There was only one known model in existence. So, yes, it was going to have some serious trade value. "Your grandfather never told you he had this?"

"*No. He never mentioned it.*"

"He must have said something to your parents."

"*My dad says no. He never knew it was there until he went into the closet to put some wrapping paper on the top shelf. There were already a couple of boxes on top of it, and a sweater. There wasn't enough room, so he took everything down.*" She looked at the transmitter. "*This was in a case. It was the first time he'd seen it. In fact, he came close to tossing it out. Fortunately, he showed it to me on his way to the trash can.*"

"All right. We'll get back to you."

"*The museum says if I contribute it, they'll put up a permanent plate with my name on it.*"

"Is that what you want to do?"

"*Depends how much I can get for it.*"

"You say your grandfather gave them some artifacts?"

"*Yes.*"

"But they didn't recognize this when you showed it to them? I mean, he hadn't shown it to them at some point himself?"

"*Apparently not. Maybe it was just something he decided to keep. Maybe he forgot he had it. He was getting old.*"

I nodded. "Jacob, can you give me a three-sixty on this thing?"

Jacob magnified the transmitter and closed in on it. I got a close-up of the controls. Then he rotated the angle. It wasn't especially striking, and it looked like a thousand other pieces of communication gear. About the size of a bread box. The exterior had a plastene appearance. There was a push pad, some dials, selectors, and a gauge. Imprints and markers were all in ancient English. And a plate on the back. "Jacob," I said, "translate, please."

"It says 'Made by Quantumware, 2711, in Canada.'"

One side appeared to have been scorched. I ran a search on Quantumware. It had been the manufacturer of the early FTL communication units. I was hoping to see *Judy Cobble* engraved on it somewhere, or the name of one of the other early starships.

"The people at the Brandenheim," said Marissa, *"say it's just an identification plate."* She looked momentarily unhappy. *"They can't match it up to anything because it's so old."*

Most people establish an online avatar, creating a more or less permanent electronic presence that can represent them if they're out of town. Or after they've passed away. Usually, the avatar looks exactly like the person for whom it substitutes. But like the original, it can be unreliable. People create them to make themselves look good, possibly to mislead others, and to lie like a bandit, if that's what it takes to make the desired impression. And it provides a kind of immortality. "Marissa," I said, "would you object to our contacting your grandfather's online presence?"

"He didn't have one."

"Really?"

"According to my father, there was *an avatar at one time. But he must have gotten rid of it."*

"Okay. Did he come back on a transport?"

"Back from where?"

"Earth."

"I don't know. I can check with my father. Probably."

"Okay. Do that. See if he remembers. Did your grandfather ever say anything that might have led you to believe he'd made a major find?"

"Not to me. At least not that I recall. My folks said he was disappointed when he came home. That he was depressed. It didn't exactly sound like a guy who was returning after making a major discovery."

I looked helplessly at Marissa.

"Finished?" she asked.

"Who can we talk to about him? Any of his colleagues who might know something?"

"Lawrence Southwick, maybe." Head of the Southwick Foundation, known principally for underwriting archeological initiatives.

"He was a friend of my grandfather's. He's retired now. I don't know that Grandpop was close to anybody else."

Garnett Baylee had been a much-admired charismatic figure. He'd been a popular speaker at fund-raisers, but had apparently never accepted any remuneration other than expenses. The money had been funneled primarily to the Southwick Foundation, but he'd also made contributions to other organizations that supported archeological work, especially with a concentration on the Golden Age.

I was surprised to discover that Baylee had never collected a degree. He'd claimed to be an archeologist but had never gotten around to meeting the formal qualifications. Everyone seemed to know that, but it hadn't mattered. His passion had replaced the formalities. He'd made a running joke of the pretense, using it to display his respect for a profession, frequently playing off comments that implied he wasn't smart enough to join. I watched a couple of his performances. He would have made a superb comedian had his passion for recovering lost history not been also on display. The archeological community loved him. And watching him, I regretted never having met him.

There were thousands of photos, covering his lifetime. There he was at about four years old, already digging holes in the lawn. And at about sixteen in a canoe with an attractive but unidentified redhead. They showed him in school and at parties. At weddings and ball games. Some pictures showed him with his dark-haired wife, whom he had apparently lost early. Playing games with his kids, and later with his grandchildren, including Marissa. And I saw him on safari, cruising deserts in a skimmer. He stood at dig sites, held up artifacts for the viewer, gave directions to his work crew, and gazed up at pyramids.

People who knew him said that he'd never pursued a degree because he was simply too knowledgeable, too brilliant, leaving him no patience for routine academic work. He simply bypassed it. And apparently lost nothing thereby.

Baylee was more than moderately handsome. Even in his later

years, his features resisted the usual tendency toward gradual decline and ultimate collapse. He was tall, broad-shouldered, and there was something in his eyes that made it clear he was in charge. I could see a distinct resemblance to Marissa, who also showed no reluctance to take over.

It was impossible to imagine this guy's coming up with a major discovery and failing to mention it. I sat there looking at a picture of the transmitter.

The second eruption was delivered by Shara Michaels, who called and invited me to dinner at Bernie's Far and Away.

"Sounds like a last-minute operation," I said. "What's going on?"

"I have some news. Will you be there?"

"What time?"

The Far and Away was crowded. A piano played softly in the background. Shara was seated at a corner table with another young woman, probably in her twenties. She waved me over. "Chase," she said, "this is JoAnn Suttner." Suttner had chestnut hair and wore a gold blouse and light blue slacks. She and Shara had already drawn the attention of a couple of guys at an adjoining table. I sat down, and we shook hands. "JoAnn's working with the SRF," Shara said. "She's the top gun in megatemp research." That was shorthand for time-space structure. SRF, of course, was the Sanusar Recovery Force, a team of scientists dedicated to tracking down the lost ships that had gotten tangled in warps caused by the passage of superdense objects. Sanusar was to have been the final port of call for the *Capella* on that fatal last flight. "Her husband," she added, "is one of the top mathematicians in the Confederacy."

JoAnn rolled her eyes. "She always talks like that, Chase. Anyhow, it's nice to meet you."

"The pleasure's mine, JoAnn. What's going on?"

Interstellars had been disappearing since they first came on the scene back in the third millennium. It's probably inevitable, when you have hundreds of vehicles traveling among the known systems, and beyond, constantly. Losses have been attributed to a variety of causes. Engine breakdown. Power failure. Deflector malfunction, causing a ship to emerge from transdimensional space into an area already occupied by rocks and even too much dust. When that happens, when two objects try to occupy the same space, you can look for a large explosion. A few incidents were even attributable to hijackings.

But it turned out there was another reason for at least some of the disappearances. Black holes and other superdense objects traveling through space tend to leave damage in their wake. Not the kind of damage we'd always known about—disrupted stars, planets ripped from orbit, and so forth—but something else entirely. The space/time continuum itself could become twisted. Warped. The result has been that some vehicles, jumping into or possibly out of transdimensional space, got sidetracked. And lost control. They became wrapped in the time/space distortion, and carried a piece of it with them. It continued to affect the vehicle, moving it along its projected course, but causing it to reemerge periodically in linear space. It was also apparent that, on board the ship, the passage of time also became distorted. It was, scientists had come to believe, what had happened to the *Capella* eleven years earlier.

We'd recovered three ships since discovering what was happening. In each of them, crew and passengers had known they'd suffered a malfunction, but they'd been totally unaware that weeks and years had been passing in the outside world. One of the three, the *Avenger*, was a destroyer that had disappeared during the Mute War two centuries ago. For the crew, only four days had passed between making their jump and being rescued. The first recovery had been the *Intrépide*, which had, incredibly, left its home port seven thousand years earlier. From the perspective of the passengers, the flight had lasted only a few weeks.

The lost ships were by then commonly referred to as Sanusar objects, named for the world that was to have been the *Capella*'s final port of call.

"I'll tell you what's going on," said Shara. A big smile took over her features. "We think we've found the *Capella*."

"Really?" I said.

"Yes. It looks good this time."

They'd predicted an arrival more than a year earlier, but the lost ship hadn't shown up. "You're not going to get everybody excited again, are you? And then leave them watching blank screens?"

"Chase," said Shara, "I'm sorry. We're still in the early stages of research on this stuff."

They thought they'd known where it would be coming in, but the evidence had never arrived, nor, when they sent out a couple of vehicles just to be certain, had the ship. For Alex and me, it was personal. Gabriel Benedict, my former boss and his uncle, was among the passengers. He'd left a message for Alex, informing him about the *Tenandrome*, which had seen something during an exploratory voyage that the government wanted to keep quiet. It had been the *Tenandrome* that had brought Alex and me together. "What makes you think you have it this time?"

JoAnn picked up the conversation. "I'm sorry, Chase. I can imagine what you must have gone through. We'd have kept it quiet until we were certain had we been able to, but there was just no way to do that. But we should be able to do something positive this time. I know everybody thinks we gave up on it. But we didn't. One of the things we did was to check the record for every sighting that came anywhere near the *Capella*'s projected course over the last eleven years. And we got lucky. There was a sighting through one of the telescopes in the Peltian System. We couldn't be sure that it *was* the *Capella*. All we got was a glimpse of radiation, but it was located where we'd expected to see her. We sent a ship out, and they picked up a radio signal. And it *was* the *Capella*."

"Beautiful," I said. "What did the signal say?"

"About what you'd expect. That they were lost and were requesting assistance."

"When did it happen?"

"A little over five years ago. The original sighting, that is. Nobody thought anything of it at the time. I mean, we weren't looking for

Sanusar objects then. Nobody really even knew they existed. But when we saw it, we went out and tracked the signal down. It was aimed toward where Rimway would have been if this were still 1424." The year when the *Capella* had vanished.

"So," I said, "you know when it left Rimway, and when it reappeared. So you know—"

"—When we can expect it again and where it should be. Yes." Both of them were beaming. I probably was, too.

"When's it going to happen?"

JoAnn passed the question to Shara, who apparently handled the trivia. "In a bit more than three months," she said. "It'll be here on the first day of spring, give or take a day or two."

"First day of spring? That sounds like a good omen."

The callbox inquired whether we were ready to order. We took a minute to comply, then I asked the critical question: "What are we going to do when it happens? Judging from what we've seen with the other vehicles, we'll only get a few hours' access. That's not much time to locate it, get to it, and take twenty-six hundred people off."

Shara nodded. "That's the bad news. We probably won't be able to rescue everyone this time around. Although JoAnn's been working on something."

Our coffee arrived. JoAnn picked up her cup, looked out at the snow, which had eased off a bit, and put it back down without tasting it. "It might be possible," she said, "to manipulate the drive unit and shut down the cycle."

"You mean to keep the ship from going under again?"

"Yes. We might be able to stop the process dead in its tracks."

"How optimistic are you?"

"We have a pretty decent chance, actually. Somewhere around a ninety percent probability."

"Wow," I said. "That's great news."

JoAnn nodded, but didn't look happy. "There's a downside."

"Oh."

"There's also a possibility we could send the ship out somewhere

where we'd lose it again." Her eyes blazed. "Or we might destabilize everything and destroy it altogether. That's why we haven't been making a lot of noise about it."

"Is there any way you can eliminate that possibility? I mean, can you run an experiment or something?"

This time she *did* taste the coffee. "Unfortunately, there's a level of uncertainty about all this that we may never get rid of. Not completely. I don't know. The ranking genius on all this is Robert Dyke."

"I've heard of him," I said. "But wasn't he—?"

"That's correct. Like your uncle, he was also on the *Capella*. He's maybe the one person in the Confederacy who could work all this stuff out."

"So what are we going to do?"

"Well, you said the right word, Chase. We're going to run an experiment."

"Good. I hope you guys will keep us informed."

"We can do better than that," said Shara. "You and Alex have been a big part of this since the beginning. You can come along if you like. We're going to put a yacht into the warp, hopefully get it tangled, then see if we can unwrap it. Stabilize it."

"That sounds like a good idea," I said. "And we have an invitation? When?"

"We'll be getting set up tomorrow," said JoAnn. "So figure we leave the day after."

Shara smiled uncomfortably. "Sorry about the short notice, Chase. But we just got clearance, and time is a priority."

TWO

The black hole is nature's ultimate assault on the notion of a reasonable, friendly universe. No advantage can be extracted from its existence. It adds nothing to the majesty of the natural world. And if there is evidence anywhere that the cosmos does not give a damn for its children, this is it.

—Margaret Wilson, *Flameout*, 1277

I called Alex that night and told him about the *Capella*. "*That's good news,*" he said. "*I hope they can make something happen. Suttner has a pretty good reputation.*"

"She seemed kind of young for a genius."

"*That's the way it usually goes with physicists, Chase. Make your mark before you hit thirty, or you're out of the game.*"

"They're running a test of some sort in a couple of days," I told him, "and they've invited us to go along."

"*In a couple of days? No way I can make that. But you're going, right?*"

"Sure."

"*Okay. Everything in shape at the office?*"

"Yes, Alex. Everything's quiet."

"*What kind of test?*"

"I don't really have details. They want to find out whether they can tinker with the drive and stabilize the thing."

"*Okay. But be careful. Don't volunteer for anything.*"

"Relax, Alex. Everything will be fine."

"I'll see you when you get back."

"There's something else," I said. "We might have found a Corbett transmitter."

"A what?"

"A Corbett transmitter."

"Would you want to brief me on what that is?"

That was an enjoyable moment. It's not often I come in ahead of the boss on an archeological find. "It's a twenty-sixth-century hyper-comm transmitter. This was the breakthrough unit."

"You mean for FTL transmissions?"

"Yes." What else could I mean?

"Really? You sure?"

"According to the Brandenheim."

"Where'd it come from?"

"That's the really interesting part of the story. Marissa Earl showed it to me."

"Marissa?" He grinned. *"It has something to do with Garnett Baylee?"*

"That's correct."

"I wasn't entirely serious, Chase. Baylee? Really?" He scratched his temple. *"He's been dead about nine years."*

"Eleven, in fact. They found it in one of the closets in his house."

"Nobody knew he had it?"

"Right. His family still lives there, and they came across it by accident. I have a picture of it if you want to take a look."

"Yes," he said. *"Of course."*

I love watching his eyes light up. *"Chase, did you say whether the museum's made an offer?"*

"No, Alex. I don't know about that. I didn't really want to ask."

He shook his head. Not surprised. *"Well, it doesn't matter. Our clients shouldn't have any problem beating whatever the Brandenheim would be willing to pay. The whole story amazes me, though. Not much of that Golden Age stuff has survived. People have been looking for it for thousands of years. Baylee spent a substantial amount of his life searching for artifacts from that period."* He was frowning. *"I met Baylee a couple of times. He was a nice guy, but he wanted to be the premier archeologist on the planet. I can't imagine he'd have come up with something like this and stuck it in his closet and forgotten about it. I wonder if he was possibly suffering from delusional problems?"*

"I don't know. Marissa didn't say anything to suggest that." For a moment, we stared at each other. Alex was in a time zone three hours later than I was. He looked tired, and it was obvious he was ready to crash for the night. "So," I asked, "do you want me to do anything about this? Should I make an offer? Just to make sure she doesn't let it get away?" Normally, we restrict ourselves to playing middleman in these arrangements. But for something like this—

"It's too early. We don't want to look anxious. Call Marissa tomorrow, though, and tell her not to do anything without checking with us first. Tell Jacob that if she tries to call me, he should put it through."

"Okay. But I should probably mention that she didn't seem to be consulting us about a sale."

"Really? What do you think she wanted?"

"I think she just wanted to get a sense how much it was worth. And maybe talk with somebody who might have an idea why her grandfather would forget he had something like this."

"I can't imagine why she'd expect us to know."

"You've a reputation, Alex. But anyhow, if you prefer, I can call and tell her we can't be of any assistance."

He laughed. *"Ask her to make the transmitter available to us so we can run some tests. Let's just be sure this is what it seems to be."*

The following morning, I called Marissa and relayed Alex's wishes. She told me that she wasn't planning on taking any action for the moment and would wait until we'd had a chance to examine the transmitter. Then, while I was having breakfast, an announcement came over the HV that Ryan Davis, the president of the Confederacy, would be making a statement at the top of the hour. The president was visiting Cormoral, and there was, of course, no way he could speak to us directly from a distance of forty light-years. That meant the message had already been received, and they were trying to expand their audience.

President Davis was a charmer, with brown hair, brown eyes, chiseled features, and a smile that always gave me a sense that he was talking directly to me. But there was no smile this time. *"Friends and citizens,"* he said, *"we are all concerned about recovering, if we can, the people on board the* Capella. *I want to assure you that we have a topflight scientific team, the Sanusar Recovery Force, working to bring its twenty-six hundred passengers and crew home. You can be certain that we are doing everything possible to make it happen.*

"Unfortunately, we are in unknown territory. We have not encountered warped space and time before. I know there is much concern across the Confederacy about this lost ship. And about the others that may be adrift out there somewhere. We are told that time seems to pass at a different rate on the lost ships than it does for us. That is, time passes much more quickly for us. Judging from what we have seen on the other three lost ships that have been recovered, it is likely that only a few days will have passed on the Capella *since they left Rimway eleven years ago. That's difficult to grasp, but our scientists assure us it is a valid picture of what has been happening. It is, they say, likely to be the case with the* Capella. *The situation could be even more extreme. We rescued two girls from the* Intrépide *last year. Cori and Sabol Chaveau. They boarded the ship seven thousand years ago. But while they were in flight, only a few weeks passed. Let me reiterate that we are doing everything possible to protect the lives of the passengers and crew. It is our first priority. We will take no action that will endanger them. And we will do everything possible to bring them home."*

THREE

No matter whether we think of lover, gold, or good times, do not cling to that which is gone. That path leads only to tears.

—Kory Tyler, *Musings*, 1412

I rode the shuttle up to Skydeck. Shara and JoAnn had arrived the day before and were waiting in the restaurant at the Starlight Hotel.

"What actually are we going to do?" I asked.

"We sent a test vehicle out yesterday," said Shara. "It's unmanned, strictly robo. As soon as it gets into the infected area, it'll attempt a jump. We have the drive set so that, if it gets tangled, it should come back into linear space within a few hours—"

"*Our* time," JoAnn said.

"And it'll stay up, we think," Shara continued, "for about four hours."

"And that process will continue?" I asked.

"Yes."

"How far will it travel between appearances?"

"We can't be certain yet, Chase. But we're estimating about one hundred twenty thousand kilometers. The problem develops due to an interface between the drive unit and the warp. When we get to it, it will already have been through the process a couple of times. What we hope to do is adjust the drive feed so that it is not responsive to the change in the continuum."

I was having trouble following. "What does that mean exactly?"

JoAnn obviously thought it was a dumb question. Her eyebrows rose, and her gaze went momentarily toward the overhead. But she managed an understanding smile. "Change the energy feed," she said. "The power level of the drive unit has to be within certain parameters for the ship to stay contained by the warp field. If we adjust the feed, we should be able to stop the process."

"That sounds easy enough."

"If we can get the right setting, yes. It is—"

"And if you get the wrong one—?"

"Probably nothing will happen. If we get it seriously wrong, we might lose the ship. The problem is that we're still learning about the settings. The *Capella* did its transdimensional jump in an area of space that had been damaged a quarter of a million years ago by a superdense object. Probably a black hole but not necessarily. A section of it literally wrapped itself around the ship. The drive unit dragged the vehicle and the section of warp forward. Time is effectively frozen on board. Fortunately, it surfaces at regular intervals for a few hours, before the interaction between the star drive and the warp drags it back under."

The pilot was waiting in the passenger cabin. He said hello, welcomed us on board, and told us his name was Nick Kraus. "Are you related to John?" I asked. John Kraus was the director of the SRF.

"Yeah. He's my brother."

Shara grinned. "Nick usually pilots the big passenger cruisers."

"Like the *Capella*?"

"I've been working the *Morning Star* these last few years," he said. Nick looked good. Brown eyes, amiable smile. A bit taller than you'd normally find in a pilot.

"So you're here as the in-house expert?"

"Something like that," he said. "I'm on loan from Orion Transport. And I'm glad to be here. It's much more interesting work than hauling around a couple of thousand sightseers."

Nick obviously knew Shara and JoAnn. "Chase," he said, "have you been up here before? On Skydeck?"

"On occasion."

Shara smiled. "She's Alex Benedict's pilot."

"The antique dealer?" He showed surprise.

"Yes."

Nick was clearly impressed. "That must be interesting work. Have you gotten a chance to land on ancient space stations?"

"One or two."

"Beautiful. I envy you." He checked the time. "Okay, guys, good luck. You have the course directions?"

"They've already been inserted, Nick."

"Okay. We'll be leaving as soon as we get clearance. Should only be a few minutes. There'll be about forty minutes of acceleration once we get started. I'll let you know before we head out. Meantime, you might get belted down." He disappeared onto the bridge.

We settled into our harnesses. I was happy about getting to ride as a passenger for a change. I could hear Nick talking with the ops people. Then the engines started. "Okay, everybody," he said. "On our way." He had a quiet voice and an easy manner. "Everybody relax and enjoy the flight." So I did. I eased back and looked out the window at the dock as it began to retreat.

"Good luck to us," Shara said to JoAnn. "You pull this off, and they'll be giving you the Presidential Citation."

We passed out of the station. "Okay, ladies," said Nick, "hang on."

The *Capella* was expected to surface about twelve light-years from Rimway, in the general direction of the Veiled Lady. "I'm a little uncomfortable," Nick said, "about getting anywhere near this entanglement. There's no chance we'll get stuck, I hope?"

JoAnn shook her head. "No. The only drive units affected by these things are the Armstrongs. They were being replaced long before we knew about the issue with the space/time warps. We have a Korba drive. Which everybody has these days. But you know that, Nick. So no, there's no need to worry."

"As soon as the *Carver* appears," Shara said, "it'll start transmitting. We should be able to get to it within a day or so."

"That's our experimental yacht?" I asked.

"Yes. The AI's running things."

"I hope this works," I said.

"It'll work." Shara gave me a thumbs-up. "Don't worry."

"If we bring this off, is it over? I mean, will we be able to get everyone off the *Capella* when it shows up? Or will there still be some reservations?"

"What we really need," said JoAnn, "is to run a test on one of the *Capella*'s sister ships. That would eliminate all doubt. We're trying to talk Orion into loaning us the *Grainger*. They've been reluctant because they're afraid we might lose it."

"There's no chance of that happening, is there?"

"Actually, there would be," said JoAnn. "We're in unknown territory."

"It's unfortunate," said Shara, "that TransWorld didn't survive. They wouldn't have had any choice but to cooperate." TransWorld, which had owned the *Capella*, had been bankrupted by the incident, a combination of lawsuits and a general business collapse. Nobody had trusted them afterward.

Nick's voice came over the allcomm. *"Okay, ladies, we'll be making our jump in ten minutes."*

After we got into hyperspace, Shara and JoAnn got talking physics, so I looked for my chance and went onto the bridge. Nick was reading a book and eating a muffin. "How you doing?" I said. "Mind if I join you?"

"Please do." He picked up the box and offered it to me. "They're good."

I took one. "Thank you."

"You're welcome. So is your life as adventurous as it sounds?"

"I wasn't aware it sounded adventurous. Mostly what I do is sit at a desk."

He looked at me for a long moment. "Chase, I'm worried about her."

"Who are we talking about?"

"JoAnn."

"This thing's getting to her?"

"Yes. She feels personally responsible for the lives of the people on the *Capella*."

"How well do you know her, Nick?"

"We've been friends for a few years. We met on the *Grainger*, when she was one of my passengers." He was checking his instruments. "She's the reason I got this assignment."

"How do you mean?"

"The SRF needed someone who was familiar with the operational side of the cruise ships. John was reluctant to ask for me. It didn't look good, I guess. I was his brother, and there'd be some question about his objectivity. But I'd been working with JoAnn on aspects of this for three years. She put in my name, and here I am."

"She seems fine to me, Nick. But I can understand she'd be feeling some pressure. I'm not sure I can do much to lighten the load, but—"

"I know, Chase. Just be aware."

We surfaced on target and, within an hour, picked up an automated transmission from the *Carver*. Nick opened the allcomm: "It's up and running," he said. "Stay belted in. As soon as I can lock down its position, we'll be turning toward it."

It took a while, of course. When he'd gotten a second read on the transmission, he looked at me and shook his head. "We're too far out." Then he was talking to JoAnn again. "We'll need about five hours to get to it."

"*That won't work, Nick,*" she said. "*It will probably have moved on before we'd get there. Head for the next target area. The delta site.*"

"Will do." He looked down at the control panel and went to the AI. "Richard? How far do they expect the next appearance to be?"

"*About forty thousand kilometers, Nick. If it's on schedule, it will be there at 1400 hours.*"

That gave us six hours. He went back to the allcomm: "JoAnn, Shara, we'll be doing some maneuvering, then going through another acceleration. Once we get started, you'll be stuck in the harness for about three-quarters of an hour."

"*Nick,*" said Richard, "*we have another transmission. This one is from Barkley.*"

"JoAnn," said Nick, "we've got Barkley." He signaled me that he was talking about the *Carver* AI.

"*Put him on,*" said JoAnn.

Barkley had a deep bass voice: "Casavant, *everything has gone precisely according to plan. I am caught in the megatemp warp, have already been up and down twice. I am moving within the projected parameters.*"

"Okay, Barkley," said JoAnn. "*We can't get to you before you go under again, so we'll meet you at the delta site.*"

"*Very good. I'll see you then.*"

"*How long have you remained in linear space after coming back up?*"

"*Three hours, fifty-seven minutes, and fourteen seconds on the first appearance. The second one was about three minutes less.*"

"Okay. How much warning have you been getting before you become aware that you're being taken back down?"

"*Less than a minute, JoAnn. About fifty-seven seconds.*"

"*Okay. We'll see you shortly.*"

"*One more thing, JoAnn: What time is it?*"

"*It's 7:57 A.M. Why?*"

"*It's just after midnight here. I wanted to set the clocks to reflect reality.*"

We reached the delta site in advance of the *Carver* and began closing toward the area where it was expected to arrive. But we were uncertain, so Nick kept a slow pace. We got out of our seats and returned to the passenger cabin, where JoAnn and Shara were talking about a rumor they'd heard that President Davis was going to apply pressure on Orion in an effort to obtain use of the *Grainger*.

"Let's hope it happens," said JoAnn. "We really need access to it to lock this thing down." She looked up at Nick. "When the *Carver* shows up, we want to get within visual range. Then, when Barkley feels the process starting again to take him down, *that's* the moment to intervene."

"How exactly do we do that?" he asked.

"We'll be getting readings from Barkley about what's going on in the drive unit. When we have those, I can give him some adjustments. Maybe it'll break the process. Maybe not. We'll have to see what happens. Probably, he'll get hauled down, but he should reappear again within, I hope, a few minutes. And, if we're lucky, that will be the end of it. If it works out—" She stared at me, and those dark eyes glittered. "If everything goes as planned, we'll be a step closer to keeping the *Capella* from taking another five-and-a-half-year dive."

"Pity it's not safe to go on board ourselves to do this," I said. "It would be a little quicker than passing information to an AI."

That brought a glare from Shara, and I realized I was talking too much. "We had a discussion about that," she said. "JoAnn wanted to do it, but John said no." Now she was looking at Nick, but the irritation was fading. "It's too dangerous."

"It would have given us a better shot," said JoAnn.

"Let's let it go, okay?"

"Well, anyhow," I said, trying to recover, "this'll probably work fine."

JoAnn nodded. "I hope so. It took almost four years just to get the math in place. The truth is there are too many elements to be certain. It's not only design and mass, but there are details associated with the drive unit, how much power it generates and how quickly it comes online. And, of course, the nature of the damage that's been done to the continuum. We haven't figured out yet how to lock *that* down. We need more time." She sighed. "This is a place we've never been before, Chase."

The *Carver* reappeared on schedule. *"He's about an hour away,"* said Nick, speaking over the allcomm. I was back in the passenger cabin.

"So far so good." JoAnn looked pleased. "Barkley, is everything okay?"

"Everything seems to be running as planned, JoAnn."

The *Carver* was a low-cost Barringer yacht. They'd been popular at one time, but the company had stopped making them twenty years earlier. Gabe had owned one when I succeeded my mom as his pilot. It was clunky in comparison to the *Belle-Marie*, but it brought back some happy memories. There aren't many of the Barringers around anymore.

It took a bit longer than an hour, but eventually we pulled to within a few kilometers of it, off its port side. "Close enough," JoAnn said. "Let's stay where we are." Barkley's lights were on both inside and out. The ship looked occupied.

"The thing should take effect again in about an hour and a half," said JoAnn.

We watched the display, which gave us a clearer view than we could get looking out the ports.

Nick pointed out that no one had eaten, but he seemed to be the only person aboard with an appetite. He got some chocolate chip cookies from the dispenser, and we all ate a couple.

The *Carver* floated quietly on the monitor, transfixed against the background of stars. I sat staring at it, literally praying, thinking how the evacuation problem was maybe about to go away. The *Capella* would arrive in three months, and we would get everyone off, and it would be over.

And Gabe would be back.

Shara commented that it was a new experience for her. "It's the first time I've been involved in an experiment that had life-and-death consequences."

JoAnn turned away from the display and looked out through the portal at the *Carver*. She wanted to be over there. I could see it in her eyes. My own thoughts were centered on whether we were too close.

I treated myself to a couple more cookies. There wasn't much conversation. JoAnn seemed caught up in her notebook. Shara stayed by the portal for the most part. I thought about going back onto the bridge, but Nick hadn't really suggested he'd welcome that, and I didn't want to intrude. So I stayed in the passenger cabin and watched while the time ran down. JoAnn eventually pushed back in her seat and sighed. "Looks like about fifteen minutes."

The AI posted a countdown on the display.

"Barkley," JoAnn said, "let me know as soon as you feel something starting to happen, okay?"

"Yes, JoAnn. Of course. I'm already sending the readings from the drive unit."

"Okay. Good."

Nick's voice came from the bridge. "You want them posted, too, JoAnn?"

"Yes," she said. Then she turned to Shara. "I don't think it'll make much difference since I don't really know what I'm looking for."

"It's beginning," said Barkley.

The readings were starting to move. Fuel input. Conversion levels. JoAnn leaned forward, tapped the screen with an index finger. Quantum resistance. "We're in business. Damn it. I wish I were over there."

"Why?" demanded Shara. "You can't do anything there that can't be managed from here."

"Maybe not. But the reaction would be a bit quicker. Okay, Barkley, cut the feed by point two two."

"Complying. But everything's becoming transparent."

JoAnn was studying the numbers on her display. "It's still too high. Back off to one seven."

"Done—"

The *Carver*'s hull was losing visibility. It faded from the display, but a ghostly silhouette remained. "Shara," she said, "I wanted to be there because time of response is everything."

And the *Carver* was gone.

"All right," said JoAnn. "Good so far."

Nick came in off the bridge. "You mean because it hasn't exploded?"

"I mean because nothing has happened. That's okay. I would have preferred seeing it stay visible. But let's relax. Time is passing at a different clip inside the ship. If we got it right, it may take a while for us to see some results."

Nick looked puzzled. "You said a few minutes."

"I was being optimistic."

So we sat and watched.

"It might just go downstream and surface at the epsilon point," said Shara.

JoAnn chewed on her upper lip. "That would indicate it was still caught in the warp. It would be a failure, but not a disaster."

It had been gone twenty-one minutes when we got a transmission. *"JoAnn, I am back up. Not sure where I am."*

Nick was back on the bridge. *"I've got him,"* he said. *"He's on track. About eleven thousand kilometers."*

"Okay," said JoAnn. "Not a complete success, but we've slowed it down."

Shara's eyes closed. "We still don't know where we are."

FOUR

The bird of time has but a little way
To flutter—and the bird is on the wing.

—Edward Fitzgerald, tr., *The Rubaiyat of Omar Khayyam* (c. 1100 C.E.)

Three days later, the *Carver* was still adrift in linear space. The experiment had been partially successful, and people across the Confederacy were toasting JoAnn.

Meantime, I was back at the country house, while Alex's taxi drifted in at midafternoon and descended through bright cold sunlight into the snow cover. He hauled his bags up onto the deck, came inside, and dropped them by the door. "Congratulations, Chase," he said. "Looks as if we're on our way."

"I hope so," I said. "JoAnn says she still can't guarantee anything."

"I'm sorry to hear it."

"So," I asked, "how was the trip?"

He shrugged. "Okay. Fairly routine until you and JoAnn and Marissa got into it." He led the way to the conference room, which also served as a dining area, and sat down in one of the armchairs. "Tell me about the experiment."

"It wasn't quite what they'd hoped for, but JoAnn sees progress." I got us some coffee and described what had happened.

"I'm sorry it wasn't a complete success," he said. "It would have made everything a lot easier."

"JoAnn's looking over the numbers, and they're hoping she'll figure out a way."

"I was talking with John." He meant John Kraus. "This was before you guys went out. He's frustrated. They've been trying to get more ships from the fleet to help. He tells me it will be harder than they realized to break the *Capella* out of the warp because the damned thing is so big. JoAnn has it right, I guess. All they have to experiment with are yachts. They just don't trust the results."

"Maybe they should bring in one of the warships. They don't have any use for them anymore."

"John tells me even those are too small. They need another *Capella*."

"Well, there are a few cruise ships."

"They're working on it. However that goes, John doesn't want to take any chances on losing the ship. He's not going to allow any experimenting with the drive unless they can guarantee the safety of the passengers. It doesn't sound as if that's going to happen."

"So what's the option?"

"The problem is that, because of its mass, the area where it may reappear has gotten a lot bigger. They'll likely need five or six hours just to get somebody alongside."

"That'll probably be a yacht, and take off about ten people."

"That is probably true. Given the time constraints, they won't be able to get more than a couple of hundred people off, at best, when it reappears."

"How long will it be accessible?"

"John says about ten hours."

"It's a nightmare," I said.

"It's why they've been hoping JoAnn could come up with something."

"The fleet won't provide any more?"

"The fleet maintains they don't have any more. Some of the media people claim they're keeping a force available in case the Mutes try to take advantage of the situation."

"Alex, the bad times with the Mutes are over. Doesn't anybody realize that? I mean, the Mutes have announced they'll be sending ships to help with the search."

"I'm not sure everybody in the media recognizes that. President Davis says he's not worried about the Mutes. But he says they have other responsibilities, like keeping ships on station to respond to emergencies. John is so frustrated, he's talking about resigning."

"You don't think he'll do that, do you?"

"No. There's too much at stake. But I suspect he's not very happy that they didn't get more from the experiment." He put the cup down, stared into it for a moment, and got up. "Well, I have some work to catch up on. Talk to you later. And by the way—"

"Yes?"

"If you hear anything more about JoAnn, let me know."

That afternoon, I was scrolling through archeological journals for material on sites that might yield what we like to think of as payoff artifacts when Jacob broke in. *"Chase, CMN is running a program you might find of interest."*

"Okay, Jacob," I said. "Put it on."

A middle-aged woman in a green blouse blinked on in the middle of the room, with Walter Brim, who did human-interest cases for the network. *"Describe it for us, Tia,"* he said.

Tia looked very much like the sort of woman you'd see in a park with kids. She was healthy, probably worked out regularly, and wore her blond hair cut short. But there was a sadness in her eyes. *"It's hard to talk about, Walter, because I've never heard of anyone going through this kind of experience. Eleven years ago, my son Mike took his family, his wife and two sons, on an interstellar trip. They were going to visit Sanusar and Saraglia. They wanted the kids to get a sense of the universe, to see other worlds. I remember being uncomfortable with the idea, but nobody asked me, so I stayed out of it.*

"Next thing I knew, I was hearing reports that the ship, the Capella, *was overdue at Sanusar. Then they said it was lost. My family was dead. I've had to live with that for a long time. Now they're*

saying they're still alive. Not only alive, but that the kids are still kids. That for them it's not 1435, it's still 1424. It's crazy but I assume they know what they're talking about."

"How have you been reacting to that, Tia?" Walter was tall, with dark hair and features that tended to inspire confidence and a willingness in his guests to express their innermost feelings. He looked sadly at her.

"I'm still trying to get my head around it. But okay, good, sure, I don't know how to describe what I felt except that I was so happy I was screaming. The ship was coming back, and a rescue effort was under way. I couldn't believe it. Then they said that they'd only be able to rescue a hundred or so of the passengers. Until the next time it shows up. Which they say will be in 1440. Walter, the ship has twenty-six hundred people on board. And they can only take off a hundred or so every five years." Her voice broke, and she stood wiping her eyes. *"Every five years, Walter. They'll be at this for more than a century."*

"Tia," said the host, "I'm sorry. I know this is hard on you."

"They tell me the kids will still be kids when they get home. That I shouldn't worry because at least they're safe. And I'm glad for that. But I'm not sure I'll live long enough to ever see them again."

"I wish I could help," said Walter.

Tia stiffened. *"Maybe you can. The reason it will take so long is that they don't have enough ships. They have to be able to get to the Capella as soon as it comes back. They're saying it'll take six or eight hours for rescuers to get to them. But after about ten hours, it goes away again. They need more ships. Where's the rest of the fleet?"*

Next came a young man whose parents had been stranded on the disabled vessel. *"I doubt they'll be able to get off right away. They're going to be stuck on that damned thing for nobody knows how long. When they do get back, I'm going to be older than they are. If I'm still here to see them."*

And Admiral Yakata Fox. *"The problem we're having, Walter,"* he explained, *"is that when the tensions with the Mutes ended several years ago, we put most of the fleet in storage. Despite what's being reported, we've made available nearly every ship we have. We've had to keep a few back because we have other responsibilities.*

"The real issue here is not so much a lack of ships as it is the sheer immensity of the target area. We can only estimate within a pretty wide range where the Capella *will appear. When we first started talking about this, it wasn't supposed to be that way. They were telling us we'd be able to pinpoint where it would come back, and we'd just be sitting there waiting. But that turns out to be wrong. They're saying it's too big, and for reasons I don't entirely understand—I'm not a physicist—that widens the area of the search. By a lot."*

Then Headline News, with Roster McCauley, came on. He was seated at a table opposite a black box. *"Earlier this week,"* he said, *"a test mission by the government could have left an AI stranded on a ship that might have disappeared into the warp. Our guest this afternoon"*—he glanced at the black box—*"is Charles Hopkins, representing the National Association for Equal Rights for All Sentients. Charles, what's your reaction?"*

"Roster, I am outraged." I recognized the voice. Charlie, the AI whom Alex and I had brought home from Villanueva, had acquired a last name. *"And I can assure you, we'll be taking action to prevent anything like this from happening again."*

"Okay, Jacob," I said, "you can shut it down."

"There *is* one more clip you might want to see."

It was Alex. He was also a guest on Brim's show.

"Alex," said Walter, *"you were one of the principals who discovered what had happened to the* Capella. *And you have a relative on board. Did you have a suspicion all along that your uncle was still alive?"*

"No. We'd assumed he was gone. We were looking for a missing physicist. Chris Robin. He was the guy who made the discovery about the lost ships."

"Well, Alex, in any case, I know you're happy at least that your uncle has been accounted for. And that eventually, if not in the immediate future, you'll get to see him again."

An odd thing happened then. Alex seemed to look directly at me. *"Yes,"* he said. *"I can't believe it's happening."*

He was careful to say nothing about the delay that would be involved. That the rescue was probably going to go on piecemeal over the better part of a century.

"I was surprised to see the interview," I told him.

"Chase, this is the biggest story the press has had in our lifetime. Of course they're going to give it massive coverage."

"Do you buy the admiral's story? That they're committing the entire fleet to this?"

"I don't think there's any question. President Davis tried to calm the people who are still scared of the Mutes, but that's a hard case to make. People don't forget." He propped his chin on one hand and sighed. "We need a better solution."

"Which is—?"

"Damned if I know."

"Shara said something about a backup plan, but she didn't explain it."

He was frowning. "I hope they have *something*." A cold rain was drumming against the window. "You know, the media have been talking about the effect it will have when people we'd written off as dead are suddenly back in our lives."

"I know. I'm trying to imagine how it would feel to have Gabe walk in."

"Yes. Gabe and the rest of them. Or from *their* perspective. What will it be like to return to friends and relatives who are at least eleven years older than they were just a few days ago? It won't be so bad for the ones we can get off this time around. But imagine the people who will be stuck out there for another quarter century or more. They will have lost the world they know."

FIVE

It's hard to imagine what it will be like opening homes to sons and daughters, to mothers and fathers written off years ago as dead. To seeing again old friends thought lost. There will be a powerful effect from this strange event because we can hardly help being reminded of the impact on our lives of the people around us.

—Editorial, *Andiquar Herald*, Janus 3, 1435

Casmir Kolchevsky showed up the following day on *Jennifer in the Morning*. Kolchevsky was small and compact, a guy who always looked as if he were about to explode. He had scruffy black hair and eyes like those of a cat watching a squirrel. That was when he was feeling friendly. He liked to preach, to make it clear that very few could meet his high intellectual and ethical standards. Whenever he showed up on one of the talk shows, I got uncomfortable because Alex was one of his favorite targets.

Kolchevsky was an archeologist. He claimed to have been a friend of Gabe's though I never saw any evidence of it, and he resented Alex because he made a living trading and selling artifacts that he felt belonged to everyone. He'd said on several occasions that Alex had betrayed the family name. That he was nothing better than a grave robber. But this time, he did not come after us.

The conversation was about the historical information that had already been gleaned from the passengers who'd been aboard the *Intrépide*. "We're now able to talk to people who were actually alive *during the Dark Age. Think about that for a minute. We can acquire some historical knowledge, some serious insights, by sitting down with someone who was there. I'll tell you, Jennifer, we live in a remarkable time."*

Kolchevsky's tone made it clear that he knew everything of significance. No one else's opinion mattered. Which was why listening to him go on about somebody else's perspective came as something of a jolt. Jennifer agreed that he had a point, and asked what he thought could be learned from people who'd begun life in a different era.

"So far," he said, *"they've shown us they were as indifferent about what was happening in their time as we are in ours. Imagine being alive during the Dark Age, when civilization was crumbling. When it looked as if everything was coming apart. When we had starships but no control over the economic and political systems. All I've heard these survivors talk about is what was going on in their personal lives. Were they concerned that things were getting worse and would probably deteriorate completely? That humanity might never recover? I've heard almost nothing about that. It was all about whether they had a job."*

"Come on, Casmir," said Jennifer, *"there've only been two people who go back that far. And they're only kids. You're going to have to wait awhile to talk to the adults from that period. The* Intrépide *won't be back for, what, seventy or eighty years?"*

"That's true, Jennifer. But do you really think the parents of these kids will be any different? No. We know what these people did. How they just stood around and let the world go to hell. Let the oceans rise. Let whole species go extinct. You think they're going to care? They probably won't have even noticed unless their paychecks got cut off."

I stayed with the show not because I wanted to hear what he had to say but because I was waiting for him to give Alex some credit. Without him, I wanted to scream at the little idiot, none of this would be happening.

And finally, near the end, he actually reached out. *"I guess we owe all this to Alex Benedict. I've been a bit hard on him in the past.*

Although he certainly deserved it. But to be fair, I should admit that he's done a serious service for these people. Saved their lives." He smiled across the room at me, that wooden, forced grin that moved his lips without creating any sense of warmth.

When Alex came downstairs, I asked whether he'd seen the show.

"No," he said. "Why?"

"Your buddy was on."

"Which one?"

"Kolchevsky."

Alex immediately looked weary.

"No," I said, "he was okay. In fact, he gave you credit for finding the *Capella.*"

"You're kidding."

"Cross my heart."

"All right. Good. Remind me to send him a Christmas card this year."

One of the panel shows, *Four Aces,* spent time discussing whether they shouldn't go ahead with manipulating the drive unit to prevent the *Capella* from disappearing again. They seldom agreed on anything. But on this occasion, they'd obviously heard about JoAnn's experiment. And they were united in opposing any effort to manipulate the star drive. *"They got lucky with the yacht, they admit that, and they're saying there's no way to be sure what would happen if they start playing around with the* Capella. *So if that's the case, why would anyone want to take chances with the lives of twenty-six hundred people?"*

Shortly after that, Casmir Kolchevsky went missing. I saw the first report on the morning news two days later. Jennifer brought in Jeri Paxton, an anthropologist and a friend of Kolchevsky's to talk about it. Jeri was probably well into her second century, but she retained much of the vigor of youth. *"The only thing I know, Jen,"* she said, *"was that his AI became concerned when he didn't come home for two consecutive nights. Drill—that's the AI, and don't ask about the name—called police. As of now, we just have no idea what happened to him."*

"Have you ever heard of his doing something like this before?"

"No, I haven't. Casmir has always lived by an orderly schedule. I had a chance to talk with Drill last night. He says this is a completely new experience."

"So there's reason to be worried."

"I'm afraid so, yes. And I'll tell you, Casmir seems to some people to have a rough edge, but he's really one of the kindest, gentlest men I know. He's one of a kind, Jennifer. I really hope, wherever he is, that he's okay. If you can hear me out there, Cas, call. Please."

The rational thing to do would have been to leave it to the police to find him. But Alex has never been willing to stay out of this type of affair. "I'm surprised," he told me, "that he has no avatar. Guy like that, with that immense ego, you'd expect there'd be one to represent his various contributions to research and tell us about his awards. But there's nothing."

"Why were you looking?"

"He's disappeared, Chase. Or didn't you notice?"

I ignored the question. "I remember his talking about it one time. The avatar, that is."

"Where was that?"

"Give me a minute." I did a quick search and came up with a three-year-old episode of *The Charles Koeffler Show*. Koeffler notes that Kolchevsky has no avatar, and that it would be easier for hosts to prepare better programing if one were available.

"Most people," the host said, *"especially those who are well-known, maintain an online presence. I wonder, could you—?"*

"Of course they do, Charles." Kolchevsky's smile revealed that he was tolerant of his host's lack of insight. *"Some of us, most of us, I guess, feel a need to establish that we matter. That we leave a mark. But putting a babbling version of yourself out there for every idiot to*

talk to doesn't get the job done. In fact, all it does accomplish is to waste time." Koeffler looked about to jump in, but Kolchevsky waved him off. "*I'm not saying everyone who puts a version of himself online is an idiot, Charles. What I am saying is that our time is limited. If we really want to accomplish something, then by God we should do it. And stop the posturing.*"

"*Are you saying you've never had an avatar?*"

He snorted. "*When I was sixteen, I had one. The girls all laughed at it.*" He sat back, amused at the recollection as the mood lightened. "*There was one girl in particular whom I just loved. In the way that only a sixteen-year-old can. She told me that she could go for the avatar and wished I were more like him.*"

"*So you took it down?*"

"*Charles, do you have one of those things?*"

Koeffler turned it into a joke without answering, and they went to another subject.

Alex shook his head. "If you're in business," he said, "you *have* to have one of those things."

I couldn't resist laughing. Alex was also amused. "I wonder," he said, "what happened to him? To Kolchevsky."

"You don't sound very sympathetic."

"Well, I suspect he's made a few enemies."

"You don't think somebody actually took him down, do you?"

"No, not really. The people he usually went after weren't the type to resort to violence."

"So what do you think?"

"I've no idea. For all we know, he might have fallen into the Melony. But that probably didn't happen or we'd have gotten a pollution problem."

"Alex—"

"Okay, I'll stop. Let me know if you hear anything. If anybody calls, tell them to check with our clients. He might be out berating one of them." He checked the time. "Have to go," he said. "Got an auction."

He rarely brought anything of value back from the auctions, but it happened occasionally. And business was slow. He'd been gone about an hour when we got a call from Fenn Redfield, the police inspector.

"Hi, Chase," he said. *"Is Alex there?"*

"He's downtown on business, Fenn. Can I help you?"

"You know that Kolchevsky's gone missing?"

"Yes. Is Alex a suspect?" I couldn't resist myself.

"Not yet," he said. *"Kolchevsky seems to have just walked off the planet. We're talking to everybody we know who had any kind of connection with him. I'm hoping Alex might have an idea where he could have gone."*

"If he did, Fenn, he wasn't telling me about it. But I'll put you through to him. Hold on a second."

That evening, I closed the office and headed for dinner with friends. Afterward, we went to a concert, drank a little too much, and enjoyed ourselves thoroughly. Later, when I got home, I felt moderately guilty for having a good time while Kolchevsky was maybe dying somewhere. I don't know why that was. I had no more affection for the guy than Alex did. Still, I guess, when people get in trouble, you forget about the kind of treatment you've received from them.

He'd lectured me a couple of times, and hadn't been the only one to warn me that one day I'd regret helping Alex loot the past. That was actually the way he'd phrased it.

I don't know. Sometimes I'm not sure how I feel about the operation we run. I understand that it would be nice if all these artifacts were placed where anyone could see them. But I've also seen the pure joy that accompanies ownership. I've watched older people, who've achieved pretty much everything you could ask from life, just light up when Alex delivered an artifact they'd been pursuing. Especially one touched, or used, by an historical figure. It's not the same as being able to stand in a museum and admire something in a glass case. It has to do with *owning* the thing. With being able to take Byrum Corble's link—the little silver one shaped like a dragon—being able to take it home and put it on display over the mantel.

There are a lot of artifacts. It seems to me there are plenty for public display, and more than enough left over for private collectors. So why not? Why do museums have to control them all?

Why do I feel I have to justify what we do?

When I went to bed, nothing had changed regarding Kolchevsky. He was by then missing almost three days.

In the morning, though, there was news: His skimmer had been found. On the parking lot at a restaurant at the foot of Mt. Barrow. Barrow was about fifteen miles northwest of Andiquar. The police were concentrating their search in that area.

"Why are you so caught up in this thing?" I asked Alex. "That guy never had a kind word for either of us."

"Just curiosity, Chase. I'll admit I didn't care much for him."

"I think he was jealous of you. Take it as a compliment."

His face took on a tolerant expression. "I'd have a hard time believing that."

"Were you able to give Fenn any information?"

"Not really. A couple of names of people Kolchevsky was associated with. He probably already had them. But otherwise I had nothing. I didn't know anything about his personal life."

We sat down in the kitchen at the country house, and he poured coffee for us. "Did you get anything at the auction yesterday?"

"There were a couple of minor items I thought about picking up. A dress that belonged to Sonia Calleda. She wore it in"—he checked his notes—"*Virgin Spring*. It was in good shape, and I thought they were underestimating the value."

"But you didn't opt for it?"

"It's not exactly our style." He tried the coffee. "There was also a locket that Pyra Cacienda wore on her Victory tour back at the turn of the century. Again, probably seriously undervalued."

"But—?"

"I don't know. I backed off. Pure instinct, I guess."

He left to go confer with one of our clients. It had something to do with artifacts from the Mute War. Rainbow didn't actually own any, of course, but we specialized in putting clients together. And, on occasion, when we'd gotten some information, we'd converted ourselves into archeologists and gone out to see what we could find. We were actually pretty good at that. Gabe, of course, had been a dedicated archeologist, and Alex had learned from him. We both had.

Larry Earl called. "I don't really have anything more on my father-in-law, Chase," he said, "except that I remember his telling me that he'd gone to the site of the Florida Space Museum."

"Okay, Larry, thanks."

"He also mentioned that it's underwater. He had to use diving gear."

"I'll tell Alex."

His face creased. "Chase, I wish it hadn't taken all these years to find that thing."

"You mean the transmitter?"

"Yes. We were wondering if we shouldn't just sell it? Take what we can get and forget the whole thing?"

"I'd recommend you give it some time."

"I'm not surprised," said Alex. "He was the kind of guy who couldn't have resisted going down to the museum. I don't think he could have found much, though. People have been looking through it for thousands of years."

"Does he mention it anywhere?"

"Not that I've come across. I've watched a good many of his addresses and gone through most of his papers."

"You find anything significant?"

"He had a passion for the Golden Age. But you already knew that. He spent most of his life at archeological sites that were connected with the early years of space exploration. He did some work at the NASA launch area in what used to be Florida. It's almost all underwater now, not just the museum. But that didn't stop him."

"Did he find anything?"

"Nothing of any value. Whatever was left had been ruined by the ocean. He was seriously angry that the NASA people didn't make a more serious effort to salvage things. Of course, to them, most of the stuff they left was junk. They'd have seen no value in, say, the computers that were used during the first Moon flight."

Something like that, today, would have been worth a small fortune. Even if it weren't one of the actual computers. Just one that was the same *type*. "Pity," I said. "But that's why artifacts command a price. If everybody held on to everything, they wouldn't be worth much."

"That's a point, Chase."

"So what else did Baylee do?"

"He was central to some of the recovery work in Washington."

"That was the United States capital, right?"

"Yes. During the second and third millennia. He did some of the excavations at the Smithsonian. And was part of a team that rebuilt the White House along the banks of Lake Washington. And before you ask, that was where the executive offices were."

"I'm impressed."

"He was still young then. Pretty much just along for the ride. He also spent a year on Mars at Broomar. The first colony. And he did some work at the NASA site in Texas."

"Texas was part of the United States originally, too, if I recall?"

"Yes."

"He did pretty well."

"He also helped find the submarine they used on Europa."

"*That* was the big one. First discovery of extraterrestrial life."

"Very good. You *did* pay some attention back in high school."

"Only when it was raining."

"He's got one other major credit. He led the mission that found the *Ayaka*."

"Which was?"

"A twenty-first-century automated ship that got lost while surveying Saturn. It stayed lost for nine thousand years. Until Baylee found it."

"Where was it?"

"Still orbiting Saturn. It became part of the rings. Baylee thought that no serious effort was ever made to recover it. In fact, it had been completely forgotten until he came across an old record."

"Makes you wonder what else is out there."

Alex nodded. "Incidentally, on another subject, some of the *Capella* families are banding together. They want to stop any effort to shut down the drive unit. They don't want the government to take any action that would put the passengers and crew at risk."

"I can understand that," I said. "JoAnn's afraid that what she wants to do could sink them permanently."

"What do *you* think about it? If it were your call, Chase, would you take the chance? Try to shut it down?"

"What are the odds again?"

"Right now they're saying that the chances for success are around ninety percent."

"That it will succeed? Or that it won't kill everybody?"

"That it won't kill everybody."

Lord. "I don't know," I said. "I don't think I'd try it."

SIX

Oh, for a lodge in some vast wilderness,
Some boundless contiguity of shade,
Where rumor of oppression and deceit,
Of unsuccessful or successful war,
Might never reach me more.

—William Cowper, "The Task," 1785 c.e.

They found Kolchevsky on the fourth day. The body was on a hiking trail, three-quarters of the way up the north side of Mt. Barrow. He'd apparently suffered a heart attack and fallen into some bushes, which had concealed the body from climbers. He hadn't used his link to call for help, so it seemed likely that the end had come swiftly. "What we do not understand," said Fenn, who came by the country house that afternoon, "was what he was doing up there. He had a history of heart problems, and he'd been warned about causing undue strain. The last thing in the world his doctors wanted him to do was go mountain climbing. And worse, that he would do it alone."

"Why didn't he have it replaced?" I asked.

"His doctors said he was in denial. Whatever, he refused treatment."

Alex closed his eyes for a moment. "Have you ever been on Mt. Barrow, Chase?"

I shook my head.

"Me, neither." He turned back to Fenn. "Is there a restaurant or a tourist area or something up there? On the mountain?"

"No. Not on the mountain. The closest one is down at ground level. Where his skimmer was parked."

"And he was on foot?"

"That's correct."

"That suggests he wasn't really trying to get somewhere. He was just out walking." He shrugged. "Or hiking."

Fenn frowned. "How do you know he wasn't trying to get somewhere?"

"Why walk? Especially with a health problem. Why not go in by air? Use the skimmer?"

"No." Fenn shook his head. "You weren't kidding when you said you weren't familiar with the area, were you?"

"You mean there's no place to set down?"

"Not unless you want to land in a tree."

Alex looked puzzled. A lovely blue arglet landed at one of the windows and peered in at us. "Were you able to get anything from his AI, Fenn?"

"Just that when he left the house, he said he would be a while. Nothing more."

"I don't guess he's ever done any archeological work on the mountain?"

"None that there's any record for."

"Okay. What was the restaurant where he parked?"

"Bartlett's."

"Did he eat there?"

"Yes. At about one. Nobody saw him after he left."

"Fenn," I asked, "why do you care about this? It's not a police matter anymore, is it?"

"No." He delivered that broad smile. "Call it professional curiosity. I can't believe a guy who's been warned about a weak heart has a hefty lunch. And then goes mountain climbing. He did eat pretty well, by the way. Meat loaf and mashed potatoes."

"I don't guess you know," Alex said, "if he reached wherever it was he was going?"

"No. We don't know whether he was going up or coming back down when he had the attack. But he got pretty high in any case. He was only a couple of hundred meters from the top when it hit."

"Well, Fenn," said Alex, "I wish we could help. I never had much in the way of personal dealings with him, except when he was lecturing me. So I can't really contribute anything."

"All right, guys, thanks." The inspector got up. "If you think of anything, give me a call. Okay?"

He left. And I knew what would be coming next. "Want to go for a ride?" Alex asked.

"Don't tell me. We're going for an uphill walk."

"I thought you might enjoy lunch at Bartlett's."

We checked the news reports first, which showed us where the body had been found. Then we headed out. Alex has a philosophy that you cannot work effectively on an empty stomach.

The restaurant was located where Route 11 plunges into the mountain chain. It was still a bit early when we got there, so there was plenty of room for the skimmer in the parking area. We touched down, went inside, and ordered. It was an unusually warm day for midwinter. The sky was clear, and Lake Accord had more than a few boats. While we waited for the food to appear, I offered my theory. "Kolchevsky was a crank. You know that as well as I do. I'd bet the reason he went up the mountain was precisely because the doctors told him not to do it. I had an uncle like that. He'd get the same kind of directions, and it always set him off. I was about twelve when he was telling my folks about how he was supposed to keep calm and not get excited and he kept going, his voice rising, getting seriously enraged that anybody would tell him how to live his life."

"How'd he make out?"

"He eventually got his heart replaced."

"Yeah. Well, I don't think Kolchevsky fits that kind of personality."

"Really? Why not?"

"There was always a kind of coldness in the guy. Especially when he was on the attack. No, he was too methodical. He didn't fly into a rage. That was all part of the act. I'm not saying he didn't get legitimately angry, but he struck me as a control freak. I usually knew what was coming next with him, and I can't recall ever seeing him get off script." His eyes drifted toward the window. We had a view of the parking lot, and beyond it, the rising slope of Mt. Barrow, which was covered by heavy forest. A couple of men carrying camping gear had just come out of the trees and were getting ready to cross the highway. "No," he said, "Kolchevsky had a reason for going up the slope."

"Was he married?" I asked.

"His wife died twenty years ago."

"Maybe," I said, "he was going to meet a girlfriend."

Barrow was by no means the highest mountain in the area, but I could see why it would have been popular with climbers: It was about fifteen hundred meters above the surrounding country, providing a magnificent view of Lake Accord, which is really a small ocean, stretching almost 140 kilometers to the west.

It's wide-open country, with only a few houses scattered in remote places. I've always thought that, when the time came, this was the sort of area I'd want to retire into.

We finished eating, left Bartlett's, and got our backpacks out of the skimmer. We crossed Route 11 and started up the hiking trail. About two kilometers in, it split in two. One track turned northwest into the heart of the mountain range. The other, the one on which Kolchevsky had been found, plunged into ever denser forest and headed for the summit. We stayed with it.

It grew steeper, until we were moving carefully, placing one foot in front of the other and sometimes using branches to pull ourselves uphill. And finally Alex pointed off to the right side at a cluster of trees and bushes. "This is it," he said.

It was easy to visualize. Whether Kolchevsky was going up or coming down, this would have been a difficult patch of ground to navigate. He had apparently staggered off into the shrubbery and collapsed.

We stood quietly for several minutes. Finally, Alex shrugged. "I don't know," he said. "Let's go up the trail for a bit."

"Any particular reason?"

"What was he doing up here?"

"I have no idea."

"Right."

As we got higher, the slope eased off somewhat, the trees thinned, and the trail moved out along a cliff overlooking the lake. A group of rocks formed a cradle embedded at the rim. It was a place where you could sit down and enjoy a sandwich with a view. In fact, several people were there when we arrived.

Clouds had begun building while we were on the trail. And now a soft rain began to fall. The people on the cradle—there were five of them—looked up. They gathered their gear and, as we watched, moved out and started down the trail. They said hello as they passed. We stayed in the shelter of the trees.

When it slacked off, we followed the trail the rest of the way to the top. Somebody had planted a WCC flag on the summit. The World Conservation Corps. I'm sure you've seen one, but in case you haven't: It portrays a gomper with big round eyes sitting beneath a rosebush, and their axiom, SAVE THE PLANET. The WCC, of course, is actually a Confederacy-wide organization that tries to remind people about maintaining the environment.

There was nothing else at the summit.

Alex stared out at the lake far below. "Why did he come up here? Why didn't he at least bring someone else along?"

Carensa Paterna asked the same question next day on *Jennifer in the Morning*. "*I'm not denying,*" she said, "*that Casmir had a rough edge. He said what he thought. That hurts sometimes. But think how much better the world would be if we all behaved that way.*"

Jennifer looked skeptical. "*Are you sure about that?*"

Carensa smiled. "*Well, yeah, I know what you're saying. But we claim to be all about truth, don't we? I'd like to be able to believe that*

*when people say nice things, they mean it. Rather than that they have
some ulterior motive. That they're trying to get something. Or they're
just sparing my feelings. And that's my point about Casmir: You
could trust him. He meant what he said. I'll confess I loved the guy.
There were times he hurt my feelings. But I'm really going to miss
him, Jen. I hate to think of what his final hours must have been like.
Wandering around on that mountain. What was he doing there anyhow? He knew his health was failing, and it just makes me wonder if
he felt lost. That maybe he didn't care anymore."*

The Hillside was an exquisite, lush club on the Riverwalk. They had a
human hostess, which is standard in most of the better restaurants,
and human waiters, which, of course, is not. They also had a pianist,
who was playing the theme from *Last Chance* when I walked in. Jas-
mine candles glittered on the tables. Prints in the style of the last century, and dark-stained wooden tables and walls provided a sense of
nostalgia. I sat down and ordered a pizza, propped my notebook in
front of me, and was reading the newsclips when a familiar voice asked
if she could join me. It was JoAnn. "Sure," I said, folding the notebook.
"How are you doing?"

"Not real well." She eased into a chair.

"What's wrong, JoAnn?"

She pressed her lips together. Shook her head. "I don't trust it."

"You mean tinkering with the drive?"

"Yes."

"I'm sorry to hear it."

She sat quietly for a minute, staring out the window at the Riverwalk. Tourists were strolling past, kids with balloons, people in
coaches. "Have you talked to Shara?"

"Not since the flight."

She leaned close to me and lowered her voice. "I'm pretty sure we
could make it work, Chase. Odds are extremely good we could stop
the *Capella* right in its tracks. But damn it, I can't be certain. And I
just can't bring myself to put all those people at risk. Shara wants me

to run the experiment again. Her argument is that if we get it right twice, we should be okay."

"Are you going to do it?"

A waiter arrived. "Could you give us a few minutes?" JoAnn asked. "I haven't really had a chance to look at the menu yet." Then she turned back to me. "There's no point in repeating it, Chase. Even if it worked fine, if the timing on a second run was perfect, I still wouldn't be in a position to guarantee it would work for the *Capella*."

"What are you going to do?"

"I don't know." Her voice shook. "I can't take that kind of chance. They want me to run a successful experiment, then assure them everything will be okay. Management is scared, Chase. There's a lot of pressure on them now. The politicians want to get this thing settled. They want the problem to go away. John is the only one who's resisting."

"John Kraus?"

"Yes. He recognizes there's a quantum factor in all this, that there's no way we can be certain. He's right. But try to explain that to the politicians."

I wasn't sure exactly what to say. My gut-level reaction was that I should simply keep out of it. Which I guess is what I tried to do. "JoAnn, John's ultimately responsible to make the call. Just do what you can and let him take it from there."

"I know. But he'll want my opinion, and I'm pretty sure that's what he'll go with." She brought up the menu, but she wasn't really looking at it. "You know, I came here thinking I could make this work. I understood from the beginning there was a slight possibility it could go wrong. But the chance seemed so infinitesimal that I thought we could live with it."

"What changed? Did you find out something?"

"Seeing the families. That's what changed. Seeing pictures of the passengers." They'd been all over the news feeds. "It was *always* five percent. That just seems like a much bigger number now." She looked in pain. "I don't want to be responsible for killing these people."

The waiter came back. JoAnn was still looking toward the menu, not really reading it. "I'll have a Camara salad," she said. It was a specialty of the house, and I suspected it was what she usually ordered.

"What does Shara think?"

"She wants to play the odds. Which is fine if it works. But it's easy for her. I'm not sure she'd be so ready to do it if it were up to her to make the call."

I wanted to tell her there's always a level of uncertainty. In everything. Nothing's a hundred percent in life. But I kept my mouth shut.

Her eyes darkened. "The stakes are too high."

SEVEN

Solitude is okay, as long as you have a friend to share it with.

—Agathe Lawless, *Sunset Musings*, 9417 C.E.

Linda Talbott had been a special client because she had also lost someone on the *Capella*. Her husband, George, had been a talented novelist. He'd written narratives centered on politics and religion, had won some major awards, and had been a rising star in serious fiction when he boarded the cruise liner eleven years earlier. He was from Dellaconda originally, and, Linda had told me, he'd been an admirer of Margaret Weinstein, its president at the beginning of the century. Weinstein had captured his attention by pushing a term-limits bill through an antagonistic legislature. After that, according to the common wisdom, the universe had grown brighter. Government on Dellaconda had become more straightforward, and, significantly, similar bills had been passed or were periodically being introduced throughout the Confederacy. That achievement alone had raised her to the front rank of Dellacondan presidents and should have ended with her becoming chief executive of the Confederacy. It didn't happen, of course. She shared a characteristic with Kolchevsky: She tended to say what she thought. She'd gotten away with it while rising to the top on Dellaconda, but there was no way she could have disregarded politics the way she did and become the Confederacy's chief executive.

Consequently, when Weinstein's chair became available, I contacted

Linda. It would command a steep price, but she had resources. She and her husband had a palatial residence along the coast in Ocean Gate, a kilometer north of Andiquar. And they owned an asteroid home. It was the place, she'd told me, they always retreated to when George was making the final pass through his current novel.

"I just thought," I told her as we sat in the Hillside, "you might be interested."

"Interested?" She almost squealed. "Oh, yes. How much?"

"They're still bidding on it," I said. "But I can connect you with Alex. Let him know how much you're willing to go. He'll take it from there. And get you the best price he can."

"I'd love," she said, "to have it sitting in the middle of our living room when George walks in."

"It's pretty valuable. I'm not sure you'd want to have it where your cats could chew on it."

"Oh," she said, "I wouldn't put it here. I'd take it out to Momma. By the way, would you and Alex be able to arrange delivery? At my expense, of course."

"Of course. You're going to give it to your mother?"

"*Momma's* our asteroid."

"Oh."

"I could explain it, but you'd need an hour or so."

I laughed. "I'll tell Alex you're interested."

They delivered the chair to us a few days later. We put it in the conference room. I was disappointed by its general appearance. It was in decent condition. But it was mostly black faux leather, and there were some scratches. But it looked comfortable, and maybe that was all that mattered. "What do you think?" Alex asked me.

"How much is she paying for it?"

"Three quarters of a million."

"That seems like a lot of money for a chair that looks so ordinary."

"That's what pumps up the value, Chase," he said. "This was where she sat when she changed Confederate politics." He was obviously pleased with himself. "It's actually a good buy."

"I'm glad to hear it."

He made no effort to hide his disappointment at my attitude. "When's Linda coming?"

"She said she'd be here this morning."

"Okay. I have to go out for a while. If she comes while I'm gone, congratulate her for me. And have her sign the documents. Morris Delivery will pick it up this afternoon, and they tell me they'll get it to Momma within three days." He delivered the line without cracking a smile.

I did a search on Weinstein and looked through pictures and displays. There was an excerpted comment by George, who had said of her in one of his novels that if she had been running Dellaconda two centuries earlier, there would never have been a war with the Mutes. I looked at photos. Here she was giving awards to celebrated literary figures. And treating famous scientists to dinner at the presidential estate. And at Everhold shaking hands with a few Mutes while she tried to keep the peace. And the famous picture of her sitting at a table with a Mute child in the world capital.

Linda showed up while I was still glossing over the history. I took her back to the conference room, showed her the chair, and was relieved at her reaction. "It's *gorgeous*," she said.

"It *is* nice, isn't it?"

"Chase, he's going to *love* having that in the house." She took a deep breath. "I hope we're able to get him home."

"Me, too." She stood behind it and pressed her fingertips into it. Then, when she'd had enough, we gave it some distance and sat down at the conference table. "How often do you get to the asteroid?" I asked.

"We spend about two months a year up there. It's never been my favorite place. But George likes solitude. At least he does when he's finishing a project."

"Why was he on the *Capella*?"

"He was doing research, Chase."

"Really? What kind of research?"

"You're not going to believe this, but he was writing a novel in which an interstellar with a bunch of politicians on board develops some sort of mechanical problem and sets down on an alien world, where they have to cooperate in order to survive."

"So it's a thriller?"

"More like a comedy." She checked the time. "Well, anyhow, I have to go. Tell Alex I said thanks. Do I pay *you*?"

"We can do it that way. And I need you to sign some documents." I led the way back to my office. "May I ask a question?"

"Certainly, Chase."

"Who named it *Momma*?"

"I don't know. Probably the previous owner. Somebody with a dark sense of humor, I guess. It was one of the things that attracted us to it. That, and the fact that it's an almost perfectly smooth sphere."

"I'd be interested in meeting him. George, that is."

"He's an odd guy in a lot of ways. But you'd like him, Chase. He told me once about the secret of life. You know what it is?"

"I'm not sure what George thinks it is."

"It's having lunch with friends. I think most people never got to see that side of him." Her voice had gotten shaky.

There were several hundred residences set up on asteroids. Most have plastene domes, but a few are apparently shielded only by a force field. I wouldn't be too comfortable with that arrangement. Power goes out, and you have a serious problem.

I went outside with her and watched while she climbed into the skimmer. "When we have the coming-home party," she said, "we'd like very much if you and Alex could attend. We'll be happy to provide transportation, Chase."

"Thank you, Linda," I said. "I'll let Alex know."

"You'll both be receiving formal invitations." She waved. "Thanks, Chase."

I backed away as she lifted off. She turned north, and I thought how much I would have enjoyed meeting President Weinstein.

EIGHT

When love comes down the trail, everything else—wealth, ambition, security, even one's career—retreats into the shadows.

—Walford Candles, *Marking Time*, 1229

Alex never did get back to the office that day although he left a message. *"He expects to be on Jennifer tomorrow,"* Jacob said.

"Anything special going on?" I asked.

"Yes. He says he knows why Kolchevsky was on the mountain."

"Really?"

"He called Inspector Redfield this morning to offer his theory."

"And what is the theory?"

"I was not included in the conversation."

"Did you ask him?"

"No. He would have told me if he wished me to know."

Which meant that he was really keeping me out of the loop. Alex does enjoy playing games. I thought about calling him, but that was probably what he wanted me to do. And if I did, he'd find a reason to put me off. He could be an infuriating boss when he wanted to. "Did he have any visitors this morning?"

"No, Chase. And no calls connected with the matter."

I knew he'd been going through Kolchevsky's history, and obviously he'd found something. I'd read the guy's bio and some comments by his colleagues. I'd even gone back and watched some of his more current media appearances, but I hadn't seen anything helpful. Anyhow, it became a busy afternoon, so I put it out of my mind and spent the rest of the day talking with clients about artifacts that had become available.

I stayed late on the chance he would return and have no choice but to tell me what he knew. But he didn't show, and, finally, I closed up and went home.

My morning routine is to watch *Jennifer* while I eat breakfast. Usually, I get downstairs just as the show is starting. That morning, though, I was a half hour early, so I'd finished before she blinked on in my living room, along with two chairs, a table, and the studio background. She was seated in one of the chairs and began by doing her standard opening lines welcoming her viewers to the show. Then she reminded us of the unfortunate death of Casmir Kolchevsky, who had been her frequent guest over many years. She told us she might have a breaking story that would explain what had caused his death. Then she showed several clips of him laughing, lecturing the audience, and playing the morally upright figure who attacked anyone who did not subscribe to his code of behavior. Which consisted largely of taking umbrage with those who had the temerity to pursue and sell artifacts.

She described the strangeness of his passing. "*He was not a mountain climber,*" she said. "*He did a little bit of that when he was younger, but as far as we can tell, this was the first time he'd gone up a steep slope in more than thirty years.*

"*Anyway, he's been a frequent contributor to this show, and we've enjoyed having him on board. I'll miss him. A lot of us will. Among them is Alex Benedict, the antiquarian who was an occasional target for Kolchevsky. That was probably because Alex was so successful at what he did and because he believed that artifacts rightfully belonged to whoever found them, and not necessarily to the museums.*" She looked off to her right. "*Alex, do I have that right?*"

Alex strode into the room. "*I think that's a fair summation, Jennifer. And good morning.*"

"*Welcome to the show, Alex.*"

"Thanks for having me." He took a seat at the table. *"It's always a pleasure."*

"Before we go any further, when I called yesterday to ask whether you had a comment on the loss of Casmir, you surprised me."

"In what way?"

"You expressed a degree of sympathy for him that I would not have expected. Despite the fact that—I don't know any other way to say this—he was on occasion extremely critical of you."

Alex smiled. *"Well, I suppose you could say that. I don't think Casmir approved of my line of work. But that's okay. Some people think* accountants *commit profane acts. In any case, Jen, I'm sorry we've lost him. He expressed his views as he saw them. We didn't agree on some basic issues. But he was essentially a good man. I think we can let it go at that."*

"Alex, when I asked you how you'd reacted to the manner of his death, a man with a bad heart walking on a mountain trail, you told me you thought you knew exactly what happened."

"Well, that may have been an exaggeration. But I have a theory." He leaned back in the chair and smiled.

She waited for him to proceed. But he fell silent, and she rolled her eyes. *"Alex,"* she said, *"you should have gone into show business."*

He managed to look puzzled. *"I'm not sure what you mean."*

"Let's let it go. Would you be willing to share that theory with us?"

"Of course. I've been delving through everything I could find on Casmir. As I'm sure you know, there's a substantial amount of material."

"And what did you find?"

"Some pictures."

"You brought them, I hope."

"Oh, yes." The studio scene blinked off and was replaced by a young couple standing on a porch. It took a moment to recognize the guy, but he was Kolchevsky. Probably in his mid-twenties. The woman I didn't know. She might have been two or three years younger, with dark eyes, amber hair cut short, and attractive features. *"The young lady,"* said Alex, *"is Anna Kushnir. Roughly a year after this picture*

was taken, they married." The picture was replaced by another, of the couple on a beach. Then participating in a graduation exercise. And coming out of a church. And another at their wedding.

"*All very nice,*" said Jen. "*But what has this to do with the way he died?*"

"*Unfortunately, he lost Anna twenty years ago.*"

Jennifer's smile had already faded. I guessed she'd known about Anna's premature death. The wedding scene was replaced by the young couple looking out over an ocean vista from a considerable height. They were seated in a rocky embrasure. Which looked eerily familiar. Then I recognized the shoreline. The ocean was actually Lake Accord. And the embrasure was the cradle we'd seen on the Mt. Barrow cliff.

A second image showed the couple at the same location, in different clothes, gazing into each other's eyes.

And a third one, also at the embrasure, portrayed them laughing while they ate what might have been popcorn. Again with different attire.

"*They loved this place,*" Alex said. "*There are numerous pictures of them here. I suspect, after he lost her, this was as close as he could get to her.*"

"Alex," I said, "I always had you pegged for a romantic. Did Fenn buy it?"

"He says it makes as much sense as anything *he* can come up with."

"Incredible. I never would have guessed that from Kolchevsky, though. He seemed like such a cold individual."

"I don't agree at all, Chase. He was always overheated. I think you're mistaking his resentment of us for a lack of feeling."

NINE

Oh, to be a time traveler! To land with Columbus in the Americas, to circle the rings of Saturn with Doc Manning, to ride the *Centaurus* on that first voyage to another star. But most of all, given the chance, I would opt to be there on the Moon when Neil Armstrong and Buzz Aldrin show up, and shake their hands. No moment in human history matters more.

—Monroe Billings, *Time Travelers Never Wait in Line*, 11,252 C.E.

Despite all that was happening, Alex could not get the Corbett transmitter out of his mind. "I should have realized," he said, "the thing's in a class of its own. What's Rifkin's blowtorch or the last flag at Venobia compared with the first hypercomm unit?" He'd looked at the visuals, but he finally decided he wanted to see the actual device.

Marissa needed a couple of days, but she eventually showed up at the country house, carrying it in a cloth bag. She and Alex exchanged greetings. Then she put the bag on a table in the conference room. The transmitter was a black box, big by modern standards, about the size of a man's shoe. It wore a battered plate with an inscription in ancient English which, after translation, indicated a manufacturing date of 2712.

It looked battered, which you could expect after eight or nine thousand years.

Alex pressed his fingertips against the casing. "It's been in a fire."

Marissa nodded. "I thought so, too, Alex. But I couldn't be sure. It might just be ageing." She sat down. "So what do you think? Have you any theories as to why my grandfather might keep something like this quiet?"

Alex let her see he had no idea. "Marissa, my guess at the moment is that *you'd* be better able to answer that question than we are. I can't think of any possible explanation other than that he was in failing health and simply forgot about it. Or that he misunderstood the significance of his find. But he was a major player among archeologists. I just can't believe that could have happened."

"No." She chewed her upper lip. "Neither of those is possible. My grandfather was in good health for a few years after he came back. He was a bit morose, but he kept his mind right until the end. I just can't imagine how he could have forgotten to tell us he had *this*." Her eyes focused on the transmitter. "There must be something else. Something we're missing."

When Marissa was gone, we went into my office. "I guess you're aware," Alex said, "Baylee was another one of these guys who had no avatar."

"Yes, I know."

"We need to start looking into this. Baylee must have had some friends. Somebody we can talk to."

"Marissa mentioned a Lawrence Southwick." He made a note of the name. "You want me to set up an appointment?"

"No. I'll take care of it. How about family members? Somebody probably knows something."

"His daughter's name is Corinne. She married Larry Earl. Larry's a technician. Corinne is the chief executive of Random Access."

"Health services," said Alex.

"Correct. Marissa tells me neither of her parents were ever all that interested in the archeology. At least with regard to what her grandfather was doing. They just wanted him to come home safely. They were apparently as surprised as Marissa when they found the transmitter."

"All right. Let's talk to them, too." His mood darkened a bit. "By the way, there's a movement to have families and friends of the people stuck on the *Capella* write messages for them. To be delivered in a single package."

"They going to do a burst transmission?" I said. "They'll get a lot of traffic, so they'll have to."

"It's a bad idea. I don't know who started it. But the people on board the ship may not be aware of what's happening, and almost certainly don't know it's not 1424 anymore. I'm not saying it would start a panic, but if they're trying to get people off in an orderly fashion, that kind of news won't help."

Marissa came in to talk with Alex. He told me later that there was no new information. But she wanted to keep us on as consultants. "I need to know what happened here," she told him. Alex agreed to do everything he could.

Later that day, we sat down with her parents, Larry and Corinne. Larry was convivial and easygoing, a low-pressure type who showed no inclination to get caught up in the possibility that something the family had found in a closet could make him wealthy beyond his dreams. "I'll believe it," he said, "when they transfer the money."

"Who found the transmitter?"

"I did," Larry said. "It was on the top shelf of a closet, under some blankets."

"And you never knew anything about its existence before?"

"No. Nothing."

"Are there any other artifacts around the house? Anything else your father-in-law brought home?"

"Not that I know of. Now, I'm not so sure." He looked at Corinne.

Like her daughter, she was a charmer, with dark brown hair and animated features. But she shook her head. "There's nothing else that I'm aware of. After we found out about the transmitter, realized what it might be worth, we turned the place upside down. Found nothing."

"Professor Baylee," said Alex, "was on Earth for a long time, wasn't he?"

"My dad was there for probably six or seven years on that last trip," said Corinne.

"Did he ever talk about what he'd been doing there?"

"Not really," she said. "In general terms, maybe. Mostly what I remember was his saying it had been a waste of time. He'd been there before, of course. He probably lived there for twenty years altogether. He'd come back once in a while and talk about the pyramids or the Shantel Monument or something. But after that last one, he seemed depressed. Worn-out. He always denied it, claimed everything was fine, but he never really told us what had been going on."

"It's true," Larry said. "Something happened. Something changed him. He never went back. Never showed any inclination to."

"Did he keep a diary? Any kind of record at all?"

"None that I knew of," Corinne said.

"Marissa mentioned a guy named Lawrence Southwick. Do you know him?"

They looked at each other. "Not well," said Larry. "We've met him. He's an archeological enthusiast. A rich one. And he was a close friend of Dad's for years. Even funded some of the expeditions."

"Do you think he might know anything about this?"

"I've asked him. He was as stunned as we were to hear about the transmitter."

"Okay. Marissa said your father didn't have any health problems. Is that correct?"

Corinne shook her head. "If he did, he concealed them pretty well. For five or six years, anyhow. Then he was gone."

"What happened to him?"

"A stroke. We never knew he had a problem until it killed him."

"Did he ever say why he stayed on Earth so long? Was there something special he was looking for?"

"We knew," said Larry, "that he was primarily interested in the Golden Age. He had a picture of one of the early space museums on his bedroom wall."

"The Florida Space Museum?"

"Yes, that's it."

"Chase told me that you'd mentioned he'd been diving there. He told you about that, but he never mentioned why he was doing it?"

"No." Corinne closed her eyes. Her cheeks had grown damp. "I never really thought to ask." She looked at Larry, who shrugged and shook his head. "All this business about the transmitter has made me realize I never took the time to talk to him. He sat up in his room every night and read or watched HV. He almost never went out. That was nothing like the man who'd been my dad. Who took me to zoos and parks and beaches." She took a deep breath. "Look, Alex, I was never into all the archeology. Neither of us was. He knew that, and he was disappointed in me. Looking back on it now, I wish I had it to do over. That I'd shown a little interest."

Alex understood. He shared a similar sense of guilt over Gabe.

Lawrence Southwick III lived in Shelton, which is about forty miles southwest of Andiquar. Alex asked me to do background checks on everybody we were talking to, and Southwick was the only local who, as far as we could tell, had ever joined Baylee on one of his expeditions to the home world. He was a retired manufacturer, one of the major people behind the success of the Banner skimmers. He'd been friendly with Baylee since both were kids.

If anyone outside the family could help us, Southwick seemed like the guy. That meant Alex would prefer to meet him casually rather than call him. He tended to spend time at the Idelic Club, on the shoreline. I checked our records, and came up with two people who had connections with the Idelic Club. One was a journalist, and the other a client. Either, I thought, would be open to inviting Alex along to an event that might lead to a chance meeting. Naturally, Alex chose the client. But Southwick didn't show up as expected. A second attempt also failed, so in the end we just played it straight and called him. I stayed back out of sight during the conversation.

Lawrence Southwick came from money. I knew that as soon as I saw the way he dressed and his furnishings. A Kopek painting hung on the wall behind him over a lush black sofa. He was tall, lanky, with sapphire eyes and thick brown hair, and the easy manner of a guy who had always been in control. His appearance suggested that he worked out regularly. *"It's been a long time,"* he said, *"since I've heard Garnett's name. He was a good guy. He loved sports. Especially golf."*

"He was an archeologist, wasn't he?" asked Alex.

"*Yes. He did most of his work on Earth.*"

"You went with him on one occasion, didn't you? To the home world?"

"*Actually on several occasions.*" He stared at Alex. "*May I ask what this is about? Has something happened?*"

"We're doing some research for Marissa Earl. She assured us you'd be happy to help."

"*Well, yes, of course I would. Garnett was among the major players.*" His tone softened. "*I accompanied him a few times. On terrestrial missions.*"

"When was that?"

"*Well, as I say, I did it several times. I went to Egypt with him once. To Asia, Europe. The Americas. All over the planet, really. Sometimes we just traveled around and visited historic sites. We saw the Parisian Tower. Or what's left of it. And Kyoto. And Feraglia. Some of the places I'd really have liked to visit are, unfortunately, underwater. Like London. And I would especially have enjoyed going to Thermopolae.*"

Alex asked some general questions about Baylee's reactions to various sites, then inquired when they'd last been on the home world together.

"*About nineteen or twenty years ago,*" he said. "*A long time.*"

"I wonder if you could tell me what that was all about? That last visit?"

He had to think about it. "*There was really nothing specific. He'd been there at that time for a couple of years, I guess. I just went to do some sightseeing. I only saw him once or twice. He was in Africa. Yeah, that's right. North Africa. Mostly I just wandered around visiting museums and picking up stuff from gift shops. And from auctions. And visiting friends.*" He glanced off to one side where a wall shelf came into view, adorned with a replica of a rocket. I couldn't be sure, but I thought it was one of the Saturns. Lunar-era stuff. Hard to tell from a distance. Rockets all look pretty much alike.

"While you were with him on that last trip, did he come into possession of any major artifacts?"

"*Well, sure. I mean, that's what he did. There are whole sections of several museums dedicated to him. But—*" His eyes took on an appearance of frustration. "*Are we talking about the Corbett transmitter? Is that what this is about?*"

"I'll confess that's what stirred my interest. Sure. It's nine thousand years old. Do you have any idea where he might have gotten it?"

"*None.*" He laughed. "*Garnie was full of surprises. But I certainly never expected he had anything like that. The truth is, he wasn't inclined to tell you everything right away. He surprised me a few times. Like with Holcroft's biography of Doc Manning. He had that for weeks before he showed it to me.*"

"Did you keep in touch during the years he was on Earth?"

"*Well, we both know that talking with someone that far away doesn't work very well.*"

"So you didn't hear from him?"

"*Occasionally. He'd come home once in a while and spend a few weeks with his family. And I'd get to see him. Then he'd be off again. Sometimes there'd be a message. It would usually be about a project he was working on. Or just a few general comments about how things were going.*" He smiled. "*We exchanged birthday greetings usually.*"

"Mr. Southwick, you underwrote some of his expeditions."

"*Well, it's probably more accurate to say I contributed to them. I still do what I can to support archeological research, Mr. Benedict.*" He glanced at his link. Let us see he was checking the time. "*Now, if you don't mind, I have some business to attend to—*"

"One other question, before we let you go. Do you know why he came home?"

"*I think he decided to retire. He never really said that, but I think that's what happened.*"

"He was still in good health, though, wasn't he?"

"*As far as I know.*"

"So why do you think he decided to retire?"

"*Mr. Benedict, it was the Golden Age that intrigued him. He was especially interested in the early years of spaceflight. He was always looking for artifacts from that era. I think his most exciting experience was diving down to the Florida Space Museum. There'd been a lot of material there at one time. As I'm sure you know. But I think what happened was that he finally decided there was nothing more to be recovered. He'd pursued all the leads, had spent most of his life looking for the artifacts that had originally been on display in the Space Museum and in Huntsville, and I suspect he just gave up."*

Southwick had gotten me thinking about what it must have been like when the world was coming apart during the Dark Age. Population was exploding, disease and starvation were rampant, religious and political fanatics ran wild everywhere. Anyone who could get off the planet was doing so. It prompted the first serious interstellar-colonization period.

"When exactly did everything get lost?" I asked Alex.

"If you mean the contents of the Space Museum, most of them were moved to Huntsville as the seas rose. The stuff at Moonbase went to Huntsville, too. But that was probably eight hundred years later. At the beginning of the Dark Age. And eventually they had to abandon Huntsville. The story is that a guy running a storage facility in Centralia helped move the Huntsville artifacts. Supposedly everything went back to Centralia." His head dropped onto the back of his chair.

"You okay?" I said.

"I'm fine."

"What's wrong?"

"I was thinking about Gabe. That artifact. The transmitter. He'd have loved to have found that. He spent a lot of time looking for something from that era. And he never got anything except bricks and assorted junk." He took a deep breath. "Yeah. He'd have liked to see it. Just *touch* it."

"I guess he was a lot like Baylee," I said.

Alex had a reputation as a guy who did not get sentimental over artifacts. According to the common wisdom, the four-thousand-year-old Aguala Diamond, which Tora Canadra had conspicuously worn while being interviewed for *The Gorpa Diaries*, meant nothing more to him than profit. Ditto Henry Comer's notebook, which Comer had famously thrown at Dr. Grace during the Arkhayne Award ceremony. It was a perspective I'd bought into for a long time. The truth, though, was simply that Alex tended to conceal his more emotional side. He shared Baylee's passion for the Golden Age. And he was becoming tangled in the guy's obsession with the lost artifacts. What had happened to the contents of the Huntsville museum? Did they still exist somewhere?

During the next few days, he spoke to every living relative who'd had any kind of connection with Baylee. Most hadn't known him very well. *"He was away all the time,"* they said. A few weren't even aware of his connection with the Golden Age. Others knew, but it had no real significance for them. He had spent so much time away that no one had maintained contact with him. And we found nobody who had even heard of a Corbett transmitter.

I got a call one afternoon from Juanita Biyanca while I was closing up. *"I represent the* Capella *Families,"* she said. *"Is Alex available?"* She was probably well into her second century. And she looked like a woman on a mission.

"What is the *Capella* Families?"

"It's exactly what it sounds like. The families are coming together. We don't trust the government to handle the rescue properly. We don't want them trying anything that will get everybody killed."

I could hear Alex in the kitchen. "Hold on a second, Juanita. Let me see if he's back yet." I signaled Jacob to ask Alex whether he wanted to take the call.

Moments later, he walked into my office. "Hello, Juanita. What can I do for you?"

"Mr. Benedict, it's becoming obvious they are not going to be able to get everyone off when the Capella *comes back. We want to make sure they don't do something silly and maybe lose the ship altogether. Consequently, we'd like you to sign a petition demanding they take no chances. That they do not touch the engines. Would you be willing to do that?"*

He looked my way with a pained expression. "Juanita, I understand your concern, and I know John Kraus will take no risks with the passengers' lives. But the issue is more complicated than you make it sound. I'm sorry, but I won't be able to help you with that."

"*I see.*" She let him see she was disappointed. "*I'm sorry to hear it.*"

"I don't think you need to worry about them taking unnecessary chances."

"*There's something else. We're soliciting for two volunteers to board the ship and stay with it when it goes down again. We need to let the passengers know what's happening. You've been a significant figure in this business from the start, and we were hoping you would be willing to help.*"

"You mean you want me to go on board?"

"*It could save the situation, Mr. Benedict.*"

I looked at him and shook my head *no*. Don't do it. He rolled his eyes. "Juanita, I don't think it's a good idea. The SRF will have radio contact with Captain Schultz, and I think you can trust them to inform her about what is happening."

"*Well,*" she said, "*you have more confidence in these people than I do.*"

"I may know them a little better."

She broke off with a cold good-bye and was gone. Alex turned laser eyes in my direction. "You didn't actually think I might go along with that, did you?"

"I just wanted to be sure," I said.

"I appreciate your confidence."

TEN

The measure of a prize is often its elusiveness. What we really care about is to possess something no one else has.

—Salazar Kester, *On the Hunt*, 4211

With the *Capella* rendezvous approaching, excitement in the media and the general public was ramping up. And interest in the other lost ships was reviving as well. Sabol and Cori Chaveau, the two girls who had been rescued from the *Intrépide*, were in the news again. The *Intrépide* had left the French outpost at Brandizi eight thousand years ago. The passengers were not only alive, but for them only a few weeks had passed.

Unfortunately, it had taken too much time to catch up with the ship, and the two girls were the only passengers we'd been able to rescue before the ship was dragged away again. Sabol was thirteen and Cori three years younger. Probably they were the youngest guests ever to turn up on *The Charles Koeffler Show*.

"*How did it feel,*" Koeffler asked them, "*when you found yourself in a place that must have seemed so strange to you?*"

"*It was scary,*" said Sabol. "*We'd grown up in Brandizi, which had only a few thousand people. It's so crowded here. And everyone we knew back there is gone.*"

"*The worst part of it,*" added Cori, "*is that Dad is still on the* Intrépide. *And it's not like the* Capella, *which will show up every five and a half years.*" She wiped a tear from her cheek. "*The* Intrépide *won't be back again for sixty-five years.*" Both girls had mastered Standard, but the ancient accent held fast. Neither would ever be mistaken for a native.

"*I'm sorry,*" said Koeffler. "*I'm sure your rescuers did everything they could.*"

"*Oh, yes,*" said Sabol. "*Dot Garber brought us across. But she went back for others and got caught.*"

"*You live with Dot's daughter, don't you?*"

"*Yes. She's been very nice. Out of this world.*"

"*I suspect, Sabol, that a lot of people would say you and Cori have been out of this world.*" Both girls smiled and blushed.

Cori's eyes closed momentarily. "*You know, this whole thing is hard to believe. I mean, it was only a little more than a year ago when we left Brandizi. And we get here, to a place that didn't even exist when we left home. And people tell us that Brandizi is gone. That nobody lives there anymore. What's really hard to accept is that everything we knew as kids, all those people, the house where we lived, our friends, that they're just not there anymore. Haven't been there for thousands of years. I can't believe that. And what's even sadder, nobody except us*"—she glanced at her sister, who nodded—"*nobody except us even knows they existed.*" More tears were coming.

"*Well,*" said Koeffler, "*you remember them. You and Sabol. As long as you are here, they won't be forgotten.*"

Baylee might not have left an avatar, but he had a serious presence on the net. Check out almost any archeological occasion, a convention, a luncheon, a conference, a strategy meeting at a university, anything at all of that nature that had happened before about 1416, and you could find him. He received awards, appeared as a speaker, performed as host, presented the prizes. The events had usually occurred on Earth, but there were occasional entries from Rimway as well. The records from Earth had been imported since, of course, no direct connection between the webs of the two worlds existed.

There was no denying that everybody loved him. He was greeted with enthusiastic applause on every occasion. People crowded up to the head table to shake his hand, to whisper words of encouragement, to get their picture taken with him. Incredibly, at an awards dinner at Polgar University on the Alpine Islands, I caught a glimpse of *Gabe* talking with him.

Baylee, in his younger years, looked good. He was short, but he had a full head of hair, blue eyes, and a smile that inevitably lit up the room. He told jokes on himself, describing how he blundered about the various dig sites but consistently "found good stuff" because he always traveled with smart people. *"I've been fortunate,"* he said at the dedication of the Cambro Museum in St. Louis. *"I've had a good run. We've tried to do what archeologists are supposed to do, which is to rescue the past, to keep history alive, and if I've been able to do that to a reasonable degree, it's been because of people like Lawrence Southwick and Anne Winter, both of whom are here today. Anne, Lawrence, would you guys please stand?"* They did, and the place rocked with applause.

I enjoyed watching Baylee perform. He had a sparkling sense of humor and a warm personality. But what really came across was his passion for history. At the Luganov Museum in Belgrade, he was shown a nineteenth-century vase. His eyes glowed as he looked at it, and he obviously wanted to touch it. His hosts urged him to go ahead, and finally he did, pressing his fingertips against it as if it were sacred. One of them even apologized, explaining that they'd have given it to him to take home if they could.

I watched him tour the Great Pyramid. And, on the Greek islands, stand with tears running down his face staring at the government building that now occupies the grounds which had once been home to the Acropolis. *"Hard to believe,"* he said to an interviewer, *"that we could have been so stupid."* The Acropolis, of course, was destroyed during the Dark Age. Nobody knows the details.

"The most important thing we've done," he said to an audience at Andiquar University, *"was to get off-world. That was the single act that opened the universe to us. We owe all that to the men and women who made the Apollo flights possible and especially to those who put their lives at risk, and who sometimes paid the price, to actually ride*

the vehicles. They got us started. Once we'd set foot on the Moon, it was inevitable that we'd go on to Rimway and Dellaconda and the edge of the galaxy. We knew it would take a while. That we'd get in our own way. That we'd be discouraged by the vast distances involved simply in going to Mars. We understood that we were probably facing an empty and cold universe. But it was the beginning, and in our hearts we must have known we would not be stopped." At that point, he paused and looked out across his listeners. *"It is our severe loss that so little remains from that Golden Age. What would we not give to be able to hold in our hands the helmet Alan Shepard wore on that first fateful flight?"*

He visited Coranthe, the city that had served as the headquarters of Mary Latvin, who brought light back to the world at the depths of the Dark Age. There's a picture of him standing beside her statue, her mantra inscribed on its base: NEVERMORE.

It's possible to watch him and his team at various dig sites, recovering artifacts. And celebrating after a visit to the Hadley Telescope, which is still in orbit, though of course it has not been used for three thousand years. The Hadley, of course, provided our first real clues about the conditions that led to the Big Bang.

Baylee loved to celebrate. Recover an artifact, locate a promising dig site, translate an inscription in a lost language, possibly just get under cover before the rains came, all were good reason to raise the glass.

Southwick and Winter showed up consistently. And on one occasion there were nine or ten of them in a modular hut drinking to Southwick, who, according to the caption, had saved Baylee's life. No details were given, but Baylee's left wrist was wrapped, and he looked unusually somber.

One celebration took place on the deck of a boat. It belonged to the Southwick Foundation, and was almost as big as the *Belle-Marie*. Baylee, Southwick, and a half dozen colleagues had just recovered the notebooks of Adrian Chang.

The record indicated that when Baylee returned to Rimway permanently in 1417, he'd been a different person. He declined speaking invitations, avoided conferences that, in earlier years, he'd attended with enthusiasm, and on two occasions he sent representatives to accept awards for him. He had never done that before. People who qualified as old friends found him difficult to reach. Southwick seems to have been the exception.

In a few personal letters published by others, Baylee revealed a sense of rage at the political leaders at the beginning of the Dark Age who, in his view, had through corruption and sheer stupidity allowed a glittering civilization to come apart. It wasn't always clear precisely who he was talking about, and he probably wasn't certain himself. Too much of the history of the period has been lost. It's known the collapse was brought about primarily by economic failure and by the inclination of leaders to employ force over diplomacy. One comment by Baylee shows his frustration: *"They had a technology that had taken them to the stars. They had stable governments, or at least most of them did. How could they possibly have given it all away? Look in their histories, and there are numerous comments about the development of a new Rome, about trying to do too much. Is that possibly what happened?"*

He was talking about the West.

Most historians believe that there are historical cycles. They point to the Time of Troubles, which was still another collapse. Not as complete as the Dark Age (the second dark age, really), but nevertheless we came pretty close to going under again. Maybe it just happens every four or five thousand years. But Baylee's bitterness extended beyond the general breakdown. He makes a particular point in arguing that maybe historians are right and we do live in a cycle, but there are some things that should be preserved. He doesn't specify what, and I didn't get the impression he was talking about artifacts. I suspect he had in mind the accomplishments of those who gave us science, who wrote the great books, who stood up to fanatics, and who took us to the stars.

Many historians credit the space effort with ultimately saving the human race. It could not have survived, they argue, had it been confined to Earth, with its population problems, its deteriorating climate, and the human propensity to make war. Baylee was not among them. He argues that we would have found a way without the interstellars. Population growth, he says, was already easing around the world before those first manned missions went out beyond the Oort Cloud. We'd backed off most of the practices that had damaged the environment. We'd have eventually stopped the warfare, as we have in fact done over these last few thousand years. With a few minor exceptions, of course.

"*You don't need faster-than-light,*" Argent Pierson quotes him as saying. "*All you need is enough sense to know when you're in trouble. We have that. Sometimes it comes in a bit late. But when the chips are down, we're pretty good at drawing the aces. What interstellar travel did for us was show us who we really were.*"

"Hard to believe, isn't it?" Alex said. "I can't imagine this guy coming home with a Corbett transmitter, dropping it into a closet, and forgetting about it."

"Does that mean we're going to pursue this thing?"

He looked amused. "It's exactly the kind of thing that Gabe would have loved to get involved with."

"Maybe when the *Capella* shows up—"

"Yeah."

It was supposed to be a joke. But I guess I should have thought before opening my mouth. It was unlikely Gabe would be getting off anytime soon.

Shara and I were back at the Hillside the following day. She seemed subdued. "Everything okay?" I asked.

"John's desperate."

"Why?"

"Because Plan A looks like a disaster."

"You mean where we take as many off the ship as we can and let the rest go down the road for another five years?" I didn't mean that to be as callous as it must have sounded.

"Chase, we can't even be sure how long it will stay accessible. Nobody talks about that. At least not in public."

"I thought you'd settled on ten hours." The estimate kept changing, but it had never varied very much.

"That's based on our experiences with the other ships. And with some experiments. But those were much smaller and they were in different time/space streams and the bottom line is that we don't know what we're doing. Not for certain.

"It's a passenger vessel, so they have a connecting tube that will allow them to cross directly into another ship. We're getting a break there. The last thing we'd want is to be opening and closing an airlock every few minutes. What scares me is the possibility that the *Capella* will fade out in the middle of the operation. If that happens, we could lose a couple of hundred people. It's a nightmare."

"So what are they going to do? You said something before about a backup."

"I was talking about lifeboats."

"Lifeboats?"

She stared down at her plate of strawberries and potato salad. "Yeah." She scooped up some of the salad and bit into it. "They might work. There's a downside, though. We'd be using the ship's appearance this time to set things up. We won't really be able to get many people off until it comes back."

"In five years."

"Right."

"Well, that's better than the *hundred* years some people are talking about. What are the lifeboats?"

"They've been under construction for a while. Some of us, including John, wanted a way to avoid stretching this thing out indefinitely. The boats should work. They're self-inflatable. Each lifeboat can support sixty-four people for twenty-two hours, which should be plenty of time for the rescue vehicles to reach them. I've been inside one. It's like the interior of a small shuttle. Sixteen rows of four seats divided by a center aisle. With washrooms. They have transmitters, lights, and a pair of jets to take them away from the *Capella*.

"The plan is that when they get here, they open their cargo bay and we stack forty-four boats inside. Or as many as we can. That's the mission. If we can get a few people off at the same time, so much the better."

"You're going to be able to fit forty-four of these things into the cargo bay?"

"Yes. They're small packages and, as I said, they self-inflate. We're hoping the space isn't taken up by too much cargo. There's no way to check that. We've talked with Orion, and they think we'll probably be able to make it work. They've got three decks, and they should be able to inflate three vehicles per deck. So they inflate nine of the boats at a crack, and get their people on board. Meanwhile, for us, four and a half years go by." She shook her head. "Then they're back. We're waiting for them. They open up, launch nine boats, and close the doors. We pick up the people in the boats. Then repeat the process. It should take about forty minutes to set up a second launch. That means if we get any kind of break we should be able to get everyone off in about three hours." She lifted a strawberry on the tip of her fork and took a bite. "Did I tell you that Wainscot Pictures is threatening us?"

"Who's *us*?"

"The SRF."

"What?" I almost spilled my iced tea. "About what?"

"You know Guy Bentley is on the *Capella*?"

"The comedian? Yes, I remember hearing that."

"The studio wants him back. They want us to arrange things so he's one of the first people off the ship."

"They're crazy."

"Bentley's one of the most popular people in the Confederacy."

"So what? They can't sue you, can they?"

"No. But they're suggesting that they'll target John Kraus and a few of the other people at the top of the organization. Make them laughingstocks."

I tried my tuna sandwich. And put it back down. "I wouldn't worry about it," I said.

"Why not?"

"The SRF will take some heat if they can't get everyone off this time around. But if they can manage five years down the line, they'll all be heroes. And Kraus especially will be untouchable."

"Maybe," she said. "We're getting a lot of requests. People asking us, pleading with us, to get relatives and friends off, and do it *now*. Some are offering money. We got a call from a woman yesterday who couldn't stop crying." She took a deep breath. "I feel sorry for them. But there are limits to what we can do." She glared past me at nothing in particular. "The strawberries are good."

Two guys and a young woman were sitting at an adjoining table, behind Shara. They exchanged whispered comments. Then one of the guys got up, walked over to us, and waited until he'd caught Shara's attention. "Pardon me," he said. "I couldn't help overhearing." He was average size, mid-thirties, with black hair. He looked unhappy. "I'm Ron Aquilar. My fiancée, Leslie Cameron, is on the *Capella*. I understand what you're saying, but I'd do anything to get her off. Is there really no way it can be done?"

Shara looked lost. "Ron," she said, "we won't have any control over which passengers get off first. We can't even contact the ship until it shows up. So there's no time to make special arrangements. I'm sorry."

"No, no," he said. "I understand that. I'm not asking you to move her to the head of the line." He glanced in my direction, then his eyes locked on Shara. "She was twenty-two when she got on that damned thing. I was twenty-seven. If you guys have it right, her age hasn't changed. I'm thirty-eight now. She probably won't make it off this time. Which means that the next time around, I'll be forty-three. She won't have changed. Doctor—?" He groaned. "I'm sorry. I don't know your name."

"Michaels," she said.

"Dr. Michaels?"

"Yes."

"Dr. Michaels, she isn't likely to be very interested in marrying somebody twice her age. This is probably my last chance with her. What I need you to do is to let me go *on* the *Capella*."

"Ron," she said, "I can't do that. The time we'll have available is too short. Putting you on board will only take a few seconds. But the loss of those seconds will prevent someone else from getting off. Probably more than one person, in fact, because you'll be bucking traffic. Look, I'm sorry. But putting more people on the ship just makes the problem bigger."

He stared down at one of the empty chairs, hoping she'd ask him to sit. She didn't. He looked my way again. And I remember thinking how this was a situation to stay out of if there'd ever been one. But I didn't. "Ron," I said, "there's a chance if you went on board that, in the confusion, she'd get off."

"Okay," he said. It wasn't clear any longer which of us he was talking to. He touched his link. "Thank you both. Dr. Michaels, you have my code, in case you change your mind. Please think about it."

ELEVEN

Take the plunge, or hesitate at the brink,
Seize the moment, or stop to think.
Make the call, and know for certain
That to stand on the side will bring down the curtain.

—Richard Hobbes, *Moonlight Lessons*, 2417 C.E.

"Alex," Marissa said, "I feel the same way you do. I'd love to know why Grandpop never said anything." We were at her house, which was an exquisite manor with Greek columns and circular windows looking out across the ocean. "There must be a way to find out."

"Unfortunately," said Alex, "as things stand now, we don't even know where to begin. I've been looking at everything I can find about him. But I still don't have a handle on what happened. We just don't really have much to work with."

She was sitting in a sofa, looking weary. "I hate to give up that easily."

"We're not giving up. Maybe someone who knew him will remember *something* that will help us. You and your folks should continue to think about who else there might be."

"You don't sound optimistic, Alex."

"To be honest, I'm not."

There's a piece of advice my mom offered one time that has stayed with me: Never back off something you really want to do because you're afraid of failing. You don't want to get near the end of your life and wonder whether you might have succeeded if you'd only tried harder.

I knew that would be the case with Alex. If he let this thing go, it would always haunt him. But I didn't say anything. If I tried persuading him to do something, his position would only harden. Anyhow, we're all aware that the subconscious knows what's best for us. As long as the conscious mind doesn't get in the way. So I sat back and waited for him to tell me he'd found something, or whatever, and that we were headed for Earth.

And I waited.

When, after a couple of weeks, nothing happened, Marissa let me know how disappointed she was. "The reason I came to you guys," she said, "was your boss's reputation. He's supposed to be a guy who gets things done."

We had a rule at the country house: You never, ever, for any reason, summon the avatar of Gabriel Benedict. He was gone, and maybe we'd get him back and maybe we wouldn't. That's another issue. In any case, the experience had been painful, and neither of us needed to have an electronic version of him showing up to remind us of how much we'd lost.

This whole thing with avatars has always puzzled me. Why people would want to get simulacra of themselves onto the net, or, worse, why we'd want to sit and talk with people we once loved who were no longer really there, just seems crazy. They have some value for people conducting an investigation, but other than that, the whole process seems counterproductive. The number of marriages breaking up, for example, because people are more interested in younger versions of their spouses, has gone through the roof.

All right: Back to the issue at hand. Gabe had known Baylee. There was a possibility his avatar might be able to provide some helpful information. I thought about breaking the rule and bringing his avatar in, but Alex would have taken umbrage. So I dug a photograph out of the collection, one in which Gabe was wearing his charge-the-hill expeditionary hat, framed it, and put it on my desk.

Next time Alex came into my office, it caught his eye immediately. "What's that?" he said.

"Just came across it this morning. You know, I miss him."

"I know." He was playing it straight. "I do, too." Then he surprised me. "We need to talk to him."

"To Gabe?"

"Yes. He might have an idea about this thing with Baylee. Jacob, get him for us, please."

I braced myself, but Alex sat down and smiled politely when the avatar appeared moments later.

"I don't think I can be of much help," Gabe's avatar said. *"I never really knew Garnett Baylee that well."*

"Welcome to the club," said Alex.

"He was a decent man, as far as I could tell. You could trust him. I was pretty young when I met him. What I particularly liked was that he really cared about being an archeologist. In fact, he might have been the reason I got so interested in the profession myself." Gabe was dressed the way I remembered him, in fatigues with a hat very much like the one in the picture. And he had a laser strapped to his belt.

"Can you think of any reason," Alex asked, "why he'd have brought the Corbett home and done nothing with it other than toss it into his closet?"

"No. I can't imagine how that could have happened." He closed his eyes and shook his head. *"If you don't have a specific lead, and it sounds as if you don't, I'd just let it go. Trying to chase this down sounds like a waste of time."*

"There might be more artifacts out there."

"That's unlikely, Alex, and you know that as well as I do. If there were more, they'd have been in his closet, too. To be honest, I can't imagine why you are pursuing this."

"Are you kidding?"

"*Ineffective use of your time. Occasionally, things happen that we can't account for. Just let it go.*"

"Okay, Gabe. One more question: When Baylee was on Earth, there must have been someone he spent time with. A friend."

"*I can help you there,*" he said. "*Try Les Fremont. He was director of the North American Archeological Institute. The problem is that he wasn't young when Baylee was running around. He may not even be alive now. But if Baylee had anything he would have been willing to share, Fremont would be as good a bet as anyone.*"

I called Marissa. "We have a couple of good offers for you on the transmitter. But Alex thinks you should be patient. We're pretty sure others are on the way."

"*My dad thinks we should do what Grandpop would have done. Decline the museum's offer and give it to them.*"

"Marissa, I wouldn't want to get in the middle of this, but keep in mind it's worth a lot of money."

Alex makes it a point to take me to dinner once, and sometimes twice, a week. We vary the restaurants, but on that night we headed off to Mully's Top of the World. Mully's is located on the summit of Mt. Oskar, and it provides a magnificent view of surrounding mountains, the Melony, and Lake Accord. There were a couple of boats on the lake. They were lit up and apparently partying.

We're supposed to have an arrangement that we don't talk business on these occasions, but, of course, that's an impossible objective. Although I should give him credit: He tries. He was talking about *Payton's Follies*, a show he'd seen the previous evening. It was a musical satire on inept guys trying to figure out ways to bed women. You know, the usual. When he'd finished, he mentioned as a kind of by-the-way that he'd had a call from John Kraus. "He tells me the *Capella* Families is organizing a virtual protest. You know why?"

I shrugged. "I can guess."

"Apparently your buddy JoAnn ran another experiment. And it worked. They shut down the drive completely, and the ship just stayed where it was. They're going to try it again. Try to get a sense of how safe it is, I guess. The *Capella* Families wants them to stop, to touch absolutely nothing and bring the families out as best they can."

TWELVE

The mind has a thousand eyes
And the heart but one.
Yet the light of a whole life dies
When love is done.

—F. W. Bourdillon, *The Night Has a Thousand Eyes*, 1873 C.E.

Shara called to explain why I hadn't been informed. *"There's so much political pressure right now,"* she said. *"They didn't want to take a chance on the word getting out before they had a chance to run the test. But it was beautiful. Everything went exactly according to schedule. But there's still a problem."*

"It was another yacht," I said.

The news was all over the talk shows by noon. The reactions of the pundits ran the gamut from being horrified to observations that at last someone was showing some sense. Jerry Dumas, on *The Dumas Report*, called it, "finally, the breakthrough we've been waiting for." Lucia Brent thought it was "a disaster waiting to happen." Hosts and guests on *The Daytime Show* and *Jennifer in the Morning* were appalled and grateful, sometimes simultaneously.

Several days after it started, Jacob informed us we had a call from a Mr. Culbertson. *"He'd like an appointment to talk with you, Alex. He's a lawyer. Represents the Capella Families."*

"I know who they are, Jacob," said Alex. "Tell him I'm busy." Alex shook his head. "I don't know what to tell these people." We were in the conference room, where he was looking through an inventory of eleventh-century Jamalian antiques that had just become available.

He marked off a couple that we would pursue. Then Jacob was back. *"Sir, he says it's very important."*

Alex sighed. "Okay. Put him through." He sat back and looked out the window at the old cemetery stones on the perimeter of the property. I got up to leave, but he waved me back into my seat.

Leonard Culbertson seemed like a decent guy. I guess I expected one of those smarmy lawyers who always show up in the police procedurals and the law-firm commercials. But he was quiet and unassuming, both qualities I didn't associate with his profession. He had thick silver hair that he had to keep brushing back. And blue eyes that had all the appeal of youth. After he'd been introduced to Alex, he asked who I was.

"Chase Kolpath," he said. "She's my associate."

He studied me for a moment. *"Ms. Kolpath, do you have a connection with Gabriel Benedict?"*

That surprised me. "He was my former employer," I said. "And a friend." I was still talking about him in the past tense.

"All right. I assume you both know what our concerns are. And Ms. Kolpath, you're welcome to participate in the discussion, if you like. Assuming Mr. Benedict has no objection."

"I don't have time for a discussion," said Alex. "Please keep it short, Mr. Culbertson." He looked my way. Did I want to get clear?

I hesitated because I didn't know what was coming. But there was no way I could walk away from it.

"You've had an extraordinary career, Mr. Benedict," said Culbertson.

Alex turned his let's-move-it-along gaze on the lawyer. "It's been a good run. The downside was losing my uncle."

"I'm sure. You must have been very happy when you learned he was still alive. That it might be possible to bring him back."

"Of course. May I ask you to get to the point?"

"*Since you've been connected with this from the beginning, you understand more than most what's involved. The scientists want to experiment with the star-drive unit. They think that they can fine-tune it, and the ship will no longer be dragged into that odd area they call transcendental space.*"

"*Transdimensional* space, you mean. But actually, we're talking about a warp."

Culbertson laughed it away. "*I'm sorry. My physics has always been a bit on the weak side. The point is they're not sure. There's a possibility we could lose the ship permanently. Along with its passengers.*"

"I don't know whether they're certain or not, Mr. Culbertson. You'd have to ask them."

The lawyer was leaning out of a large, cushy armchair. "*I don't have to ask them. They are telling us that there's no guarantee. They like the odds. That's what they're saying. Mr. Benedict, I represent the families of more than four hundred passengers. The families do not want anybody screwing around with the drive unit. They don't want anyone taking any chance on stranding their loved ones permanently on that ship.*" He looked across at Alex, then at me. "*I'd be surprised if you don't feel the same way.*"

"Mr. Culbertson, I don't believe they are going to take any chances with the lives of the passengers."

"*I hope you're right. We would all like to get these people back to their families as quickly as possible. But I'm sure you'd agree that risking all those lives to hurry the process along when otherwise they seem to be in no danger is at the very least reckless?*"

"Possibly. The problem is that, as things are now, a lot of families are broken apart. Some kids face the prospect of not seeing their parents for twenty-five years. Or more. I know you represent families who want to exercise caution on this. But there are several hundred other families who are saying that their family members have already been gone eleven years. That they want them back. In some cases, husbands are separated from wives. There are teenagers on board, without their parents." Alex's eyes were locked on the lawyer. "For that matter, there's no guarantee that the cycle will hold indefinitely. It's possible that no matter what we do, the ship could go down and not come back. They just don't know, Mr. Culbertson."

"What about you, Ms. Kolpath?" he asked. *"Where do you stand on this?"*

"I hate it," I said. "I'm grateful they don't need me to make the decision because I don't know what the right call would be."

"I understand," he said. *"But somebody's going to have to decide. Now either we—the concerned families—can make it, or we can leave it to the physicists. If they get their way, and we lose all those people, they'll simply comment that these things are not definitive, and they took the most appropriate action. They don't have a serious stake in the game."*

I kept going: "Do you really believe that, Mr. Culbertson? Nobody has a higher stake than they do. JoAnn Suttner is putting everything on the line. She feels personally responsible for the lives of those people. If she can't make the right thing happen, it will follow her through the rest of her life."

Culbertson was looking into a corner of the room. At a photo of Gabe. *"Is that your uncle?"*

"Yes," said Alex.

"You look alike." He rearranged himself in the chair, trying to get comfortable. *"Mr. Benedict, if they asked* your *advice, what would it be?"*

Alex sat, unmoving. I looked out at the tree branches swinging gently in the wind. "I honestly don't know," he said finally. "I've asked myself what I'd want if I were *on* the ship. In that case, I think I'd just as soon wait. Play it safe. I mean, it's not as if I'd actually *have* to wait. It would be just a case of sitting it out for another couple of hours. But I don't have a family that needs me back *now*. In fact, if I had to stay out there for a quarter century, the only person who'd notice I was gone is sitting right here." He glanced over at me and smiled.

"That's certainly a rational response. You've become a public personality, Mr. Benedict. People trust you. Moreover, you're a big part of the reason we learned about the lost ships. The reality is that, to a

substantial degree, this is going to become your decision. You're going to be pressed on both sides. Which I guess is what I'm doing now. And I apologize if I'm making you uncomfortable. But a lot of people will go along with what you have to say in this matter. I hope you'll make your views public. We need you. We need you to take a stand, to ensure that we don't, through impatience, kill all those people."

"I think you're overestimating my influence."

"I don't believe that's the case, sir. This thing may even go to court. But, whether it does or not, in the end it will be a political issue. There's no applicable law here. In any case, Mr. Benedict, Alex, I want you to know we will appreciate any support you can give us."

THIRTEEN

Few people achieve greatness. One reason is that the opportunity, for the vast majority of us, never even shows up. Another is that if it does, it will inevitably look like a long shot. And the temptation invariably is to play it safe.

—Schiaparelli Cleve, *Autobiography*, 8645 C.E.

Alex was out of the building later that day when we received a call from the Meridian Library in Areppo. Despite the fact it's located on an island, the Meridian Library is probably the major storage complex for historical data on the planet. The voice was male. *"We located the information Mr. Benedict called for. We can forward the entire result if you wish. Or if you want us to do a specific search, we can manage that as well."*

"No, no," I said, with no idea what we were talking about. "Why don't you just send the entire package? And thank you."

Jacob's professorial image appeared in the middle of the room, quiet smile, gray beard, dark jacket. *"It's coming in now, Chase."*

"What is it?"

"It's Armand Rigolo's Western Collapse. *I guess Alex doesn't have enough to read these days."* Rigolo's book was the classic on the subject. It's one and a half million words, written during the recovery period that began at the end of the Fourth Millennium. He paused. *"Wait. There's more."*

"What else?"

"Still coming in. Books about the two space museums, Huntsville and Florida. Also third-millennium catalogs and publicity documents from both places advising visitors why they would profit from a tour. Personnel sheets. Some inventories. Gift-shop ordering forms. There's quite a lot really. And a note from one of the Meridian librarians."

"Let me see the note."

It appeared on the display:

Alex, this is everything we have on it. I hope you find what you're looking for.

—Jami

I was paging through the material when Alex returned. He had a client with him, so it was another half hour before he actually had time to stop by the office. "Did they send us anything interesting?" he asked.

"I don't know. What are we looking for?"

"Anything that might provide a clue to what Baylee was trying to do before he came home."

"Yeah. Okay. That's going to need someone smarter than I am."

"Chase, I think we're looking at a major discovery." He sighed. "What did we get?" Jacob provided the list of enclosed materials, and Alex needed only a moment before something caught his attention. "The Huntsville inventory. Do we have a date, Jacob?"

"September 30, 3111."

"Is that significant?" I asked.

"The inventory had some transmitters. It doesn't say what kind. Wait a minute. But they have serial numbers."

And the slowest person in the room came out of her coma. "The Corbett," I said.

Alex's voice reflected his excitement: "Yes. And the numbers match. Baylee's hypercomm unit is on the list. There were three of them." He raised a fist. "Yes! Magnificent!"

"So are we saying," I asked, "that Baylee found the stuff that was at the Huntsville museum?"

"That's what it looks like."

"All right. Where do we go from here?"

"I think we owe ourselves a vacation on the home world, don't you?"

"That's a long haul, Alex. And we still have no idea where to look."

"That's not entirely true. But you can stay here if you want to. I'll understand."

Sure he would. "All right. But how could Baylee have found the artifacts from Huntsville? That would have been the biggest archeological discovery ever. So he comes home and just throws the transmitter in the closet? And doesn't say anything?"

"Doesn't make much sense, does it?"

"Not that I can see."

"So all right. Let's just forget about it and get back to our accounting."

"You know, Alex, you can be sarcastic at times."

That brought a modest smile. "My feelings are hurt."

"Okay," I said. "When do we leave?"

"The *Capella* isn't expected for several weeks. We should be back long before then. But let's try to get a running start."

"So where exactly are we going?"

"Gabe gave us one suggestion: Les Fremont. Luciana Moretti's another possibility."

It took me a moment, but I remembered: She was an advisor to the Southwick Foundation. "Believe it or not, Chase, she's also a music professor. She and Baylee played together in an amateur band. One or the other should have some idea what he was up to."

"Okay," I said.

"Call Marissa. Advise her there's a good chance the value of the transmitter will go up over the next few weeks. Tell her to hold on to it."

The following morning, we caught the shuttle to Skydeck. We had just left the ground when Alex asked me if I knew who Monroe Billings was. I'd heard the name, but that was all. "He's a science fiction writer," he said. "He's pretty well-known in the field."

"Okay," I said. "I'm not big on fantasy. But why are you asking?"

"It's not exactly fantasy."

"Okay."

"He's written some seriously off-the-wall novels. In one, an expedition goes to Andromeda and discovers it's *alive*."

"What is?"

"Andromeda."

"And you're telling me it's not fantasy."

"In another, people are stored in computers and become immortal."

"I'd certainly look forward to that."

"He also wrote *Good Times*."

"I assume it's not as upbeat as it sounds."

"It deals with genetic manipulation designed to make everybody happy."

"That sounds pretty good."

"Nothing ever works out well in these books. Can you imagine living with someone who's always happy?" He sighed. "Anyhow, to answer your question, one of his books is *Time Travelers Never Wait in Line*. His characters go back to the Fourth Millennium. You know why?"

"I have no idea."

"They're looking for what they call the Apollo Sanctuary."

"That's where the Huntsville artifacts are hidden?"

"Yes."

"You're kidding. Do they find it?"

"Yes. And they bring everything back with them to our time. And the artifacts are all taken to a safe place."

"That sounds like a happy ending. Where was the safe place?"

"Winnipeg." Earth's global capital. Well, that seemed appropriate. "It strikes me," he continued, "it would have been a happier ending if they'd auctioned everything."

We were just rising above the clouds. "Maybe," I said, "we should look there first."

FOURTEEN

O happy day, to follow that long, winding track
Down the mountain and across the bridge,
To wander through woods and across wide fields
And come at last into the warm embrace
Of the place where I began.

—Mara Delona, *Travels with the Bishop*, 1404

I'd been to Earth a few years earlier and hadn't enjoyed the arrival process. As was normal routine throughout the Confederacy, we turned control of the *Belle-Marie* over to their operations center so they could bring us in. At other worlds, that was pretty much the end of it. Not at Earth's Galileo Station.

"Belle-Marie," said a radio voice, *"what is the name of the pilot, please?"*

"Chase Kolpath."

"Ms. Kolpath, are you carrying any passengers?" The voice was a bored baritone.

"One. Alex Benedict."

"Please spell the last name."

I spelled it for them.

"How long do you expect to be here?"

"We're not certain. Possibly a month or so."

"And what is the purpose of your visit?"

"We'll be doing some historical research."

"Do you have any animals on board?"

"No."

"Very good. Thank you."

"I've a question."

"Go ahead."

"I'd like to take our lander groundside instead of using the shuttle. Can we arrange that?"

"Just a moment, please."

The Earth filled the sky. We were on the nightside. The globe sparkled with lights. But I couldn't be sure which continents we were looking at.

"Belle-Marie, did you make prior arrangements to use your lander?"

"No. Should I have done that?"

"I'm sorry. It's required." His voice softened. *"Air traffic is heavy. Unless you have a good reason, they aren't likely to allow it."*

"Let it go," said Alex.

As far as I know, the home world is the only place with customs and immigration operations. Everybody is a citizen of the Confederacy, but Earth has laws left over from the old days, when they had serious problems with population, pirates, terrorists, smugglers, and I'm not sure what else.

We docked, and I opened the hatch. A customs officer was waiting. "Ms. Kolpath," he said, "do you have anything of value that you plan to leave behind?"

"No, sir."

"How about you, Mr. Benedict?"

"No, I don't."

He scanned the luggage. Then he pointed at one of Alex's bags. "Open this one, please."

Alex complied, and the officer looked in, moved some clothes around, and retrieved Alex's scanner. "Why do you need this?"

"We'll be doing some archeological work."

"I see. Do you have a license?"

Alex produced it, but the officer shook his head. "This is not applicable here, sir. I'm sorry, but we'll have to take this. Privacy restrictions." He produced a ticket and handed it to us. "You can pick it up when you're leaving."

Alex put the ticket in his pocket. "How can I get a license?"

"You can apply for it in the services office, sir, which is located in the Altair concourse. But be aware that approval will take a while. They're a little nervous about devices like this."

"I guess I can understand why," said Alex.

"You'll be staying about a month? Is that correct?"

"That's right," said Alex.

He entered the information into a computer and produced two red cards, which he gave to us. "I'm allowing you six weeks. If you expect to remain longer, follow the instructions on the back of the card." He smiled and made it clear he was being generous. "When you leave, you'll want to turn this in."

We walked under a large sign blinking WELCOME HOME and strolled out into the Centauri Concourse, where we joined a crowd of sightseers, mostly young couples and families. Our shuttle would be taking us down to Arkon. But we were looking at a ten-hour wait.

"Do you want to get a room?" he asked.

"It's okay. We don't have our luggage, and I can sit around out here as easily as in a hotel." It was midmorning Eastern Time on the American continent, which was our destination, so I'd reset the time on the *Belle-Marie* to match. Which is to say we'd gotten up shortly before coming into port.

Pictures of major cities and tourist sites lined the walls, along with exhortations to look good by using Miranda Body Spray for healthy skin. The tourist sites included the Grand Canyon, New York Island, Mt. Everest, Berlin Park, the pyramids, and the Great Wall of China.

Major cities, places like Balaclava, Yung-Wei, Kladno, and Tucson ran programs explaining why tourists would enjoy visiting. They displayed historical and cultural sites, theaters and parks, silver towers glittering in sunlight and kids splashing around in pools. "We should turn this into a vacation," I said

Alex looked pleased at the suggestion. "If we can figure out where Baylee got that transmitter," he said, "I'll be happy to spring for a week off."

We wandered through gift and clothing shops. I couldn't resist buying an aqua-colored blouse with both faces of Earth emblazoned on it. There were game shops and entertainment centers. Eventually, we went into the Vanova Dining Room, found a table near the window, and ordered lunch.

I think we were both a bit overwhelmed. We'd been there before, but there'd been distractions then. This was the first time I really had an opportunity to just sit around contemplating the home world, the place where everything had begun. I tried to imagine what life had been like when we were confined to a single planet. Or, to go back even earlier, to a time when we thought the Earth was the center of the universe.

It got me thinking about how much we take for granted. Sightseeing in those early years was restricted to what you could see from a boat or an aircraft. If you wanted to get a look at, say, Saturn, you needed a telescope. People sometimes talked about the end of the world. And for a while, during the atomic standoff of the twentieth century, it looked as if it might happen. I know if we started piling up nuclear weapons on Rimway, I'd move somewhere else. I sat there and looked down and thought how lucky I'd been to have been born when I was.

The sandwiches came, and we exchanged comments on the food. "How's yours?"

"It's good. I thought about getting the pork roll, but the tuna was probably a better idea."

Now we're spread out across several hundred worlds, and we've left our footprints on countless others. I wondered whether, in those ancient times, when they made those first flights to the Moon, if they'd ever dreamed of going to the stars. They knew by then how far the closest stars were, so it must have seemed impossible. The first off-world flights had required three days to get to the Moon. Incredible. The Moon was only a quarter million miles away. You could almost have walked it. They'd have needed over a year to get to Mars.

I couldn't help wondering why they would even have bothered. There was nothing on Mars. And the rest of the solar system had looked sterile. If they'd tried to go to the nearest star, Proxima Centauri, at those velocities, it would have taken fifty thousand years.

What would have happened if they'd just given up? They'd come close. But they'd stayed with it. Manned flights had eventually headed out for Mars and then moved to Europa and beyond. They'd lost a few people along the way. But the vehicles had gotten better, and Maureen Caskill, in the twenty-fifth century, had figured out how to break the rules, to get past light speed. And after that, the stars had opened up.

"Makes you proud," I said.

Alex didn't ask for an explanation. "It's why we need to hang on to our history. It tells us who we are."

I sat there, munching my sandwich, thinking what Alan Shepard would have given to have known that one day I'd be visiting from another place so far away that no one in his time could have dreamed of going there. The restaurant wall carried photos of some of the early astronauts. Neil Armstrong, of course. And Viktor Patsayev. Yuri Gagarin, the first person in space. Valentina Tereshkova, the first woman. Gus Grissom. Gordon Cooper. John Glenn.

What would they have thought? Did they have any sense they were preparing the way for people who'd think of interstellars as *yachts*?

Science had been on the move in those years. It was the Golden Age, but they probably never realized it.

And maybe not so much simply because of the scientific advances, especially the breakthrough work in physics and medicine, the arrival of communications technology and advances in engineering, but because they had the people who knew how to make it pay off. They'd gotten past the nuclear threat, extended life spans, and generally made their world a better place. It hadn't been perfect. Wars continued.

They had problems taking care of their poor. They had lunatics who thought God wanted them to commit mass murder. But on the whole they did pretty well. And Alex and I were collecting the benefits.

"Chase, are you there?" He was looking at me, his brow creased. "You all right?"

"Oh. Sorry. I was just thinking."

"They want to know if you'd like some dessert."

FIFTEEN

Time's the king of men,
He's both their parent, and he is their grave,
And gives them what he will, not what they crave.

—William Shakespeare, *Pericles*

The shuttle brought us down over the Atlantic. We dropped out of the clouds into driving rain and headed over open water toward the American coast. Alex was seated by the aisle, consulting his notebook. "We're over the Jersey Islands now," he said. "That big one *there* is Manchester Island. I think." He peered out the window and checked his notebook again. "Yes. And just north of it is Plumsted. They're popular vacation spots." A cabin cruiser was moving west, leaving a wide wake. Nothing in that direction except ocean.

Ardmore was a spectacular city, blending Golden Age architecture with ultramodern spires and cones. Broad parks and walkways were visible as we came in off the sea and landed at the terminal, where Jay Carmody, an old friend of Alex's, was waiting. He was a methodical guy with blond hair and golden eyes. Handsome by anybody's standards, except that he could have used some animation. He said how good it was to see us again. "I'm not sure how much I can help, Alex," he said. "But I'll be happy to do whatever I can. I never actually met Garnett Baylee. I knew about him, of course. He was a big name here.

I saw him a couple of times at conferences. But always from a distance. When did he die?"

"About eleven years ago." He thought about it. "Maybe a bit more in terrestrial years."

We were at the baggage section. I tried to pick up my luggage, but Jay wouldn't hear of it. He got both of my bags and led the way toward the exit. Outside, we put everything down and waited while he went to get his car. Forty minutes later, we were pulling up under a full moon in front of a modest two-story cottage about a quarter mile from Sabat University, where Jay was a history professor. Lights went on, we climbed out, passed through a gate in a picket fence, and went up three steps onto an enclosed porch. The door opened, and a smiling middle-aged woman came out and waved. "It's good to see you again, Alex," she said. "It's been a long time."

They embraced, and Jay introduced me to his wife Kali.

"I've looked into a lot of this stuff," Jay said. "The Corbett you mentioned was one of the artifacts they moved off the Moon at the beginning of the Dark Age. They closed everything down and brought back what they could. That included the Apollo 11 lander. They put most of it, including the transmitters, in the Huntsville Space Museum. There was never a mention of the Apollo 11 after that. Nobody knows what happened to it."

We were seated in their living room, surrounded by family pictures, Kali and Jay with their two kids, and with an older couple who were probably the parents of one or the other. Lots more of the kids. And a German shepherd. The shepherd's name was Vinnie. He was on the floor beside Kali's armchair.

Jay turned toward his wife. "Huntsville," he said, "also had most of what had been in the Florida museum. Stuff from the very beginning."

"That's the one," she said, "that was located near the launch facility, right?"

"Yes. At Cape Canaveral." He looked my way. "It's still a tourist attraction although you have to take a submarine to see it." All of Florida save the northernmost hundred miles or so had gone into the sea during that period. "What we need, Alex," he said, "is for somebody like you to come up with Cutler's diary. You know who Cutler was?"

Alex did. "Abraham Cutler," he said, "was the director at the Huntsville museum when the situation got critical."

"That's right. Mobs moved in, looted some of the stuff, and set some fires. That was enough for Cutler. Within the next few months, he moved as much out as he could. Sometimes under fire. There's some evidence he might not have survived the experience, that he was killed by the thieves. We just don't know." Jay's frustration was apparent. "You mentioned how valuable the Corbett is. I'd give two of them to get my hands on Cutler's account of what happened. The standard story is that everything was taken to Centralia and put in a storehouse in Union City. That's probably true, but what happened after that is a mystery.

"There's a report that Cutler's sister published his diary. But you know the situation. When the electronics went to hell, everything was lost. In some respects, we know more about the ancient Egyptians than we do about the United States of that era."

Alex smiled sadly. The Egyptians had carved everything in stone. There had been a second United States, a few centuries later. Most of the major nations that had collapsed during the Dark Age came back. None of them still existed, of course. At least not in the same form. Somebody finally figured out that as long as there are independent nations, there will be friction, and all that's necessary is one idiot in charge somewhere, and you get a war. Not good with the hyperweapons that kept getting more lethal. Which is why there's a single government now, overseeing several hundred worlds and outposts.

"Cutler," Jay said, "was effectively a minor figure. We don't even have proof, at least none that I know of, that he was the one who actually cleared the museum. But however that may be, *someone* did."

Kali looked good. Dark hair, bright eyes, and a smile that suggested she lived in a world that was endlessly amusing. They introduced the kids, who within a few minutes retreated upstairs, ostensibly doing homework. We could hear soft music and occasional conversation and laughter.

"Can I get you guys something to drink?" she asked.

I was unfamiliar with the choices and went for something called *a Virginia bullet*. It was okay, but a little strong for my tastes.

"Do you by any chance know Les Fremont?" asked Alex.

"I know him to say hello to. That's about all."

"He had a connection with Baylee. I understand they spent a lot of time together."

"Yeah. Wish I could help, but I don't have anything on that. I can tell you that Fremont shares the same passion for Golden Age archeology that Baylee did. But that's about it."

"Do you know where we can locate him?"

"Herbert," he said, addressing the house AI, "what do you have?"

"He still lives in Chantilly, Jay." Herbert gave us an address. Chantilly was on the shore of Lake Washington.

"Okay," said Alex. "Good. How about Luciana Moretti? Do you know anything about her?"

Jay repeated the name to himself. Frowned. "I've heard it somewhere."

"She's an adjunct of the Southwick Foundation. And a music professor."

"Oh, yes. A music professor with an interest in archeology. She used to show up at conferences."

"Did you ever run into her?"

"I did. Nice lady. But it's like Fremont. Strictly hello, and it's been nice to meet you. You want Herbert to check?"

"Please."

"Herbert?" he said.

"She was formerly an instructor at Beckham University," he said. *"Left there three years ago. Took up a similar position at the Amazon College of the Arts."*

"Where's that?" asked Alex.

"Corinthia," said the AI.

"It's in South America," added Jay. "On the Amazon, of course."

SIXTEEN

No single place in the world so embodies the spirit of the age as New York. If a time ever comes when its name is unknown, when it has disappeared from the maps, we will have forgotten who we are.

—Marianne Coxley, *On the Road*, 2044 C.E.

We caught a maglev into Chantilly. The last ten minutes of the ride took us along the lakeshore. We saw piers and boats and a few people fishing. And then, without warning, the Washington Monument rising from the water. It was supposed to be taller than the original one although there was no way to be sure. But reconstructing it constituted the ultimate act of defiance by the American people against the rising seas that were engulfing them and the rest of the world.

The cupola and dome of the old Capitol building had at one time also risen above the lake waters. But they were deemed to suggest a broken nation. They detracted from the grandeur expressed by the obelisk, so they were taken down.

I knew, of course, what the Golden Age capital had looked like in its halcyon era. When we'd visited Atlantis in the tour sub a few years earlier, there'd been no emotional reaction to the submerged ruins because there was no record of Atlantis in its prime. But this was different. Riding along that lakefront, I wondered what visitors to Andiquar, arriving in ten or eleven thousand years, would see? You wander around near Independence Park and the Hall of the People, and you get a sense that they will be there forever. But forever is a long time. The people who lived in Washington before the waters came probably thought that about their city. But it's all temporary, baby. Perpetuity is an illusion.

The planet was no longer a place Neil Armstrong would have recognized. Most of the historic Golden Age cities had been located on or near water. Consequently, they were for the most part gone. Paris and Rome remained. And Madrid and Tehran. A few others.

The international borders were gone as well. They'd dissolved during the Fourth Millennium, and with them the nation-states they'd defined. All prior attempts to form a world body had ultimately failed, resulting in international disruptions, until the rise of the World Union at the beginning of the Fifth Millennium. The much-feared global government had finally appeared, but it turned out to be, at worst, no more inefficient or corrupt than the governments that had preceded it. Its major contribution, during those early centuries, had been that it kept the peace. Gradually, when the turmoil subsided, and the Dark Age had passed, a quiet and efficient civilization emerged. On Earth, everyone lived, effectively, in a county or its equivalent. It may have been that a fair level of tranquillity finally arrived because people had decent lives. Controls were in place to keep power-grabbing loons at a distance. Professional politicians no longer existed. And maybe, as Ingmar Moseka commented, liberal education was available to all, and the result was a responsible population that wasn't as easy to fool as it had been in earlier times. Laws were made and policies developed by citizens who served a limited term, then returned to their lives. And people were free to live as they wished, without having to worry about where their next meal was coming from.

Advanced technology made food and housing available for all. AIs and robots did most of the work that no one else wanted to be bothered with. Most people managed careers, some simply lived lives of leisure. And humanity's movement to the stars, which had begun in the twenty-sixth century, accelerated. The half dozen worlds we occupied at the beginning of the Dark Age blossomed, a thousand years later, into a vast network.

People lived at leisure everywhere if they so desired. Even on the home world, it wasn't necessary to work if one wasn't inclined. Education was available for all, as was opportunity, and in the end, success was defined primarily by one's contribution to the community. Major achievements, scientific, literary, artistic, began to come in from distant worlds.

The people of Earth, however, never forgot who they were. They were never quite ready to accept equality with those whom they still thought of as colonials. Despite that, throughout the several hundred worlds of the Confederacy, the human race gradually evolved into a family.

Well, at least we'd gotten closer than ever before.

Les Fremont was still active with the North American Archeological Institute. He'd written two books on what he called expeditions into time, and he still participated in fieldwork. We arrived shortly after noon at a modest chateau located in a neighborhood filled with oaks and hedges. Kids tossed balls around at a corner playground. Fremont's home had a small lawn, surrounded by a plastene fence. A swing hung from a tree limb.

The cab pulled into the driveway, and Fremont came out the front door. He was a large, elderly man who walked with a limp. He waved as we got out of the cab and moved carefully down the steps leading off his deck. "Alex?" he asked.

Alex waved back. "Hello, Dr. Fremont." He looked around. "Beautiful place."

"Thank you. My name's Les, by the way."

They both turned toward me. "My colleague, Chase Kolpath."

"Pleasure to meet you, Chase." Fremont extended a hand and led us inside. "Hot out there." It was.

We sat down in the living room, and he asked what we'd like to drink. "We only have wine and fruit juice," he said. "I'm sorry. I just didn't think of it. I tend to overlook stuff now."

He offered no further explanation. But he glanced at a woman's framed photo. We all went for the wine.

He brought it out and settled into a large chair that might have been custom-made for him. We raised our glasses to Garnett Baylee, "who was," according to Fremont, "one of a kind." Then he folded his hands. "Alex, how may I be of assistance?"

Alex explained about the Corbett.

Fremont almost went into shock. "Really? Are you sure? He found a Corbett transmitter and didn't tell anybody? Is that what you're saying?"

"That's correct, Les."

"Why?"

"That's why we're here. We're hoping to get an answer."

"When you do, I'd like to hear what it is."

"Did you have much contact with him when he lived here?"

"I saw him pretty often. Garnie and I were friends. And we were both interested in Golden Age archeology. Although, if you want the truth, I think he was a little over-the-top."

"That's pretty much what we've heard generally."

"The thing he really cared about was the Huntsville museum artifacts. He spent a lifetime trying to figure out what happened to them."

"And what did he conclude?"

"I don't know if he ever *did* reach a conclusion. The last time I saw him, which was a year or so before he left us, he was still on the hunt. You know he lived near here, right?"

"No. I wasn't aware of that. Do you have the address?"

"Let me write it down for you." He reached for a pad, wrote on it, and handed the sheet to me. He'd have had to get up to pass it to Alex.

Alex looked at it. "Thanks," he said. "He lived nearby, but you lost contact with him for a *year*?"

"He just wasn't around much."

"Okay. By the way, Les, the Corbett transmitter Baylee's son-in-law found in his closet was on the Huntsville museum inventory."

"Why did I think you were going to say that? Is that really true?"

"Yes."

"That's hard to believe, Alex. If he'd found something like that, he would have told me. There's no way he'd have kept it to himself."

"Can you recall anything specific? Did he ever express any theory about where he thought the artifacts might be?"

"Well, he entertained different theories at different times. But none of them ever worked out. He was still wandering around trying to get an answer when I lost touch with him. So I don't know where he was looking during his last year or two here. He might even have backed off. He did that periodically. He'd join a mission to the Middle East, or Germany or somewhere. I was always glad to hear about that, that he was doing something else, because the whole thing seemed hopeless. I mean, we're talking about ancient history. What kind of condition was the transmitter in?"

"Actually, it was in pretty decent shape."

"Really? That seems strange."

"I know. I wondered about that, too. Wherever he found it, it had been in a safe place."

There was nothing more to be gained from Fremont, so we rode over to Baylee's former house. It was a modest place, a cottage with a view of a river, and, in the distance, a bridge. Several trees rose above the lawn. Two women were seated on the porch, one in a canvas chair, the other in a rocker.

Alex told the cab to stop. We got out and stood at the end of a walkway. The women looked in our direction, and we waved. One raised her hand in a halfhearted return of the gesture.

We went about halfway to the porch and stopped. "Hello," Alex said amiably. "We're doing some research on Garnett Baylee. I wonder if we could talk with you for a minute?" They glanced at each other. Neither appeared to have any clue who Baylee was. "I believe he owned this place at one time. About eighteen years ago."

The woman in the rocker frowned as we went closer. "Who are you?" she asked.

"My name's Alex Benedict." He smiled at me. "This is Chase Kolpath."

"Hello," I said, putting as much good cheer into it as I could manage.

The other woman got to her feet. "Is there a problem, Mr. Benedict?"

"No," he said. "No problem. But Garnett Baylee was a famous archeologist. He used to live here."

"I never heard of him. I'm not even sure what an archeologist does." She laughed as she saw Alex's reaction. "Just kidding," she added.

"We're writing a paper on Baylee, and I wanted to get a look at where he used to live. It's quite nice."

"Thank you. We like it."

Alex said something about the beautiful view and what an attractive neighborhood it was. "Did you buy the property from him?"

"I really don't recall what the owner's name was," said the woman in the rocker.

"Are you the current owner?"

"Yes, I am."

"May I ask how long you've been here?"

She had to think about it. "About seventeen, eighteen years. So it probably was him."

"Mr. Baylee died a few years ago, on Rimway. His family found a valuable artifact in one of the closets of his home there. It was a mechanism used by the early starships."

"Oh."

Suddenly, both women looked interested. The one in the canvas chair asked whether that translated into a lot of money?

"Thousands," said Alex. "The reason we stopped by is that we wanted to let you know. Have you by any chance found anything he might have left?"

"No," said the owner. "I don't recall anything. Other than a couple of rakes out in the shed."

"Okay," said Alex. "If you *do* find something, would you let me know? I'm an antiquarian. I can give you a good idea what it would be worth."

"Sure," she said. She put her thumb under a link-bracelet, and lifted it slightly.

Alex moved his hand in front of his own and sent her his code. "Good luck," he said. "I hope you come up with something."

"I'll let you know if we do."

They looked relieved to see us leave. And Alex was obviously unhappy. "What's wrong?"

"I'd give a lot to be able to look through the property. But I don't think they'd be very receptive."

"That's probably an accurate call. We could always arrange to have them win a dinner somewhere, then wait for them to leave the house."

Alex likes to say I have a great sense of humor. On that occasion, he said nothing.

"In case you're thinking about buying your way in," I said, "they'd have no reason to lie. And I know it happened once, but it's not likely there'd be anything on a closet shelf they hadn't noticed."

SEVENTEEN

We love artifacts because they provide a connection with the past and permit us, for a moment, to share in ancient glories. To own a pen that once belonged to Winston Churchill is to bring the man himself into our living room. A helmet worn by Andrey Sidorov allows us to climb out of the hatch with him onto Europan soil and to take that first up-close glance at Saturn. To touch the cup of Christ, could we find it, would put us in touch with Jesus himself.

—Kirby Edward, *Traveling in Time*, 1407

Moonbase had been in place almost a thousand years when they closed it down. It had become irrelevant to interplanetary travel as anything other than a monument. You could probably argue it had *always* been effectively irrelevant. But it must have been a glorious accomplishment when they first raised the flags. One of the old videos is still available, the clip that people must have watched around the world, the speeches, the ribbon-cutting ceremony, the raised glasses, the confetti drifting down ever so slowly.

The big celebrations had all been held there, marking the early flights to Mars, Europa, and Venus; the first manned vehicle to glide through the rings of Saturn; the first expedition to reach Mercury and send back images of its battered landscape and swollen sun. Visits to the outer planets. And, employing the long-awaited FTL technology, the first manned interstellar voyage. They'd gone to Alpha Centauri. It had required fourteen weeks, round-trip. They didn't have the Corbett transmitter then, so they had to wait for the mission to return before anyone knew whether it had succeeded. Unfortunately, there was no video record of that one.

There was another celebration four years later when a radio transmission, sent by the *Centaurus* crew from Alpha Centauri, was received by that same crew in Huntsville.

Moonbase apparently lit up on every possible occasion. And at home, streets from Moscow to Yokohama to Cairo filled with people and music.

The base even survived the global economic collapse during the twenty-fifth century, and the brief ascension of dictators throughout the world. The United States suffered under four of them before launching the revolution that hanged Marko the Magnificent on July 11, 2517. They launched fireworks at Moonbase that evening, as the news became public. And someone named Cass Mullen is quoted as having said that as long as there's a U.S.A., the lights at Moonbase would never go off.

Unfortunately, that turned out to be true.

Another global economic cataclysm hit early in the thirty-second century. Moonbase was by then a relatively trivial expense, but it was one the various supporting governments decided they couldn't afford. All but Russia, the UK, and the United States withdrew their support. As conditions at home deteriorated, and terrorist attacks struck the station, all six of the original lunar descent modules were brought back. And many of the artifacts. These tended to be personal items: the pressure suit worn by Neil Armstrong on that first landing, a notebook kept by Roger Chafee, a reproduction of the bridge of the *Centaurus*, the original mission plates for the first eight interstellar flights, arm patches from the Apollo missions, and an array of other gear belonging to individual crew members. There were also framed photos of ships and astronauts and comets and the Martian base, whose primary value lay in the fact that they had once decorated the walls of the original Moonbase.

Moonbase survived another forty years, until the three supporting nations dissolved.

It reminded me again how lucky we are to be living in this happy time. And I guess ultimately we owe it to the people who hung in throughout all the turbulence. Who kept the lights on at Moonbase until they went out on the ground.

That evening, Alex called Luciana Moretti and introduced us. "We're trying to figure out something about Garnett Baylee's work," he said, "and we're hoping you might be able to help."

Moretti looked surprised to hear Baylee's name. Her face was lined by too many years. Her frame was bent, and she looked tired. *"It's been a while since anyone's mentioned Garnett to me,"* she said, in a voice that seemed much too strong for its frail source. *"May I ask what your interest in him is?"*

Alex explained about the transmitter. "His family's wondering how he got possession of it. We were hoping you might have some idea where he might have found it."

"None," she said. *"But I'm happy to hear about it. He deserved a final success."* She was seated in an armchair, an open book in her lap.

"Were you in contact with him during the last year or two before he went back to Rimway?"

"Occasionally."

"And he never said anything to you about it?"

She laughed. *"No. I'd certainly remember it if he had. Are you certain about your analysis?"*

"Yes." He paused. "I understand you're an accomplished musician."

"That may be giving me too much credit, Alex. But it's nice to hear. I don't play professionally anymore, but I'm still active. My primary responsibility these days is directing the school's music program."

We talked about concerts and symphonies for a few minutes, with Alex asking most of the questions. It was a standard approach for him, putting Luciana at ease and allowing them to get to know each other somewhat. He was good at it.

Her husband Rod appeared and joined the conversation. Which was Alex's signal to get me into it also.

A string instrument I didn't recognize was stored in a glass cabinet behind her. *"It's the one she used to win the Cortez Prize,"* Rod said proudly. *"That was the first time I'd seen her, onstage at the Galabrium."*

"And that was how you guys met?" I asked.

"Oh, yes." Rod exchanged smiles with his wife. *"I was in the orchestra."*

"But," said Luciana, *"that's enough of that."* She looked at Alex. *"You wanted to talk to me about Garnett."*

"Yes," said Alex. "I understand you're an advisor for the Southwick Foundation."

"To a limited degree. I'm pleased to say we're doing reasonably well. Would you be interested in making a donation?"

"I'm an antiquarian, Luciana. You really want me to make a donation to an organization I'm in direct competition with?"

"You might not get another chance."

"Of course," Alex said. "After all, you're contributing your time to my current project." He tapped his link.

"No, Alex, that's really not necessary. I was just—"

"It's a good cause," he said.

She checked her own link and her eyes widened. *"That's very generous of you. I'll arrange to send you periodic updates on current projects."* She paused. *"Oh, but you're from Rimway, aren't you?"*

"That's correct."

"Well, so much for the updates. Now, if you will, satisfy my curiosity and tell me about the Corbett. Was it really found in Baylee's home?"

Alex described in detail what had happened. When he finished, Luciana sat in a state of disbelief.

"My inclination," she said after a long pause, *"is to tell you it's not possible. Something's wrong somewhere. But obviously it's true, or you wouldn't be here. I can't think of any way to account for it. I can't imagine where he got it or why he didn't say something to me. Or to Lawrence. You did tell Lawrence about this, right?"*

"Yes, I did."

"Well, it just beats the hell out of me."

"When was the last time you saw him?"

"*I think it was a few months before he left. Before he went back home. I thought he'd return, but he never did, then five or six years later, I heard he had died.*"

"Did you hear anything from him at all after he'd returned to Rimway?"

"*No,*" she said. "*And that was strange. I expected him to keep in touch, but he just seemed to disappear.*"

"Did you make any effort to contact him?"

"*I sent a couple of messages. Nothing special, just hello, how's everything? I don't recall whether he even responded. I don't think he did.*"

"Do you have any idea where he'd been spending his time during his last year here?"

"*He was in Centralia for a while. You know about the Prairie House, Alex?*"

"That's a storage facility. The place where the Huntsville artifacts were supposed to have been taken."

"*Correct. It was in Grand Forks. Grand Forks isn't there anymore. But the town still is. They call it Union City now. He was there for a while. I'd guess he was trying to decide whether there was anything to the claim.*"

"And—?"

"*I don't know how it turned out. I never got to talk to him about it. I assumed if he'd found anything, he'd have told me.*"

"One final question, Luciana: Can you think of *anyone* else who might be able to shed some light on this?"

"*No. I'd say if anybody would know anything, it would be Lawrence. But you've already talked with him. And I assume he wasn't able to help?*"

"No."

"*Then I can't imagine who can. Lawrence and Garnett were very close.*"

"Okay, thanks."

"*There might be one other possibility, Alex.*" She checked her notebook. "*There's a charter boat outfit in Cumberland. Eisa Friendly*

Charters. Garnett used to go there a lot. Liked to dive down to the Space Museum. You know the one I mean?"

"Sure. The Florida museum."

"Right. Anyhow, Eisa's run by a brother and sister. He got pretty close to them. It's possible they'd know something. I wouldn't bet on it, but it's all I can suggest."

EIGHTEEN

A treasure has value far beyond what can be taken to the bank. But it cannot be divided without losing its essence. Cut it into fragments, and there remains only money.

—Schiaparelli Cleve, *Autobiography*, 5611 C.E.

In the morning, we caught a maglev to Fargo, in Centralia. We arrived in the early evening, rented a car, and rode north through a flat landscape that consisted mostly of cottages and town houses and rosebushes and parks. The lawns weren't as lush as we'd seen elsewhere, but Centralia had a reputation for being cold. I'd seen pictures of the area in an earlier age, and it wasn't hard to believe it had once been home to vast, windswept prairies.

We'd been under way about half an hour when we received a message from Rimway.

Interstellar communications are, of course, not cheap. Consequently, if someone wants to send a transmission across the stars, he will frequently look for others who might also wish to make contact with the party at the other end, thereby dividing the cost by bundling the messages. There'd been no bundling with this one, no apparent concern about cost.

It was from Leonard Culbertson, the lawyer for the *Capella* Families. Alex looked at it and passed it to me. *"Alex,"* it said, *"I hope you've seen the wisdom of stopping the people who want to play lethal games with the drive unit on the* Capella. *We are still gathering support for our initiative. We have tried to go through the courts, but no action will be forthcoming in time to prevent a disaster. In any case, the scientists are being very reassuring. In fact, they're making a strong case. They are going to bring in young teens and argue that they have been deprived of a parent for most of their lives, and that, unless the court allows the procedure to take place, some of them won't see their parents until they're in their thirties or forties.*

"Your voice means a lot in this struggle. A statement from you will not necessarily carry the day, but it would have considerable weight. If you can help, the sooner you are heard, the better.

"However you decide, I appreciate that you've at least listened. A reply to this message has already been paid for. Again, thank you for your time."

We were seated in back while the car navigated through heavy traffic. Alex was staring straight ahead. The roadway was sealed off from pedestrians or animals, raised three or four meters off ground level.

I'd never have described Alex as being indecisive. But at that moment, he looked like a man in pain.

"Maybe we could try contacting John," I said. "It's possible they've had a breakthrough, and they could guarantee everybody's safety."

"No." He was scowling, as if some dark creature fluttered outside the windshield. "If they'd managed something like that, he'd have let us know."

The car got us to Union City shortly after sunset. The visitors' center was closed, but we'd done the research. The Prairie House had been located on what was now the northeastern edge of town, a few blocks from the Red River.

We checked in at a hotel and drove to the site, which was occupied by an abandoned church. It was away from streetlights and flanked by a vacant lot on one side and a grocery store on the other. The front doors were at the top of a half dozen steps. A sign off to one side identified the grounds as the Good Shepherd Baptist Church. Another sign stated that it was closed. A stone angel, with folded wings, waited on one side of a walkway, and a large cross rose from the steeple. The grounds were freshly cut, and there were a few headstones in back. Lights were just coming on in the houses, and people were sitting out on porches while kids chased one another along otherwise-quiet streets.

We got out of the car. The church had been there a long time, almost a century. The data for the site went back almost a thousand years. The location had usually been occupied by a church. But there had been private homes, a couple of retail shops, and even, at one point, a hardware store.

Prior to that, the record was unclear. It wasn't even certain this had been the location of the storied Prairie House, which, in its time, had served as a community center, a warehouse, and a militia outpost. It had been burned down once, or maybe twice, during the Dark Age. No picture of it existed.

The Baptist church had closed down twenty years earlier, when the city took over the property and tried, with no success, to cash in on the Apollo artifacts legend by establishing an Apollo gift shop. The former gift shop still stood, pale and desolate, beside the church, where it now functioned as a grocery store.

The rock walls of the church were dark and gray. "I don't think we're going to learn much here," I said.

"You never know, Chase." He took a deep breath. I could see frustration in his eyes.

"What?" I said.

"The scanner would have come in handy. I'd like to see what the lower levels look like."

"You don't think there could still be something here, do you?"

"Anything's possible. But no, it's not very likely. Still, I'd like to take a look. Maybe we could at least find some evidence that the artifacts had actually been brought here."

Some of the kids who'd been playing stopped to watch us. As did a few of the adults on their porches. One man stood up, came down the steps onto a sidewalk, and started across the street in our direction. He was small, with a ridge of gray hair around his skull. His ears stuck out, and he probably needed a better diet. He took a long look at our car as he passed it. "Hello," he said. "What's going on?"

"We're tourists," said Alex. "I see we're too late to get a look at the church. Do you know if there's any way we can get inside?"

"Well, you're right. It *is* a little bit late. Why would you want to go in *there*?"

"We're interested in the Prairie House."

He laughed. "That's been gone awhile, Mister."

"I know. But it was a famous place. I'd love to be able to tell my family I was inside the building that's on the grounds now."

"Why don't you come back in the morning?"

"We could do that if it would work. We just want to look around a bit. We wouldn't damage anything."

"I doubt you *could* damage anything." He looked at the church and then at me and then back at Alex. "Who are you, Mister?"

"My name's Alex Benedict. This is Chase Kolpath. Is there anyone here—?"

"I'm the curator. My name's Edmunds."

"Oh. Good. We're doing research work. If you could provide access to the building, I'd be happy to pay you whatever it might entail."

"Give me a few minutes," he said. "I'll be back."

He returned with a lamp. "There's not really much to see, Mr. Benedict." He unlocked the gate, and we walked up to the church door, which he also opened. He held the lamp inside. We were looking at gray stone walls and a pulpit. The pews had been removed. "Careful where you walk," he said. "The floor's uneven."

An electronic wall plate began to glow. And a voice spoke: "*Welcome to the Golden Age Sanctuary, where the artifacts from the scientific era were protected during the dark times. These priceless treasures are believed to—*"

Edmunds waved a hand, and it stopped. "We'd planned for a while to turn this into a kind of museum. But the board of commissioners decided it would just be a waste of money. *That*"—he pointed at the plate—"is as far as we got."

"Mr. Edmunds," said Alex, "what do you think actually happened to the artifacts? Were they really here at all?"

"Oh, I don't think there's any doubt about that. But it's thousands of years ago, Mr. Benedict." He raised both hands. "Who knows?"

"Are there any legends about what happened to them? Any theories?"

"Sure. They took them to Winnipeg. There's another notion that they got taken to the Moon." I knew Alex didn't expect Edmunds to be able to give us anything helpful. But at a moment like this, his natural inclination was to keep people talking. You just never knew what you might pick up. "I've heard every kind of crazy story you could imagine," the curator continued. "They're lost, and nobody has any idea what happened to them."

"Somebody thought they might have been taken to the Moon?"

"Yeah. That's been a pretty popular notion here. That the government's got them hidden up there."

"Why would the government hide the artifacts?" I asked.

Edmunds shrugged. "Who knows? Some people will tell you that's just the way governments are."

"What do *you* think?"

"About what?"

"About whether they were actually able to get the artifacts safely away."

He laughed. "I doubt it."

"Why's that?"

"It would have been a hellish situation. Those people would have been too busy saving their lives to worry about a lot of museum pieces. It's a nice legend. But I can't imagine that it really happened. And I'm sorry. I know that's not what you want to hear. I think the truth is that people at that time were going crazy everywhere. They didn't have anything, and they probably stole everything they could carry off and burned the rest. Now, do you still want to look around?"

We followed him up the center aisle, turned left past the pulpit, and exited through a side door into a passageway. "The storage area, what's left of it, is below."

"Most of it is filled in?" asked Alex.

"That's correct. Nobody knows who did it, or when. It might even have *caved* in at some point. We don't even know for certain that the basement was part of the original Prairie House. It was probably added later. But that doesn't fit well with the official story, so I won't push the point."

He opened a door, and we looked down a stairway. He put one foot on the top stair and waited. "You want to go down?"

"Yes," said Alex. "If you don't mind, I'd like to look around a bit."

We followed him down into what seemed nothing more than a very large cellar. Boxes and crates lined the walls and were stacked in piles across the area. "Can we look in one?" Alex asked.

"Sure."

Alex pointed at a crate, and Edmunds lifted the lid. It seemed to be filled with moldering blankets. Another crate had more. And a third was filled with pipe and metal bars. A plastic box revealed two Bibles and several hymnbooks. "Has anyone ever gone through all this stuff?"

"I'm sure Rev. MacCauley had his staff look at everything before they left. In any case, Union City ordered a general inventory when they picked up the property back around oh nine. If they found anything, they kept it to themselves."

We went back upstairs and talked about how some people had thought the artifacts had been distributed among a few private homes during the Dark Age. That they'd been hidden in attics and basements. "I'll tell you," he said, "the town commission would love to come across some of them. But that's crazy.

"The entire area," he continued, "gets scanned about every few years by somebody who wants to make sure they didn't miss anything."

"How much total space was there?" asked Alex.

"Who knows? The church never had that much."

Alex used his link to produce an image of Baylee. "Mr. Edmunds, do you by any chance recognize this man?"

He looked and shook his head. "No," he said. "I don't think so. Who is he?"

"Garnett Baylee. He'd have been one of your—"

"Oh, yes," he said. "Yes, I did meet him once. Sorry, it's been a long time, and I don't remember faces real well. But I *did* meet him."

"Do you remember any of the conversation?"

"I think it was pretty much like the one *we* just had. But it's been a long time. Probably twenty years."

"Did you know who he was when you met him?"

"Yes. That's why I remember him. He was a professor up at Bantwell University. Wrote a couple of books. I heard him speak a few times."

"Was that at the university?"

"No. The Historical Society gave him some kind of award. And he came down here to receive it. And he made a few other appearances. He was a funny guy. I *do* remember that about him."

"Do you remember what he spoke about?"

"No, not really. The award was given at a dinner, and he only talked for a few minutes. Mostly, I guess, he just said thanks. The other occasions, as best I can remember, he talked about artifacts. But I don't remember any details."

We came out of the church and walked into the arms of a reporter. She had just come through the gate. "Mr. Benedict?" she said. "My name's Madeleine O'Rourke. From *The Plains Drifter*." She was tall, as tall as Alex, with amber hair swept back, and green eyes. "I wonder," she said, "if I could ask a few questions?"

Alex was not a guy who normally fumbled his composure in front of beautiful women, but he was taken aback by this one. "Hi, Madeleine," he said. "I, um, this is Chase Kolpath. And sure. About what?"

"You're a famous guy. I was wondering what brings you to Union City?" She had a distinct accent. Tended to draw out words, sometimes adding an extra syllable.

"I assume you already know the answer to that, Madeleine." That was a stall while he thought about how he wanted to reply. "We're interested in the Prairie House. And the story about the Golden Age artifacts."

"Well," she said, "I guess you've come to the right place." She looked around. People were watching from their porches. "Do you mind if I record the conversation?"

"No, that's okay."

"Thank you. Can I assume you're trying to find out what happened to the material that disappeared back in the Dark Age? Is that correct?"

"I'm surprised you know we're here at all, Madeleine. May I ask how that happened?"

"Oh, Mr. Benedict, I doubt *you* can travel anywhere without the media becoming aware of your presence."

"Actually, the media isn't usually all that interested in antiques. But you're right, we'd like to find out what happened to the artifacts, sure. But I'm surprised you'd know about that."

She smiled again. "Why else would a celebrity of your stature be down here?"

"Well," Alex said, trying to look modest, "we could be here for any number of reasons."

"Sure you could. Your Aunt Susan lives down the block, for one." Another quick smile. "So, do you have any idea what might have happened to them? To the artifacts?"

"Not at the moment, no."

"But you do hope to solve an eight-thousand-year-old mystery?"

Alex laughed. "Madeleine, I'd love to."

"Do you have a lead?"

"Not really, no."

"Mr. Benedict, where will you go from here? What can you hope to find that everyone else has missed?"

"Probably nothing. But there's never any harm in looking."

"But you must have something to work on?"

"Madeleine, if we find anything, I'll be sure to let you know."

The conversation continued like that for another few minutes. Alex avoided mentioning Baylee. I suspected she knew about him, but if she did, she didn't bring up his name, either. Finally, she thanked him and left.

We walked out of the church grounds and returned to the car. "You okay?" I asked him.

"I'm fine." He took a deep breath.

"She's quite a package, isn't she?" I said.

"Oh." He smiled. "She's okay. Not in your league, though."

NINETEEN

We do not always behave in a reasonable manner. Sometimes we are acting out a role we wish to play but know we cannot. Sometimes we are simply responding to a distant echo.

—Adam Porterro, *An Idiot's Rules for Life*, 7122 C.E.

We spent the night in Union City and, in the morning, started for Bantwell University. It was located in Winnipeg, the world capital, which was located about 170 kilometers north. Alex called them shortly after we got started. He identified himself and asked to speak with the head of the archeology department.

"That would be Professor Hobart, Dr. Benedict. Hold one, please." People frequently granted Alex degrees he didn't have.

Then a new voice: *"Dr. Benedict, this is Jason Summerhill. Professor Hobart isn't available at the moment. May I help you?"*

"Yes," he said. "Professor Summerhill, the doctorate is a mistake. Call me Alex. I'm working on a research project regarding Garnett Baylee. He used to be a professor at Bantwell."

Laughter at the other end. *"Alex, I know who Baylee is. Everyone in the department does. But he never worked here. Not as far as I know."*

"Really? I was informed last evening that he did. It would have been quite a few years ago."

"Can you hold a moment, Alex? Let me check."

A woman took over: *"This is Shirley Lehman, Alex. Baylee never worked for us."*

"Okay. Misunderstanding somewhere, I guess. Did you by any chance know him, Shirley?"

"I met him. He spent some time here, but that was years ago. But he wasn't in the classroom. As best I can recall, he was doing research."

"Do you have any idea what he was looking for? I'm doing some research on *him*. Trying to fill in some blank spaces."

"No, Alex. I wish I could help. You might check with the library. That was where he spent most of his time."

Winnipeg was all green landscapes, broad parks, beautiful homes. Thick forest on the north and west shielded the city from the cold winds of long winters. The Miranda Cone, named for the woman who had brought the North American Federation back during the Time of Troubles, rose 187 meters over Grantland Park on the southern side. Monuments, some dating back thousands of years, dominated fountains, parks, and government buildings across the city. The university sprawled over a wide area on the west side. Its architecture had been created in the mode of the last century, using cylinders, cubes, triangular pyramids, and polygons.

The campus was crowded with students when we arrived. Two mag streetcars were disgorging passengers as we pulled into the parking lot at Union Hall, which housed the library. Something, presumably a subway, rumbled past underfoot. We got out of the car, went inside, and made for the central desk. A librarian, studying a display, looked up as we approached. "Can I help you?"

"Hello," Alex said. "My name's Benedict. We're working on a book about Garnett Baylee. Do you know who he is?"

She was middle-aged, thin, and well pressed. Her hair, tied in a knot, was beginning to gray. "Yes, I've heard his name," she said. "What precisely do you need?"

"He came here regularly at one time. About eighteen or nineteen years ago. Do you by any chance remember his being here?"

She smiled. "Not really. That's a long time ago."

"Of course," said Alex. "Is there a way to find out what he was working on here?"

"Wait a minute." She seemed to be having a conversation with herself. "Sure. I'm not sure I can tell you anything, but I can show you the library record. It would have what he was looking at."

"Beautiful," Alex said. "Would we be able to get access to the same material?"

"Just a moment." She got up and disappeared through a doorway.

The record consisted of a list of titles of histories, essays, and papers, authors' names, and dates. The dates would have been those on which Baylee examined the document. There were also two collections of poetry. Alex looked pleased as we walked away from the desk. "Marco Collins," he said. "No surprise there, I guess. Shawn Silvana. Frederick Quintavic." There were maybe fifty more authors.

"You know all these people?" I asked.

"I know their reputations. Some of them. I'd guess they're *all* historians or archeologists. Some of them have been dead for centuries. Let's get started and see if any lights go on. This shouldn't take long."

I laughed. "Alex, you may not have noticed, but that's a lot of material."

"With luck, we'll be finished in time for lunch. We'll start at the end of the list. If he found anything here, that's most likely where it'll be, just before he cleared out."

"You're making an assumption."

"Well, it's hard to imagine it happened any other way."

"Okay," I said. "I hate to be the dummy, but what precisely are we looking for?"

"Anything that touches on moving the artifacts, either from the Huntsville Space Museum, or from Centralia. Preferably the latter."

Baylee had spent his last four days at Bantwell going through material left by the historian Marco Collins. "He's the one we want to talk to," I said.

Alex nodded. "That would be ideal. Unfortunately, he died about twenty years ago."

We looked through the Collins inventory. He had wide-ranging interests, but he seemed to have specialized on the New Dawn, the recovery from the Dark Age. "What we need to do," said Alex, "is try to narrow down any of his work that touched on the artifacts." He gave me a series of search terms, Apollo artifacts, Cutler, Grand Forks, Zorbas. "Dmitri Zorbas is probably the most critical one. He's the person associated with the last days of the Prairie House. He was the crusader, the guy who tried to salvage artifacts when things turned ugly in Grand Forks."

"I've heard the name before," I said.

"He's pretty well-known for his efforts to recover books that had gotten lost." We sat down at a table, in front of a pair of displays. Alex brought up a list of the Collins material. It included a diary covering twenty-seven years, final versions and early drafts of seven histories, several hundred essays, and more than twenty thousand pieces of correspondence.

"Collins is easily our most likely candidate. So we should be careful going through this."

To make things more daunting, the books were all doorstops. I looked at the titles: *The Grand Collapse: The Last Days of the Golden Age*; *Beaumont* (Margot Beaumont, of course, was the British president who played a key role in initiating the New Dawn); *Incoming Tides: How Climate Change Brought Everything Down*; *A Brief History of Civilization*; *Looking Back at the Future* (a title suggesting Collins was not an optimist about our own chances); *Beyond the Moon: The Great Expansion*; and, finally, *How to Create a Dark Age*.

"Where do you want me to start?" I said.

"Go with that one." He indicated *The Grand Collapse*. "That's the one Baylee was spending most of his time with near the end. That and the correspondence. I'll check that."

While there were only seven books, there were twenty-two drafts. "If you write a book," said Alex, "I doubt you can do it in a single draft. The writers I've known won't even let anyone *see* their first draft. We probably don't have anything earlier than a third draft."

"This one's marked first draft."

"Don't believe it."

"Whatever," I said. "Fortunately, since the books are probably all available, we shouldn't have to go through the drafts at all."

"That sounds reasonable. But we're trying to find something that's been overlooked. There's a good chance that would have happened because it didn't make the final cut." His expression suggested he sympathized. "You obviously don't know much about how writers work."

That hit home.

"What?" he said. "Did I say something wrong?"

"Alex, I have a confession to make."

Those intense eyes locked on me. "About what?"

"I've been recording some of the stuff we've been doing. Writing memoirs."

"Oh. I thought for a minute you were going to say you believed this is a fool's errand. No, that's okay. If you want to do that, it's not a problem. Maybe eventually you'll be able to contribute them to somebody's archives."

"Well, actually it's probably past that point."

He swung his chair around to face me. "What do you mean?"

"The first one will be released in the spring."

"The first one? You mean you sold one of the memoirs?"

"Actually I sold the first three."

His jaw dropped. "The first *three*?"

"The Polaris incident. And two others."

"Chase, you can't be serious."

"You're a big name, Alex. The publishers think they'll sell pretty well."

"Shouldn't you have cleared it with me first?"

"I wasn't sure you'd approve."

"I'm not sure I do."

"Rainbow Enterprises will get a lot of publicity out of it."

"I understand that, but—"

"What?"

"We have to be concerned about the privacy of our clients. Did you stop to consider that?"

"Sure. I've changed all the names."

"Chase, I'm not so sure that's a good idea."

"Maybe we should get back to *The Grand Collapse*. Or did we just have one?"

There was a distinct growl. But he said, "No, we're fine."

"Good. I'm working on the Sunset Tuttle one now."

"All right. Let's try to concentrate on Garnett Baylee, okay? And do me a favor?"

"Sure."

"If anyone asks, I never knew about any of this."

I started paging through draft one of *The Grand Collapse*. And glanced down at the bottom of the screen, where the word count was over three hundred thousand. "This is impossible, Alex," I said. "We'll be here for a year trying to go through all this."

"You don't have to read everything, Chase. Just scan—"

Unfortunately, Marco Collins was impossible to scan. I had never read him before, but the book just sucked me in. I couldn't believe I was looking at an early draft. (There were two, plus the book itself, to go through.)

I've read the standard histories that most people have, but I'd never seen anything like this one, which was a tour through the general collapse. I was present when the global economy, almost without warning, crashed on Thursday, March 8, 3021. Collins explained how it had happened, and even though I've never had any interest in economics, I couldn't break away from it. I was in the North American Stock Exchange when the sale orders began to arrive. A few days later, I watched angry mobs in Chicago rampage through the downtown area in defiance of a government too weak to respond.

We didn't get out for lunch. Alex picked up some cookies somewhere, and we got by on those.

I was seated in a living room with a small family in Casper, Wyoming, when the internet went down. Within hours, personal-communication devices began to fail. Suddenly, a group of people who had been connected all their lives to the rest of the world found themselves completely cut off. Angry voices filled the streets. No one had any idea what had caused the problem.

It didn't go away. A few hours later, the lights went out. The power system failed, and the only way people could talk with each other was to go outside and knock on doors. It was chilling, a life I couldn't imagine.

Fortunately, the weather was mild. A militia unit showed up to provide security. But within a few days, food deliveries began to fail, and the militia seemed unable to do much to ease the problem. Gradually, they faded from the scene. And the first raiders appeared. For a time, the raiders traveled in trucks and cars, but with the electricity down, they had no way to recharge. Eventually, they switched to horses. They ignored money, which was becoming irrelevant. They stole supplies and killed at will. The town organized its own defense force, but it was running out of food. Another blow came when the water system shut down.

They had to learn the farming and hunting skills earlier generations took for granted. And how to make bullets and shoes. Many of them died in the process. People wandered into Casper on occasion with news of civil war, plague, utter chaos.

It never ended. New generations appeared, adapted, and hung on as best they could.

"Chase, you there?"

"Oh, yes, Alex. Hi." The windows were dark, and the lights had come on.

"They're closing. We have to go."

"Okay." I took a minute and finished the section. Then I shut down the screen. "Ready when you are."

It was raining when we went outside. We stood on the portico, out of the downpour. The campus grounds were empty, save for a couple of girls waiting in a lit doorway. Alex looked up at the sky. The storm was not likely to dissipate soon. "You find anything at all?" he asked.

"No. To be honest, I got caught up in the reading."

"Maybe it would be a good idea to stay with the searches."

"I know. Dumb."

He laughed. "I understand. Collins is pretty good, but we don't have time to go through it all."

"I can't imagine living the way those people had to."

Alex smiled. "We take a lot for granted, Beautiful."

I found Zorbas's name in the second draft of *The Grand Collapse*.

He was born in Giannouli, in a Greece that, like the rest of the world, was coming apart. His parents were wealthy, and when he was ten, they moved to North America in an effort to get away from the general instability. But the Americas were as tumultuous at the time as everybody else. When he was twenty-two, he went back to Giannouli, but the place was in chaos, so he aborted and returned home.

Not much is known about him from that point until, about twenty years later, he has become director of the Prairie House. He first appears in Huntsville as a stranger approaching Abraham Cutler, with a plan to save the Apollo artifacts at a time when the Space Museum, and the entire area, was under siege by desperate mobs.

"Collins describes the attacks by thugs determined to loot the museum. The security people held on, but the area was coming apart. He quotes Mary Castle, a historian living in that period, as saying that Zorbas was determined to save the Apollo artifacts. The Dakotas weren't especially safe either, but Zorbas was convinced he could protect them. In any case, it was far more stable than Huntsville. Cutler apparently knew him, or in any event trusted him. They put together a working generator and used it to recharge a small fleet of trucks. Then they loaded everything onto the vehicles and took it to Grand Forks, where it was stored in the Prairie House. When conditions deteriorated there, Zorbas moved the artifacts again. Cutler is out of the picture by then.

"Zorbas puts together another truck convoy. And they load it with the artifacts. But where does it go? Collins doesn't say. He admits that there's no way to verify that it even happened."

When we looked at the published version, the section about Zorbas took the action as far as the Prairie House in Grand Forks. But after that, there was no further mention of what happened. We could not find a copy of *Lost Cause*, the Mary Castle book cited by Collins.

We spent several more days going through the material and were about to give up when *I* caught something. Usually it's Alex, but my turn had come. "Shawn Silvana," I said.

"What about him?"

"Shawn's a female. And the big thing is that she's still alive."

"What else?"

"I was looking at her *Coming Home to Aquarius*. It's a history of the early colonial years in space."

"Why do we care?"

"It's dedicated to *my good friend and mentor Marco Collins*."

"And you think that she might know—"

"—What Collins really believed about the artifacts. Why he deleted the material about Zorbas. It's a long shot, but maybe we'll get lucky."

TWENTY

The problem with *The Dark Age* is that we're sitting here a hundred years after it went away, and nobody yet has turned the lights on.

—Hamid Sayla, *Lessons Learned*, 3811 C.E.

Shawn Silvana had fashioned a long career tracing the development of human worlds from their early outpost stage through the middle years as communities and cultures took hold, and finally evolving to their present state, in which they functioned simultaneously as independent entities and members of the Confederacy. She was based at the North American Historical Center, in Brimbury, 120 kilometers west of Winnipeg.

Brimbury was a beautiful city, a glittering array of soaring towers and wide streets, aesthetic schools and houses, most in geometrically precise positions, separated by gardens and meadows. The Historical Center was headquartered in a wide building with a flowing dome and elevated walkways.

We thought we had an appointment to talk with Professor Silvana, but when we went inside, an administrative aide apologized and informed us that she was on a field trip and that the data system had not been updated. "I'm terribly sorry," she said. "We don't expect her back for several months."

My first reaction was that, since Silvana specialized in the development of planetary cultures, we would have to do some serious traveling to talk with her. But we caught a break. "No," said the aide, "she's in Europe. They're doing a dig at Koratska."

"Would it be possible to talk with her?" Alex asked.

"I can try," she said. "Give me a minute."

We were led into a conference room and, moments later, Shawn Silvana blinked on. We knew her, of course, from the pictures in the books. She was well into her second century, with red hair and dark skin, and a lot of animation. She looked at us curiously, took off her field hat, and sat down on a large log. We could see behind her a section of the dig site, by which I mean a large hole. Beyond that was heavy forest.

"What's your name again?" she asked. "I didn't have a good connection."

"Alex Benedict. This is my associate, Chase Kolpath."

It was dark, and the moon gleamed in the branches behind her. "Alex and Chase. That rings a bell."

"We're antiquarians," Alex said.

She laughed. "Good. Excellent. Do you know what we've found here?"

"I have no idea," said Alex.

"The headquarters of Andrew Boyle."

That caught his attention. "Marvelous. Are you sure? They've been looking for that for centuries."

"Oh, yes. There's no question about it. This was his base."

"Who's Andrew Boyle?" I asked.

Alex responded: "He's one of the heroes of the Dark Age. Died too soon. He was betrayed by one of his own people. If he'd survived, they might have been able to avoid some of the worst effects of the collapse."

"Well," said Shawn, "that's very good, Alex. You know your material. That's certainly part of the mythology, but God knows it's unlikely that any one person, even Boyle, could have headed off much of what was coming. It was too late by the time he got into the fight."

"Boyle," said Alex, "lived during the period when the corporates and the governments were trying to get up and running again. There was a lot of turmoil, but it really seemed, for a short time, as if a transition to a more stable society was actually happening. He was a leader for the ages, and he was there at exactly the right moment. The situation had reached a tipping point, and it could have gone either way. He had a lot of support. Worldwide. After he was killed, everything came apart."

"Well," said Shawn, "it was all a long time ago. Alex, to what do I owe the pleasure of this call? And I should tell you that I'm sorry I'm not there to see you in person. I don't guess I could talk you into coming over here to Koratska?"

"We appreciate the invitation, Shawn. Might some artifacts be available?"

"We'd be happy to show you what we have. But everything we find is already designated. The university would run me out of town if I compromised any of the find."

Alex smiled. No surprise. "Shawn, are you familiar with Garnett Baylee?"

"Of course," she said. "He was a close friend."

Alex explained about the transmitter while her eyes widened. "We're trying to figure out where he found it."

"You think he might have located the rest of the artifacts? The ones that were at Prairie House?"

"It's a possibility."

"Incredible." She was silent for a few moments. "How can I help?"

"I was hoping you might have some idea where they were taken? Some hint?"

"I have no idea, Alex. I'm sorry. I wish I did."

"You knew Marco Collins?"

"I did."

"Did you ever discuss this with him?"

"Sure."

"We read an account of the transfer from Huntsville to Grand Forks in an early draft of The Grand Collapse. And then that they were getting ready to move everything again away from Grand Forks.

But it didn't say where. And that whole section was cut out of the final version."

"*Did he do that? I wasn't aware of it. Well, that might have been because there was no specific evidence. No indication where they might have taken all that stuff. Assuming they did. He probably didn't have anything more than the tradition.*"

"What do you know about Zorbas?"

"*Enough that I can believe the story, that he'd do anything necessary to rescue the artifacts. When the thieves and vandals arrived in Grand Forks, he became one of the leaders of the defense. He was one of the heroes of that era. We do have documentary evidence of that. But I suspect during that period he had a lot more to worry about than some artifacts.*"

"I was wondering," said Alex, "if his heroic stature wasn't the reason the tradition formed. That people thought sure, it was the sort of thing he would have done. Except, yes, maybe he was too busy saving lives."

Somebody handed Shawn a cup. Probably coffee. She sipped it. "*It's possible.*"

They both fell silent.

"Okay," said Alex, "thanks, Shawn. We won't take any more of your time."

"*Well, there is one thing that Marco mentioned.*"

Alex's jaw tightened. "What?"

"*He told me he'd seen a comment attributed to Zorbas's brother Jerome that he'd taken the artifacts to Greece.*"

"To Greece?"

"*To a place near where he was born. Larissa. But Marco didn't buy it. Greece was even more disrupted then than North America was.*"

"Larissa," said Alex. "Did Marco have any direct contact with Baylee?"

"*I have no idea, Alex. But it's certainly possible. Marco would have been teaching at the university at about the same time Baylee was doing his research there.*"

TWENTY-ONE

Historians are not to be trusted. They believe what they wish, crushing facts underfoot and twisting outcomes to fit preconceptions. History, as it is presented to us, is no more than a point of view.

—Algernon Eddy, *Notebooks*, 1366

The final version of *The Grand Collapse* reported only that Dmitri Zorbas was "believed" to be at the Prairie House when the decision was taken to shut it down. Whether they were "shutting down" a trove of artifacts or simply a communal establishment is left unclear.

"Do we head for the Aegean now?" I asked. Larissa was located north of the Pagasetic Gulf.

"I don't know," said Alex. "What do you think?"

That kind of indecisiveness was unlike him. "I assumed that was automatic. Why do you ask?"

"It doesn't feel right. I can't believe he'd have taken the artifacts to Greece. They wouldn't have been any safer. And he'd already given up twice on the area." He took a deep breath. "Maybe it's time to go home."

I can't explain what happened next. I wasn't ready to give up, but I was also inclined to agree that charging off to Europe with several truckloads of artifacts during a time of worsening instability didn't seem like a smart move. On the other hand, what other course did we have? "Your call, Alex."

"Let's talk about it in the morning."

He retired to his room, where I knew he'd go back to plowing through the library books, while I turned on the HV. I needed a break. I probably sat for an hour or so watching *Last Man Out* and *The Harvey Gant Show*. They're pretty weak comedies, but I wanted something light. When they were over, I put on a talk show just as Alex, wrapped in a robe, came out of his room carrying his notebook and wearing a broad smile. "Chase," he said, "did you look at either of the poetry books they gave us?"

"No. I never got to them. Why?"

"They're both Marcel Kalabrian collections. I'd never heard of him before, but he was alive during the thirty-third century."

"Okay," I said. "Does he have anything helpful to say?"

The smile widened. He opened the notebook. "It's called 'Coffee,'" he said.

> *In the cold gray morning light,*
> *They loaded our history into their trucks*
> *And cars, and turned into the rising sun.*
> *They drank their coffee*
> *And rode out of town while the rest of us slept.*

"That's a bit of a coincidence," I said. "Was he there when they took the artifacts out of Huntsville?"

"I don't think he's referring to Huntsville."

"Why not?"

"Wrong image. The Huntsville transfer was made by plane."

"Then you're thinking Prairie House?"

His eyes met mine. "Kalabrian lived in Grand Forks."

TWENTY-TWO

It's Greek to me.

—Shakespeare, *Julius Caesar*, 1599 C.E.

Like the other nations of the ancient world, Greece had long since ceased to exist. Nor was there any longer a place in that area known as Larissa. We knew, though, where it had been.

The plane came in over rolling green fields, patches of forest, and occasional towns. Off to the east, the countryside turned rugged. Beyond it, the Aegean sparkled in the morning sunlight. Alex had spent most of the flight reading whatever he could find about Dimitri Zorbas. "Most historians don't think he actually existed," he said. "But at a distance of eight thousand years, the evidence for anybody's existence, except major kings and presidents and people like Einstein and Kalaska, is questionable."

"Did you look up *Larissa*?"

"'Ancient Greek city located near present-day Elpis. Destroyed by Moravian rebels during the Sixth Millennium.' It was a famous cultural center for a long time. There's a list of major artists, playwrights, poets, and composers associated with the city."

"You think there's much chance we'll actually find something here?"

"Probably not," he said. "But it's a place to start."

*   *   *

We touched down at Elpis, checked into the Parakletos Hotel, and rented a car. Before leaving America, Alex had set up a meeting with one of the professors in the archeology department at Papadopoulos University, indicating he'd like to get some information about local archeological activity.

After we'd gotten settled, he called the school and got through to the professor, Theta Taras. She was an older woman, probably well into her fifteenth decade. *"When would you like to come over?"* she asked.

"At your leisure, Theta," he said. "I suspect we've a much more flexible schedule than you do."

"Well," she said, *"I'll be free any time after three thirty."*

"Perfect. We'll be there."

The university was of modest size. Three or four buildings, boasting classic architecture, which suggested that the Greek spirit was not dead. The campus was filled with hedges and flowering bushes and fountains. When we arrived, students were on the run, and bells were ringing. The car let us off in one of several parking areas and gave us directions for reaching the Student Union Building.

Theta's office was on the second floor. Sunlight poured in through two sets of windows. There were pictures of Theta posing with students and colleagues at dig sites and award ceremonies. Plaques and bronze cups looked out at us from a cabinet. "It's a pleasure to meet you, Chase," she said, with a broad smile. "And Alex Benedict. I never expected to have a chance to say hello to *you*. That's a marvelous service you provided with those missing interstellars. I can't imagine what those people must be going through."

"Thank you, Theta. And you're right. I hope we're able to get them clear."

A door opened, and a young lady came in with a tray full of snacks. I wasn't sure what they were, but they were brimmed with icing.

There was a ruggedness about Theta that suggested she'd done a lot of fieldwork. She had amber-colored hair that literally gleamed when the sunlight touched it. "Alex," she said, "you indicated that you wanted to talk about archeological projects here in Elpis. If you've no objection, I want to invite one of my colleagues to sit in. He's been more involved in local efforts than I have."

"That's fine," said Alex.

"I don't think anything of archeological significance has happened in Elpis over the past century that Manos wouldn't know about. Assuming that something actually *has* happened."

Manos was considerably smaller than she was and probably a few years older. He seemed much more the classic academic type, with inquisitive brown eyes, sharp features, and a goatee. We did another round of introductions. His last name was Vitalis, and he was the chairman of the archeology department.

"We're looking for a project," Alex said, "that would have taken place approximately eighteen years ago. Garnett Baylee would have been running it. Has either of you ever met him?"

Theta indicated no.

"I did on one occasion," said Manos. "Just to say hello to. But that would have been—" He stopped to think. "It was at the award ceremony for Benjamin's retirement. That would make it a quarter of a century. Give or take a couple of years. Theta tells me you are doing a hunt for some space artifacts."

"That's correct. From the Prairie House in Centralia. It was originally material from the Huntsville Space Museum."

"Why do you think they would have been brought here?"

"The evidence isn't exactly overwhelming, Manos. Just a comment by Marco Collins to a colleague. You know who he was?"

Manos nodded. "Of course. And Collins thought these artifacts had been brought here?"

"He admitted the possibility. That would probably have been enough to bring Baylee looking. It's possible, by the way, that if he *did* come, he might not have revealed what he was actually looking for."

"Why would he have done that?"

"We don't know. But there may be a layer of secrecy about this."

"We have a list," said Theta. She put it on the display. "These are local projects initiated during the period in which you're interested." There were seventeen of them, extending between twenty-five and seventeen years earlier. One by one, they took us through them. The Welka Initiative was sponsored by the Athenian Historical Society, and had consisted of an excavation in an area that had once been the headquarters of Mikos Valavos and his rebel group. They'd been active during the period in question. Next was the Olmert Project, which was funded by the Southwick Foundation. That, of course, immediately caught our attention. "They were looking for a *library*," Theta explained, "a collection of physical books that was believed to include classics all the way back to Homer. They thought they might recover *The Iliad*. And several hundred other titles that we've lost." He sounded genuinely frustrated. "But they got nothing."

We looked at the documents from the Olmert Project. They contained nothing suggesting the excavation team was trying to find anything other than what they claimed. In addition, people who knew Baylee had been at the dig site. Baylee had never been seen and, if we could believe the record, had had no connection with the effort. And, in fact, the project had occurred after he had returned to Rimway.

Theta and Manos continued through the entire list. Nothing else came close to qualifying.

We weren't even off the campus before Alex commented that, by the way, there were three other places named Larissa.

"Oh," I said.

"We assumed because he was from the Greek one—"

"I get it. Where are the others?"

"Canada and West Africa. And a Pacific island."

"Are we going?"

"You think there'll be a sunrise tomorrow?"

TWENTY-THREE

Be cautious of a man whose eyes never reflect joy.

—Armand Ti, *Illusions*, 7212 C.E.

The Pacific island and West Africa didn't take much time. The Canadian town had gone out of existence thousands of years ago. The location was now occupied by South Kolva, one of the largest cities in North America. We were able to determine within reasonable boundaries that Baylee had never been to any of the three locations. Nor had anyone else arrived during the last twenty-five years to establish an archeological site.

"It looks like a dead end," Alex said.

"I guess so."

"Okay," he said. "Before we pack it in, we have one more person to talk to."

Eisa Friendly Charters was located at the southeastern tip of Aquatica, a hundred kilometers northwest of where the ancient city of Jacksonville had been. It was as close as you could get on land to what had once been the Space Coast. Eisa occupied a pier on Golva Bay. A pair of flags flew over their office, one representing Aquatica and the other the corporate banner, displaying a laughing dolphin seated behind the wheel of a yacht. The dolphin wore a scarf and a captain's cap.

A young woman sat behind a counter when we walked in. "Can I help you?" she asked.

The room seemed to be constructed of wood and was filled with pictures of sailboats and cabin cruisers. A blinking sign advertised special rates and assistance for divers.

"Hello," Alex said. "How are you doing?"

"I'm fine, thanks. Can I be of assistance?"

"I hope so. We're doing some research on Garnett Baylee. He was an archeologist. Pretty well-known. And he was a customer here some years ago. We're working on a book about him, and we were wondering if anyone here might remember him?"

"You'd have to see Ms. Peterson. What kind of information are you looking for?"

"Anything personal. Everybody liked Professor Baylee, and we're hoping to find some background material. Anecdotes. Anything at all."

"Hold on a second." She got up and went into an adjoining office.

The sign changed, and a submersible appeared. *Let us take you for the cruise of your life. Visit Miami. Reasonable rates.*

And moments later: *Enjoy time at sea with your friends. Friendly Rates from Friendly Tours.*

She returned, accompanied by a lean, smiling woman in a blue-and-white blouse. "Your name, sir?" she asked.

"Alex Benedict."

She glanced in my direction. Hazel eyes framed by soft brown hair. There was something almost mischievous in her smile. "You're working on a book about Garnett Baylee?"

"That's correct."

"My name's Polly Peterson. It's been a lot of years since we've seen Garnett. How is he doing?"

"He died quite a while ago."

"Oh. I'm sorry to hear it. He was a good man."

"He was. He also earned a solid reputation as an archeologist. But you probably knew that."

"Yes. I believe I *did* hear something along those lines."

"Could you tell us anything about him? Did he talk to you about any projects he was working on? Anything like that?"

She went behind the counter and consulted the computer. "May I ask what kind of book?"

"A biography."

"I see. Well—" She shrugged. "We took him out on a number of different occasions. Usually, he just wanted to go for a cruise. He loved the sea. He usually brought friends with him. They'd go out and have parties. I got the impression they were usually coming off a work assignment of some sort. There's only one time that we have listed where he had a specific destination."

"And that was—?"

"The museum."

"The Space Museum?"

"That's correct."

"Did he go in a submarine?"

She consulted the computer again. "No. They went diving."

"You say *they*. Can you tell me who was with him?"

She squinted at the display. "He was apparently alone on that occasion. The only one with him was my brother, Khaled. He would of course have accompanied him on the dive."

"Of course." Alex looked up at the sign. A schooner was now visible under a full moon. *Try our moonlight cruise.* "Okay. Do you know what he did at the museum? What he saw? What affected him?"

"Why don't we go into my office?" She held the door for us. "You really need to talk to Khaled about that, Alex." She smiled.

The office was small, but the chairs were comfortable. There were more pictures of people in scuba and diving gear, of the company pier and office, and of groups of happy-looking customers in nautical clothing.

"I'd like very much to do that. Can we set it up? What I'd really like to do is arrange to have him take us to the museum site. Is that possible?"

"Khaled's out on a cruise right now. Give me a chance to talk with him, and we'll get back to you."

*   *   *

Later that evening, as we were sitting down to dinner, she called. *"Khaled will be free this weekend if you still want to charter a boat."*

"Excellent," Alex said. "Yes, let's do that."

"Okay. The museum tour, right?"

"Yes. Please."

"Unfortunately, our submersible won't be available. Is that a problem?"

"No, that's okay."

"Good. Can you be here by eight Friday morning?"

"Sure. We can do that."

"All right, Mr. Benedict. The agreement has been forwarded to you. Sign and return, and we'll take it from there."

I brought up a picture of the Florida Space Museum as it had been before the ocean took it down. It had been a plain three-story U-shaped brick building fronted by a parking lot. A statue of an astronaut stood near a flagpole. Two landing vehicles and a rocket were in the immediate area. And that was about it. Nothing fancy. There was a myth that the building had originally housed a girls' school, but there was no evidence to support that.

We ate on a balcony looking out over the ocean. It was a clear sky, no moon, but the stars were brilliant. I was watching lights moving on the horizon when Alex broke in to ask if I was okay.

"Oh," I said. "I'm sorry." I glanced down at my plate. "I was thinking about the museum. And Cape Canaveral. The ultimate historic site. And it's underwater. How could they not have noticed what was going on? They went to the Moon, and they couldn't see that the glaciers were melting?"

"I'm sure they did," said Alex. "But you know how people are. They're going to resist changing a lifestyle unless the danger is looking them directly in the eye. The glaciers must have seemed like somebody else's problem."

It was time to change the subject: "You really think Baylee might have said anything to Khaled Eisa that would be of any help?"

"Probably not, Chase. But the two of them would have spent considerable time alone on a boat. They dived to the museum together. What do you think they were talking about?"

"Probably the artifacts."

"Maybe we'll get lucky."

TWENTY-FOUR

Believe the illusion, and it *becomes* reality.

—Ivira Taney, *My Life and Look Out*, 2277 C.E.

We ate breakfast at the hotel. "I need a bathing suit," said Alex. "There's a beach place back down the road where I should be able to pick one up."

"We're going down to look at the museum?"

"Yes. *I* am."

"I'll go, too."

"You have any diving experience, Chase?"

"Not exactly."

"Any at all?"

"No."

"I'll have the imager along, so you can watch. This is no big deal, and you'll be safer in the boat."

"Have *you* ever done any diving?"

His eyes took on a sheepish appearance. "Khaled will have enough trouble just having one of us to look out for."

We were back in the Eisa Friendly Charters Office Friday morning when Khaled came in. He was tall, gorgeous, a guy who caught my attention immediately. He had the same brown hair and hazel eyes as his sister. He might have been a twin. "Polly told me you were looking for me," he said, ushering us into the office and offering some fresh fruit juice. "You want to go out to the Space Museum, is that correct?"

"Yes," said Alex.

"And there's something about Garnett Baylee?"

"Yes, Mr. Eisa. Do you remember him?"

"Oh, sure." Khaled was more casual, more amiable than Polly. But both exuded authority. "We saw a lot of him. He'd take his people out for an evening of good times. They loved partying at sea." His eyes touched mine, and he delivered an inviting smile.

I returned the gesture.

Alex saw the exchange and couldn't entirely hide his amusement. But he plunged ahead: "When was it that he went to the museum? Can you give us a date?"

"Sure," he said. "Give me a second." He checked the record. "June 16, 11,257." Nineteen years ago.

Alex glanced my way. That made it a year or so before Baylee returned to Rimway.

We boarded a cabin cruiser, the *Patriot*, and headed out to sea under bright, sunny skies. Behind us, the shoreline was mostly beach. A few kids stood in the surf and waved as we pulled away from the pier. Alex and I made ourselves comfortable in the passenger cabin. Minutes later, Khaled turned the boat over to the AI and joined us.

"You guys know Garnett very well?" he asked.

"No," said Alex. "I never really met him."

"But you're going to be his biographer?"

"Something like that."

The conversation subsided into Alex's standard methodology. We talked about Khaled's background, how he'd grown up on the coast, had gone to Aquatica University, where he'd majored in literature. But he'd always loved the ocean, and eventually he'd joined with his sister—who *was*, it turned out, a twin—to form Eisa Friendly Charters, which had four cabin cruisers and a sub.

We'd been out about an hour when Khaled pointed to a passing boat. "There's *Silvia*," he said. "It's one of ours."

*   *   *

Eventually, Alex got back to Baylee. "So you took him out once to see the Space Museum?"

"Yeah."

"You say that as if it's unusual."

"Well, look, guys, there *isn't* a museum. I mean, it's been sitting down there for thousands of years. The tides took it apart long ago. There's nothing there now. Probably hasn't been for centuries. Just a few lumps in the ocean bottom. You can see where it *was*. But that's the most you can hope for. If you want to go sightseeing, there are whole cities down there. Jacksonville, Orlando, St. Petersburg. They're a mess, too, but at least they're big enough that you can actually see them."

"Did you suggest looking at one of those instead?"

"Yeah." He grinned. "He laughed at me. That was before I knew him very well."

"He was only interested in the museum."

"You got that right. Look, Alex, I've seen guys get emotional about that place before. I understand what it means. But I've never seen anybody react the way he did. We went down, and after we came back up, he was almost in tears."

"He had a fixation about the place," Alex said.

"He was mad that they'd lost the stuff that had been in the museum. We stayed out here three or four days. He went down with a sensor and went all through the area, hoping to find something. But there wasn't anything. I mean, they took everything out to—what was it?—Huntsville. And all right, I knew they wouldn't have gotten *everything*, but it's been nine thousand damn years. The guy just wasn't making sense." He shook his head. "It's the only time I ever saw him like that.

"On the way back, he talked about trying to find the stuff that had been in the museum. That he'd looked everywhere. He started drinking, and I got worried. He's a big guy, and once he almost fell overboard."

"Khaled, did he ever give any indication that he'd found any of those artifacts? Anything at all?"

"No. I saw him a couple of times after that. Just going out to have a few drinks. Alone both times. I asked him if he was still looking for the Apollo stuff. He just got a kind of sad grin on his face and shrugged it off."

Alex nodded. "You guys have a sub, right?"

"Yes, we do. Her name's *Lola*."

"Did you offer to take him down in *Lola*?"

"We had a different sub then. But sure. I remember we'd been having problems with sharks in the area. I wanted to avoid taking any chances, so we stopped taking people down for a while. If people wanted to see the museum, we only took them in the sub. I offered him a substantial discount. But he said no."

"What's a shark?" I asked.

Khaled's eyes glowed. "You really do come from another place, don't you? You have an accent."

"We're from Rimway," I said. "What's a shark?"

Alex responded: "It's a big fish that would enjoy having a Kolpath sandwich for lunch."

"That's sort of what I thought."

"Alex," said Khaled, "why did *you* pass on the sub?"

"No special reason. I just want to do this the same way Baylee did."

"All right. Whatever you like." He looked my way. "Will you both be going down?"

"No," I said. "I think I'll sit this one out."

The sea was quiet, and the sun was sinking toward the horizon when we arrived at the museum. There was no wind to speak of. Khaled lowered an anchor into the water while Alex asked how he could be sure where we were. "There's just ocean in every direction."

"We planted a homing device here years ago, Alex. We knew there'd be a fair amount of interest. There are a few other pieces of tracking equipment here although I think ours is the only one that's still working."

He suggested that Alex not try making a dive until morning. "We'll want as much light as we can get," he said.

Another boat passed close to us, filled with college kids singing and having a good time. "It's spring break, I guess," I said.

Khaled nodded. "In this part of the world, it's always spring." He was obviously enjoying himself. "Usually, our customers just want to cruise along the shoreline and go sightseeing. In fact, Polly's out now with a bunch of them. She'd have preferred to bring you guys out here instead, but I was the one who'd taken Baylee, so I got the assignment."

"Sightseeing where?"

"They're going north, up to Monica Bay." Khaled was keeping his eyes on me while he talked. Alex got the message and announced that he was going out on deck to enjoy the breeze. So Khaled eased us into a conversation about the sea, about the romances of the boating business, about life along the coast. He was smooth, and I guess I made no effort to discourage him.

Eventually, I tried to turn the conversation back onto Baylee. Had he ever seemed as if he was making any kind of progress? Did he ever look happy?

"Well," he said, "that's a tough call. He laughed a lot. He knew how to enjoy himself. But he never let go of the museum. You know what I mean?" Khaled understood he didn't have much time, so he plunged ahead. "I hope this doesn't make you uncomfortable, Chase, but you're the loveliest woman I've seen around here in years, and I wouldn't forgive myself if I just let you walk away. But I guess you're not planning on staying in this area, are you?"

"No, Khaled. We won't be here long."

"May I ask what sort of relationship you have with Alex? And I hope I'm not out of line here."

"He's my boss."

"Oh, good." Big smile. I found myself wishing he lived in Andiquar. "So, would you allow me to take you out for dinner, say, Monday evening?"

"We won't be here Monday evening, Khaled," I said. "Sorry."

"Well, okay." Another smile. "How about Sunday then?"

"Khaled, I don't think it's a good idea. I'll be gone after Monday morning. It can't really go anywhere."

"Back to Rimway?"

"Well, probably not right away. But—"

"Let's not just let this go away. If we can get some time together Sunday evening, let's do it. Then we can say good-bye. Or whatever."

My heartbeat was picking up. "Don't you have any boats to take out?"

"I'll get a replacement. It's the advantage of being the owner."

In the morning, he and Alex appeared on deck in swimsuits. Khaled strapped a pistol-shaped weapon onto his belt. I assumed it was a blaster. "We haven't been seeing any sharks lately," he said. "But caution never hurts."

"What does it do?" I asked. "Blow them up?"

He laughed. "It screws up their nervous system. It won't do any permanent damage, but they won't hang around."

"Good," I said. No other boats were in sight.

"It's not too deep here," said Khaled. "All set, Alex?"

"Let's do it."

They pulled oxygen masks down over their faces and tested the radios. "Good luck," I told Alex. He gave me a thumbs-up and turned on the imager, which was fastened to his vest.

I opened my notebook, and the handrail and ocean blinked on. There was a gate in the rail. Khaled opened it and stepped aside. Alex went through, climbed down a ladder, and slipped into the water. Khaled followed, and both quickly disappeared beneath the surface.

The boat rocked gently in the waves.

I sat down on a deck chair with the notebook and watched the images. The water grew darker as they descended, and the bottom came gradually into view.

"*If you look over to your right, Alex,*" said Khaled, "*you can make out some of the mounds. Underneath all that are steel and concrete.*"

Alex turned on a lamp. "*Has anyone ever actually looked, Khaled? I mean, have they dug up the area?*"

"*Every fifty years or so, an archeological team shows up and goes down to poke around. As nearly as I can make out, they've been doing it off and on for thousands of years. If there was ever anything here, it's long gone now.*"

Alex looked to be moving smoothly. I saw the lumps in the bottom that Khaled had talked about. And a broken wall. A couple of struts stuck out of the ocean bottom.

Khaled pushed on one, demonstrating that it wasn't going to move. A few fish passed through, apparently drawn by the lights.

Gradually I became aware of a white skimmer moving toward us. It was coming slowly, and descending.

"Over here," said Khaled. He was digging at the mud, and after he got about a foot down, he found something solid. *"It's a floor. I think we're inside the museum."*

Alex came over to look. Then he began swimming in a circle, gradually moving farther out, examining the bottom, sometimes touching down, digging in.

I was tempted to comment that I didn't think they were going to find anything. But I decided to stay out of it.

Alex tugged something out of the mud. It looked like a piece of metal.

The skimmer began turning away, heading west.

On the display, the piece of metal caught the light. It was a beer can.

"I guess you're right, Khaled," Alex said. *"This place does attract visitors."*

"Yes, sir. Absolutely."

"Ahhh," said Alex. *"What's this?"*

A pair of angled poles jutted out of the mud. One was bent. Both were about a meter long and heavily corroded. In fact, it was unlikely anything remained of the original material. "What is it, Alex?" I asked.

"Not sure yet. Khaled, is there a way to figure out which part of the museum this would have been?"

"I'm sorry, Alex. But no. We could come back with a compass and maybe get some direction. At least it would tell us—" He stopped. *"Well, no, that wouldn't really help."*

Eventually, they surfaced and came back onto the deck. Alex went to his notebook without drying off.

"What's going on?" I said.

He held up a palm. Give him a minute. He was looking at a picture of one of the original lunar descent modules. I tried to imagine what it had been like going down to the lunar surface in one of those things. How did they manage any kind of serious spaceflight with no capability for gravity manipulation? It blew my mind.

Khaled pulled a towel around his shoulders and turned to me. "I probably should have warned him. Most of the people who come here get disappointed."

"He's okay," I said.

Alex looked up from the notebook. "Those rods," he said. "They're from one of the Apollo descent modules." He split the screen and brought up a picture of the poles sticking out of the mud. "The metal is completely corroded. But look at the angles. They're the same."

"Not much left of it," I said.

"No. We probably wouldn't have that if it hadn't been inside the museum. It was protected from the tides for a long time. Until the walls went away." He sat quietly for a few moments, just watching the sea. "Baylee would have known what that was," he said finally. "It must have torn his heart out." He looked up over my shoulder. "What's that?" he asked.

The white skimmer was back, ahead of us and off to starboard. I shielded my eyes from the sun. "It's been hanging around for a while," I said.

Khaled watched it while he continued drying himself. "We get a lot of those out here. They just fly over the museum so they can say they've been here."

It was moving in a wide circle, angling around until it was directly ahead of us. Khaled threw the towel over one shoulder and watched as it turned in our direction. "You guys aren't wanted by the police or anything, are you?"

"Not that I know of," said Alex.

The skimmer was descending. Coming toward us now. It leveled off at an altitude of about a hundred meters. There was no longer any doubt that it was interested in us. "I'm not comfortable with this,"

Khaled said. He walked onto the bridge and started the engines. "Pat, pull up the anchor." Pat was the AI.

The chain began to move.

The skimmer kept coming. Its engine grew louder.

A hand appeared through an open front window. It was holding something. A weapon. It looked like a blaster.

"Heads up," said Alex. He and I retreated toward the stern.

Khaled leaped back down onto the deck. He shoved Alex and me behind the after bulkhead and fell on top of us. I couldn't see anything from there, but the engine kept getting louder. Then an explosion rocked the boat. The skimmer soared past, rose, and began another turn.

"Chase!" Alex's voice. "You okay?" The overhead was blown off the cabin, and we were beginning to take on water. The deck was sliced wide open.

"Yes," I said. "I'm okay. What the hell's going on? Khaled, you all right?"

"I'm good." He sounded enraged. "Heads up! That son of a bitch is going to do it again."

We were on fire, and sinking.

Khaled pulled the antishark weapon out of his belt, scrambled onto the bow, and aimed it at the skimmer. By then, I was calling into my link: "Code five, yacht *Patriot*. We are under attack. Request immediate assistance. White skimmer unprovoked. Using a blaster."

"Khaled!" Alex grabbed one of his legs. "Get down from there, you idiot. You're giving him a target."

"No, I'm not," said Khaled. "I'm showing him a blaster."

"That's not a blaster," I said. "*He's* got the damned blaster. That's only a stinger. Or whatever. Will it do any damage to him?"

"It *looks* like a blaster. And yes, if I can hit him, it will."

"You'll get yourself killed," said Alex.

The skimmer came out of its turn and was angling toward us again.

The Patrol got back to me: "*Patriot*, we are on our way. Keep transmitting." I slipped into the water in an effort to keep the hull between me and the skimmer.

Khaled was standing in as cocky a manner as he could manage, swinging the shark disrupter as if it could actually do some damage. Meantime, my link was connecting with our attacker. *"I have its registration number,"* it said.

"Open a channel to them," I told it. Then: "I don't know who you are, you nitwit, but your number has been forwarded to the Coast Patrol. Back off. We have a weapon!"

They raced overhead again, but this time they did not fire. Instead, they began to turn away and accelerate.

Khaled tossed me a life vest.

The Patrol got there in eight minutes. By then the *Patriot* had slipped beneath the surface, and the nutcase who'd jumped us was long gone. They hovered overhead in two vehicles and hauled us out of the water. Then one of the officers informed us that the skimmer's registration number was invalid. "You didn't actually get a close look at it, did you?"

"I didn't think I needed to," I said. "I thought I had its number."

He looked sympathetic. "It's bogus. They're pretty easy to manipulate. We've been trying to do something about that for years, but the techs haven't been able to figure out a way without violating all kinds of security laws." He paused. "You have any idea who that might have been? You guys have any enemies who want you dead?"

He was talking to Khaled and me. Alex was in the other skimmer.

"I don't know anybody," said Khaled, "who'd want to do this." He looked at me.

"Alex and I don't even know anyone on the planet," I said. It had occurred to me that it might have had something to do with Baylee, but that made no sense. Why would anybody care whether we found what we'd come looking for? "I have to think it was just a random nut on the loose."

When we got back to shore, Alex admitted he'd given much the same answer. "But," he added, "I don't hold with coincidence."

We thanked our rescuers. Everyone got a good laugh when they heard the attacker had been scared off by a shark stinger. Then we completed some documents. Polly showed up at the Guard station just as we were finishing. She apologized, as if it were her fault. "It's a first for us. If you tell your friends about this incident, Chase," she said, "I hope you don't mention Eisa Friendly Charters."

TWENTY-FIVE

Love isn't everything. But it renders the rest of the human experience virtually irrelevant.

—Edmund Barringer, *Lifeboat*, 8788 C.E.

When we got back to the hotel, Alex steered me over to a sofa in the lobby. "Chase," he said, "I don't think *we* were the targets this afternoon."

"Why do you say that?"

"Khaled wasted no time getting the engine started and trying to get us out of there. In fact, he started the engine before the attack began."

"You think this isn't the first time it's happened?"

"I'm not sure what to make of it. But we'd be smart to assume the worst. That it *was* aimed at us. But I think there's something Khaled isn't telling us. We should stop somewhere and pick up a couple of scramblers."

"I was just about to suggest that."

"Are you still going out with Khaled tonight?"

"Yes."

"I wonder if that's a good idea?"

"We'll be okay," I said.

"All right. Enjoy yourself. But keep your eyes open."

Khaled took me to a cabaret for dinner. We ate while a group called the Late Nighters played and sang about the wonders of love. Then we got a comedian who was actually entertaining. And the place filled with music again, and we went out onto the dance floor.

It made for an exhilarating evening, rendered poignant by the knowledge that we would probably never see each other again. Khaled looked at me with an air of wistfulness. And to be honest, I couldn't decide whether my emotions that night were brought on by the circumstances or whether I really liked the guy. And the fact that I was carrying a scrambler gave the entire affair an added dimension. "You know who you look like?" I asked. "Zachary Conner."

He really did. The rumpled brown hair, the square jaw, the electric eyes. He had everything but the mustache. I don't know if he could have handled the romantic lead in *Last Man Standing* or *Starburst*. But he was close enough.

"You know," he said, with a grin, "I hear that a lot."

He had no easy means to travel to Rimway. And all my instincts barred me from even thinking about initiating something that had no chance of going anywhere. We talked about the attack off and on through the evening. While we were out on the floor, I asked whether he'd ever even *heard* of anything like this before?

"No," he said. "That's why I thought it might be directed at you and Alex."

"There's no reason," I said, "why anybody should want to come after us. But I suppose it's possible."

"Well, I plan to be careful for a while. I'd suggest you guys be heads-up, too. Maybe you should back off this Baylee thing for a while. *That* might be the problem. In any case, I'd hate to see anything happen to you."

"Don't worry," I said. "We'll be fine."

He was warm and gentle, and, unlike most guys, he wanted to talk about things I cared about, rather than about himself. He would have been worth hanging on to.

The evening ended on a note of lost opportunity. "If you get back here, Chase, or you have some free time before you go home to Rimway, let me know, okay? I'd love to do this again."

"I don't think there's much chance, Khaled. But if it happens, I'll let you know."

"Good enough."

We kissed, at first tentatively, then I took things into my own hands.

In the morning, we wandered down to the hotel restaurant and Alex asked me if I was ready to head out. I had mixed feelings, but a part of me was hoping we'd get an extra day in the area. "Why don't we relax a bit?" I said. "Take some time for ourselves?"

"Oh." He grinned. "It went that well, huh?"

"He's a good guy. Saved our lives."

"Okay. You can stay in the area if you want. I'm headed for Atlanta."

"What's in Atlanta?"

"The Albertson Data Museum."

"Another museum?"

"They try to recover information that was lost when the first internet collapsed. That's all. This has nothing to do with Baylee. I want to see if they have anything we can take back with us. For our clients."

"Okay." I hesitated. "I'll go."

"You don't have to."

"I know."

"Good. I think it's safer."

An autotray rolled up to the table, and our breakfasts were placed in front of us. *"Anything else you would like?"* asked the bot.

Alex waited until I'd indicated I was fine. "No, thanks," he said. "This is good." We'd just started eating when Alex frowned and touched his link. He listened for a moment and formed the words *Madeleine O'Rourke* with his lips. I needed a moment to place the name. She was the reporter from *The Plains Drifter*. "Yes, Madeleine," he said, "what can I do for you?" He increased the volume so I could hear.

"Alex, I just heard about the attack. You and Chase are okay, right?"

"Yes, we're fine. Just got dumped in the water, that's all."

"*I'm so glad. Who was it anyhow? Any idea?*"

"None."

"*Wow. Alex, is this the first time it's happened?*"

"Yes, Madeleine, it is."

"*You know any reason why someone would be trying to kill you?*"

"To be honest, I assumed someone was angry with Eisa Friendly Charters. I don't think it was aimed at us. No reason it would be."

"*Be careful about assumptions.*"

"I try to be."

"*Good.*"

Pause. Then: "How'd you find us?"

"*Oh, come on, Alex. You're a big name. And now you've been involved in* this *incident. You think you're not visible?*"

I went back to my eggs while Alex touched his link. "Connect me with *The Plains Drifter*. It's in Centralia."

"Why are you calling her back?" I asked.

"Hang on a second, Chase."

Then a man's voice: "*Good morning.* Plains Drifter. *This is Cam Everett.*"

"Mr. Everett, I was trying to reach Madeleine O'Rourke."

"*Who?*"

"Madeleine O'Rourke. She's one of your reporters?"

"*Umm, no. I never heard of her.*"

"Oh, Sorry, Mr. Everett. Must have been a communication breakdown on my end. Thanks." He disconnected and looked at me. "I think we might have just discovered who was in the skimmer."

TWENTY-SIX

History is the witness of time, the torch of truth, the memory of who we are.
It is the ultimate teacher about life, the messenger from the past.

—Cicero, 80 B.C.E.

Alex thinks the worst disaster in the history of the human race occurred
when the internet shut down, apparently without warning, early in the
Fourth Millennium. "The breadth of the loss," he said, as we went in
through the museum's front doors, "is best illustrated by the fact that
we don't even know what disappeared."

The vast majority of books, histories, classic novels, philosophical
texts, were simply gone. Most of the world's poetry vanished. Glimpses
of Shelley and Housman and Schneider survived only in ancient love
letters or diaries. Their work doesn't exist anymore. Just like almost
every novel written before the thirty-eighth century. We hear references
to the humor of James Thurber, but we have nothing to demonstrate it.
Unfortunately, there was no equivalent this time of the monasteries that
salvaged so much during the first dark age. Within a few generations of
the electronic collapse, a few people knew Pericles had been important,
but hardly anyone knew why. And Mark Twain was only a name.

There'd been internets on the colonial worlds, but unfortunately
they were all in their early years and the titles they carried tended to
be largely limited to local novels.

The Albertson Museum, apparently, had locked down its reputation when it recovered a copy of *The Merry Wives of Windsor*. That had given us a total of six Shakespearean plays. A bound copy of the six, titled *The Complete Plays*, was for sale in the gift shop. I couldn't resist.

That got Alex's approval. "It's interesting," he said, "we still use the term *bookshelves*, but we don't put many books on them."

Books aren't generally available. You have to go to a specialty shop or a museum to find bound books. We'd kept the Churchill volume that we had come across several years ago on Salud Afar. It was *Their Finest Hour*, the second volume of his history of the Second World War. The rest, of course, is lost. At first, Alex had talked about selling it, but it wasn't hard to persuade him to find a spot for it in my office, where it remains.

The museum had also posted a list of recently uncovered historical information. Most of it came from internets around the Confederacy. They aren't connected, of course, so information thought lost in some places occasionally turns up in others. Anyhow, that was the day I discovered why the term *waterloo* meant bad news. And how it happened that *rubicon* had something to do with a point of no return. And I'd always known what people meant when they called someone a Benedict Arnold. That day I learned why.

We wandered through the displays, looking at household items dating back thousands of years, athletic equipment for games I'd never heard of, and kitchen gear from the days when people did their own cooking.

They had a theater where you could watch one of the movies from Hollywood's early years. Hollywood was where they manufactured most of the films when the technology was just getting started. Only seven have survived from that era. All are shown in the theater, and are also available in the gift shop. In case anyone's curious, they are *High Noon*, *South Pacific*, *Beaches*, *Close Encounters of the Third Kind*, *Casablanca*, *Gentlemen Prefer Blondes*, and *Abbott and Costello Meet Frankenstein*.

Alex spent several minutes gazing at the display. "You going to get any of them?" I asked.

"I don't know," he said. "I'm not a fan of ancient movies. But *Casablanca* looks interesting."

"Why don't we get the entire package?"

I was surprised to discover that two songs I'd thought were more or less current, that I'd grown up with, had come from the films. "I'm Gonna Wash That Man Right Outta My Hair" was from *South Pacific*. And "Wind Beneath My Wings" came from *Beaches*. So we got the package.

They had some hardcover books for collectors. A few histories. Several copies of the Bible. Twenty or so novels I'd never heard of. Several commentaries on religion. A few histories, including a book titled *It Never Happened*, by Russell Brenkov. Brenkov was a Dark Age historian. His name had been mentioned during my college years, but I'd never read him.

There are also fictional characters who were once famous but who have been forgotten. Tarzan swung through jungles in a series of books that, in their time, are supposed to have outsold everything except the Bible. The search to identify him—it's assumed he is a male—is still on.

Dracula, as far as we know, appeared in only one novel, but his name survives. He was apparently a physician. His name is associated with blood extraction. If that seems grim, it helps to recall that he practiced in an era during which invasive surgery was common.

Sherlock Holmes was lost for six thousand years before being rediscovered thirty years ago by people working with the Goldman Institute. Now, at least on Rimway, he's enormously popular. His name never really disappeared from the language. It remains synonymous with deductive skills.

Superman and Batman got their start, we think, during the twenty-fourth century. Except for a brief period during the Dark Age, they've never gone away.

We joined a guided tour. The guide was explaining why so much had been lost, and how active efforts at recovery have been under way for centuries and would probably continue indefinitely. "When the early colonists first went out," she said, "they took a lot of things with them, especially books and movies. A lot of it is still out there, we think, but we have never really organized things to bring it all together."

A teenager wanted to know why they hadn't combined the internet data yet. "After all," he said, "it's been thousands of years."

The tour guide laughed. "I'd guess it's because they keep growing.
Keep acquiring information. I'm not sure what kind of effort it would
take to figure out what's missing from our system. Part of the problem
with losing material is that very often you also lose the memory that it
existed. In time, you no longer have a record of what's gone. Digging
through other data systems sounds like a good idea, but we don't
always know what we're looking for. It tends to happen by accident.
We don't know, for example, how many Shakespearean plays there
were. When we discovered *The Merry Wives of Windsor*, nobody here
had ever even heard of it. It was a complete shock. They had it at the
City on the Crag, but nobody here had come across it."

"Are some of his other plays out there?"

"Possibly," said the tour guide. "We hope. We have people visiting
every world in the Confederacy, looking for that and whatever else
might be available."

"At one time," said Alex, "archeology was just pick-and-shovel operations. Today it's also a series of electronic searches." We were standing
in front of the statue of a man in the main entrance hall. It had been
recovered from Lake Washington, but its identity was lost.

The museum has pictures of athletes in various types of uniforms,
some wearing helmets, some outsized gloves, some carrying long
sticks. People still play soccer, and we know a little about the other
sports, but they're long gone. Nobody's even sure when they died out.
He stared up at the statue. A phrase was engraved across the ceiling
which is associated with him: *I have sworn upon the altar of God
eternal hostility against every form of tyranny over the mind of man.*

I'm not sure who he was, but I suspect I'd have liked the guy.

Baylee and Southwick were included with a list of contributors framed
in the entry. "I'm not sure what we'd do without people like them," I
said. "Gabe's name should be up there, too."

I regretted the comment immediately. It was halfway out before I thought to shut it down, and by then it was too late. "You have to contribute to *this* museum to get that kind of recognition," said Alex. "His name is up in a few places." He was close to saying something more, but he cut it off. "Yeah," he said finally, "he's in good company."

Time to change the subject: "How about we get something to eat?"

"Okay. That sounds like a good idea."

We left the museum and crossed the street to the Barrista Grill. Soft music drifted through the dining area.

"So what's next?" I asked, as we took a table near a window. The sky was filled with clouds.

"I don't know. If it weren't for the attack on the boat, I'd be about ready to give it up and head home. But somebody wants us to stop. Why?"

"I have no idea."

"Madeleine O'Rourke changed the game." The candles blinked on, and the table described a couple of specials and asked what we'd like. We ordered a bottle of wine with our meal and sat back to relax. Alex was lost in thought. I stared out the window, watching as rain began to fall. Two people had paused outside trying to make up their minds about coming in. The rain settled the matter for them.

The wine arrived.

Finally, I asked him what he was thinking about.

"*Close Encounters of the Third Kind*," he said.

"Did you want to go watch it tonight?"

"That's not what I mean. It struck me that when we were trying to find Larissa, we limited the search too much." He picked up the bottle and popped the cork.

"You mean we should have looked off-world?"

"Very good."

"There's no colony with that name."

"No, there isn't. But there are six *places* in the Confederacy. Two states, two islands, and a mountain. We can eliminate them because they're all on worlds that we hadn't reached during the Dark Age."

"You only named five."

"The sixth one is a moon. Orbiting Neptune."

"In *this* system?"

"Yes."

"Beautiful."

Alex smiled. "Let's hope." He took a deep breath and filled the glasses. "By the way, the place has a site that would have been perfect for hiding the artifacts."

"Really?" I said. "What's that?"

"There was a research station built out there during the twenty-fifth century. It was abandoned after about eighty years. Or four centuries. Depends whose history you read. In any case, it would have been a tempting place to store the museum artifacts."

"Sounds more promising than the Aegean."

"Yes. We assumed the reference was to the Greek area because Zorbas was born near there. But that might have gotten us thinking small."

I picked up my glass. "Sounds good to me."

"Maybe we have it this time." He lifted his and took a deep breath. "Let's hear it for the Neptunians."

TWENTY-SEVEN

The human experience, for us, is a period stretching back over a few thousand years, starting with the Sumerians and extending to the first manned Mars flight. And already we have lost parts of it. What happened to the Minoan civilization? Or the one that prospered thousands of years ago in the Indus Valley? Who created the Sphinx? How did an ancient people move the Stonehenge rocks? Or construct mathematically correct pyramids? Did the Ark of the Covenant ever really exist? One has to wonder how much will have gone missing when another few thousand years have passed.

—Joseph McMurtrie, *Looking Forward*, 2312 C.E.

The jump out to Neptune took almost no time at all, but we surfaced almost a million kilometers from Larissa. "Make yourself comfortable for a couple of days," I told Alex. And he did, settling in with a twenty-second-century book he'd picked up that insisted there was nothing left for science to do. I've mentioned that Alex, like his customers, enjoys the feel of objects that have passed through hands in ancient times. But he doesn't stop there. He also has a passion for ideas from other eras, concepts, points of view. I don't know anyone else who reads Plato for sheer pleasure.

If you sit by a couch that had once served Owen Watkin, he'd say, or Albert Einstein, you can almost feel their presence. He never tried to explain the psychology of it. It was simply, for him and for his clients, a reality. It was the reason that he never felt guilty about selling artifacts to his customers rather than donating them to museums. Put it in a museum, he'd say, and people wander past and stare at it. But that's nothing other than a superficial reaction. The people who come to Rainbow Enterprises want something more. They hope to share their time, their *lives*, with an historical figure they've come to know. To reach across the centuries, the millennia, and *touch* Serena Black. And I know how that sounds. There's no way I can explain that to anyone who doesn't already understand why some people love antiques. But Alex concedes that sitting in light emanating from a lamp once owned by a celebrity doesn't really allow you to hold a conversation with that person. To do that, you need an avatar. Or, for someone from an earlier era, a book. I should mention, by the way, that it's especially difficult to explain the passion when I don't really share it. Alex tells me that he feels sorry for me. And when I tell him maybe in time I'll acquire the taste, he says no. He tells me the boat has left.

I'd picked up a jigsaw puzzle at the space station. A *real* one where you actually need a table. It was two thousand pieces, and depicted the Hadley Telescope against an array of stars and a service vehicle. I set it up in the passenger cabin. Alex watched as I started on it, said nothing for a few minutes, and finally asked whether I could finish it before we had to change course or velocity, which would scatter the pieces. "That's what makes it interesting," I said.

He laughed. But it didn't take long before he joined me.

We worked on it for much of the first day. That evening, he suggested we watch *Casablanca*. I wasn't exactly reluctant, but I'd been looking forward to seeing *Gentlemen Prefer Blondes*.

Alex said, "Whatever you like." But he looked disappointed. I knew the game, but I caved anyhow, and we went with *Casablanca*.

I'll confess that I loved the film. And I was surprised to discover that another of my favorite songs, "As Time Goes By," provides the central theme. When it was done, I watched with tears in my eyes as Rick and Captain Renault walked off across the airfield.

In the morning, I went back to work on the puzzle while Alex stared at the incoming pictures of Larissa. We were still twenty hours out. The moon isn't much more than a large chunk of rock shaped like a potato, with a length of about two hundred kilometers. It orbits Neptune twice daily.

After a while, I went over and sat down beside him. I looked at the images of a bleak moonscape coming in through the scopes. "Where do you think they would have put the station?"

"The accounts don't say, but I can't believe they didn't have it on the side facing the planet."

"Okay. That makes sense. Did the station have a name, Alex?"

He had to look it up. "Landros. He was the commander of the first mission to get out this far."

There was a sudden flash directly in front of us. A rock, maybe, or even some dust, had drifted in and gotten eradicated by the laser.

Alex cleared his throat. "You know," he said, "I'm not sure it wouldn't have been better to leave the artifacts to the looters rather than bury them out here. If that's what they did. There's something basically indecent about hiding things in a place like this."

"Especially," I said, "if you forget about them and leave them here."

He nodded. "That's what I mean."

We turned the scopes on Larissa as we approached but saw nothing other than rock, broken ridges, promontories, and craters. Then it slipped behind Neptune.

It needed only a few minutes to reappear. I sensed an air of desperation as Alex manipulated the images we'd been getting, shifting angles and adjusting magnification and seeing nothing but desolation. "We need to be closer to make anything out," he said. "Just put us in orbit around the moon, and we should be able to find the station easily enough."

Neptune has five rings. Larissa, at a range of eighty-five thousand kilometers from the planet, lies outside the ring system.

The gravity level on the moon is almost nonexistent. I'd have weighed about four pounds on the surface. When, finally, we got close, I folded a sheet, placed it over the puzzle (which was about half-finished), and taped it down. Then I eased us into orbit.

Alex sat by a portal staring out as the moonscape moved slowly past.

We spent the better part of a day in orbit and saw nothing but craters and rocks. "We have to get closer," he said.

"That means we'd have to burn a lot of fuel. It doesn't have the gravity to support—"

"Give me a suggestion."

"How about we leave *Belle* in orbit and use the lander."

We climbed into the lander and launched. I took us down to an altitude of about six hundred meters. "This place looks so dreary," I said. "It's hard to believe anybody would have left something valuable out here."

"That's precisely what makes this the perfect sanctuary," said Alex. He was sitting up front with his jaw propped against one fist, staring out at the ground passing beneath us. We were moving faster than we had been in the ship. "Have faith."

"Somebody told me once that's a good way to get into trouble."

We didn't know what the base looked like. The only thing we could be relatively sure of was that it would have been constructed on an elevated area.

Alex was beside me in the right-hand seat. We were both wearing goggles which, at least theoretically, made it easier to see in the azure glow of the giant planet. His lips were set in a thin line. "It has to be here somewhere," I said.

"Let's hope so."

Larissa was, of course, in tidal lock. The sun was too far away to be anything more than a bright star. The lighting, enhanced by a ring system that rose almost vertically into the sky, produced a terrain that seemed utterly unreal. We were constantly seeing shapes that did not exist, braking, going down, moving to starboard, doing whatever was necessary to change our angle. Each time, as our spotlights touched jewel-like azure objects, they went away, and we were left only with rocky escarpments and crags.

After about two hours, Alex pointed. "There it is." There was a note of triumph in his voice. We were looking down at what appeared to be a cluster of connected cubes and domes spread across varying levels of the moonscape.

I took us lower. This time the object did not blink out.

There was a reasonably flat area within a few hundred meters. I took us in and touched down. We sat for a while, studying the structure. It was perched across the top of a pair of ridges. There was a telescope and scanners and radio antennas. Dark ports looked out at us. Eventually, we got up and climbed into pressure suits. We checked air supplies and radios, and when we were ready, Alex led the way out through the airlock. We walked carefully through the almost nonexistent gravity, resisting the temptation to do any jumping. We climbed to the top of the ridge, looked up at a wide, flattened dome. A walkway that took us directly to a hatch.

There was a portal on either side. Both were dark. We pointed wrist lamps into them and saw furniture. Tables, chairs, sofas. "I think," said Alex, "there might be some valuable stuff here."

A pad was located beside the hatch. He touched it. When nothing happened, he pressed harder. "Not working," he said.

We rounded the building and saw more structures of varying shapes. There was nothing elaborate, just modular parts that fit together like a large puzzle. They were all connected and stood at varying elevations on that uneven ground. A block-shaped building supported a group of scanners and dishes. It was at the highest point in the network and was linked to the dome by a bridge. In the distance, separated from everything else, we saw a collapsed telescope, the tube still attached to the mount but lying on a few rocks.

The block-shaped building had another airlock. This one worked.

I jumped when lights blinked on. And I heard Alex swallow. "Somebody's done some maintenance," I said.

"Maybe." The lights were all outside. A luminous line had also appeared, framing the hatch. And a single lamp hidden in the wall lit up the entry. The hatch rolled into the overhead, and more lights came on inside the airlock. Alex looked back at me. *"Stay here,"* he said. *"Let's make sure this thing works before we go any farther."*

He went inside, touched something, and the hatch closed. *"So far so good,"* he said. *"It's running air into the chamber."*

"Be careful."

"I will."

"You think this is really *it*?"

He took a deep breath. *"Let's not get excited."* He was silent for a minute. Then: *"Okay, it's completed pressurization. We're good."*

After we were sure the hatches worked, I joined him inside. The building was filled with chairs and tables. Some clothes had been left, and some basic equipment, and something that must have been a data-processing system. Which had no power. But the lights came on as we went room to room. It was a place where time had barely moved. Whoever had been there might have left only a week earlier. *"They've got to be here someplace, Chase."* He was talking about the Centralia artifacts. *"This place would have been perfect."*

But we didn't see anything. Eventually, we went back outside, surveyed the area, and found two storage buildings. Neither had power, so we used the lasers to cut our way in. They contained some large tanks, a lander that I would not have wanted to try traveling in, and some spare parts. *"If this was where they brought everything,"* he said, *"somebody cleaned it out."*

"Maybe Baylee?"

"No. Baylee would have had to cut his way in. Same as we did."

We checked the other buildings. All were, as we expected, empty. They were basically nothing more than living quarters. *"I really thought we had a decent chance this time,"* said Alex when it was over, and we stood outside in the soft blue light. Reluctantly, we turned away and climbed back into the lander.

"Is there any other Larissa in the solar system?" I asked. "Maybe an abandoned orbiter or something?"

"Not that I've been able to find."

"What about an asteroid? There are *millions* of them."

"I checked. They don't use names. They have an alphanumeric system, which was introduced after the Dark Age. I couldn't find a record of what preceded it."

After we got back to the *Belle-Marie*, Alex sat staring wearily, sometimes at the magnified images on the displays, sometimes out at the rocks. Finally, he shook his head. "Let's go home," he said.

TWENTY-EIGHT

In the end, there is no higher praise than that which comes from a dedicated detractor.

—Casmir Kolchevsky, *Why Archeology Matters*, 1428

The expected arrival of the *Capella* was more than five weeks away when we got back to Rimway. Alex dropped me off at my place, told me to take a few days' vacation, and headed for the country house. I was relieved to get to my cottage without having to think about how much work had piled up at the office.

It wasn't the first time we'd failed on a serious outing. Alex usually accepted defeat without remorse. Hunting for artifacts, or sometimes just lost information, never came with a guarantee of success, so he never had a problem shrugging things off. It was part of the business. But this time was different. I wasn't sure whether it was that the stakes were so high. Or that he felt he'd let Marissa Earl down. Or that he was convinced he'd missed something. Whatever was weighing on him, he'd grown increasingly quiet during the flight home.

In the morning, I went down to the gym and restarted my workout routine. Afterward, several of us met for lunch. Then I went back to my apartment, read for a bit, watched some HV, and was drifting off to sleep when a call came in from Brockton Moore, the host of *Morning Roundtable*. "I hope I'm not disturbing you, Chase," he said.

It was unusual for any of the media people to call me at home. "Not at all, Brockton," I said. "What can I do for you?"

"Well, we know that you and Alex just came back from Earth. And that it had something to do with Garnett Baylee. I was wondering if you'd care to share with me what it was about?"

Moore, I decided, thought I would be more likely to talk with him than Alex would. "We were just on vacation. Who's Garnett Baylee?"

"Well, his granddaughter's one of your clients."

"Oh. *That* Garnett Baylee."

"Very funny, Chase. Seriously, though, what's going on? Can I persuade you to come on the show to talk about it?"

"I'm not sure why you're calling *me*. Alex is the person you should talk to."

"Alex isn't taking calls, Chase. Anyhow, you look a lot better than he does. We'll get more viewers."

"That's very kind of you, Brockton. If you like, I'll tell him he has an invitation from you."

"Is that really the best you can do?"

"I'm sorry. A client's business is confidential."

"Then it is connected with Marissa Earl?"

"I didn't say that."

"Sure you did. Listen, Chase, we'd love to have you on the show."

"All right. You want the truth?"

"Sure."

"We were looking into something. Nothing came of it, so there's no story. There's just nothing there that would interest your viewers."

"Why don't you come in and tell them that yourself? Tell them what the story was that didn't pan out?"

"Because it would be boring. I hate being boring."

In the morning, I decided I'd had enough sitting around and headed for the country house. I walked in the front door and Jacob said hello and told me that Shara had just tried to reach me. I was still in the act of sitting down when my link sounded. It was Shara. *"Glad you're back, Chase,"* she said. *"How was the trip?"*

"We did a lot of sightseeing. What's happening with the *Capella*?"

"*We might have a breakthrough. Orion is making the* Grainger *available for testing.*"

"How'd that happen?" I asked.

"*What we're hearing is that President Davis leaned on them. They're claiming he had nothing to do with the decision, that it's being done purely in the public interest. If that's the case, it took them a long time.*"

"So you're going to use it in a test?"

"*Yes. We're going out again. You and Alex want to come along?*"

"This one's not secret?"

"*No way Orion would overlook publicizing its commitment to the public welfare.*"

"When are you going?"

"*End of the week.*"

"Hold on." Music was coming from the conference room. I stuck my head in and saw Alex seated in front of one of the displays. "Got a minute?" I said.

"Hi, Chase. What are you doing here?"

"Just thought I'd drop by. Listen, SRF has the *Grainger*. They'll be making another effort in a couple of days. You want to go?"

"I'd like to, but I have all kinds of commitments, and I don't see how I could do anything except get in the way. You want to handle it?"

"All right."

"Good. By the way, Southwick will be here in an hour or so."

"Okay. Why?"

"Don't know. He called and asked if he could come by."

He arrived in an aircab, directed it to wait, and strode up the walkway to the front door as if he owned the place. Jacob opened up for him, and I escorted him in. "Good to see you, Chase," he said with an amenable smile. "I have an appointment with Alex."

"He's in back." I showed him. "Straight ahead on your right."

Southwick entered the conference room. I turned away and started back to my office, but Alex called for me to join them. "You've been part of this from the start, Chase. If Mr. Southwick doesn't mind, I'd like to have you sit in."

Southwick nodded. "Lawrence, please. And absolutely. Glad to have Chase stay. I hope I didn't mislead you guys. I don't really have any information to add. I was just hoping you'd met with some success. That you'd picked up some sense of where Garnie got that transmitter."

"I wish, Lawrence," said Alex. "But no, we didn't really find anything. At one point I thought we were in business. But we got nothing." He shrugged. "Can I get you a drink?"

"No, thanks. I'm fine." He looked disappointed. "So do you think it's worth pursuing any farther?"

Alex shifted around in his chair. Looked down at the table. "We just don't know."

"You said that you thought you'd come across something?"

"Does *Larissa* mean anything to you?"

"You mean *Marissa Earl*?"

"No. *Larissa* with an 'L.' This would be a *place*. I think."

He stiffened. "I have no idea. Never heard of it."

"It looks as if Baylee got interested in some historical notes that claimed the Apollo artifacts had been taken from the Prairie House to a place called Larissa. It was a Greek city close to where Dmitri Zorbas was born. You know who Zorbas was?"

"Yes. More or less. He was the director at the Prairie House."

"Right. We went to Europe and looked, but there's no indication that Baylee ever showed up in the area. So I think we can write that off."

"That's a pity. I'm sorry it didn't lead anywhere." He looked out at the trees. Something was chirping. "You have a beautiful view, Alex."

"Thank you."

"Okay. I won't take any more of your time. I know you went to a lot of trouble to try to chase this down. I just wanted to say thanks. I appreciate it. And I know Garnett's family does, too." He got up. "Time to let it go, I guess. If there's anything I can do, anything at all, let me know."

I walked back to the front door with him. "You know, Chase," he said, "I wish I'd known about that communication device, the transmitter, when he was alive. There's probably a simple explanation that would have settled all this pretty easily."

A few minutes after he'd left, Alex came into my office. "Do you have any details about the *Grainger* test? What are they planning on doing?"

"I can check with Shara."

"No, that's okay. We don't want to be giving them stuff to do. By the way, something I meant to tell you earlier and forgot. I was doing some research. We might have had a closer call than we realized."

"What do you mean? Did we get dumped in the ocean during shark season?"

"I'm not talking about the attack on the boat."

"What then?"

"The research base on Larissa. You remember one of the buildings still had power?"

"Yes."

"Some of the power sources they used in ancient times could become seriously dangerous if they didn't get shut down. They were effectively self-sustaining, and they could continue to function pretty much indefinitely."

"That's hard to believe, Alex. They'd continue to function over thousands of years? I'm more inclined to think somebody's been doing some maintenance."

"We have energy sources now that have the same capability. But there's a difference. Modern ones have, or are supposed to have, a safety feature. After a while, they disconnect on their own. The older ones were supposed to have that, too. But according to what I've read, it didn't always work. And when it didn't, they tended to become unstable. They were especially dangerous if, after a long period of just sitting there, somebody activated them."

"You mean like by opening an airlock?"

"Yes. Then there was a fair chance they'd blow the place apart. A few people have been killed."

"Maybe it would be a good idea to disable them."

"Most *are* disabled. But stations get put all over the Belt. Our client Linda Talbott and her husband live on an asteroid. Who knows where all these places are? Anyway, if we do something like that again, we should be careful. Not do anything that might turn on the power."

"Alex, that wasn't the first time we've done *that*."

"I know. That's why I'm mentioning it."

TWENTY-NINE

"Próso Olotahós!"

Classical Greek phrase, meaning to get the wind in one's sails, to race forward with all possible acceleration.

—*Dictionary of Standard Speech*, 32nd edition, 1422

I rode up on the shuttle with Shara. "Are Nick and JoAnn," I asked her, "already on Skydeck?"

"They left three days ago," she said.

"*Three days ago?* Aren't they riding with us?"

"They're both on the *Grainger*, Chase."

"Okay. They're not still going to be on board when it makes its jump, are they?"

She gave me a clenched-teeth nod. "Yes."

"I don't think that's a good idea. Why don't they let the AI handle everything?"

"JoAnn says she has to be there so she can get a feel for what's happening and react on the spot. Which means she needs a pilot with some passenger-ship experience. That's Nick."

"They're taking their chances."

"That's why we're going along. If it doesn't work out, we'll take them off the *Grainger* and bring them home."

"It's not a good idea," I said again.

"JoAnn thinks there's no other way to do it. And we're running out of time. We need to know whether she can fix the problem. And demonstrate it to everybody's satisfaction."

"How confident is she?"

"She says they'll be okay."

"I hope."

"She's the best we've got. If she can't shut down the cycle, it's not going to happen."

It wasn't exactly a topic that was going to make for light conversation, but all efforts to change the subject failed. We went over it and over it, and the mood got darker. "Does Nick know what he's gotten himself into?" I asked finally.

"You think he wasn't paying attention during the first test?" We were leaving the atmosphere by then. Below us, there was nothing but clouds and ocean.

"That's not what I'm saying, Shara."

"We don't really have much of a choice."

Our voices had been getting loud, and we were drawing stares from a woman across the aisle. I said something about how I was sure everything would be fine. We were both quiet for a minute or two. But there was no avoiding the issue. "How's JoAnn been?" I asked.

"How do you mean?"

"Nick thought this whole process was getting to her."

"I don't think you need to worry about *her*," Shara said. "She's committed. There's no question about that. And she's pretty tough."

"Who's *our* pilot going to be?"

"We can get one at Skydeck. But I thought you might want to volunteer—"

We arrived on the platform with some time to spare, so we stopped for lunch at Karl's Dellacondan, where the atmosphere lightened a bit. Maybe it was the string music, maybe it was that the place was filled with tourists talking about the view. Whatever had happened, we relaxed and tried to pretend everything was under control. The sandwiches were good, the manager stopped by our table to ask whether we were satisfied with the service, and a young man in a station uniform who had been one of Shara's students appeared and told her what a great teacher she'd been, and that he was confident her presence on the *Capella* team would guarantee a happy result. "If," he added, "anything would."

We were just finishing when Operations called. *"Chase,"* they said, *"the* Casavant's *ready. It'll be at Dock Six."*

Fifteen minutes later, we boarded the yacht and sat down on the bridge. I ran the systems check while the luggage arrived. We took it back to our cabins, returned to the bridge, and got ready to leave. As best I can recall, we were trying to divert a general sense of unease by talking about guys when the radio blinked on. "Casavant," said a female voice, *"you're cleared to go."*

"Acknowledge, Ops. On our way." I switched over to the AI. "Richard, release the magnetics and take us out." On the far side, the doors were opening. "So what's the plan, Shara?"

"They've put the original drive unit back into the *Grainger.* That makes it vulnerable to the warp. Nick and JoAnn left early because they didn't want to emerge from hyperspace anywhere near the affected area. So it took them almost three days to get to their destination. Which is the same place we were last time. When we get close to *our* target, which is eight million kilometers downrange, they'll submerge. The drive should react exactly as the *Capella*'s did. It'll get them tangled. If that happens, they'll get pushed forward like the *Carver.* Except a lot farther. JoAnn has it worked out so they'll come back in about seventeen hours, in an area where we'll be waiting."

"Good. I'm glad to hear it'll only be a few hours and not five and a half years." That was supposed to be a joke.

Shara didn't react. "When they come out of it, they'll contact us, and we'll join them. JoAnn says she'll be able to get some readings on how the drive gets affected, which should help. She expects that after they come out that first time, it will take about five hours before they get pulled under again. When that happens, she'll put the drive into acceleration. She thinks they can run the ship out of the warp. There won't be much time to do it because she says it has to happen during the first minute or two of the process."

"What happens then?"

"If it's successful, they'll come out of it immediately. They'll surface again, and it will be over." Her lips formed the words *I hope*.

I didn't like going anywhere near warps. Most, if not all, interstellars are now equipped with drive units that theoretically don't line up with the damaged area and consequently prevent you from getting dragged under. We've only lost one vehicle in the last three years, and that didn't seem to be connected with the issue. But I'm never going to believe we're entirely safe around those things.

We rolled out under the light of the Moon, adjusted course, and accelerated. After about a half hour, Richard announced we were ready to make our jump.

"Do it," I said. The lights dimmed, and we passed into transdimensional space.

We'd been back on the surface less than an hour when the AI announced that he had located the *Grainger*. "*Range is eight million kilometers.*"

I looked at the navigation display. But it was too far to get a picture.

Richard again: "*Incoming transmission.*"

It was Nick: "*Hello,* Casavant. *Good to see you guys.*"

"Hi, Nick," I said. "How's it going?"

There was a delay of about a minute before his response got back to us. "*Chase, is that you?*"

"Sure. Who else did you expect?"

I covered the mike. "Shara," I said, "does John know Nick's doing this?"

"Yes. And he's not happy. Nick said his brother threatened to cancel the attempt."

JoAnn's voice came in: "*Right now,*" she said, "*we're adrift. We're on the bridge, which is probably bigger than the entire ship you guys are riding in.*"

Shara leaned over the mike. "Everything okay, JoAnn?"

"*So far. Of course, we haven't really done anything yet.*"

"Okay. If there's any problem, we can pick you up."

"*Negative. We'll see you downstream. There's a slight adjustment in the area where we should come back out. Nick has forwarded it to you.*"

Richard indicated we had it, and I acknowledged.

"*We're accelerating now,*" said JoAnn. "*We'll make our jump in about thirty-five minutes. Nick says we'll arrive tomorrow at approximately 1100 hours.*" The current time was 1813. Seventeen hours would pass before they'd show up although for them it would be only about thirty minutes. "It's spooky," I said.

Shara passed my comment on to JoAnn. She laughed. "*Tell Chase that what's spooky is walking around in this giant ship and finding absolutely nobody.*"

Eventually, Nick got back on the circuit and told us they were about to make their jump. "*See you in a half hour.*" He flashed a wide grin.

I brought up a picture of the *Grainger*. It could have *been* the *Capella*. The colors were different, silver rather than light blue. But those were only details. The external design of the two ships was identical.

"*Everything is in order,*" said Richard. "*If all goes according to the plan, we will arrive in the target area approximately one hour before they do.*"

We spent the evening watching comedies. Neither of us felt much like sleeping, but we would need to be awake in the morning. Nobody wanted to be alone either so we both slept in the passenger cabin. I spent much of the night staring at the overhead. Then, in the morning, we were up early. Richard would have awakened us had anything happened, but I couldn't resist asking him anyway. "*No, Chase,*" he said. "*There's been no activity.*"

We had breakfast and went up onto the bridge, where we sat trying to think up things to talk about other than how unnerving the situation was. With two hours remaining, Richard posted a countdown on the auxiliary display. "Does anybody really understand time/space structure?" I asked.

Shara laughed. "Anybody who says he does is deranged. The math works, Chase, and that's all we have. Maybe all that matters." We watched the stars. We'd long since gone to cruise mode, so there was no sense of movement. The *Casavant* could have been frozen in place.

Shara took to walking around the ship. I tried reading. Couldn't do fiction. Not under those circumstances. I did a search for Apollo artifacts. Alex, guessing I'd do that, had loaded several books on the subject into the library, but they were all highly speculative. One argued that Dmitri Zorbas had sold them to his father-in-law, another that Zorbas had tried to transport them east, but they'd been taken from him as they passed through Chicago, a large and lawless city at the time. Even more so, apparently, than other big cities.

The arrival time came and went. Shara was back in her seat by then, staring at the clock on the display. "Don't worry, Chase," she said, "they'll be okay. There's a fair amount of give-and-take in the estimate." She was obviously scared out of her wits.

But at 11:22, Richard's voice broke through the silence: *"They're here."*

"Hello, Chase." It was Nick. *"What time is it?"*

"You're twenty minutes late, Nick."

"It's JoAnn's fault."

"Everything okay?"

"We're fine."

JoAnn got on: *"Shara, Chase, everything looks okay. We'll be with you for about five hours, then the process will start again. We'll go under, but we should be able to shut it down. If it works as I expect, as I hope, we'll be back in linear space within a few minutes. Your time, that is. If that happens, we should be able to go home and have a parade. And then see if we can convince everybody that we can rescue the* Capella. *You're here in case it doesn't work. If that happens, you'll have to wait another—what?—seventeen hours so you take us off."*

"Let's hope that won't be necessary."

They were farther out than we'd anticipated. We'd just arrived within visual range when JoAnn got on the circuit. *"Best you not come any closer, Chase. If things go wrong, there's a chance you'd get dragged down with us."*

I pulled onto a parallel course, about ten kilometers off their port side. The ship was *gigantic*. "We'll be okay," I said. "When it starts, how quick is the process? Do you have enough time to manage the controls?"

"When the cycle begins, we get tremors throughout the ship. We should have about a thirty-second window to make this work."

"Okay. Let us know if we can do anything."

"Of course."

She handed it over to Nick. *"She's right,"* he said. *"You really feel alone in this thing."*

"Well, when we get back to Skydeck, I suggest we do a party."

"I'm in favor of that, Chase." He paused. *"Something else."*

"Okay."

"When we get home, I'd love to take you to dinner. Maybe Cranston's."

Cranston's was one of those restaurants where they didn't put the price of the food on the menu. It wasn't supposed to matter to the clientele. "I'd enjoy that," I said.

"Beautiful. I'll look forward to it."

"Me, too." Nick, I decided, was my kind of guy. Along with Khaled. Life was good. But we needed to stay on topic. "Did it really take you only a half hour to get here?"

"It was about thirty-four minutes. We were talking to you guys, then the ship shook a couple of times. But whatever it had been went away, and everything quieted down. A half hour later, here we are."

"Incredible."

"Yeah, it is. It'll be even more so if next time you can stop it dead in its tracks." He had turned and was obviously talking to JoAnn. *"By the way, when it starts again, I'll have to sign off in a hurry. We don't get much time to react."*

"Maybe we should get off the circuit altogether, Nick. So you can concentrate on what you're doing."

"Your call, Chase. But it's not likely to happen for a few hours

*yet. By the way, I don't know whether you're aware, but everything
we do over here with the drive unit is being forwarded to you. Just in
case there's a problem."*

"That sounds a bit scary."

*"It's just a precaution. JoAnn wants to make sure nothing gets
lost."*

A transmission came in from John Kraus. *"JoAnn,"* it said, *"good
luck. Keep us informed."*

Nick responded a minute or two later: *"JoAnn's doing math right
now, John. But we're fine. Waiting for the warp to kick in. We're still
four hours away."*

Richard set another countdown going to mark the time since *Grainger*
had arrived in the target area. If everything went according to plan, it
would reappear shortly after being taken down, we'd get JoAnn and
Nick off and return to Skydeck. Then we'd sit it out for a few days. If
the *Grainger* remained stable, we'd go back and retrieve it. Eventually,
it would be returned to Orion which, Shara told me, was already com-
plaining that its customers wouldn't want to travel on it after this.

As the countdown proceeded, we simply sat on the bridge, exchang-
ing encouragement and assurances with JoAnn and Nick and with
each other.

The long silences made everyone uncomfortable, on both ships,
but every topic other than the one that hung over our heads seemed
trivial. Nick and JoAnn, at different times, both said how they wished
it was over. That they wanted it done with.

So did I. I resisted making any more suggestions that they should
clear out of the *Grainger* while there was still time. That we could swing
in close, and I could take the lander over and get them off. Of course, I
knew the answer I'd receive, how they *had* a lander on board if they
needed one. I thought about approaching the subject sideways by inquir-
ing whether their lander would be safe, or whether it would also be
caught when the warp activated. But that, too, had an obvious answer.

I looked over at Shara. "Do they really have to stay on board during all this?"

"Yes," she said. "JoAnn has a Keppinger detector with her and—"

"What's a Keppinger detector?"

"It reacts to conditions in the warp. It gives her the information she needs to make the adjustments to the drive unit."

"Couldn't they just install the thing and let the AI take care of it?"

"There's more to it than that, Chase. JoAnn needs to make judgments about the readings."

"Great."

JoAnn and Shara were talking quantum theory or something when the conversation suddenly went quiet.

"What's wrong?" Shara asked.

"It's starting. Gotta go."

The *Grainger* floated serenely among the stars. Nothing seemed to have changed. I could hear Shara breathing beside me, staring out through the wraparound. "Even if it works," she said, speaking neither to me nor the microphone, "I'm not sure I'd trust it."

"I can understand why," I said.

"We'll need more than a single trial to convince anyone. To convince *me*, for that matter. But let's get past this first and see what we have."

A faint glow appeared along the *Grainger* hull. And brightened. We could see what appeared to be stars *inside* the ship. It was becoming transparent. Then the light faded. And, finally, there was only the field of stars.

THIRTY

Twilight and evening bell,
And after that the dark!
And may there be no sadness of farewell
When I embark.

—Alfred Lord Tennyson, "Crossing the Bar," 1889

Theory indicated that if everything went as expected, they would return within minutes. Or maybe seconds. We held our breath.

Richard started another countdown on the auxiliary screen. "Shut it off," I said.

"*I'm sorry, Chase. I was only trying to help.*"

"Just leave it alone."

Shara was holding tight on to the arms of her chair. I sat there looking out at the night, watching for the silhouette of the giant ship to reappear. Please, God. "We should do this more often," said Shara.

"You want some coffee?"

"No. Not at the moment."

We sat, listening to each other breathe. We didn't really know if, when the ship reappeared, we'd be close enough to see it. The vehicles that got tangled in the warp tended to maintain a direct course, so we could assume it would come back along that same vector. But it was possible that it would be several million kilometers away. Which meant that the news might come by radio.

"*Chase.*" Richard's voice. "*I am scanning for it. Nothing so far.*"

"Okay," I said. "Thanks."

"*Do you wish to receive periodic reports, Chase?*"

"No," I said. "Just let me know if you see something."

I moved farther to port as a safety precaution, but otherwise maintained the same course and speed. I know this makes no sense, but my natural tendency was to assume the *Grainger* would show up in the same position relative to us that it had held when it went under. But the minutes dragged on, and no lights appeared.

I began to notice that the sounds in the *Casavant* were a bit different from what they were in the *Belle-Marie*. The engines had a different tone, somehow more masculine, more inclined to growl. I heard more beeps and boops from the electronics than I was accustomed to. And the ventilators put out a louder hum.

"Come *on*," whispered Shara.

The chairs squeaked.

"*I have it,*" said Richard. "*It's on course, range approximately six thousand kilometers.*"

"Beautiful," I said. "Open a channel to them."

"*Done, Chase.*"

"Nick, we see you. Welcome back."

We got nothing but static.

"Nick, answer up, please."

Shara was frowning.

Still nothing.

"Nick," said Shara. "Say something!"

"*It must be at a considerable distance,*" said Richard. "*I can't see any lights.*"

"Nick!" Shara again. Her voice tight with mounting desperation. "Are you there? Come on. Say something."

"Belt down, Shara," I said. "Their power may have gone down. Let's go find them. It shouldn't be a problem." I switched over to Richard. "Are we getting any kind of radio activity at all from them?"

"*Negative, Chase. I will let you know if I detect anything.*"

"Try the AI."

"*I already have. That's also negative.*"

"Not good," said Shara. "We've got to get them off before it goes under again."

We sent a message to the SRF, informing them of the situation.

We had a reply within the hour. From Lynn Bonner, chief of the SRF presence on Skydeck. "*Chase, do not take any unnecessary risks. Determine as best you can what has happened and report to us before taking any action.*"

The *Grainger* was still showing no lights when we pulled alongside. I moved in closer than was comfortable. But I wanted to be within a couple of minutes of the *Grainger*. Just in case. Shara was getting out of her seat to head for the lander when a second message arrived. It was from John Kraus: "*Exercise extreme caution. What is the current situation?*"

I sent a picture of the dark ship. "No response yet. We are going over now."

"No," said Shara. She got up and shook her head. "You stay here. I'll let you know what's going on."

"Forget it."

She paused in the hatch, turned, pointed an index finger at me. "*Stay here,*" she said.

I had no wish to go with her and get into a vehicle that had become so unpredictable. "You can't go over there alone."

"Chase, we need somebody here on the radio. To keep in touch with John."

"Richard can relay anything we need to send. We don't know what's happening, and you may need help. Anyway, I suspect I have a little more experience with starships and pressure suits than you do."

We climbed into the suits and added wrist lamps and jet packs. We were so close there was no point taking the lander. I picked up a cutter to ensure we didn't get stuck somewhere.

We left the *Casavant* and floated across to the *Grainger* airlock.

Usually, when you touch the hull of a ship, especially a big one, you can *feel* the power. There are engines and compressors and monitors and a thousand other devices that support life. This one felt dead. Shara looked at me with her eyes wide as I pressed the pushpad beside the outer hatch. The pushpad is supposed to work even in the case of a power failure. And it did. The hatch clicked, and I pulled it open and stepped inside. It was dark, and there was no artificial gravity. "Careful," I said. Shara joined me, we closed up, floated off the deck, and switched on our lamps.

The airlock began to pressurize.

"*That's good,*" said Shara. "*At least they've got some power.*"

"It's the backup system," I said. "Not sure there'll be much else."

The inner hatch opened into a passageway. Into *three* passageways, actually. One ran directly ahead across the ship; the others went fore and aft parallel to the hull. No interior lights came on.

I didn't trust what I was seeing, so I motioned Shara to leave her helmet in place while I removed mine. But the air was okay. I called out both names. "JoAnn.

"Nick."

Shara, her helmet now off, joined in: "Anybody there? Hello— Where are you guys?"

A dead silence rolled back at us.

We took the passageway that led forward. It was lined with doors. We tried one. It opened, and we looked in at a small compartment. Couple of chairs. A display screen. A fold-up bed.

I pulled the door shut. Shara looked frightened. God knows what I looked like. "Where the hell are they?" she said.

The ship was cold. Seriously cold. How could that have happened? We put our helmets back on and adjusted the heat in our suits.

The bridge figured to be up two or three decks. We kept going toward the front, passed one elevator, and stopped at the second. It wasn't working, which didn't matter because I wouldn't have wanted to take a chance on getting caught in it. I called Richard. "Hypercomm for John Kraus."

"*Okay,*" he said. "*Whenever you're ready.*"

"'John, we are on board the *Grainger*. They have a power outage. Haven't located JoAnn and Nick yet. Will let you know as soon as we have something.'" I looked at Shara. "Anything else?"

"*Yes. Richard, tell John that it's seriously cold over here. Hard to believe this thing was under power just a few minutes ago.*"

"*I have it,*" Richard said. "*Will transmit immediately.*"

Eventually, we came across a ramp connected to decks above and below. It was steep, designed for low gravity. In zero gee, we could float up the thing. And we did.

There was a theater on the next deck. We entered in the rear and looked past the seats up at a stage. There would have been a screen there somewhere as well, but it wasn't visible. We played our lights across the chairs, hoping to see some movement.

We had to take off our helmets to call their names. Which we did. There was no response.

We went back out into the corridor and continued the process. We were reaching a point at which I think if someone had answered, I'd have been seriously spooked.

"I can't believe," Shara said, "that they didn't mention the cold."

We went up another ramp into an area that included a large dining room. It had long portals, so occupants could have looked out and seen the stars. And one more deck took us, finally, within range of the bridge.

It was dark, and empty, and didn't look as if anyone had been there *ever*. I sat down in the captain's chair, leaned over the controls, and tried to turn the power on. Nothing happened.

"Look at this," I said, pointing to the comm system.

Shara's brow creased. "What am I looking at?"

"It's an allcomm. The captain uses it to speak to the entire ship. Provided he has power." I looked for an activator switch, found one, and used it. The panel lit up. Bingo.

"JoAnn," I said, "Nick. We're on the bridge. Where are you guys?"

*   *   *

Our voices echoed through the ship. After a while, we shut the lights down again. Don't ask me why. It seemed like the cautious thing to do, and that's my middle name. We walked around some more, or floated around, really, and opened more doors. We came across a couple of storage rooms, places where they had blankets and pillows and dishware. A few cabinets were open, and some of the materials had been removed.

We were sitting in a lounge area when Richard informed us we had another transmission from John: *"Get off the* Grainger *immediately. If it goes under again, I don't want you guys going with it. We have a team on the way. They'll take it from here."*

The SRF vehicle arrived within hours. They told us they'd been instructed to give it another day. Then, if the *Grainger* still seemed stable, they would board and begin a shipwide search. We were to go home.

So we started back. "I'm not sure how I let this happen," Shara said, as we left the *Grainger* behind.

"You're not responsible."

"Chase, I knew the risk was greater than JoAnn was letting on."

"So did she, probably."

"She did. She hated taking Nick over there, but she had no choice. But I doubt she thought anything like *this* could happen." She stopped and heaved a desperate sigh. "Damn it. There had to be a better way to do this. Or not do it."

John and several of his colleagues were waiting when we arrived at Skydeck. They crowded around us, asking if we were okay, telling us how sorry they were. We retreated into a conference room, and they began looking for details. Had JoAnn changed any of the protocols? I had no idea. We had a record of everything she'd done until the moment when the *Grainger* went under and communication was lost. Shara insisted JoAnn would not have changed anything without letting her know.

So the experts took over the *Casavant* to begin analyzing the data while we retired to a conference room and described the experience in painful detail to a group of about fifteen people. They asked a few questions and told us not to talk about it. And they ultimately fell into absolute silence, save for a couple of coughs.

At the end, John sat with his head propped on folded hands.

THIRTY-ONE

Whoever loved that loved not at first sight?

—Christopher Marlowe and George Chapman, *Hero and Leander*, 1598 C.E.

Alex was at the terminal when we got off the shuttle. He looked worried. "You guys okay?" he asked.

"We're all right," I said. But I walked into his outstretched arms and hung on to him. He didn't have the details, but enough had already gotten out to alert the media and the rest of the world that something had gone terribly wrong and that JoAnn and Nick were assumed lost. Shara joined us in the embrace and we stood in the concourse for a long moment while the crowd passed. "I'm sorry, guys," he said. "What happened?"

Shara just shook her head. "Let's get away from here."

We walked out to the skimmer. The sky was gray and overcast. We took our seats while he put the luggage in back. "I assume," he said, "they don't want you to talk about it."

I looked up at him and nodded.

"It won't go any farther," he said.

Shara and I looked at each other. "No way," she said, "we can keep this to ourselves."

"Yeah," I said.

We told him everything. We just sat in the parking lot and talked, tried to describe what it had felt like passing through that empty cruise

ship. He listened quietly. Closed his eyes. Finally, when we were finished, he asked if we were okay.

We both said *yes*. We'd lived to come back. But I, for one, knew I
would never be the same.

Nobody wanted to go home, so we headed over to Bernie's Far and
Away. "Some of the people on HV," Alex said, "were criticizing JoAnn
for rushing things."

"Who was doing that?" asked Shara.

"A couple of physicists. They were on several shows this morning.
Saying she should have taken her time."

Shara made an angry noise in her throat. "We didn't *have* any
time, damn it. That was just a preliminary run. If it had worked, there
would have been a lot more research to do before we could have tried
using it on the *Capella*."

"Hey," said Alex, "it wasn't *me* talking."

"I know," she said. "I'm sorry. I just wish these idiots, when they
don't know what they're talking about, would keep their mouths shut.
Do you know who they were?"

"I wasn't paying that much attention."

She was still growling. "Ding-dong," she said.

Alex wanted me to go home, but I had no interest in spending the rest of
the day in my cottage. We invited Shara over to the country house. But
she said she had calls to make, so we dropped her off and went back to
the office. After we got inside, he waved me into a seat. "Can I do anything?"

"No. Other than maybe change the subject. I need something else
to think about."

He smiled. "I love you, Chase."

"Thanks. Me too."

"All right. Let's try to do something else."

"Good."

"I've been putting together a list of available artifacts we saw on

Earth. If we get enough interest, we can go back and get some of them." He showed me his notebook, where sixty-seven items were recorded. "Why don't you take a look when you get a chance? No hurry. See if there's anything you saw that we should add? Then we can talk about putting out some feelers."

But the truth was I couldn't get my mind out of those empty corridors. I sat down at my desk and pretended to start. When he walked away, I don't think I did much other than sit there and stare at the wall. Then, without warning, he was back, standing in the doorway. "Is there anything at all I can do?" he asked.

"No," I said. "It's all right. I'll be okay."

He offered to stay with me, but I told him to let it go. "Okay," he said. "I'm exhausted. Going upstairs to crash."

After he left, I put the notebook down and turned on the HV, hoping for word about the *Grainger*. The networks were constantly announcing breaking news, but it always consisted of informing us that it was still being searched by the SRF team, and that JoAnn and Nick had not yet been found.

I hadn't had time to get to know either of them well. Just the two missions. But on that day, I'd have given anything to have them back. What would it have been like to party with JoAnn? And, of course, the dinner with Nick was not going to happen.

Finally, I settled down to work. I added a couple of items to Alex's list and had started putting together a sales pitch for them when Lawrence Southwick called. He was seated beside a virtual fireplace. Which contained a virtual fire. That probably meant he was calling from an asteroid. "Alex is asleep," I said. "Can I help you, Lawrence?"

He smiled. *"Hi, Chase. Just tell him that the person he should talk to about Zorbas is Marjorie Benjamin. She's a researcher at the National Institute. She's spent half her life doing Golden Age research. I've let her know you're interested. Her code's attached."*

A few minutes later, Jacob informed me we had a transmission from Khaled. *"Hi, Chase,"* it said. *"I've got a vacation coming up, and I'm going to head for Andiquar. I hope that's okay. I don't want* to rush things, but there doesn't seem to be any casual way to approach this. I'll be there in about a month. Will give you more specific information when I have my reservation. I'd love to take you to dinner again."

He was obviously giving me time to think about it. As much as I liked him, and felt indebted to him, it was too much too soon. I wasn't comfortable with the arrangement. But I wasn't sure I wanted to back away.

When somebody is crossing worlds to take you to dinner, and the guy has saved your life, it has already gotten serious. I needed the better part of an hour to put together a response that I hoped was appropriate: "Khaled, I enjoyed our time together. But I don't think allowing ourselves to become emotionally involved right now is a smart idea."

I went back to thinking about that empty ship while trying to explain why collectors on Rimway would love to acquire a seven-hundred-year-old bracelet worn by a woman who'd set out on a round-the-world trip in a cabin cruiser which was later found abandoned and adrift in the middle of the Pacific, with the bracelet lying on the deck. Or an ID chain that belonged to Chad Tappett, a European champion for animal rights whose career had been cut short when a lion got loose in an incident that many suspected had not been an accident.

Eventually, I called Shara. She blinked on, wearing a robe and sitting on the edge of a bed. "You hear anything more about the *Grainger*?" I asked.

"No. They've got six or seven people on board, but last I heard, they still haven't found them."

"You're crashing early."

"I'm wiped out, Chase. I can't believe I spent so much time just sitting in the Casavant, but I'm exhausted."

"You have any theories about what happened?"

"Yeah."

"What?"

"I think they were caught in the warp longer than anybody expected. I think, instead of shrinking, the time element stretched out."

*   *   *

I thought we'd gone pretty much as far as we could with Garnett Baylee. But Alex looked interested when I passed the Marjorie Benjamin message to him next morning, and an hour later, he was off to talk with her. He came back looking exasperated. "Well," he said, "she was able to provide some new information about Dmitri Zorbas."

"Anything useful?" I asked.

"He attended Larissa University."

"You're kidding. That was all she had?"

"That's it. That's, of course, where it's located. He went back to Greece to get his master's, and met his future wife, Eva Rodia, there. Apparently he planned to stay in Europe, but they headed back to America because Zorbas missed his family. She also told me that Zorbas wrote an autobiography, *Lost Dreams*. It's the perfect title because the book is also lost." He collapsed into a chair. "I wish we could get our hands on that."

"Is there any evidence the book might have explained what happened to the artifacts?"

"Marjorie didn't know, but she doubted he'd have included that kind of information. He lived and died during the early years of the Dark Age, so he would probably have had no security to rely on. She tells me that people generally believed that the economic downturn and the outbreaks of violence and all the rest of it were the end of the world. That it was Armageddon. But Zorbas never bought into that idea. He expected the problems to go on for a long time though probably not for six or seven centuries. But in any case, he was an optimist. Which is why she says he made a major effort to salvage the artifacts. She can't believe, though, that he'd have been likely to reveal their location to anyone other than his family or a few people he thought he could trust. Unfortunately, he died in the general holocaust. And maybe so did whoever he took into his confidence."

"Including his wife?"

"Nobody really knows what happened to her. The whole story lacks specifics."

"How'd he die? Do we know that?"

"Oh, yes. That's no secret. He was still living in Union City, and taking care of the Prairie House when a nearby town, Seymour, was overrun by thugs. They shot their way in, began burning everything, raping the women, you name it, I guess. The townspeople fought back as best they could and called for help. According to the legend, Zorbas rounded up a militia group they'd put together, and they went to Seymour. They drove out the thugs, but he died in the battle. Marjorie Benjamin said there were a number of stories about his helping defend the area. He was apparently almost a mythic figure at the time."

"It's a pity someone didn't record where he'd put the artifacts."

"If somebody had, Chase, I doubt we'd have anything to look for now."

"What did Marjorie think? She give any credence to his having stashed everything somewhere?"

"She's like us. She wants to believe it."

Next day, a second transmission came in from Khaled. *"I got your message, but giving up is a losing proposition. I'll let you know what my schedule looks like as soon as it takes shape. You can tell me you don't have time if you want. Or even that you don't want me to come. I'll understand. And I'll abide by your wishes. But I'm just not going to walk away from you unless you push a little bit. I hope you don't mind my taking this into my own hands. I'm looking forward to spending some time with you again, Chase. If you're willing. Incidentally, I'll only be in the area for a week. But don't worry. You won't have to entertain me or anything like that. I have sightseeing plans, so I won't be getting in your way. See you soon. I hope."*

"Jacob," I said, "message going back."

"Very good." I detected a note of approval. But coming up with the right response wasn't easy. And after a couple of minutes Jacob asked if I'd changed my mind.

"No," I said. "I was just thinking. But okay, let's go."

"When you're ready."

"'Khaled, I'll confess I'd enjoy seeing you again. But I just don't think it's a good idea. Not right now. Eventually, we'll probably get back to Earth. I'll let you know if it's going to happen.' Make sure it goes priority, Jacob, okay?"

Shara called in the middle of the night. *"They found them."* She paused, and I held my breath. *"They're saying they've been dead for thirty years."*

"What?"

"Thirty years, Chase. Probably died of starvation."

"You were right."

"Yeah. I guess. Time was moving differently for them than it was for us. But not the way we'd expected. They think that they survived for about four years, until they ran out of food."

THIRTY-TWO

There is no emotion so painful as a happy memory.

—Aneille Kay, *Christopher Sim at War*, 1288

By midafternoon, the media had the story. The victims, the networks were reporting, had died when their food supply ran out. Shock was deep and widespread. Nothing like this, everyone was saying, had *ever* been reported before.

The HV ran on and on. Physicists tried to explain how something like that was possible while political commentators predicted that there would be no further talk about manipulating star drives. Walter Brim, a guest on *Straight Talk*, asked the viewers to imagine how terrible it would be if something like that happened on the *Capella*.

I got through the afternoon as best I could, needed some medication to get to sleep that night. Alex called in the morning to make sure I was okay, and suggested we meet at the Hillside.

When I arrived, he was already there, seated at a corner table. He raised a hand and smiled. "You still okay?"

"I'll live."

"Apparently, Nick arranged things to conserve power. That's why so much was shut down. But I guess they couldn't do anything about the food supply. Believe it or not, they had enough food on board to get them through it if they could have prevented it from spoiling."

"I guess," I said. "I'm not sure though I would have wanted to live inside that thing for four years."

We ordered whatever off the menu. I don't recall what it was, just that I drank a lot of coffee. And we were back to talking about living for the day because you never know about tomorrow. Nick and JoAnn had seemed so *alive* when they were on the *Grainger* bridge.

The Hillside was crowded. "Never noticed before," I said, "but having almost a full house lends a sense of security to the place."

He reached across the table and pressed my wrist. "The world has changed, love." He was about to continue when his link sounded. He activated it, listened, and nodded. "Good, John, let me know when, okay?" And then: "Yes. She's with me now."

"What's happening?" I asked.

"There's going to be a memorial for JoAnn and Nick at the headquarters building. Middle of the week. They'll tell us when they lock in the night."

That evening, President Davis spoke. He stood behind a lectern, the blue and white colors of the Confederacy draped across the wall behind him. *"Friends and citizens,"* he said, *"you already know of the losses we incurred during an effort to find a better way to manage the rescue of those trapped on the* Capella. *JoAnn Suttner and Nicholas Kraus, members of the Sanusar Recovery Force working under the auspices of the Department of Transportation, lost their lives in the attempt. I am sorry to report also that, as a result of the experiment, we know now that the technique under development cannot be relied on. We will not risk the lives of the people on the* Capella. *Therefore, we will be falling back on the lifeboats that we have been preparing for the last few months.*

"It is a method we would have preferred not to use because it is more time-consuming than we wish. But it is our safest way to proceed. Consequently, we now face the reality that we cannot take everyone off prior to experiencing another jump. In fact, we will be able to provide an immediate escape for only about two hundred of those on board.

*"Having said that, I want to remind everyone that our first con-
sideration remains the safe return of our friends and family members,
not on rushing to get them off quickly. Our primary concern is their
safety. I regret this reality. But we are confronted with a force of
nature. We have no reasonable choice except to wait. It is a price we
must be willing to pay to bring this unhappy state of affairs to a successful conclusion."*

Three nights later, we went downtown to the Riverside Hotel for the
memorial service, which had been originally scheduled for the Department of Transportation Building. But the planners had been surprised
by the public response to the event. "I don't think we realized," Senator Caipha Delmar told us, "that people would turn out the way they
have." Obviously, the sacrifice JoAnn and Nick made had an impact.

Several thousand persons jammed into the hotel. About half got
into the Starlight Room, where the ceremony was to be held. The rest
filled the lobby, the restaurant, the bar, and a second showroom where
the event was put on-screen. John came out onto a raised platform
precisely on time, thanked the audience for their support, and introduced himself as Nick's brother and as the director of the operation
that had taken the two lives. "At first," he said, "I'd planned to
describe this simply as an effort gone wrong. But it served to show us
that the potential downside of trying to stop the process is too high,
and in that sense, because of JoAnn and Nick, twenty-six hundred
people will not be put at risk. I'm proud to be Nick's brother and to
have been JoAnn's colleague."

That drew somber applause. "Whatever it takes," he continued, "we
will not waste the sacrifice these two heroes have made. We *will* get those
people off the *Capella*. The lifeboats are ready to go. We'll take advantage
of its return to get the lifeboats to it, to get them on board, and when it
comes back in five years we'll get the passengers and crew off, *all* of them,
and we'll throw the biggest party Rimway has ever seen."

The place exploded.

He waited until things calmed down and invited Shara onstage to
say something.

She took her place behind the lectern. "I'll never forget JoAnn," she said. "She was young and brilliant, and had so much to give, and in the end, she gave it all. And Nick. He'd been a peerless friend. And he was a professional interstellar captain whose first concern was his passengers and crew. If he were here tonight, he'd consider that the ultimate compliment."

Prize-winning physicist Akala Gruder said that she had known JoAnn and could not believe she was gone. "In a sense, she never will be." She had never met Nick, she said. And added, "My loss."

A few others expressed similar sentiments. Then we got a surprise. John introduced President Davis. He came in through a side door and, like everyone else that night, he spoke without notes. "We are gathered here this evening," he said, "to pay tribute to our friends JoAnn Suttner and Nick Kraus. I don't know that I can add anything that hasn't already been said. Other than that it gives me great hope for the future to know that these two friends were by no means unique. Where, I wonder, do we get such men and women?

"One more thing. The parents of both are present with us tonight. They were invited to speak this evening, but they declined. We can all understand that. The emotional pressure is high. And I think their natural inclination is to let others do the talking. But that said, I would now like to invite them to come up to receive the Presidential Medal of Honor, which is hereby granted to JoAnn Suttner, and to Nicholas Kraus, for extraordinary heroism in the cause of providing assistance to those in desperate need."

JoAnn's husband, Jerry, was halfway across the Confederacy and had not been able to attend. But both sets of parents, Laura and Joseph Dayson, and Sandra and Jack Kraus, made their way onto the platform. The President handed them the awards, they exchanged a few comments, everybody wiped their eyes, and it was over.

In the morning, I was just settling behind my desk when Jacob announced that I had a call from Nick's mother. *"I saw you at the memorial last night, Chase,"* she said. *"I tried to get to you, but we lost you in the crowd."* That brought an uneasy moment.

"Hello, Ms. Kraus. It's nice to hear from you. Please accept my condolences on Nick's loss." I paused, not sure where the call was going. "What can I do for you?"

"Call me Sandy, please. I know Shara, and she told me how things went." My heart picked up a beat. *"I wanted to say that I'm glad you and she were there. And that I hope you're not too upset."*

"I'm okay," I said. Suddenly I was back in the passenger cabin with Nick while he asked whether he could take me to Cranston's. "I wish I could have helped."

"You were there. It's all you could do. Jack and I just wanted to say thanks. And to make sure you're okay." Jack, of course, was Nick's father.

"Yes. Thank you. I'm all right. How about you?"

"We'll get through it, Chase." Her voice caught. She said goodbye, and she was gone.

THIRTY-THREE

History fades into fable; fact becomes clouded with doubt and controversy; the inscription molders from the tablet; the statue falls from the pedestal. Columns, arches, pyramids, what are they but heaps of sand; and their epitaphs, but characters written in the dust?

—Washington Irving, *The Sketch-Book*, 1820 C.E.

Alex showed up next day on *Morning Deadline*, whose host was Cal Whitaker. The topic, of course, was the *Capella*. Its projected arrival was now two weeks away. Also appearing on the program was Levi Edward, a celebrated newscaster who'd retired twenty years earlier and was now visibly near the end of his life. His face was lined, and he grunted with pain every time he moved. "*Too much running for interviews,*" he said, trying to turn it into a joke. The familiar baritone was still there.

Everyone in the audience knew that Edward's wife, Lana, was on the lost cruise ship. He'd been at the forefront in pushing for a way to bring the *Capella* home. "*I'd love to see her again.*" He looked across the glass table at Alex. "*If she has to wait another five years to get back—*" He delivered a forced smile.

"*What do you think, Alex?*" asked Whitaker. "*Is there any chance at all they might find a way to stop it from moving ahead another five years? Or has the* Grainger *incident ruled that out beyond any chance?*"

Alex was clearly uncomfortable. "*I don't think there's any chance now that* we'll *find a quick fix,"* he said. *"If there's any alternative plan in the works, I haven't heard of it."*

"But they're still saying that manipulation would probably work. Despite the Grainger, *physicists are claiming that if we simply reduce the power in the engines, the odds are ninety-five percent that everything would be okay, and the process will stop. Am I right?"*

"That's what some of them are saying, Cal. But I don't think the people who have to make the decision are willing to take that chance."

Edward nodded. *"It's certainly a rational approach. I don't know whether I agree with it or not, but I can understand it. Alex, if it were your call, what would you do? Would you mess around with these lifeboats? If you were a passenger on the ship, what would you want them to do?"*

Alex's eyes took on that distant look I knew so well. *"If I were on board, with those odds, I think I'd want them to take the chance."*

Overnight, Project Lifeboat had become the focus of everyone's attention. The news programs carried pictures of the "lifeboats," and the various hosts walked us through them, counted the sixty-four seats in each, and assured their viewers that the vehicles seemed perfectly safe. Easy to say, of course, while they were perched on the landing strip at the Clayborn facility, where a substantial number of them were being manufactured.

Each lifeboat was folded into a gray, cube-shaped, plastene package with rounded edges. The cube measured slightly less than four meters on a side, which made it too large to fit into the *Belle-Marie* or most of the yachts that would be involved in the rescue effort. They were also too large to be carried by the shuttles that routinely took people and cargo to Skydeck. So special shuttles were being built. From Skydeck, the packages were loaded onto anything in the rescue fleet that could accommodate them. Some ships could carry two. A few of the cargo vehicles would be able to take an entire complement of forty-four, which would constitute enough to take care of everyone on the *Capella*. The complication was that there'd be only a few hours to find the *Capella* and load the lifeboats. If the operation was conducted successfully, which is to say if we were able to load forty-four lifeboats, then everybody should be able to get off when the ship returns in five years.

Each package was equipped with a pair of jets, which would be used to guide it into one of the *Capella*'s three cargo decks.

We watched as a member of John Kraus's team strolled around one of the packaged vehicles. The cube was marked TOP, BOTTOM, FRONT, and REAR. Four tanks were attached to the rear, and a half meter of black cord hung out of the front of the package. He reached for the cord, held it for a moment, then pulled on it.

The cube literally unrolled as it filled with air and morphed into a lifeboat. Two aides attached small jets to the rear and sides of the vehicle. That would enable the AI pilot to control movement.

A section of Skydeck had been set aside to manufacture the lifeboats, but because there was no way to know which ships would reach the *Capella* during the few hours they expected it to be accessible, *thousands* of them were needed, and that was far beyond anything that could be done on the station.

Also, operating out of Skydeck, rescue teams were practicing moving the lifeboat packages from rescue vehicles into a replica of the *Capella*'s three cargo decks.

In a conversation with Alex and Shara, John Kraus admitted that he saw little likelihood they'd be able to get forty-four of the packages on board during the short time they would have. "If they get unlucky," Alex told me afterward, "they might not get any in there, and the entire project could be pushed back still another five and a half years."

"That would be a disaster," I said.

"It would be. But the truth is there's no way around it. The alternative is to go back to manipulating the drive unit. Nobody wants to do that."

"No more ships available?"

"They apparently have as many as they can handle. Some Mute vehicles are coming in, too. John says a lot of people are unhappy about that. We still have politicians who think the Mutes can't be trusted."

"Alex, what about President Davis? He doesn't buy into that, does he?"

"If he did, they wouldn't have been invited in the first place."

"Good. I'm glad we have somebody with some sense."

"Absolutely. And I hope he's got it right."

"Alex—"

"Just kidding."

Later that morning, Shara came by the country house. "I was talking to John," she said. "They're caught up in another battle."

"About what?"

She took off her jacket and sat down in the love seat. "I shouldn't be telling you this."

"It won't go any farther."

"Promise?" I put my hand over my heart. "I'm serious," she said.

"I won't say a word. What's going on? Something about tinkering with the star drive again?"

"Yes."

"I thought what happened with JoAnn had settled it."

She laughed. "JoAnn's responsible for launching the new round."

"All right," I said. "What happened?"

"It looks as if she did a lot of research while she was caught in the warp. Years' worth, I guess. She left the results for us, along with a request it be made available to Robert Dyke."

"Wow," I said.

"Right."

"And John doesn't want to let him see it?"

"I think he'd be willing to go with it, but if he does, he'll be bucking the President. Davis has taken a public position, and I don't really know what's going on behind the scenes, but I'd be shocked if, after what he said, he'd be giving John a green light. So John will probably not ask."

"He'll make the call on his own."

"Yes."

"You're suggesting JoAnn thought she had the solution."

"I don't have specific knowledge, except that she wanted her work passed on to Dyke."

"That tells me something else," I said.

"What's that?"

"She understood what had happened to her and Nick. She knew that time outside the ship was moving a lot slower."

I heard no more about it after that, nor, as far as I could tell, did Shara. As the time wound down, we continued moving ahead with the Lifeboat Project. The *Belle-Marie*, of course, would be part of the rescue fleet. "So what's the plan?" asked Alex.

"They want us in place four days before they expect it to appear."

"Four *days*?"

"They're playing it safe, Alex. It would be a little embarrassing if the thing showed up early and was gone before anybody could get to it."

"I guess so. I don't think I've been paying as much attention as I should."

"You're still hung up on Baylee."

"Well, there's not much I can do about the *Capella*. But I'll go with you when it's time."

"Actually, you're not invited. They're putting some limits on the yachts. Nobody but the pilot."

"Because a passenger takes up space?"

"Right."

"It makes sense. Well, okay. When are you leaving?"

"I'll give myself three days to get into the area. I don't want to be charging around at the last minute."

He nodded. "Okay. How difficult will it be for the ships going out there to pinpoint their own positions? You've always said you can't be too exact about where you are when there's no star nearby."

"That's part of the problem, Alex. Everything's too far away from any landmarks, so a few million kilometers one way or another doesn't make much difference in the way the sky looks."

"Then how—?"

"It's one of the reasons they need so many ships. There's going to be some guesswork involved in establishing the location, so they're trying to flood the area. They want to set up the fleet cruisers first. And the cargo vehicles. Both carry a load of lifeboats. They *have* to be able to get one of them close to the *Capella* with at least five hours available to transfer the boats."

"I hate to say this, Chase—" He didn't look comfortable.

"I know. We're going to need some luck."

"Well, maybe JoAnn's work will give them a breakthrough."

I took a deep breath. "Shara tells me they're beginning to think there might be an uncertainty principle involved that would take any hope of a guaranteed solution out of it. They don't have a method to analyze the structure of the warp. It can vary, and that makes it impossible to be sure about the details. She thinks the reality is that they'd be very likely to be able to shut down the process, but there'd never be a guarantee."

"So in the end—"

"Take a chance. Or use the boats."

Senator Angela Herman showed up on *The Peter McCovey Show* that afternoon. She was an attractive woman, or would have been had she not been so combative. She obviously had presidential ambitions, and belonged to the Union Party, which was then out of power. She liked to portray herself as one of the "ordinary folks" who were always getting trampled by government stupidity or its deliberate malfeasance. *"Who do you think,"* she asked Peter, *"is going to see to it that this business with Sanusar ships doesn't happen anymore? It turns out it's been going on for literally thousands of years, and nobody noticed it until a physicist doing independent research and an antique dealer, for God's sake, figured it out. And now we have to depend on the government to rescue the people stuck on the* Capella. *And they obviously don't know what they're doing. Look how this business with the* Grainger *went. Why didn't they hire a good private corporation, like Orion or StarGate, to work out a solution? I just hope that they get it right this time."*

"*Aren't you being a little harsh, Senator? I mean, there are a lot of lives at stake. Kraus and his people are trying to pull off a small miracle.*"

"*Sure they are. And who do they put in charge? I don't want to malign those who've been lost, but the reigning so-called genius was a twenty-seven-year-old who managed to get herself and her pilot stuck for thirty-some years on a ship that she disabled. Maybe they should have picked somebody with a little more experience?*"

The host was clearly uncomfortable. "*Senator, I'm sure you're aware that the most productive time for the great physicists down through the ages has always come before they hit thirty. That's when they've had their major accomplishments. Do it in your twenties or forget it. JoAnn Suttner had an incredible career.*"

"*Until it mattered. The notion that you have to be a kid to do physics is a myth, Peter. It's never been true. Never will be.*"

"Jacob," I said, "shut it down."

After it went off, I don't recall that my office had ever seemed so quiet. Outside, a few birds were chirping, and branches were swaying in a warm breeze. But somehow a general stagnation had infiltrated the country house.

"You okay?" Alex was standing at the door.

"Yes, I'm fine."

"It'll be all right," he said. "She's a crank."

"I wasn't thinking about *her*."

"I know. You just have to have some time to get past this."

"It won't be all right, Alex. It never will be."

He took me to dinner that evening at Bernie's Far and Away. We sat out on the enclosed terrace, ordered drinks and I'm not sure what else. The Moon was full. But seeing Earth's oversized satellite had spoiled me. Lara looked almost insignificant by contrast.

"I can't help thinking," he said, "how many artifacts will be created by everything that's been happening."

"How do you mean, Alex?" I asked.

"You remember the coffee cups you had made for *Belle* last year?"

"Sure." *Belle-Marie* was inscribed beneath a pyramid and the company name, *Rainbow Enterprises*.

"If we get lucky and actually become part of the rescue—"

"Not much chance of that."

"I know. But if it happens, those cups will be worth a ton of money in a few years."

"How many years?"

"Well, maybe a century or two."

"Okay. I'll hang on to them, just in case."

The drinks came. Dark wine. I raised my glass toward the Moon. "JoAnn and Nick," I said.

Alex nodded. "Yeah. However things go, the price will have been pretty high." We drank. And stared at each other. And put the glasses down. "I'll tell you what has a chance of becoming a huge collectors' item."

"I don't really care, Alex."

"Okay."

I could see I'd offended him. "I'm sorry."

"It's all right. I shouldn't be preoccupied with trivia."

We were both silent for a time. Then I finished my wine. "So what will, Alex?"

"Will *what*?"

"Become a big collectors' item?"

"Oh." He didn't want to pursue the issue. "Anything off the *Casavant*."

"Like its cups?"

"Yes." He studied me. "You don't believe it?"

"Eventually, *everything* becomes valuable."

"These are historical times, Chase."

I knew what he was doing, trying to get my mind off the losses we'd taken. "I know," I said. "The ship's name is inscribed on them, in handwritten form, beneath its silhouette."

"They'll be worth a fortune."

"I hate to say this, but—"

"What?"

"I was thinking about human nature. They'd be worth more if things go badly, and nobody survives from the *Capella*. In fact, the value would go through the roof."

"Yes," he said. "It would. It's the darker side of the business."

"Yeah. While JoAnn and Nick—" My voice caught, and I couldn't go further.

"Unfortunately," he said, "we have short memories. Most heroes are forgotten by the next news cycle."

Alex restored Gabe's office. He moved the artifacts up to the second floor and took all the stuff he'd been collecting back there down into the basement. The walls had been filled during Gabe's years with plaques and pictures, most of which had been taken down. I know that sounds a bit coldhearted, but I think the truth was that they were a painful reminder of a time Alex didn't want to think about. He told me once that he'd never thanked Gabe, who had taken him in at a critical moment in his life and had cared for him for almost twenty years. Anyhow, everything was now back on the walls. Alex had also located a photo of Gabe and himself at about ten years old and my mom at a dig site somewhere. It had been framed and now rested on the desk.

He knew, of course, that the odds of bringing Gabe home anytime in the near future were remote.

But just in case.

I was standing at the doorway admiring how it looked when Jacob broke into my thoughts: *"I hope,"* he said, *"that we get him back."*

THIRTY-FOUR

The storm has passed. Let's go to lunch.

—Kesler Avonne, *Souls in Flight*, 1114

"*Chase*," said Jacob. "*You have a call from Mr. Conner.*"

I didn't know anyone by that name, which in our business happens all the time. "Okay," I said. "Put him on."

I'm not sure what I was expecting, but I was shocked when vid star Zachary Conner blinked on. He looked exactly as he had playing opposite Roma Carnova in *Downtown*. "*Hello, Chase,*" he said in that familiar deep baritone.

"Okay," I said. "Who are you really?" Then I realized. "Khaled."

Conner vanished, and my sailor buddy appeared. "*Hi, Beautiful. How are you doing?*"

"I'm fine, thanks. You know, you don't look as much like him as I thought."

"*No, no. Too late to walk it back.*"

"Where are you?"

"*Skydeck. I got your message, so I thought I better come right away.*"

Several hours later, when the shuttle arrived at the terminal, I was waiting. It was nice to see someone smiling again. We fell into each other's arms. "I know you were a bit reluctant about this, Chase," he said. "I hope you don't mind."

"No, no. I'm glad to see you."

"If you're upset or anything like that, just tell me, and I'll go away. But I hope you won't."

"Khaled, you should have let me know. This is crazy."

"I know." Suddenly he looked scared. "I can get out of your way if that's really what you want me to do."

"That's not the problem. The *Capella*'s close. I'm going to be leaving in a couple of days."

"Oh, God. I knew about that, but I didn't expect you'd be going out again. I should have realized. Chase Kolpath to the rescue. How could I—?"

"I'm sorry."

"Not your fault." He stood there looking helplessly around the terminal as if he might find a solution in one of the service shops. "Dumb. Don't know how I could have been so dumb."

"It's okay, Khaled."

I led him to the skimmer. He threw a suitcase in back, and we took our seats. "Actually," I said, "when I left Earth, I didn't think I'd see you again."

"I know. And to be honest, I debated whether I should come. After I got your messages, I really thought about backing off, but I just didn't want to let you walk away. And I couldn't think of any subtle way to do this."

"I'm sorry this has been so difficult, Khaled."

He flashed that smile again. "Someone like you, Chase, I knew right away it wouldn't be easy." He buckled himself in. "I'm sorry you had to go through that experience with the *Grainger*. It must have been terrible."

"It was," I said.

"I had no idea you were doing this kind of dangerous stuff."

"You must have gotten a clue after that lunatic sank your boat."

"Yeah. I don't know what that was about. I thought that was aimed at you and Alex. Have you figured out yet why anybody might be trying to do that?"

"No," I said. "Maybe it was just a nitwit out for a good time." I lifted us out of the parking lot. "Where are you headed, Khaled?"

He raised both hands. "Can you recommend a hotel for me? Something not too expensive."

That, of course, was an invitation for me to take him in. But I wasn't prepared to commit to that. "Sure," I said. "I think you'd like the Cosmo. It's a nice place, and the prices are decent."

If he was disappointed, he managed not to show it. "Sounds good."

He checked into the hotel, which was located in South Tasker, an Andiquar suburb. "The ride to the theaters and the historic sites is a bit longer than from some of the tourist hotels," I explained, "but it would cost a small fortune to stay downtown."

"No, this is good. Can we do dinner?"

"Sure," I said. "You want to eat here? At the hotel?"

"Yes, if you don't mind. I've had enough running around for one day."

We were shown to our table by a bot, who produced two glasses of water. "Andiquar's a beautiful city," he said.

"Is this the first time you've been on Rimway?"

"Yeah. In fact, it's the first time I've been off the ground at all. I'm surprised."

"About what?"

"Well, they say that a lot of people get sick on the star flights."

"That's probably an exaggeration. Some people do, but not many."

"Well, anyhow, I was glad to come through it without a problem." He rotated his shoulders. "The gravity's a little higher here, isn't it? I'd expected to feel heavier, but I don't really notice anything."

"It's only a couple of pounds," I said.

The callbox asked if we were ready to order. We looked at each other, and I went with spaghetti and meatballs. "Sounds good," said Khaled. "I'll have the same." We added some wine. Then he sat back and looked seriously into my eyes. "Chase, this trip is obviously not going to go exactly as I'd hoped. But that's okay. Even if I only get this hour or so with you, it will have been worth it."

"Khaled, that's sweet."

*   *   *

If he really was tired of traveling, he showed no sign of it through the balance of the evening. After we finished eating, we went dancing. I took him to the Moonlight Ballroom, then to the Golden Rose, and to Whitfield Park. Eventually, we stopped in at a small club off Lavender Row, where we finished the evening drinking cocktails beneath the stars. "I don't suppose," he said, "I could persuade you to run off with me to the Caribbean?" He smiled, to let me know he was kidding, but not really.

"Where's the Caribbean?" I asked.

"It's a group of islands in the Atlantic. Close to Aquatica. They're really nice. You'd like the music. Moonlit beaches. You'd *love* Jamaica."

That constituted the wildest moment of the entire evening because I found myself almost considering it. "Is this what you always do?" I asked. "Gallop into a town and sweep some unsuspecting young woman off her feet?"

He leaned forward and pressed my arm. "Can I read that as a *yes*?"

"Khaled, what would I do at Eisa Friendly Charters?"

Another grin. "You'd be the best-looking sailor on the East Coast."

"Oh, yes. Sailors mostly swab decks, don't they?"

"Seriously, that would be an easy issue to manage." His tone had changed. His eyes were still locked on mine. "Chase, I know this is all very sudden. And I don't expect you to answer now. But what I'm asking is that you think about it. Give me a chance. I love being with you."

"This is only the second time we've been out together, Khaled. We're practically strangers."

"You don't believe that any more than I do. And anyhow, it's the *third* time."

"Not by my count."

"We were on the *Patriot* together." He laughed. "That's always been my experience with beautiful women. They tend to forget me."

"Well, I guess we could count the boat ride as a time out together. Since you saved my life."

"Oh, Chase," he said. "You were never really in danger."

"I see. So what you're saying is that the nutcase who attacked us was really a plant, so you could make an impression?" I expected a laugh.

"Of course not," he said. "You think I'd let somebody sink one of our boats to—?" He shook it off. "No, what I meant was that I was there, and there was no way I was going to let anything happen to you."

I'd informed Alex that Khaled was in town, and he was wearing that occasionally smug smile when I showed up at the country house next morning. "Well," he said, "how'd it go?"

"It was fun. I have to admit, he *is* a pleasure to be around. And I needed an evening like that."

"Where is he now? Do you know?"

"He was talking about going down to tour the Hall of the People."

"Well, things are pretty slow here. Why don't you take the rest of the day off? Go over there and join him?"

"Thanks, Alex. But I'm not sure that would be a good idea."

"Oh." He shrugged. "Well, whatever you want. Just let me know if you leave, okay?"

THIRTY-FIVE

There is no ultimate truth. There is only the moment and what we choose to do with it.

—Marik Kloestner, *Diaries*, 1388

I left the country house in the early afternoon and picked up Khaled at his hotel. I took him to Kornikov's German Restaurant for some sauerbraten. Afterward, we went downtown and toured the government buildings and the cultural center. We attended a concert, had dinner, and headed for the Hall of the People, a magnificent, sprawling, marble structure, four stories high, roughly a half kilometer long. As always at night, it was bathed in a soft blue luminescence.

We strolled through the surrounding grounds. Flags and banners of the Confederate worlds snapped along its front in the winds off the ocean. Tourists filled the area, taking pictures, explaining its significance to kids. The Council meets there, of course. The executive offices are located on the lower floors, and the World Court convenes in the eastern wing. The White Pool, with its myriad fountains, runs the length of the building, and the Silver Tower of the Confederacy stands at its north end. The tower was barred to visitors, as is normal after dark. In the daytime, people can take the elevator to the top, where a balcony circles the building.

We went inside the Hall to visit the Archive, which houses the Constitution, the Compact, and the other founding documents. "You know," Khaled said, "I've taken the virtual tour, but it's nothing like actually being here."

"I guess," I said, "that living a few kilometers away kind of dulls the effect. I think most locals take everything for granted. I came out here for the first time with my seventh-grade class. We walked through the building, went back to the school, and, if my memory is right, we wrote essays about our reactions. Which probably meant making stuff up."

"So you said how you were overwhelmed?"

"I suppose. And I probably talked about how good the pretzels were."

He laughed and commented that it reminded him of some of his own best work. We came out and sat by the pool for a while. We talked about my experiences with Alex, and Khaled described how fortunate he was to be able to make a living taking people for boat rides. And how much he was enjoying being on Rimway. And, finally, he brought the conversation around to *us*.

"Do we have a future?" he asked.

It wasn't an easy question to answer. "Probably not," I said finally. "I love my job here, Khaled. There's just no way I would leave it."

He stared down at our reflections in the water. "Well," he said, "there *is* another possibility."

I became aware of a cool breeze blowing out of the west. And a sprinkle of rain, there for a moment, then gone. Like a fly-by-night romance. "Khaled, we don't know each other very well yet. We don't know enough to make major decisions."

"What you're saying, Chase, is *no*." He was still looking down at the water. "You're closing the door to every possibility. Am I reading that right?"

"Look: Why don't we do this a day at a time? Let it play out a little? I know we live kind of far apart, but that doesn't mean we have to make major decisions tonight."

He nodded and finally lifted his eyes. "How many days do we have left?"

"Tomorrow," I said. "I'll be leaving after that."

"Okay." He took a deep breath. "Then you *will* see me tomorrow? You've been kind of reluctant to—"

"Yes, we can get together tomorrow. If you want to. I'd been concerned because I have to go up to Skydeck and make sure our yacht gets its maintenance service." Actually, that can all be taken care of without my being personally on the scene. But I was trying to send a message. Though I didn't want our last possible day together to get away from me. So if you ask what the message was, I wasn't sure.

"What's a good time?" he asked.

It seemed like the moment to take advantage of Alex's offer. "I have the day off."

"Really?"

"Yes."

"You know what I'd like to do?"

"What's that, Khaled?"

"I'd like to go for a ride out on the Melony." I looked out at it, placid and quiet in the starlight.

"Okay," I said.

"It's the way we met. Maybe it should be the way we say good-bye."

"Khaled, that's not what I've been saying."

"I know," he said. "I'm sorry."

I was dressing when a call came in from a guy I didn't know. He identified himself as Kyle Everett. *"Chase,"* he said, *"I'm one of John Kraus's administrative assistants. We're trying to get this thing organized. We're dividing the Lifeboat mission into divisions and squadrons. Would you be interested in being a division commander?"*

"That sounds a little above my grade level, Kyle."

"John made the call. He says you'd be fine. You wouldn't actually have to do anything except relay information. We're going to run everything from the Dauntless. *We'll have approximately ten ships to a squadron, and ten squadrons to a division. There'll be nine divisions. When we decide to do something, we'll let you know, and all*

you have to do is pass it on to the squadron commanders. They'll relay it to their ships. When everyone complies, they'll acknowledge, it'll come back to you, and you will send it on to us. Clear?"

"Sounds simple enough."

"Then you'll do it?"

"Sure."

"Good. We're going to have almost a thousand vehicles out there. We don't want pilots making individual decisions, so we're going to maintain a tight control from the Dauntless. *Any questions?"*

Sunlight poured through my windows in the morning. A beautiful, unseasonably warm, bright day. Perfect for a ride on the river. I showered, got dressed, and was sitting down to breakfast when a call came in. It was Khaled. As soon as I saw him, I knew something was wrong. *"Chase."* He tried to smile. *"I'm going to back off today. I'm sorry. But I don't want to go through a last day with you."*

"Okay, Khaled. I'm sorry, too. But I understand."

"I've got a ride out of Skydeck this afternoon."

"All right. Is there anything I can do?"

"No. You've been honest with me. I guess that's enough." That brought on a long silence while both of us struggled to find something to say.

"You have a reservation on the shuttle, Khaled?"

"Yes. I'm all set. I just wanted you to know that I enjoyed the time we had together. Here and back home."

"I did, too."

"Good." He was standing off to one side of the kitchen table. *"Have a good life, Chase. I'll miss you."*

THIRTY-SIX

The enormous multiplication of books in every branch of knowledge is one of the greatest evils of this age; since it presents one of the most serious obstacles to the acquisition of correct information, by throwing in the reader's way piles of lumber, in which he must painfully grope for the scraps of useful matter, peradventure interspersed.

—Edgar Allen Poe, *Marginalia*, 1844 C.E.

Finally it was time to go. John conducted a briefing for the pilots from a conference room at the Department of Transportation. Approximately thirty people were there. The rest of us watched by HV. *"Since we don't know precisely when it will appear,"* he said, *"we'll arrive four days early and maintain the search around the clock. That means you should be on station at 1600 hours on the twelfth. Check in with your squadron commander as soon as you arrive. The formation will be spherical and centered on the* Dauntless, *which will be placed as close to the anticipated arrival site as we can manage. Unless you're on the outer boundary of the formation, the six ships closest to you will be at a range of fifteen thousand kilometers. Those will be operating above and below you, fore and aft, and on either side.*

"One other thing: Unless you're carrying lifeboats, we want only the pilot in each ship. If you need an additional person for any reason, check with your squadron or division commander. We need to conserve our life-support capabilities.

"Your position in the formation will be assigned this evening. We

don't expect the Capella *to appear before 1600 hours on the sixteenth. But we could be wrong about that. We could also be wrong in our estimate that it will arrive inside the search area. So we need everyone to maintain vigilance in all directions. If anyone locates it, or notices anything out of the ordinary, notify your commander immediately but take no action until you receive instructions."*

A hand went up. *"If it doesn't show up, John, how long will we wait?"*

"We're hoping everyone will be willing to give it three or four days, if necessary. The Dauntless, *and the StarCorps ships, will wait as long as it takes. StarCorps, by the way, already has units in place in case it arrives early. In that event, we will probably be unable to load lifeboats, but we will do what we can.*

"We anticipate that when it does arrive, it will be accessible for approximately seven or eight hours. If you become part of the contact group, you will likely be closer to the action than the Dauntless. *But be careful. It will get busy very quickly. If you do not have lifeboats on board, your mission will be to take off as many people as you can as quickly as you can. Once you have them on board, get clear so someone else can move in.*

"Be aware that our principal objective is to get the lifeboats loaded onto the Capella. *If we can rescue some people at the same time, that's good. But do not under any circumstances get in the way of the teams that are trying to transfer the boats. Vehicles with boats will have radio ID's and blue-and-white blinkers. They will be given right of way."*

Another hand went up. *"Do the people on the* Capella *know they're in trouble?"*

"We haven't had contact with them, Maureen. So we have no way of knowing. But probably they do. From their perspective, they will have surfaced off schedule and gone down again without initiating the action. So I'd be surprised if Captain Schultz is not aware she's in trouble.

"I'm sure most of you know that Robert Dyke is among the passengers. We'll have several teams of physicists and engineers spread around in the rescue force. What we want to do is talk to him. Give

him what we have and find out if he might be able to help. Do not, however, initiate contact with the Capella. *If they contact you, pass it on to your squadron commander immediately. Since we do not know the situation aboard ship, do not allow yourself to get into a conversation with them. News of radio contact should be passed to the* Dauntless, *and we will take it from there. Is that clear to everyone?"*

I took the shuttle to Skydeck a few hours later. The normal routine for anyone who maintained a ship at the station was that you notified them in advance when you would be using it, and it was waiting for you in one of the eight docks. But under the pressure of the rescue fleet being assembled, traffic was so heavy that they directed me to report to one of the operations offices, from which I was conducted to the maintenance area. There I boarded the *Belle-Marie*. There were probably twenty other ships, all crowded into a relatively small space. Two freighters and a fleet cruiser were floating outside the station.

I sat down on the bridge, said hello to Belle, and started running the checklist. Outside, a few lights broke through the darkness. "Do you know how to get us out of here?" I asked Belle.

"*Yes,*" she said. "*No problem.*"

I finished the preflight and checked in with ops.

"Belle-Marie," said a male voice, "*it'll be a few minutes. We'll get back to you.*"

"Copy that."

Sitting on the bridge in a sparsely lit enclosure is different from being under a dark sky. It can become oppressive. I was glad when my link buzzed. It was Alex. "*How's it going?*"

"I'm waiting to launch."

"*You have a minute?*"

"As far as I know. What's going on?"

"*I've been doing some research. Thought you might be interested in what I found.*"

"Sure. What is it?"

"*I've been reading Harvey Foxworth's* Walking Through the Rubble. *It's a history of archeological efforts to reconstruct the major*

*events of the Dark Age. It was written a thousand years ago, but it's
the classic work on the era. Foxworth has some details regarding Dmitri Zorbas that I haven't seen before. He kept a diary, Zorbas did, but
never allowed it to be published. After his death, Jerome Zorbas, his
brother, apparently under instructions, destroyed it."*

"You think they destroyed it because it revealed the location of the
artifacts?"

"There's no way to know."

"So what good does it do us if it's been destroyed?"

*"It provides credence to the probability that Zorbas had the arti-
facts and hid them."*

"Maybe. On the other hand, maybe they destroyed it because he
had too many women in his life."

*"I didn't say it was a confirmation, Chase. But Foxworth thinks
he salvaged the contents of the Prairie House. Zorbas came from a
wealthy family, so he had resources. We've known that. The family
maintained a home, according to the book, 'in a safe place' well away
from their quarters in Union City. Unfortunately, there's still no hint
where that might have been. Foxworth comments that, at the height
of the period, there were no safe places. There are a couple of pictures
of Rodia, standing with her husband. These were the first pictures I'd
seen of Zorbas himself. He always seems to be wearing a backpack.
He's on a horse in a couple of them. And there's one with him standing with a group of guys beside what appears to be a lander. It's hard
to be sure because the technology was so primitive. But they're laughing, and everybody's got a bottle."*

"Something else," said Alex. "About the internet failure." Terrorist attacks had gradually disrupted it and eventually took it down
worldwide. It was one of the causes of the Dark Age. Some historians
think it was the prime cause.

"They lost almost everything," he continued. *"I'm talking about
books now. A lot of the minor stuff, administrative records and avatars and medical data and whatnot, stuff that was maintained on
local data nets, survived. But they lost pretty much every book that
didn't exist as a print copy somewhere. And print copies don't have a*

good survival record over time. Anyhow, Zorbas set up a team to res-
cue whatever books they could. Foxworth has put together a long list
of titles that he credits Zorbas with saving."

The list appeared on my auxiliary screen. It included Cicero and
several Greek and Roman plays, Chaucer, Rabelais, two Dickens novels, and three of the six surviving Shakespearean plays. And a book
that one of my high-school teachers had used, she'd said, with the
hope that it would create a passion for reading: Ray Bradbury's *Martian Chronicles*. I remember how disappointed I'd been later when I
learned the Martian canals had been pure fantasy.

There were probably two hundred titles in all. They weren't all
classics, but the mere fact that they'd survived gave them considerable
value.

"Zorbas," I said, "must have been one hell of a guy."

*"Yeah. He was. But I suspect he'd be unhappy if he knew how
things have turned out with the museum artifacts."*

"Have you had any luck locating Madeleine O'Rourke?" The
woman who'd pretended to be *The Plains Drifter* reporter.

"No. She's done a decent job of keeping out of sight."

"Pity. She might be the key to this business."

"My thought exactly." He paused. *"What are you going to do
about Khaled?"*

"What do you mean?"

*"Well, you know we'll be going back to Earth when this business
with the Capella is over."*

"Actually, I *didn't* know that. Why will we be going back to Earth?"

"Because we haven't found the artifacts yet."

"Oh. Does that mean you know where to look?"

"Not yet. But we'll find out."

"How will we do that?"

"I'm not sure yet. But Baylee figured it out."

"Maybe we're not as smart as he was."

"Maybe not. Chase, are you still not moving?"

"That is correct. I'm sitting in a basement."

"Well, enjoy." He paused. *"Listen, keep me informed, okay? And*

if by any chance you get seriously lucky and have Gabe among your passengers on the way back, let me know. I'd want to be there when you come in."

I waited almost half an hour before clearance came. Then doors opened, and we passed through into the docking area and out through another set of doors into the night. Belle set course, and, finally, we were on our way.

I made my jump, divided my time between reading and sleeping, and eventually surfaced just outside the target zone. At least that was Belle's best estimate.

Belle worked to get an angle on our position while I checked in with the *Dauntless*. When I'd finished, she informed me we'd need thirty-six hours to arrive on station. *"Find a good book,"* she said.

We had some material about Baylee in the library, and I settled in with it. There were a couple of histories that had information on his assorted treks around terrestrial archeological sites. I sat looking at pictures of him standing with a spade in one hand at an Egyptian dig site, directing excavations at Chicago, examining ancient English inscriptions on a building in the American Southwest, talking with locals near Roman ruins. There were pictures of him and his team working at the Broomar site on Mars. And investigating an early space station orbiting Jupiter.

Lawrence Southwick had obviously spent more time with him than I realized. He was in many of the photos. And there was somebody else. In a picture from the Nevada desert, near the Phoenix ruins, a young woman stood between Baylee and Southwick. A fedora was pulled down to block off the sun. It was hard to make out her face. But I knew her.

"*Who is it?*" asked Belle.

"It's Madeleine O'Rourke."

"*The reporter?*"

The caption identified her as Heli Tokata.

THIRTY-SEVEN

Enjoy your time with a friend. You will not have him forever.

—Elizabeth Stiles, *Singing in the Void*, 1221

I sent a message to Alex suggesting he run a search on Heli Tokata and informing him where I'd seen her picture. A response came back within a few hours. *"Thanks,"* he said. *"It's her. I can't believe I missed it."*

And finally we arrived in the search area. The *Capella* was due in a little over four days. I informed the *Dauntless* that we were on station and checked in with the squadron commanders who were assigned to me. Six were there; four were presumably still en route.

There was no sign of movement in the sky, of course. We were too far from each other to see anything with the naked eye. I invested my time by going back over Alex's research material. He'd added not only a few books to Belle's library but also probably a thousand essays, reports, journals, and diaries. Belle offered to help, but Alex had already put her through the more obvious searches. I didn't see any familiar names among the authors, so I picked a book titled *Golden Vistas*. It was a history written by Marcia Hadron. She was a contemporary, living on Toxicon. The fact that I wasn't familiar with her name shouldn't be interpreted as implying that she was an obscure voice in the field. To begin with, despite my job, I'm not nearly as well-read as I should be. Hadron had won several major prizes for her research.

The title referred to archeological missions aimed at recovering artifacts from the early space age. The *Golden Age*. Baylee got an entire chapter. But Hadron barely mentioned the Prairie House or Dmitri Zorbas. Nevertheless, I read through the chapter, and in the process found my respect for Baylee continuing to grow. He was described as a man who inspired others, who accomplished a great deal during his career, but who consistently gave the credit to his colleagues. *"They loved him,"* Hadron says. *"He was remarkably selfless in a profession that traditionally attracted giant egos."*

"You know," I told Belle, "you tend to hear the same thing about physicists, writers, lawyers, and actors. You never hear it said about physicians, though."

"Maybe," Belle said, *"it's because physicians are in a position to inflict serious damage on a patient who criticizes them."*

Baylee was mentioned a few times elsewhere in the book, but I couldn't find anything relating to the hunt for the Apollo artifacts other than the author's regret that they had never been recovered. Hadron dismissed the Dakota "myth," as she called it. The artifacts, she believed, had almost certainly been taken out of Huntsville by thieves.

"I have something you might be interested in," said Belle. *"It does not relate to the artifacts, but it is nevertheless intriguing."*

"What is that?" I asked.

"It's from a doctoral dissertation by a young woman who cites Luciana Moretti as her source. Apparently Baylee and Southwick did an excavation at Tyuratam."

"Where?"

"It was a Russian launch site. The Baikonur Cosmodome. It sent the first satellite into orbit in the 1950s. The exact date has been lost. Anyhow, according to the account, he and Southwick led an expedition there twenty years ago. Well, technically Southwick led the expedition. He was the guy with the money. A few of them went out rafting on a nearby river, the Syr Darya. And something in the water attacked them. No indication what it was. Anyway, one guy was killed. But Baylee emerged as the hero. He fought the thing off with a pole. Saved Southwick's life. And two other people."

"I'm surprised," I said, "Southwick never mentioned that to us."

"*I am surprised as well.*"

"It might be a male thing. You don't look very good floundering around in the water while somebody else tackles the alligator. Do they have alligators at Tyuratam?"

"*I have no data on that.*"

"Most guys," I said, "would probably claim that they used an oar or something to help." Whatever the truth was, Baylee kept looking better.

I found something else. It showed up in Trevor Nakada's memoir, *Life in the Ruins*. Nakada was an archeologist who'd spent most of his career working in Asia. But he'd gotten his start with Baylee and Southwick in an underwater expedition that had brought back artifacts from the White House. The book had a substantial number of photos from the mission, most with Nakada on eminent display. One shows him standing between two young women, using a cloth to hold a tray. One of the young women has just removed her swim fins; the other has a broad-brimmed cap pulled down over her head. The caption reads: *The author holds a nine-thousand-year-old platter which he has just recovered. Margaret Woods stands to his left, with an unidentified colleague.*

The unidentified colleague was Madeleine again.

Belle's light blinked. "*Transmission coming in,*" she said. "*From the* Dauntless."

It was John. "*A few vehicles are not going to make it out here. So we're doing some minor changes in positioning.*" We acknowledged receipt and relayed it to the squadron commanders, all of whom had by then arrived. We were, however, still missing three ships.

With about forty hours remaining before the *Capella*'s expected arrival, the last two ships in my unit checked in.

I rarely spend time alone in the *Belle-Marie*. Belle is company of sorts, but it's not really quite the same as actually having a living person on board. On that flight, I did more workout sessions than usual. Took most of my meals on the bridge. After the first night, I slept in the passenger cabin. Anything to break up the routine.

I couldn't help thinking about the first time I'd boarded the *Belle-Marie*. I'd been with my mom, back in the days when she'd been Gabe's pilot. Gabe had just bought the yacht, replacing the *Tracker*, which he'd had for years. They'd brought me aboard for the maiden voyage, which had only been a short flight to Lara. I was twenty at the time. That was when I decided I wanted the same career my mother was enjoying. A couple of years later, when Mom decided to go home and live a normal life, Gabe hired me, reluctantly, to replace her. I'm pretty sure he did it to make her happy, expecting he'd have to get rid of me pretty quickly. But everything worked out, and I spent a year and a half with him before he climbed on board the *Capella*. Ordinarily, he'd have used the *Belle-Marie*, but he was looking at a long flight and wanted to turn it into a vacation. So he'd gotten on the cruise ship and gone into oblivion. I'd wondered if his decision had something to do with maybe not trusting me on an extended mission. But Mom told me he'd liked the big cruise ships, and there'd been nothing unusual in his decision.

When he and the other passengers and crew were all declared dead a year later, Alex inherited the *Belle-Marie*, and it became officially the means of transport for Rainbow Enterprises.

I'd enjoyed my time with Gabe. This should not be read as a criticism of Alex in any way, but he was easier to talk to. More amiable. There was no subject that didn't interest him. He loved to talk about history and politics and religion. He was passionate about everything but never in the sense that he'd get angry if you disagreed with him. In fact, he seemed to enjoy contrary opinions and was always willing to listen. Once or twice, I thought I even succeeded in changing his mind. He thought, or pretended to, that the human race would have been better off if everyone were kept just slightly inebriated. "People are much friendlier, much more empathic," he told me, "when they've had a couple of light drinks. But not when they get much beyond that. And there's the problem. You can't control intake."

There'd been a lot of girlfriends. He even took them on his archeological missions occasionally. At first I felt a little uncomfortable, alone in an interstellar with a guy who seemed to be a makeout artist, but he never got out of line. I was the pilot, and if he wanted a woman along on a trip, he brought one. My mom just smiled when I asked her about it. "Some things never change," she said. "But you don't have to worry about him."

I'd have trusted him with my life. I had trouble once with a technician on the Dellacondan space station. He was a big guy, and I can't say he really intended anything serious, but he mouthed off about my looking "delicious." He was with a couple of oversized friends. All of them were considerably bigger than Gabe, but he stepped in immediately and made it clear that he'd do whatever it took.

I slept late into that final morning before the *Capella*'s expected arrival time.

I couldn't help thinking about him as I showered and had breakfast and took my seat in the passenger cabin. I remembered his disappointment on the return flight from a mission to the City on the Crag. I don't recall any longer precisely what it was he'd been looking for, but it'd had something to do with a two-thousand-year-old civilization that had collapsed with no apparent explanation. Whatever he'd been looking for specifically, he hadn't found it. There were five members of his archeological team coming back with him, all annoyed, all convinced they'd missed something. But in the end, the gloom had gone away, and it had turned into a party. Sometimes, Alex partied, but it always carried with it a sense of dutiful behavior. Alex did social stuff because whatever he wanted to accomplish required it. Gabe loved having a good time. It was hard to believe that, if we could get him off the *Capella*, Gabe would be only a few days older than the last time I'd seen him, eleven years before. I was sitting there thinking what a crazy universe we live in but how we wouldn't be able to get around much if time and space weren't so counterintuitive. It was hard to understand how the structure of the universe could come about naturally. Why wasn't there just hydrogen drifting around? It was a question physicists had struggled to answer since Isaac Newton's time. There were theories, of course. But they were always hidden in equations. There was never anything you could visualize.

"*Chase.*" Belle's voice. "*Transmission coming from the* Dauntless.*"

"Okay."

"*Good afternoon, all. Be advised the* Capella *could now appear at any time.*" It was John. "*Those of you who are able, pick up passengers: After they're on board, they'll probably be asking questions. Be honest with them. No point trying to hide the truth. We'd like to prevent their communicating with people on the* Capella, *but I don't see any way to block that other than to ask them to refrain. I suggest you not let them know about the time differential unless specifically asked. Don't lie about it, but try to avoid the issue.*"

I remember thinking that, if we were successful, and the passengers and crew were actually rescued, that someone would make a movie of the experience. And I had a title: *Waiting for the* Capella.

THIRTY-EIGHT

The thing that irritates me about how the universe works is that, once we get born, it shows zero concern for us. It's a system filled with supernovas, giant gas clouds, predators, and earthquakes. We might turn an asteroid aside, but don't try to rewire the process to prevent recurrences. When a tornado shows up, just get under the table and pray.

—Schiaparelli Cleve, *Autobiography*, 8645 C.E.

"As most of you know," John said, "the captain of the Capella, Dierdre Schultz, has a solid reputation. But it's incumbent on us to stay out of her way. As soon as we make contact, we'll try to ensure that she understands what has happened. That conversation will be relayed to the fleet to keep everyone apprised of the situation. If we get this right, we'll only have to come out here to do this one more time."

"I wish it would come," I said. "I hate the waiting."

Belle asked something irrelevant. Did I want her to locate and run a good comedy? Was I getting tired? I don't recall exactly what it was. But I told her to relax.

Her lights blinked in her standard suggestion of a giggle.

We'd probably get a few people out on this attempt, and eventually, even if things didn't go well, we'd recover the vast majority. I was happy to be part of it, but I wanted it to be over. I didn't like the idea of its going on for another five years. Or maybe more.

I didn't think I was actually talking, but Belle was picking it up. "It'll be okay," she said. "There is reason to be optimistic."

"I know, Belle. I just wish we could bring them home now." JoAnn would have been bitterly disappointed at how this was playing out. Despite John's assurance that whatever had been determined by the physicists would be passed on to Robert Dyke, I doubted that would include JoAnn's contribution. Considering the President's stand, I guessed not.

I talked with some of the nearby ships. They were mostly yachts, like the *Belle-Marie*, but there were also two freighters. The freighters were the *Bentley* and the *Bollinger*, carrying twenty-eight and twenty-two lifeboats respectively. Five of the pilots told me they had either relatives or friends on board the *Capella*. There was a lot of frustration and even some tears. They all understood that the odds against recovering any specific person on this attempt weren't good. And they agreed that they were prepared to settle. *"If I can just come away from this with the knowledge that they're okay, and that we'll get them back, I'll go home happy."* It was a sentiment I heard again and again. But they didn't sound as if they meant it. Five years is a long time.

One of the entertainers on board the *Capella* was Dory Caputo. She sang, danced, and did comedy. Her husband was on the *Bentley*, and would be helping move lifeboats if they got into position. He sent me a vid of one of her performances. Dory laughed, told jokes, explained how to handle idiot bosses, and simply seemed *too alive* to have gone missing for eleven years. *"I never wanted her to sign on for the thing,"* he said. *"I hope, when she gets back, she'll have more sense."*

There was a lifeboat team of four on the *Bollinger*. *"They've got thousands of these things stashed on the ships,"* one of the pilots told me. *"They're going to use, at most, forty or so of them. What will they do with the rest? It's a goddam shame the thing won't stay on the surface long enough to make it a bit easier to do this stuff."*

Halfway through the afternoon, the timer sounded. Zero hour. Two hours later, John addressed the fleet and said that patience was in order. "This is at best an imprecise operation," he said.

I awoke on the fifth morning to the smell of bacon and eggs. *"We're going to do a minor position adjustment in about an hour, Chase,"* Belle said. *"Since you have to get up, I thought you'd like some breakfast."*

"Sounds good," I said. "I'll be there in a minute."

"And we're getting another transmission. From the Raven.*"* *Raven* headed one of the squadrons reporting to us.

It was a woman's voice: *"Belle-Marie, we have a sighting. Reported by the* Breckinridge. *Awaiting confirmation."*

I acknowledged. Belle waited a few seconds. Then: *"Chase, do you want me to pass it on to the* Dauntless?*"*

"No. Let's give it a minute. See what happens."

I got some orange juice to go with my breakfast. Then the *Raven* was back. *"False alarm. It was apparently somebody showing up late. Wait, hold on."* She clicked off, and a few seconds later, was back. *"It was the* Holtz. *They're listed among the no-shows. But I guess they got here. Anyhow, false alarm. Out."*

THIRTY-NINE

Man is not capable of forgetting. He refuses to let go of the past. However far or fast he runs, he drags the chain with him.

—Friedrich Nietzsche, unknown date

The rest of that fifth day in the target zone passed without incident, other than one more false alarm caused by another late arrival. The pilot apologized and explained that he'd been given the wrong arrival date. He didn't say how that could have happened, but as far as I know, nobody pressed the issue.

That period of quiescence ended when Belle came alive in the middle of the morning: *"Message from the* Dauntless.*"*

John's voice again: *"We have a confirmed contact. The* Capella *has arrived. Its position has been forwarded to your AI. We have not yet established a radio link with them, but as soon as we do, we will use the beta frequency to pass the transmissions on to all ships."*

"Here we go, Belle."

"Yes, indeed. Good luck to us."

"Belle," I said, "will we be changing course?"

"Not at the moment. We are directed to maintain present status until otherwise informed."

"Okay." That was a disappointment: We would probably not be part of the rescue operation. I switched to the beta frequency and heard confirmation: A voice was assuring someone on the *Capella* that evacuation vehicles were on their way.

"*What's going on?*" asked the *Capella*. "*Why are all you guys out here?*"

"*Capella, are you aware what's been happening?*"

"*We're having a problem with the drive. Can't seem to stay submerged. Every time we try to make our jump, we go down for a few hours, then we're back under the stars again. Do you know what this is about?*"

"*Can you get the captain on the circuit for me? Quickly, please. This is an emergency.*"

"*You sound rattled, Dauntless. What's happening?*"

John took over: "*Get Captain Schultz for me immediately. We don't have time to waste.*"

"*Okay. Give us a couple of minutes, all right? Capella out.*"

"Ask them," I grumbled, "what year they think it is."

"*I can understand why they do not realize their situation,*" said Belle.

"Where *is* it, Belle? The *Capella*? Do you have a read on it?"

"*We haven't been informed. I haven't been able to locate it, but I'd guess it's not within range, or they'd have started us toward it already.*"

"*Dauntless, stand by for Captain Schultz.*"

And, moments later, a woman's voice: "*Dauntless, this is the captain. Are you having a problem?*" She sounded annoyed. "*Who am I speaking to, please?*"

"*Captain, my name is John Kraus. Are you aware of your situation?*"

"*That we've been forced to surface? Of course. Our drive unit is not behaving properly, but we haven't been able to determine the precise reason. Mr. Kraus, how does it happen you're involved in this? Do you represent—?*"

"*Captain, how long has it been since you left Rimway?*"

"*Three days. Why do you ask?*"

"*You've been disabled. I'll explain in a minute. But time is short.*

You're going to have to evacuate. We have ships in the area, moving toward you."

"Evacuate? Why on earth would that be necessary? How did you even get here so quickly? We only sent out the report earlier today."

That would have been sent the last time they were on the surface. It would have been a directional signal, aimed at Rimway. Or where Rimway had been eleven years earlier. Which meant no one would have heard it.

"Captain, you've been caught in a space/time warp. It's 1435. You've been out here eleven years."

"That's ridiculous. Mr. Kraus, who are you really?"

"It's true," said John. *"Have your navigator check his position. You're not anywhere near where you think you are."*

I heard whispering. Then the captain was back: *"We're looking into it."*

"You don't have much time. So you're aware, I'm the director of a government effort to get you and your passengers and crew off that ship. You only have a few hours before you'll be dragged under again."

There was a long silence. Then a male voice with an odd accent: *"He's right, Captain. We're way off course."*

"Incredible," said Schultz. *"It doesn't seem possible. You say we've been out here eleven years?"*

"That is correct."

"Mr. Kraus, if you've no objection, I'll wait for a response to my request for assistance before I start an evacuation."

"Bear with me, Captain, but we're pressed for time. When you surfaced before, how long were you up?"

"About nine hours."

"All right. We're going to assume that's how long we'll have this time, too. When you were pulled under, how long were you down before you resurfaced?"

"About twelve hours. Hold on a minute." We could hear more talking in the background. Then she was back: *"They're telling me it was closer to fourteen before we came up again."* She was obviously

angry. "*We were trying to determine the nature of the problem when we heard from you.*"

"*Okay. We'll get to you as quickly as we can.*"

Schultz was slow to respond. But when she did, her voice had hardened: "*How could this happen?*"

"*Let's talk about it later. You'll probably be dragged under again the same way this time.*"

"*Wonderful. When will the first ship be here?*"

"*In about three and a half hours. It's the* Ventnor. *They can take twenty-eight of your people.*"

"*Twenty-eight?*" Schultz laughed. "*You have a hundred more ships coming in?*"

"*Actually, we have a thousand. The problem is that only a small fraction can get to you in the time we have available.*"

"*So what do you propose to do?*"

"*Captain, let me tell you about the lifeboats.*"

I couldn't resist trying to raise Gabe on my link. But there was no connection. I wasn't surprised; we were much too far from the *Capella*.

"*There's also nothing to relay the signal,*" said Belle.

"That's more or less what I was saying."

"*I have their position,*" Belle said. "*We have six ships moving toward her. Five are yachts. The sixth one is a fleet cruiser, the* Sadie Randall. *Some good news here: the* Randall *has the full number of lifeboats on board, forty-four. But they'll need six and a half hours to make the rendezvous. That will leave them about two and a half hours to transfer the boats.*"

And then wait another five years to finish the rescue. "Belle," I said, "how many people can the *Randall* take off? Through the airlock?"

"*Her life-support system would allow her to take about a hundred. The problem is that she probably can't unload the boats and pick up evacuees at the same time.*"

"Damn."

"*Chase, we have an incoming message. A general broadcast to the entire fleet.*"

It was John again: "*Our prospects for bringing this off look pretty good. We expect to be able to transfer a substantial number of lifeboats to the* Capella. *If it stays with us as long as we anticipate, we will move enough over to be in a position to run a complete evacuation when she reappears in 1440. In addition, we expect to take a hundred or more people off today. I want to thank all who have participated and made it possible to create the rendezvous. Without your help, it could not have happened. Unless your AI has course instructions from us, you are now free to leave the search area.*"

I thought about what was probably going on in the *Capella* at that moment. And I sympathized with her captain. Deirdre Schultz would probably be making an announcement, trying to explain what had happened to almost three thousand people who wouldn't be able to believe what she was saying. Telling them a story she was having trouble accepting herself. Once they realized it wasn't some sort of mad joke, once people understood that their worlds had grown eleven years older without them, there'd be tears and screams and probably some hysterics. And a lot of people saying how that was it for them with interstellar travel.

If I'd been in Schultz's position, I decided, I would want to leave that part of the story until I got everyone off the ship. Except that she probably figured she'd be unable to get away with that.

"*We have an additional message from Mr. Kraus,*" said Belle. "*For you.*"

"*Chase,*" he said. "*You and Alex have been major contributors to this effort from the beginning. If you'd like to stay with us, we'd be happy to have you.*"

There was no point moving closer since I could not help. But I welcomed the invitation to stay in the area and watch. I suspected a lot of other people would be lingering as well.

"John," I said, "thanks. I'll hang on. Let me know if I can do anything."

"*You already have, Chase.*"

Belle told me I looked unhappy. *"Keep in mind,"* she added, *"that he'll be back. Gabe, that is. Probably not today, but you* will *see him again."*

"I know. I just hate getting this close to him, though, and having him get away again."

"It could be much worse. You should consider yourself fortunate."

"I do." I sat quietly, imagining Gabe arriving at the country house, coming up the walkway, and seeing how everything had changed.

Again, I must have said something because Belle took a harsh tone: *"Listen, you've taken good care of the property, haven't you? I know Alex quite well, and he would not allow it to deteriorate."*

"That's not what I was thinking. Gabe won't be happy when he finds out what kind of business we're running out of it."

"There's not much you can do about that. You guys will just have to come to some sort of agreement."

I took a deep breath. "Alex will probably have to leave. Not that Gabe would force him out, but there'll be a lot of tension."

Belle was silent for a long moment. Then: *"What about you, Chase? Which of them would you prefer to work for?"*

I'd been thinking about that. And I wasn't sure. What I'd really like would be to see them come together. Both involved with Rainbow Enterprises. But I knew that would never happen.

The beta frequency was, for the most part, silent. Schultz was undoubtedly too busy to be talking on the radio. But one of her ops spoke for her now and then. *"We have twenty-eight people lined up and ready to go as soon as the* Ventnor *gets here."*

And: *"Some of our passengers have gone into shock. We debated not saying anything until they were safely out of here. But in the end that didn't seem like a good idea. We've told them about the eleven years. But they* don't *know that it'll be 1440 before most of them get out. We don't want to start a panic. Things are scary enough now."*

And then the captain herself: *"I can't believe it's been eleven years, John. Did they write us off as dead?"*

"Yes, Dierdre. Nobody knew what had happened."

"My poor husband. But at least he knows now we're all right?"

"Yes."

"Thank God. When you can, would you tell him you talked with me? I hate his having to wait another five years before I see him again."

"Sure, Dierdre. I'll tell him."

"Thanks." Long pause. *"John, is he all right?"*

"Yes, he's fine. And he's waiting for you." I was impressed when I heard that, that he'd foreseen this conversation and done the homework. I imagined myself on the receiving end of that request and stumbling around asking for his name and address and wondering if he'd married someone else. Or whether he was even still alive.

"Our passengers and crew," said Schultz, *"are going to have a hard time getting their heads around this. Everybody they know and care about will be eleven years older."*

"I know, Dierdre."

"I just don't believe this is happening."

Captain Schultz and her passengers had experienced only a couple of days of being stranded. I couldn't help thinking about the other lost ships, some of them drifting through centuries and even millennia.

Then the captain again: *"John,"* she said, *"the* Ventnor's *here."*

FORTY

If you would live to the fullest, stay off the expressways. Always go by the back roads.

—John Kraus, *Memoirs*, 1434

I watched through the *Ventnor*'s scopes as she pulled alongside the *Capella*. The lights continued spreading out, on the bridge and across thrusters and scanners and gleaming from portals. It morphed gradually into a flying city. And the hull kept getting larger until it filled the display.

And we could hear the interchange between the operational officers on the two ships:

"*That's good,*" said the *Capella*. "*Hold it there. We're opening the airlock. They're carrying some bags. No major luggage, though. You guys going to have room for it?*"

"*Shouldn't be a problem.*"

"*All right. Good. There are nine families. Twenty-eight people altogether.*"

"*Okay.*"

"*Lock is open. Tube's in place.*"

Exit tubes are constructed of plastene, supported by struts. The *Capella*'s reached across the thirty meters or so separating the two ships until it touched the airlock. The hull was replaced on-screen by the *Ventnor*'s interior. I knew the pilot, Janet Carstairs. I watched her leave the bridge and proceed into the passenger cabin, where she opened the inner airlock hatch. Then she checked to see that the tube was in fact secure. *"Okay, Mike,"* she said, *"open up."* Mike, I assumed, was the AI.

"Complying."

The hatch slid up into the overhead, and I could see into the tube. Lights came on along its length, and the interior of the *Capella*'s airlock appeared at the far side. *"Clear on this end,"* Janet said. She gave a thumbs-up and entered the tube.

The *Capella* replied: *"Opening up."*

The clicks and whirls of the other hatch became audible. Then people appeared, crowded at the entrance. And voices encouraging one another. *"Be careful, Penny."*

"I got the bag, love."

"Is this safe, Mommy?"

Janet crossed over to the other ship, where a family of four, with a boy and girl, both about six or seven, waited in the airlock. Their father grappled with bags. Janet took one and led them into the tube. *"Be careful,"* she said. *"Hang on to the rails. There's no gravity."* The father came next, then the kids, scared at first, then giggling as they drifted toward the overhead. The mother brought up the rear, securing the children.

Other families followed.

Janet came out of the tube but stayed at the hatch to help as they reentered the gravity field. The passengers came out of the airlock, uncertain children, moms and dads looking confused and worried. *"We don't have cabins for everyone,"* she said, *"but we'll manage."* She directed some of them toward the after section of the *Ventnor*, freeing up space. The last one through was a young woman who might have been alone. The twenty-eighth passenger. Janet was explaining how they'd get everyone settled as quickly as they could, but first they needed everybody to sit down, either where they were or in one of the cabins. *"We're short on seats,"* she added. *"So we'll have to make do. Parents, we'd like you to belt yourselves in, then hold on to your kids. We want to get away from here to make room for the next ship coming in."*

We heard the voices from the *Capella*, announcing they were closing the airlock. Seconds later, Janet informed them she'd disconnected from the tube.

The passengers buckled down. A new voice, presumably the AI, announced they'd have sandwiches and cookies as soon as they got clear.

"*Next ship,*" said John, "*will be the* Deloi. *They're about forty minutes out.*"

As soon as I heard the name I knew there'd be a problem. And I'm sure John was aware of it, too. But we needed all the ships we could muster. Deloi was one of the major cities on Borkarat, a Mute world. "*That's an odd name,*" said Schultz. "*Where's it from, John?*"

"*It's an Ashiyyurean ship.*"

"*Mutes?*"

"*Yes.*"

"*You're having my people taken off by Mutes?*"

"*Things have changed in eleven years, Dierdre.*"

"*I'm glad to hear it. But my passengers aren't going to want to get into a ship with Mutes. I mean, they still read minds, don't they?*"

"*Tell your passengers not to think any embarrassing thoughts.*"

"*This is going to be a hard sell, John.*" Somebody shut the transmission down at that point. I sighed. Kraus had obviously recalled that the conversation was being broadcast.

"Schultz's right," I said to Belle. "People *still* don't want to be around them."

"*Well, Chase, I suppose they have the option of staying on the* Capella *for another five years.*"

Mutes had come a long way in the human perspective over the recent past, principally through the assistance they'd rendered at Salud Afar. Nevertheless, even in this more enlightened age, their black diamond eyes, reptilian gray skin, and especially their fangs provided an unsettling appearance. But the real problem, as everyone understood, was that they knew what you were thinking. And, of course, Schultz's passengers and crew, and she herself, had never lived outside that earlier era.

The broadcast would have been picked up by the *Deloi*, which left me wondering what its Mute pilot was thinking.

"*They won't be surprised,*" said Belle, demonstrating a capability herself for reading minds.

When the *Deloi* showed up and docked with the *Capella*, they opened their airlock and we watched while thirty-three people walked through the exit tube and were greeted by the Mute pilot, who had to use a voice-box that also served as a translator. Everything seemed to go as smoothly as anyone could have hoped although the passengers were obviously unnerved. It didn't help that Mute laughter sounds forced to humans, or maybe a bit like the laughter of a vampire. But, fortunately, there was only one alien on board.

Later, John told us that Captain Schultz, after assuring the selected families that there was no reason to be concerned about the Mute pilot and that everyone knew their telepathic capabilities were vastly exaggerated, added that she was expecting a delay before the next group would be able to get off. They would, she noted, be smart to go now while they could. She sent along a female junior officer whom everyone liked and trusted. "The only problem there," said the director, "was that the junior officer was pretty nervous, too, but she was able to hide it."

"*Incoming call,*" said Belle. "*From John Kraus.*"

"*Chase.*" He showed up on-screen, looking annoyed. "*I need your help.*"

"Of course, John. What can I do?"

"*I may have misplayed my hand. You know who Robert Dyke is, right?*"

"Sure."

"*You're probably not aware of this, but JoAnn left some suggestions for him. On what she thought might work. You know, the drive-manipulation thing. It looks as if she did a lot of thinking about it while she was stuck on the* Grainger. *I passed what she had along to him. He's on the* Capella.*"

"I know."

"*Okay. What you don't know is that he's talking about putting her ideas into action. He's going to try doing what she did on the Grainger.*"

"Well, that's why you gave it to him, isn't it?"

"*No, it isn't. Well, hell, I don't know. I wanted him to be able to see what she thought, and maybe he could find a way to make it applicable. But he's telling me that her comments are helpful, 'illuminating,' he said, but that there's no way to be certain of the outcome. I've asked him to stay away from it if he can't be sure. But he isn't cooperating.*"

"So what do you want me to do?"

"*Talk to him. Tell him what the Grainger looked like when you were walking through it looking for JoAnn and Nick. Make him understand the risk he'd be taking.*"

"John, why not tell Captain Schultz?"

"*Dyke's already talked to her. He's convinced her he can make it work.*"

"I wouldn't have any influence with this guy, John. Maybe you should ask Shara to do this? At least he probably knows who she is."

He hesitated. "*I've already asked her. She won't do it.*"

"Why not?"

John looked like a man in pain. "*She's not sure what's the right thing to do. Please, Chase, the lives of these people may hang on this. You were close to JoAnn. Maybe you can let him know she didn't trust it.*"

"I can't believe anything I might tell him would make any difference, John."

"*You could be right, Chase. But you're all we've got. Think about what you saw on board the Grainger. Imagine what it would have looked like if there'd been more than two thousand people on board.*"

That provided a chill. "All right," I said. "Can you connect me with him?"

"*Give me a minute. We're going to tell him who you are and that you wanted to speak to him. Okay?*"

"All right."

"*By the way, I'll stay on audio.*" That almost sounded like a warning.

The screen went blank.

I sat there staring at it. What the hell had I gotten myself into?

The next voice I heard wasn't John's: "*Okay, Robert—We've got her.*"

And a face blinked on. "*Chase?*"

"Yes. Hello, Professor Dyke."

In photos, Dyke came across as solemn, humorless, cocksure of himself. But the image on the display belied all that. He was worried and looked as if he carried the weight of the world on his shoulders though he nevertheless managed a smile. "*Hello, Chase. I understand you wanted to talk to me?*"

"Uh, yes, Professor."

"*I'm Rob,*" he said. "*Please keep it short. I'm busy at the moment.*"

"Rob, I understand you're thinking about trying to do the same thing that JoAnn Suttner did on the *Grainger*?"

"*No. That's not correct. I'm changing the formulation.*"

"But you can't be certain it will work, is that right?"

He stared at me. The smile was gone. "*Chase, I think I understand what this is about. And I believe I can save us both some time. No, to answer your question, in a matter like this, there is no absolute certainty. But we have the next best thing. JoAnn has passed me some data, and some after-the-fact speculation that is very helpful. I don't think there is any realistic reason to be worried.*"

"Robert, walking through that dead place picturing what happened to JoAnn and Nick was possibly the worst experience of my life." That was, of course, a lie since at the time I had no idea what had happened to them. "I cannot imagine what it would be like to condemn almost three thousand people to that kind of death. Please don't do this."

"*I need to cut this short. Let me ask you a question: If you were here with us, what would you want me to do? Provide you an almost certain ticket home? Or back off and cause you to lose another five years of life with your friends and family?"*

I guess I stared back while I fumbled for a reply. "I—"

He waited. Then: *"I guess that's clear enough, Chase. Maybe we'll have a chance to talk again sometime."*

He blinked off. And John was back, glaring out of the screen at me. *"Well done, Chase,"* he said. *"If he kills everybody, it's on your head."*

It left me in a rage. I sat there staring at the mike, rehearsing what I would say to John Kraus when I called him back. How in hell had this become *my* call? I was still fuming over it, trying to figure out what I wanted to say, when Belle told me John was on the circuit again.

"Tell him I'm busy," I said.

"I think you should take it, Chase."

Why not? I had a few things to say to him anyhow. Might as well get them said.

John's face appeared on-screen. *"I'm sorry, Chase. That wasn't your fault. I shouldn't have put you into that position."* The lips softened into a smile. *"I apologize."*

"It's okay." It's all I could say.

"I owe you."

"You know," I said, "no matter what I told him, Dyke wasn't going to change his mind."

"You're probably right."

"I hope so, John. Because at the moment, it's the only thing keeping me sane."

Another general broadcast came in: First a voice we didn't recognize: *"We are on approach, John. Will rendezvous in about twenty minutes."*

"Glad to hear it, Bark. Capella has opened its cargo hold."

"The reference," said Belle, "is to Bark Peters, captain of the Sadie Randall."

"Bark," said John, *"I have estimated time to transfer lifeboats as approximately three hours. Has there been any change?"*

"*Negative that.*"

"*And you have forty-four boats?*"

"*Confirmed.*"

"*All right. The three hours will take you right up to, and maybe a little past, the projected* Capella *departure. You have no wiggle room.*"

"I'm aware of that, John."

"*One other thing: Be careful. Break off at the first sign of instability. We don't want you getting pulled down, too.*"

"*I'll take care of it, John. You can leave the details to me.*"

He didn't sound very flexible.

"*Okay. Have it your way, Bark. FYI, we also have a yacht closing. The* Mary Lou Eisner *will arrive within minutes after you guys do.*"

"I hope," I said, "it's not another Mute."

"*The* Mary Lou Eisner*?*" said Belle. "*That seems unlikely.*"

"I was kidding. What's its capacity?"

"*Nine people.*"

"We could do better."

"*It would be close.*"

"There are—what?—two more coming in after that?"

"*Yes. The* Shang-Chi *and the* Morrison. *They're about an hour apart. Both small, so they won't be able to take many.*"

"At least they'll be in and out quickly."

We were getting pictures from the *Randall* as they approached. "I have a question for you, Belle," I said.

"*Okay.*"

"Who was Belle-Marie?"

"*Her last name was McKeown. She was one of Gabe's girlfriends. A special one.*"

"What happened to her? They never married?"

"*No. She walked away from him.*"

"She walked away from *Gabe*?"

"*Yes. Damaged him emotionally, I believe.*"

"And he named his new yacht for her?"

"*I thought it was strange, too. Why do you pay tribute to some-*"

body who discards you? He could have called it the Giddy-Up *or something. But he told me she never knew about it."*

"Well, I'm sorry to hear it."

"Gabe was, is, kind of tough on the surface, but down under all the manly stuff, he's pretty sentimental."

"Did you ever meet her? Belle-Marie McKeown?"

"Yes. I have it from others who saw her that she looked good. I do not normally develop emotional reactions to people. Certainly not based on their appearance. But I will confess that I never cared for her."

"Because of the way she treated Gabe?"

"No. I didn't like her before that happened. I'm not sure I can give you a reason. She was a bit distant. I think Gabe always realized he wasn't going to be able to hold on to her, but he stayed with it as long as he could."

Bark Peters came back: *"John, we are pulling alongside the* Capella *now. Lifeboats will be on the move in three minutes."*

FORTY-ONE

It is ironic that we do not remember who invented the camera. No human creation so deeply impacts our lives as this, which allows us to capture permanently the images of those who have gone before. Those we love may pass out of this world, but their faces, and the moments we shared with them, are forever ours.

—Rev. Agathe Lawless, *Sunset Musings*, 1422

Bark Peters provided close-up pictures of the lifeboat packages as they were sent one by one out of the *Randall*'s storage compartments. Twin jets were attached to the packages. Two crew members in green-and-white jet-assisted pressure suits traveled with each unit. They guided it across a gap of about forty meters into the *Capella*'s cargo hold, where some of the cruise ship's people corralled it and took it into whatever open space they had available.

An additional four members of the *Randall*'s crew, with jetpacks, served as wingmen, hovering between the two ships, lending a hand where necessary. It was an efficient process, but it was *slow*. They lost control of one package, and two of the wingmen had to chase it down. On another occasion, one of the *Capella*'s people, apparently not paying attention, got clobbered by an incoming unit and had to be taken inside the ship.

By the end of the first hour, twelve lifeboats had been moved across and stored, and three were en route. They were slightly ahead of schedule, and the operation was improving as the two crews became more efficient.

Meantime, the *Mary Lou Eisner* arrived and took off an additional ten people, one more than expected. The *Chang-Shi* came in a half hour behind it and collected eleven more. Then we heard John's voice: "*Got a problem, Bark. One of the people from the* Chang-Shi *has gotten loose on the* Capella. *He's taken control of the drive. Says he's going to shut it down. Cease operations immediately and get clear.*"

I was still getting pictures from the *Randall*, watching its crew continuing to move the lifeboats into the *Capella*. Despite the instructions, the *Randall* showed no sign of leaving. A few minutes later, John called me. "*Chase, do you know an Archie Cicotte?*"

"Negative."

"*He's the pilot of the* Chang-Shi. *He's on board the* Capella. *He's the one threatening to shut down the engines. He's telling them it's the only right thing to do. That it will stop the ship from getting sucked under again.*"

"You sound as if you expect me to do something."

"*He says Alex told him to do it.*"

"What? That's crazy, John." Then I remembered. "Alex was on a show last week. The host—I forget who it was—asked him what *he* would want to happen if he were stuck on the *Capella*. He said he'd want somebody to shut down the engines. Take the chance. Something like that."

"*Well, wonderful. Now we have to deal with this lunatic who took him at his word.*"

"I don't think it ever occurred to Alex—"

"*Let it go.*"

"How'd he get into the control room?"

"*Can we talk about that later? I need you to talk him down. Tell him who you are. That Alex didn't mean it or something.*"

How did I keep getting into the middle of these things? "Okay, John, put me through."

*   *   *

We got a visual. I could see four crewmen keeping their distance from a short, beefy guy who was bent over the controls. Everybody's eyes, except his, turned my way.

"*Look,*" he was saying, "*I'm sorry I'm scaring the hell out of you people, but in a few minutes, you'll all be glad I did this.*"

"Archie," I said. "You don't really want to be responsible for killing twenty-six hundred passengers, do you?"

He spun around, surprised. "*Who are* you?" he said.

"My name's Chase. I work for Alex Benedict. He's my boss."

"*Really?*" He straightened, and one of the people near him looked as if she was about to make a move, but Cicotte reacted, and she backed away. "*Are you Chase Kolpath?*"

"Yes. Please, Archie, get away from that thing before you kill everybody."

Archie was about average size, middle-aged, beginning to lose his hair. He looked angry. "*I'm not going to kill anyone. Chase, I'm glad to meet you. I'm sorry it has to be under these circumstances. But I've been an admirer of you and Alex for a long time.*"

"Archie, if you shut that engine down, you may destroy everything. I'm serious. I've seen tests where they played around with the drive units, and people died."

"*Then why did Alex say that's exactly what he'd do? That he'd shut the engines down?*"

"He meant if he was alone on the ship. If he was the only one at risk, he'd take the chance. I *know*, Archie, because we talked about it afterward. Alex would never put other people at risk."

"*Chase, if I don't do this, the people here will disappear out of the lives of their families for another five years.*"

"Archie, do you have a relative on board?"

"*No, I don't.*"

"A friend, maybe?"

"*Did you and he really talk about it?*"

"Sure."

"*Okay.*" He looked around the room. It was presumably the bridge. "*Chase, I don't know anyone who's on the ship. Nobody.*"

"Then why are you doing this?"

"*Because everybody's been saying that the odds of something bad happening if we shut down is only about one in twenty. We can live with that.*"

"That's only a guess, Archie. It's only a guess." He stared at me. "If you do this, and you get lucky and nobody dies, everybody will still hate you. You really want to live with that?"

"*This isn't about me, Chase.*"

"Okay. It's about the families of the people on board. Think what you'd do to them if it goes wrong. Archie, you have no right to do this. To put other people's lives on the line."

He stood there, his face drained of all color. Then he backed away from the controls. "*Chase,*" he said, "*help me.*"

The *Morrison* came in on time and took off another dozen, consisting of three families and Guy Bentley. Bentley was the comedian who'd almost become the principal in a legal action. His studio was desperate to get him back. Their effort to accomplish his return by threatening to sue had failed, but they'd apparently cut a deal with somebody.

"I can't believe John would sell out," I said to Belle.

"*I doubt he did. But Great Lion Studios has a lot of influence with politicians. I suspect they got somebody to put pressure on him. Don't worry about it. To be honest, Bentley's the funniest guy on the planet. I'm glad he's back.*"

"You're glad he's back, Belle? You always claimed you don't have a sense of humor."

"*And you believed me? I'm shocked.*"

We watched as the *Morrison* disconnected from the exit tube and moved away. Only the *Randall* remained, still steadily transferring its cargo of lifeboats. The smaller vehicles had taken ninety-five people off. Ninety-four if we deducted one for Archie, who'd been left behind. Schultz had supplied a spare pilot for the *Chang-Shi*. So we had about twenty-five hundred remaining plus a crew and staff of approximately sixty.

I'd counted twenty-six boats transferred as we got down to our last hour. Assuming we would *have* another hour.

I could see that the *Capella* cargo hold was filling up. When she went under, Schultz would have plenty of time to talk to her passengers, and get 540 of them into the first round of boats. Then, incredibly, they would arrive in 1440.

After that, there would be some time pressure. She had three cargo decks, and three boats could be inflated at a time on each deck. She'd have to repressurize, inflate the next round of boats, get sixty-four people in each, decompress again, and launch. Estimated time for the operation: slightly over an hour. If everything went smoothly.

She'd have to repeat the process four times. That should be manageable, but I didn't envy her.

Then we were listening to John again: *"Dierdre, we can't be certain that we know when and where you'll be back. So do not launch any of the lifeboats until we've established contact, and you know we're within range."*

"I understand, John. And thank you for all you've done. You put a major flotilla out there, and we appreciate it."

"We're happy to help. And we'll be back for you—"

No one, including Captain Schultz, knew precisely when the *Capella* had reappeared. But we were working off an estimate that had to be accurate within fifteen minutes or so. We were slightly more than halfway through the eighth hour when I got within link range and decided to try to contact Gabe. I wouldn't reveal what was really happening because Kraus and Schultz wanted to keep it quiet, and we owed them that. I suspected the people on board had learned the truth by then, but I didn't want anyone to be able to point at me.

It took a few minutes, and I kept the images of the lifeboat transfer on the navigation screen. But, finally, the circuit clicked, and Gabe was *there*! He was seated in what appeared to be a passenger lounge.

The guy I'd believed for years I would never see again. *"Hello, Chase,"* he said, with a shocked expression. *"Is that really you? What are you doing here? What's happened to the ship?"*

"Engine trouble, I think," I said. "They're going to be taking everybody off within the next few hours."

"That much I'd heard. But I got the impression there was more to it than that."

"We'll talk about it when we get you off, Gabe. They've got lifeboats on board. Just grab a seat when you can, and we'll see you at Skydeck."

It's impossible to be able to make a determination from a projection, but Gabe was reasonably tall, and had always exuded a take-it-easy manner. He had a full head of hair, and he looked younger than I would have expected. Of course, he hadn't aged more than a couple of days since the last time I'd seen him. *"Are you on the* Belle-Marie?*"* he asked.

"Yes."

"Can you take me aboard?"

"Not right now, Gabe. The crew over there is a little busy."

"Okay. By the way, I'm working on an interesting incident. What do you know about the Tenandrome?*"*

I couldn't resist a smile. That was an old story, an interstellar that had seen *something* that people in authority had tried to keep quiet. It was what had brought Alex and me together. "Okay, Gabe. That's something else for when you get back. You feeling all right?"

"Sure. Why wouldn't I be?"

"Just asking. We'll be glad to see you again."

"That's an odd comment. It's only been a few days. Is there something you're not telling me? Are we in more trouble than they've been letting on?"

"No. There's no major problem. Just get on the boat when they tell you to."

"All right. How's Alex?"

"He's good. He'd want me to say hello."

He was frowning at me. "Chase, you look different somehow."

"Probably my hair. I've cut it back a bit."

"I see that. But there's something else. You look more serious. Or something."

Older, I thought.

Suddenly, his image began to fade. It came back, then went away again. Completely.

On the main screen, I could see the crew hurrying, trying to move what would be the last two packages across to the *Capella,* which was also becoming less distinct. Two of them wore the *Randall*'s green uniforms. They were going to get caught over there.

Someone on the *Randall* was screaming for them to come back. The lifeboats were the thirty-fourth and thirty-fifth. The green uniforms kept going, and as the cruise ship faded from view, they went with it.

"Good-bye, Gabe," I said.

FORTY-TWO

Parting day
Dies like the dolphin, whom each pang imbues
With a new color as it gasps away,
The last still loveliest, till—'tis gone, and all is gray.

—Lord Byron, "Childe Harold," 1818 C.E.

Alex was relieved to hear that I'd seen Gabe. "I wish I'd been with you," he said.

And with five years to wait, we took a few days off to feel sorry for ourselves and for the *Capella* families. I told Alex I wasn't sure I'd done the right thing trying to tell Robert Dyke not to monkey with the engines. And Shara told me that John Kraus had admitted to her that he now believed he'd made a mistake. Watching members of the families in tears on the various talk shows left us all with a sense that maybe, sometimes, when the odds are right, you take the chance. "It's what life is," said Alex.

Too late now.

We settled back into our normal routine. I started by running searches on Madeleine O'Rourke and Heli Tokata. Neither turned up anything although that came as no surprise. You don't show up on someone else's internet unless you're a major figure of some sort. Alex said he'd send the picture to Les Fremont and Luciana Moretti and run the names past them. "I should have done that when we were still Earthside," he said. "Getting careless, I guess."

Meantime, the Transportation Department threw an appreciation ceremony for pilots and crews, attended by about half the people involved, the rest having probably returned to their home worlds. Eight of the Mutes attended. Awards for service beyond the call were granted *in absentia* to the two *Randall* crew members who took the last boats over to the *Capella*, but had not returned.

Alex and I attended, of course. It was one of the gloomier events I'd been to, and the only one recognizing a successful operation that was nevertheless downright melancholy. Alex's mood blended right in. John sat down with us midway through the evening, and I was surprised to learn that he had intended to present Alex with an award for the discoveries that had led to the formation of the SRF. But when Alex learned of it, he'd declined.

That was out of character for him. I had never known him to shy away from public acclamation. So I asked him why. He just shrugged it off. When I persisted he said he didn't want to accept an award when two others were being given to people who had jumped into the warp. "We might not get them back," he said.

He remained unusually somber throughout the evening. As I've said, Alex is not exactly a party guy, but he knows how to enjoy himself when occasion demands. But not that night. And, finally, when we had a moment alone, I asked what else was bothering him.

"There was something John said to Captain Schultz—"

"And that was—?"

"That the world had changed. And he was talking about eleven years."

"I'm not following."

"Change is a constant, Chase. Which brings us back to Larissa."

"Again?"

"When I ran my search for Larissa, we found a few unlikely places on the ground. And the Neptunian moon. I never thought about asteroids. They don't get names. There's a numbering system."

"You think they might have had names in Zorbas's time?"

"Yes. Chase, everything starts out with *names*. Planets, stars, galaxies, whatever."

"Have you been able to confirm that about the asteroids?"

"Not yet. I've talked with people in several science and history departments. Everybody agrees that it must have been true, but nobody knows for certain."

"You think that's where Zorbas put everything? On an asteroid?"

"Where would you find a more secure location at a time when the entire planet was collapsing?"

"Linda Talbott got you thinking this way, didn't she?"

"That's a pretty remote place she has. But sure. If I had access to an asteroid and something I wanted to hide—It seems so obvious now I wonder how I didn't think of it." In fact, I had, but I let it pass.

"So how do we find it among millions of asteroids? You think there's a listing somewhere?"

"If there *is* one that Zorbas used, Baylee must have found it. So, yes, I think there's a good chance there's a record, something that will identify the asteroids by name."

"Where do we look? We've already searched the internets here and on Earth for anything named Larissa. Do we start checking internets around the Confederacy? That could take a while."

"I think there's a better way."

"And what's that?"

"Chase, you work for a company that services collectors. I'd be surprised if we can't find a book in someone's collection that wouldn't provide the answer."

Hardcover books remain popular items. Nothing shows off one's intellectual prowess more effectively than a case full of classic novels and histories in a living room where they are visible to all. I sent a message out to everyone we knew who had a collection. That included a considerable majority of our clients. If one is interested in a piece of dinnerware once owned by Margo LaQuerta, we can be certain that her midnight comedies, in two volumes, rests on a shelf nearby.

The message read as follows:

Dear Mr.———:

We are currently conducting a search for any historical or scientific book that might provide a detailed description of Earth's solar system as it would have been perceived during the Third and Fourth Millennia. Please notify us if you have such a volume and would be willing to let us examine it.

Yours,
Alex Benedict

I showed it to Alex, who suggested I remove his last name. "Keep it informal," he said. And also he directed me to delete everything in the last sentence after *volume*, and finish the request with *Thank you for your assistance.*

We didn't specify what we were looking for. We knew our clients too well. If a Larissa asteroid *did* exist, half of them would have somebody out within a few days looking for it.

I sent the message to over a hundred clients and had several replies before I could tell him it was gone.

We handled it by asking each respondent to show us the contents page and the index. We searched the index for *asteroid* and *Larissa* and anything else that might be suggestive. Most of them listed *Larissa*, but were referring to the Neptunian moon. Over the first few days, that was all we saw.

The media, meantime, were filled for days with stories about the rescue effort, interviews with everyone involved, and reports of parties thrown by the families who had gotten someone back, and even by a few who were simply grateful for the confirmation that everyone on the *Capella* was actually alive. Politicians made speeches and promises. A few people criticized John for not doing everything he could to have Robert Dyke pull the trigger.

Fairly typical, I thought, was an appearance on Charlie Koeffler's show by one of the families we'd seen taken off by the Mutes. Karl Dunn and his wife Arlene had planned a ride to the stars with their two kids, Laurie and Jack. *"And here we are,"* said Arlene. *"We were only out there a few days, and they're telling us it's 1435."*

Laurie, who was about eight, with a huge smile and curly brown hair, could not stop laughing. *"We're time travelers,"* she said.

Jack was two or three years older. He had a question for Koeffler: *"We heard they can turn the ship around, and we can ride back to where we came from. Back to 1424. Do you think that's true?"*

Koeffler laughed. *"I don't think it works in both directions."*

"So," Jack continued, *"Allie's about twenty-two?"*

Karl smiled and nodded. *"Allie is Jack's best friend."*

"I'm afraid so," said Koeffler.

"But that means he's old," said Jack.

All three adults got a laugh out of that. But Jack looked seriously unhappy. *"I've lost him."*

The shadow of 1440, when the *real* rescue would occur, hung over the shows. Serge Lebouef, on *Jennifer in the Morning*, was shattered by what had happened to his wife, Carmela. Carmela had been one of the two crew members who had stayed with the lifeboat packages and been swept along when the *Capella* was taken down. *"Five years is a long time to be without her,"* he said. *"But I understand why she did it. And I'm proud of her."*

"Your wife's a hero, Serge," said Jennifer. *"And the experts all agree that they should be able to recover her. That she is probably now on board the* Capella."

"Oh, yeah. I'm sure she's all right. Listen, Jennifer, I wasn't surprised by what she did. To be honest, it was the reason I hoped the Randall wouldn't get close to everything. I know how this sounds, but—" He stopped, took a deep breath, closed his eyes, and swallowed whatever he'd planned to say.

He'd brought images along, and we watched him and Carmela at the eighth-grade graduation of their daughter. We saw them on the beach, saw them strolling through Brockman Park, saw them overseeing their daughter while she played on a swing. *"She'll have to do a lot of growing up without her mom,"* he said.

George Talbott was, as anticipated, not among the few who'd been rescued. But Linda had thrown the party anyway, providing transportation out to her asteroid home for any who wanted it. Alex had asked me to go while he attended a conference he couldn't skip because he was guest of honor.

Approximately thirty people were in attendance. Half arrived in Linda's vehicle. I came with them, since I was not excited about riding in an empty ship again. She launched the party by introducing George's avatar, who proceeded to thank everyone for coming, then showcased the Weinstein chair. Had it stopped there, things would have been okay, but the avatar began talking about how in just five years the *real* George would arrive, and we could have a serious celebration. He kept going on like that, and some of us got uncomfortable. Five years, I suspected, was not a long time for an avatar. But George's parents were present, and neither one looked like a good bet to make it to the follow-up event.

Eventually, Linda decided the avatar was not contributing a positive note and shut it down. But the damage was done, and the party never recovered. Instead of raising drinks to the fact that everything was under control and a celebration with George actually present was now within range, people took to wandering outside and looking up at the night sky through the plastene dome that shielded the house and commenting on how far away everything looked and that they would never want to live in a place like this. They were, of course, careful who was present when they made the observation.

Nevertheless, some of it got back to Linda, who became visibly annoyed. "We don't *live* here," she said. "This is where George writes. But unless he's working on a major project, he stays groundside. With me." Linda was fond of saying that she "hung out" at Momma. I actually couldn't imagine her spending any length of time in the solitude that enwrapped that place. She's too much of a social critter for that. And I suspect that, if George comes home and continues to settle in there while he writes his novels, the marriage will not get past the first renewal date.

The invitation included overnight accommodations for anyone who wished to stay. But by 0100 hours, Andiquar time, I was played out, and I rode back to Skydeck with one of our clients.

I didn't get in to the country house until midafternoon the following day. By then we'd gotten access to nine more books. And Alex was right: During the Golden Age, they *did* assign names to asteroids. At least to some of them. We found Ceres and Victoria, Flora and Prosperpina, Bellona, Irene, and Pallas. But there was no mention of a Larissa.

Later that afternoon, a bouquet of golden roses arrived. They were from Khaled and were accompanied by a note. *"I'd hoped to see you in the reports somewhere,"* it read, *"but there were so many people involved, and so many ships. Anyhow, congratulations. Do you plan on being there when the* Capella *returns?"*

He signed it with love.

I sent off a thank-you, and told him that being able to help had been an exhilarating experience. Then I made a mistake. Alex was on the hunt again, and I knew where that was eventually going to lead. "Can't say for sure," I added, "but I suspect we'll be heading back in your direction before long."

Lawrence Southwick showed up at the country house that same afternoon to offer his congratulations. "It's a pity we couldn't have gotten more out," he said, "but at least the end's in sight. Did you guys get close enough to *see* them? The ship, I mean?"

"I wasn't there," Alex said. "Chase went."

"Why not?"

"I take up too much space."

We were in my office. It was a beautiful day, unseasonably warm, and both windows were open, so we were getting a fresh breeze. Birds sang, and a gomper was tapping on a tree. "So what's your next project, Alex?" he asked.

"Don't know, Lawrence. We've been involved in a fair amount of trading recently, and I'm thinking about taking a vacation."

"That sounds good. Any idea where?"

"Out to the islands, probably."

"Sounds perfect. You deserve one."

"I think it's Chase who deserves one. But how about you? What are you up to these days?"

"Not much. Retirement does that to you." He turned to me. "Chase, will you really be taking some time off, too?"

"No," I said. "Somebody has to hold the fort."

"Of course. I understand how that is." He smiled at Alex. "I wish, during my working years, I'd had an associate like her."

We did some more small talk, then he said good-bye. "If I can ever be of help, Alex, don't hesitate to let me know." We watched him lift off in his skimmer and head out over the river.

Alex sat quietly for a few moments. "Chase," he said finally, "did you notice anything odd?"

"No," I said, "nothing I can think of. Why?"

"The question about whether we'd given up on the Golden Age artifacts."

"Alex, he never asked anything like that."

"Precisely. Doesn't that strike you as curious?"

Responses about Madeleine O'Rourke came in from Lucianna and Les. Neither was aware of anyone with that name. But both knew Heli Tokata. *"Tall young woman,"* said Lucianna. *"Green eyes, odd accent. She's from Cormoral. A history buff. And a pilot. Came to Earth for her education, got her Ph.D. from Hemmings University in Kobula and never went home. The interesting thing is that she hooked up with Baylee for a couple of years. She might still live in Kobula."*

"She was just someone I knew to say hello to," said Les. *"She lives in the British Isles, or did last time I'd heard. Place called Suden-*

ton. *She was a member of Garnett's crowd. I think she went out on a few expeditions with him."*

Alex was at lunch when another of our clients, Jorge Brenner, called. *"I have a novel, Flex, by Cal Eliot. He was a twenty-first-century science-fiction writer, and it's about a couple of guys who chase a shape-changing monster through the solar system. It attacks research stations, colonies, and orbital bases. I don't know why it survived. The book, I mean. It's not very good, but it's kind of a ride through the planetary system. Earth's planetary system. I don't know if it could be any help to you. But these guys go everywhere. It has pretty good descriptions of the gas giants and Mercury and Mars, and at one point they land on the Venusian surface. It's a bound book. But I can ship it over if you like."*

I couldn't imagine it would provide what we were looking for. But what was the harm? "Sure, Jorge," I said. "Send it when you can. We'll take a look and get it right back to you."

Meantime, more books arrived, and we discovered still more asteroids. Spock, Hrazany, Nanking, and Arabia. The latter two were obviously named for *places*. And Transylvania for, I guess, the famous physician. Nobody's sure whether there actually *was* a place with that name. The significance of the first two names is unknown.

Other asteroids were named Anderson, McCool, Saga, Shoe-maker, Arago, Einstein, and more than a hundred others. But there was still no sign of Larissa. Until *Flex* arrived.

The book had been published eleven years ago by Babcock, which specializes in reproducing books from other eras. It was a translation, of course. The cover showed two astronauts in clunky Third-Millennium gear confronting a bulbous monster while in the background an asteroid seemed to be bearing down on a vulnerable Earth. A note on the credits page claimed that the publishing house routinely did everything it could to re-create the original packaging. And that *Flex* was no exception. The present cover was the same as the one that had originally been used.

I turned it over to Jacob, who produced an electronic version, and a search for *Larissa* gave us a positive result. In one sequence, Mark Andrews and his partner Delia Tabor are barely able to intercept an asteroid that has been flung in the direction of the home world by the invading monster of the title. The asteroid is Larissa. And the name appears only once.

"That's it on the cover," I said.

"Beautiful, Chase."

"The credits say it's not the original artwork, Alex, but that it's a copy."

"The original might not have resembled the asteroid anyhow. I doubt they'd have bothered going to the trouble to get an actual reproduction."

"But—?"

"There's a chance. At least we have something to work with."

I had lunch with Shara the following day, and I told her about the *Flex* monster. "Well," she said, "I don't know whether information about Larissa exists anywhere. But I can tell you the best place to look."

"Where's that, Shara?"

"The New Honolulu University. I should have thought of them before. They have a science history archive that would probably have it if anybody does."

I passed her comment to Alex and told him I'd get a message out to them.

"Don't bother." He went over and looked out the window. It was a beautiful morning, birds singing, a plane in the distance, tree limbs moving lightly in the breeze. "We can check when we get there."

"We're really going back?"

"Sure."

"Don't you think we should let them respond first? They might not be able to offer any help either."

"If they can't, we have another option."

"What's that?"

"We could try asking Baylee's pilot where Larissa is."

"Baylee's pilot? Who's that? Tokata?"

"Very good. Yes, I think that's very likely. Chase, you haven't been in touch with Khaled recently, have you?"

"I had a message from him last week."

"Okay. We don't want him to know we're going."

"I may already have given something away. I told him there was a possibility."

"All right. Don't say any more."

"I won't. But you want to tell me why?"

"I don't trust him."

Well, I knew he was wrong about that. I let it go, though. "Whatever you say. When do we leave?"

"There's no rush. Can you manage tomorrow?"

FORTY-THREE

Lives of great men all remind us
We can make our lives sublime,
And, departing, leave behind us
Footprints on the sands of time.

—Henry Wadsworth Longfellow, "A Psalm of Life," 1839 C.E.

We arrived at Galileo Station, worked our way through customs, and rode the shuttle down to New Honolulu. It was early morning when we checked into a suite at the Majestic, which looked out over a crowded beach and an ocean filled with swimmers. We changed clothes, and I headed for the door, assuming we would be leaving immediately for the university.

But Alex sat down. "We have a call to make first," he said. He asked the directory if it had a listing for Heli Tokata. "She lives in Sudenton. In the British Isles."

"Yes, sir," it replied. "We have it."

"May I have her code?"

"Of course. It's Hobart 2796-331-49."

"Now," Alex said, "I have to do a little artwork." He used his link to project his image, seating it in one of the armchairs. Then he manipulated it, changed it to a young woman. Blond hair, attractive. Brown-and-gray business suit. "Maybe a little more intensity in the eyes." He made the adjustment. "What do you think, Chase?"

"She looks good." I assumed he wanted to mislead Tokata. "You want me to provide the voice?"

He shook his head. "I've got it." He fiddled with the link again and whispered "Hello, how are you?" into it. The image repeated the greeting. He tried it again, manipulated the sound until it had acquired a soft, vaguely seductive feminine tone with a British accent. "How's that?"

"Not sure," I said. "What's she going to do?"

He locked her into the memory so she would be the voice and image that appeared to the person at the other end of the call. I found myself thinking of Zachary Conner. "Chase," he said, "why don't you sit over there so you don't get caught in the exchange? You don't want to be seen."

That was fine by me. Alex was much better at this kind of thing than I was. So I moved well off to the side.

"Good," he said. "Now, what's Eisa's code?"

"Khaled? You mean *Tokata's* code, right?"

"No. We need to settle something first."

I began to squirm. "Do we really have to do this, Alex?"

"Yes, we do." I gave him Khaled's code, his personal one, not the code that would connect him with Eisa Friendly Charters. "You just watch, all right? Don't say anything."

"You can count on that."

He passed the code to the link and directed it to make the call while I did some quick math. It would be midafternoon along the Florida coast. I heard a pickup at the other end. My throat tightened. And Khaled appeared in the center of the room. He was looking at Alex but seeing only the young woman. "Mr. Eisa," Alex said. "My name's Marie Baxter."

Khaled's features softened. *"Hello, Ms. Baxter. What can I do for you?"*

"I'm trying to locate an old friend. Heli Tocata. We went to school together. I've lost track of her. The address I have doesn't seem to work anymore. She mentioned you to me a few weeks ago. Told me you're a friend, right? The boat owner?"

"Yes. That would be me."

"Good. Anyway, I'm trying to find her."

My heart picked up a notch.

"*Sure,*" he said. "*I know Heli. But she doesn't live around here anywhere.*"

"I didn't think she did. Last I recall, she was headed for the British Isles. Do you by any chance have contact information for her?"

"*Hold on, Ms. Baxter. I'm getting it for you now.*"

Alex glanced over at me with a look of regret. He had to be careful because any change in his expression would be reflected in Marie's. But he understood that I was annoyed. I wanted to break into the conversation and tell Khaled what he could do.

And, finally, Khaled was back: "*Yes. She does live in the British Isles. Or at least she did last time I talked to her. In a place called Sudenton.*" He provided the code and delivered a smile. "*You want me to repeat it, Marie?*"

"No, I've got it. Thanks, Mr. Eisa. I'm in your debt." And Alex disconnected. A long silence followed. "I'm sorry, Chase," he said finally.

"The whole thing was a lie. All that talk about how he needed to be with me."

"Well." He cleared his throat. "Maybe not that part of it. But the attack was a lie. My guess is that Eisa planted an explosive on the boat, detonated it at the correct moment, then pretended to drive off the attacker."

"Tocata was the attacker?"

"I don't think there's any question. We know she was lying about who and what she was. And she's a friend of Eisa's."

"*Oh, Chase,*" Khaled had said, "*you were never really in danger.*"

My chest was heaving. "None of this makes sense, Alex."

"Tocata doesn't want us to find out what happened with Baylee. So she tried to scare us off. But what's she hiding? And I can't believe she's alone in this."

"Why not?"

"Because they destroyed one of Khaled's boats. As far as I've been able to determine, Tocata doesn't come from money." He looked out at the sky. "I was sorry to put you through that, Chase. But I had to confirm my suspicions."

"It's all right."

"I suspect you'd like to call him and tell him what you think, but—"

"No. Actually, I have no intention to call him. *Ever.*"

"Okay."

"So what's next? Do we call Tocata?"

"No. We relax and go down to the beach for a while. This afternoon, I'm going to head over to NHU. See if they can ID Larissa."

"Why not just call them?"

"I'm interested in seeing the place. Anyhow, asking questions in person usually produces better results. You want to come?"

"Sure."

The campus occupied about five acres on the outskirts of the city. Six or seven buildings, their entrances marked by geometric art, were joined by sloping rooftops and walkways. At the northernmost extremity, a pair of towers gleamed in bright sunlight. The science history section, officially known as the Casper Archive, was located in a three-story structure between the towers.

We climbed a half dozen steps and went through the front door into a circular, vaulted room whose walls were covered with scientifically related artwork, portraits of famous scientists, photos of off-world landscapes, and sketches of classical formulas. Kormanov's Origin of Life Theory was on display, as was M Theory, Carmichael's Particle Theory, Goldman's Dark Energy Formula, the Schroedinger Equations, and the Pythagorean Theorem. The Brickman Analysis, the breakthrough study of how the human brain works, occupied a prominent position over a sofa.

A few people were admiring the art, and a young man was seated at a desk in the center of the room. A name tent identified him as Rafael Iturbi. He looked up from a monitor as we approached. "Yes," he said. "What can I do for you?"

"Mr. Iturbi," said Alex, "there's an asteroid that, back in ancient times, in the Third Millennium, was called Larissa. Can you pin it down for me? Match it to a catalog number?"

"How do you spell that, Mr.——?"

"Benedict. Alex Benedict" He printed the asteroid's name on a sheet of paper.

Iturbi glanced at it. "Okay. Hold on, Mr. Benedict." He straightened his shoulders and stated the name for his computer. He crossed his arms, glanced up at me, smiled, and refocused on the screen. The smile faded. "We don't show it, sir."

"Do you have any files that are not included with the electronic data?"

He had to give that some thought. "Hold on a second, please." He got up from the desk, crossed the room, and walked out through a door.

"That's not a good sign," I said.

He gave me his eternal optimism smile. We waited. More people came and went. Then a bearded older man appeared at the same door and came toward us. "Hello?" he said. "Mr. Benjamin?"

"Benedict," said Alex.

"I beg your pardon, Mr. Benedict. I'm Morton Williams. You say the asteroid's name is Larissa?"

"Yes, Mr. Williams."

"Okay. I'm sorry, but we don't have the information. We can identify some asteroids, but unfortunately, that's not a name we're familiar with. How do you know it existed at all?"

"We have good reason to know that there *was* an asteroid with that name. In fact, I have a picture of it. Do you think you could match it?"

"Can you show it to me?"

Alex produced the cover from *Flex*. We'd removed the monster and the two astronauts. But Williams was frowning anyway. "This is a *drawing*," he said.

"It's the best we could come up with."

He studied the image for a minute or two. "May I ask why you're interested?"

"Just doing some research."

It seemed to satisfy him. "We have a substantial number of pictures of major asteroids, other than those whose ancient names we have on record. Maybe we'll get lucky."

He sat down at Iturbi's desk, concentrating on the display, which we could not see. He grunted periodically, sucked his lower lip, and eventually shook his head. "We're not getting a match. The reality is that nobody has cared about asteroids for a long time. Back in the early years, they mined them, but we don't have much left from those years. A few people live on them now, and they've given them names. Not official, of course. But is it possible you're looking for one of those?"

"No," said Alex. "This would be from the Third or Fourth Millennium."

Williams shrugged. "Sorry. Wish we could help."

We hadn't expected much, I guess, but it was nevertheless disappointing. "We still have options," Alex said. We went in through the lobby and took the elevator up to our suite. Once in our apartment, Alex began tinkering with his link again.

"What are you doing?" I asked.

He looked off to my left. I turned and saw another image of Alex smiling at me. He added some muscle and maybe a couple of inches. He lightened the hair and rearranged the features, turned himself into a stranger, then the guy began to look familiar again.

Southwick.

He was behind all this? "How are you going to manage the voice?"

"I brought along one of the HV interviews."

He plugged the voice and the image into the memory and called Heli.

We got a recording: *"Heli is not available and is not currently able to return your call. Please leave your name and code."*

Alex, speaking in Southwick's voice, explained that he was on a business trip and couldn't be reached, but that he would try again later.

*   *   *

We'd timed our arrival perfectly. The locals were celebrating the Mili-landi Fest, which, according to the hotel guide, dated back over three thousand years. Tents were set up on the beach, bands played raucous music along a seawalk, fireworks were launched, kids rode a Ferris wheel, and people gambled their money away. Comedians performed, a uniformed antigrav team dropped out of the sky, and everybody danced well into the night.

The following day, we went sightseeing, visiting several of the islands. We spent a couple of hours in the Maui Museum, where we picked up some books, mostly histories. But while we were wandering around, a couple of reporters showed up and began interviewing Alex. I drifted away and found a Wendell Chali collection. I've always enjoyed the Chali stories. They're great mysteries, but unfortunately they're six hundred years old, and two-thirds of them have been lost.

I also picked up a novel from the twenty-first century about a pilot living in the early years of interstellar travel. *That* one survives, and Wendell Chali goes missing. It's frustrating. Still, I identified with the pilot. Her name was Hutchins, and I remember thinking that I'd have enjoyed talking with her.

We needed two more calls before we finally caught up with Heli. She was seated in a lobby at a hotel. Behind her, through a room-length portal, we could see nothing but ocean. *"Yes, Lawrence,"* she said, thinking she was speaking to Southwick. *"I wasn't aware you were coming back. Where are you now?"*

"In Hawaii. I'm on business. I'll only be here a couple of days."

"Okay. What can I do for you?"

"I just wanted to alert you that Benedict is still at it. In fact, he came back here a few days ago. Have you heard from him?"

"No."

"Good. Be careful. Stay out of his way, okay?"

"Don't worry, Lawrence. That nitwit won't get anything from me. He doesn't even know my name."

"All right. Just keep down. I'll let you know when he goes back to

Rimway. One other thing, I think he knows about the asteroid. The, um, what was it, KL-something?"

"*KL-4561,*" she said.

"Yeah. Right. My memory doesn't work too well anymore. Anyhow, if you see anything that suggests he's headed out that way, let me know. The guy's a publicity hound, so if he really does have something, I'd be surprised if he doesn't make the news with it. Okay?"

"*All right, Lawrence.*"

"By the way, I won't be answering my personal link. I'm at the Majestic Hotel. If you need to reach me, just leave a message, and I'll get back to you."

He disconnected and sat back in his chair with a look of triumph. "Finally, Chase."

"How'd you know about the KL?"

"All the large asteroids in the belt have a KL designator."

"Why'd it have to be in the belt?"

"Most of the asteroids are. I was playing the odds."

"Okay. Then why did it have to be a large asteroid?"

"It had a name."

"Not bad," I said, "for a nitwit. By the way, what happens if she calls back and discovers Southwick isn't here?"

"I've already taken care of that at the desk. They think *Southwick* is my pen name."

We did a search for KL-4561. There were a couple of pictures, and some information on its dimensions. It was thirty-seven kilometers in diameter, and it was in the outer main belt, orbiting the sun in slightly more than eight years. He brought up the *Flex* cover and compared it. "Well," he said, "one asteroid looks pretty much like another."

I'd just come out of the shower when Khaled called. So I kept it on audio. "*Hi, Chase,*" he said. "*I was surprised to find out you were here. You didn't call me.*" He sounded genuinely disappointed.

I was still not supposed to be talking to him. Or letting him know what we'd learned. "We haven't had much free time, Khaled," I said, trying to keep my voice level. "And we're not going to be staying long."

"*Oh.*" He sounded genuinely upset. What the hell was it with this guy? "*What are you doing in Hawaii?*"

"We're here for the Mililandi Fest. We'd seen that a lot of artifacts were going to be on display. So we came hoping to find some we could pick up. Alex does stuff like this all the time."

"*You sound kind of funny. Is everything okay?*"

I wanted to scream. You sold us out, Khaled. Dumped us in the ocean. Played us for idiots. And you want to know if everything's okay? "Sure," I said. "Everything's fine. I'm just a little tired, I guess. We've been on the run. How did you know we were here?"

"*I saw something about Alex on HV. I assumed if he was here, you were, too.*"

"Okay. Yes, um, listen, I have to go. We're trying to make a flight."

"*When are you going back, Chase? Any chance we can get together before you leave?*"

"I don't think so, Khaled. I don't have any free time. Listen, I've gotta go. Alex is calling me."

"*All right. I wouldn't want to crowd you. I know how busy you must be.*"

"So long, Khaled."

FORTY-FOUR

The vast majority of us are far more capable than we realize. We grow up with parents, teachers, bosses all telling us what we can't do. Don't touch it; you'll break it. They mean well, but they leave us with a sense of our own incapacity. When the day comes, if it comes, that you begin to believe in yourself, the world will be yours.

—Mara Delona, *Travels with the Bishop*, 1404

We picked up a chip in the operational services office that would allow us to locate KL-4561, or any of the other listed asteroids. Several hours later, we were on our way back up to Galileo. Alex was visibly excited. "You have any idea what we're going to find?" I asked him.

"No," he said. "Best I can come up with is that Baylee inadvertently led some pirates there, and they took off with everything. They left him with the transmitter as part of a deal that he wouldn't say anything. And they agreed not to kill him."

"Alex, that doesn't make any sense. Anyway, there *are* no pirates."

"I know."

"Then why—?"

"You asked for a theory. At the moment, it's all I have."

The *Belle-Marie* was waiting when we arrived. I'd have preferred to spend a few more days in Hawaii and just enjoy the ocean and sunlight. But Alex was anxious to resolve this business, and the luaus would fall pretty flat with Baylee's transmitter hanging over our heads.

We picked up some food supplies and climbed on board. Larissa was on the other side of the sun, so we had a long ride ahead of us. Alex went back into the passenger cabin while I turned the ship over to Belle and waited for authorization to leave. I couldn't help being impressed by the amount of traffic handled by Galileo. It had close to four times the docking area that Skydeck possesses, and it wasn't really enough. Plans were under way to extend its facilities. The home world still handled more commerce than any other world in the Confederacy. It did not have the largest population. In fact, four other worlds surpassed it. But it claimed with some justification to be home to the major advances in the arts and sciences. Of course, scientific advancement had for a long time consisted of little more than taking existing technologies and making them more effective. There just wasn't much left to uncover.

"Belle-Marie, *this is operations. You are clear to go.*"

"Acknowledge, ops." I warned Alex. Belle released us from the dock, and we eased out toward the exit. It looked as if sun, Moon, and Earth were lined up. I wondered if they were getting an eclipse groundside.

We made our jump and surfaced a short time later. "How'd we do?" Alex asked.

"Not bad," I said. "We'll need about two days to get to it. We can make it a little quicker if you want, but it'll be an uncomfortable ride. And suck up a lot of fuel."

"No reason to hurry, Chase," he said. "Whatever's there has been sitting around for more than eleven years. A few hours one way or the other won't make much difference."

We relaxed and read the books we'd picked up at the Maui Museum, watched some comedy shows from the library, and kept up a decent workout schedule. Sometimes we just sat and talked. The main topic of conversation was inevitably the *Capella*, and my reaction to seeing Gabe again. We didn't speculate much on what we expected to find on the asteroid, which led me to suspect that, despite his denials, Alex had a theory. But he didn't bring it up, so I let it go.

I'd thought a lot about it, of course. The only explanation that seemed feasible to me was that the whole Larissa thing was a missed communication somewhere. That Baylee had never found the Prairie House artifacts. That when he'd come across the transmitter, it had been by itself somewhere. Probably, someone had found the artifacts thousands of years ago, had sold everything off, and it simply never made the history books. Or, like so much else, everything had simply gotten lost. If Alex had asked me what I expected to find when we arrived at KL-4561, I'd have told him there'd probably be nothing.

Belle woke me on the morning of the third day. *"We're close,"* she said. *"KL-4561 is about two hours away."*

"Okay," I said. "Thanks, Belle. I'll be there in a few minutes."

"Do you want me to wake Alex?"

"No," I said. "No need to."

I got up, showered, dressed, and headed for the bridge. Alex was moving around in his cabin. Asteroid belts are not rare, but this would be my first visit to one. I'm not sure what I expected to see, but it wasn't the progressively brighter glow in an otherwise-empty sky. *"It's the* Gegenschein," said Belle.

"What's a gegenschein?" I asked.

"It's sunlight backscattered from the dust in the ecliptic."

"Okay. Where are the asteroids?"

"They're hard to make out. They don't reflect well."

"Just the dust," I said.

"The asteroids are out there." She adjusted one of the scopes, and a dark, lumpy rock appeared on the navigation screen. *"There's one now. It's at a range of about four thousand kilometers. Too small to see with the naked eye, of course."*

"How big is it?"

"Can't be certain at this range, but not more than forty meters across."

"All right. You're keeping a watch in all directions, right? We don't want any collisions."

"Yes, Chase." She was taking a tolerant tone. *"But you needn't be*

*concerned. We could roll through it with the scanners and scopes
turned off, and the chances of our hitting anything would be minimal.*"

We'd arranged our arrival so that as we entered the belt, we'd be
moving not only to penetrate it, but also in the same direction as the
orbiting asteroids. That, of course, reduced the chance of a collision.
But it *did* look empty out there.

Eventually, Alex showed up. "See anything?"

"Just a couple of rocks," I said.

"It doesn't look like what I expected."

"I thought so, too. Belle tells me we could go through it blind-
folded and be pretty safe."

"Really? You told her that, Belle?"

"*Not precisely in those words.*"

"Well, I'm glad to hear it. Have we locked onto Larissa yet?"

"Belle?" I asked.

"*Not yet. But we should see it anytime now.*"

We went back into the passenger cabin and had breakfast. I'd gotten into the habit over the past few years of watching the morning
news shows. I missed them when we were on the road. Alex had suggested I record a few before leaving Rimway, so I could watch them
during the flight.

"They'd be old news," I'd told him.

"They're *always* old news," he'd said. "There are no good journalists anymore." Alex didn't like journalists, or at least he didn't like
talk-show hosts because they'd made a living for years inviting people
onto their shows to criticize him.

Alex had always pretended to ignore the tomb-robber comments,
but I could see that sometimes they stung. I suspect there was an echo
in there somewhere from Gabe's efforts to win him away from the
career he had chosen. Gabe, he'd explained, had never let his anger
show, but his disappointment had come through. And it lingered. By
the time Gabe got back, in 1440, I suspected Alex would have found a
way to construct a rapprochement. He'd discovered that life without
his uncle was not fulfilling. He would have denied that he craved
Gabe's blessing, but it was hard to miss.

My mom hadn't cared much for Alex, and she'd been uneasy when I went to work for him. She'd have tried to talk me out of it except that she was too smart for that. She understood there would have been no better way to lock me into the country house than to show her disapproval. So she'd concealed it as best she could, and I saw it only on those rare occasions when the subject surfaced because of some news coverage, or my misbegotten attempts to explain how he was performing a public service. She had to work hard not to roll her eyes. There'd been only one occasion I could remember that she'd actually said something directly, and that was after the near disaster on Salud Afar. I can't quote her, but she commented that people would always remember him as a hero, and she couldn't deny that it was fortunate he'd been there on that occasion, but that it didn't change the fact that he saw the world in terms of cash flow. He pretended to love historical objects, she'd said, but that passion was always tied to their sales value.

I knew Alex better than she did. He had no objection to making money from artifacts. What lay open to the world, in his view, belonged to the world. If he could recover it, he saw no moral imperative that required him to turn it over to a museum. He supplied artifacts to collectors, to people who appreciated their value. To people like Linda Talbott, who could plan a major celebration around a chair.

I've seen Alex's clients take more pleasure out of an artifact than I've ever seen anyone display walking through a museum. And okay, I know how that sounds. But that was running through my mind on that flight, when we confronted the very real possibility that we were about to uncover a find of historic proportions. Consequently, it was no surprise that I almost fell out of my chair when Belle's voice broke through: *"All right, Chase. The asteroid's in sight."*

She put it on the display. It was only a light in the sky, indistinguishable from the stars. But, as we watched, its position gradually changed.

"How long?" I asked.

"About forty minutes."

The tension rose. Even Belle seemed to become nervous as we

closed on it. She didn't, for example, set up her usual countdown when something big was in the works.

We rode in near silence for about fifteen minutes before Belle spoke again. *"It has lights."*

"Lights?" I asked.

Alex was seated beside me. "That's not what I was expecting," he said.

She increased magnification on the display. There were three or four lights on the asteroid. But we still couldn't make out any details.

"Range 120 klicks," said Belle.

"Are they reflections?" Alex asked.

"Maybe," I said. "Could be some stuff left on the ground."

As we drew closer, they brightened. And morphed into window lights. *"There appears to be a structure,"* said Belle.

It was a *house*. Like Linda's, except that it was wider, more spread out, with rounded corners and a tower on one side. "Belle," said Alex, "hail them for us. Find out if anyone's there."

Belle barely let him finish: *"Alex, we have an incoming transmission."*

"Put it through."

A woman blinked on: *"Who's out there?"*

"Belle-Marie," I said. "We were just looking around. Sorry to disturb you. Can you tell us where we are?"

She was young and attractive. Golden hair, blue eyes. And, I thought, she was happy to see company. *"Don't you know?"*

Alex, who was not visible to her, frowned at me. "Well, more or less. We didn't expect to find anybody here."

"Actually, there's a whole community here."

"I didn't know. My locator says you're KL-4561. Is that correct?"

"Yeah. That's us. You alone?"

"I have one passenger."

"Okay. You're welcome to drop by if you like. We're always happy to have visitors. Don't see many strangers, do we, Tori?" Someone laughed.

Alex nodded. Do it.

"Yes," I said. "Sure. We'd enjoy stopping for a quick visit if that's okay."

"*Beautiful. My name's Amy. Come on in. We'll turn the lights on for you.*"

We swung around the asteroid to get a good look. "I don't think it's the one on the *Flex* cover," I said. "But I can't tell for sure."

Alex was pressing his fingertips against his temples, like a guy with a burgeoning headache. "This is not going to be what we're looking for."

More lights came on, and the dome that enclosed the house became visible, along with a docked ship and a second docking area. We eased down into it, connected with the exit tube, and followed it into the dome. The interior had been transformed into a garden filled with hardscrabble plants that must have been able to get along without much sunlight. There were a couple of padded benches, a walkway, and a fountain though the water was apparently turned off. It was chilly but not as cold as I'd expected. As we approached the front door, it opened, and Amy appeared, alongside another woman.

"Hello," she said. "Welcome to Amora. This is Tori, my wife."

Alex hid whatever disappointment he might have felt. We introduced ourselves and went inside, into a lavish living room, with padded decalite furniture and a large coffee table. Thick curtains covered the windows. Amy drew them aside so we could see the garden and the stars. A piano stood on one side of the room, and pictures of mountains and rivers covered the walls.

We sat down, and a third woman came out of a doorway, carrying a tray with drinks. "This is Reika. My other wife." All three looked pretty good.

We said hello and exchanged introductions.

"Beautiful home," said Alex.

Reika looked around and said thanks while she and Tori served the drinks. Amy retreated into the kitchen and came back with a plate full of chocolate chip cookies. "Sorry, guys," said Tori, "if we'd known you were coming, we'd have been better prepared."

"You say there's a community out here?" I said.

Amy and Reika both started to respond, but Amy got out of the way. "Oh, yes," Reika said. "I wouldn't exactly describe them as next-door neighbors, but we have a homeowners group, and we visit back and forth, and, when needed, we take care of one another."

Reika was the smallest of the three, with black hair and dark eyes and, obviously, Asian blood. Tori was the tall one. Red hair fell well below her shoulders, and something in her manner suggested she was the one most likely to enjoy life in a remote place.

"So what brought you out here?" asked Amy. "Looking to move in?"

"Actually," said Alex, "we were looking for an asteroid that used to be called Larissa. Ever hear of it?"

They looked at one another and shook their heads.

"Does *this* asteroid have a name?" I asked.

"Amora," said Amy.

"Oh. Sure, I forgot. Did you guys name it?"

She smiled. "No. It's *always* been Amora. As far as I know."

I glanced at Alex. Tokata had spotted us and supplied a false lead. He took a deep breath. "Anybody know Heli Tokata?"

They looked at one another again and shook their heads. "Who's she?" said Tori.

"A young lady who has managed to stay a step ahead of us." He sighed and turned his attention to the piano. "Who plays?"

Amy smiled. "I do. But Reika is the serious one."

Alex tried his drink. "Excellent," he said. Then to Reika: "What do *you* play?"

"The violin," she said.

Tori finished her drink. "Anyone need a refill?"

Alex passed.

I opted for a second round. And Amy decided she could use a refill, too. "Reika can play anything," she said. "But she's a composer. She writes beautiful music, which is why we are here."

"How do you mean?" I asked.

Reika looked uncomfortable.

"Don't be so shy," Amy said. "You know it's true."

Alex was seated behind the coffee table on a long divan. "What kind of music do you write?" he asked.

Amy got up, walked over to a cabinet, opened it, and took out a violin. She handed it to Reika. "Show them, love," she said.

Reika looked at us as if seeking approval. Tori returned with the drinks.

"Please," I said.

Reika had been seated with Alex on the divan. She got up, shouldered the violin, and raised the bow. Then she began to play. I'm not sure what I'd expected, but the music was incredible. It was soft and majestic and wistful. It filled the room and subsided and filled the room again. Finally, somehow, it ended in heartbreak.

"It's called," said Tori, "'Tides.'"

Amy sat with a triumphant smile playing on her lips. "Tell them about it."

"It's two lovers standing near the ocean," Reika said. "Listening to the sea. And one of the two is saying good-bye. It's over. I like you, but it isn't going to work. And she walks off, leaving the other one to try to put his life back together."

"When Reika writes a song about shattered love," said Tori, "the people in the audience all get hit pretty hard."

"You're a professional," said Alex. It wasn't a question.

"Yes. I used to play with the Ningata Symphony Orchestra. Tori did, too. That was how we met. I always loved composing, but I didn't think I was any good at it. I showed Tori something I'd written. She took it and showed it to the Banner Boys. You know who they are, right? No? They're pretty big." We got a smile that suggested she was wondering where we'd been all our lives. "They asked if they could perform the piece. It was called 'Seaview.' I said okay, sure, and it became a big hit. After that, I knew there'd be no stopping me."

"Marvelous," I said. "You like oceans."

"Oh, yes."

"Yet you're out here."

"In the middle of the biggest ocean there is." She put the violin down on a side table. "I've always loved oceans because of the sense that they go on forever. When I was a kid, I used to stand on the beach and listen to the rumble of the surf, and you couldn't see anything all the way out to the horizon except water. There were no boundaries. No limits. I don't know why, but every human emotion, out here, is also boundless. And there's no reason for restraint. It's where I get to be who I really am. Does that make any sense?"

"But," I said, "you guys are entertainers. Entertainers hang out in public places."

"We don't *live* here, Chase. Amora is a retreat. *This* is where we hang out. It's where we can be ourselves."

"One final question," said Alex. "You don't have any artifacts stored here anywhere, do you?"

They looked at one another. Reika smiled. "What kind of artifacts? I have an old coat upstairs."

"Okay," said Alex, "thanks."

I turned to Amy. "I assume you run the P.R. operation."

She laughed. "Not really. In fact I'm the comedian."

FORTY-FIVE

There's no such thing as an idle threat.

—Arnold Case, *The Last Hunter*, 1114

"I guess Tokata isn't as dumb as we thought."

"I guess not."

Tori, Reika, and Amy came out under the dome and waved as we lifted off. We waved back, and I asked Alex if we were headed home?

"No," he said. "We still don't know what this is all about."

"So it's back to Galileo?"

"Yes."

"What are we going to do now? Try to beat the truth out of Tokata?"

He was seated beside me, staring out at the stars. "There might still be a way to manage this."

"I'm listening."

"We need to scare Tokata. And Southwick. They've got one vulnerability."

"What's that?"

"They're trying to keep a secret. All we need to do is put the secret at risk."

"So how exactly do we do that? We don't *know* what they're hiding. We can't even find the asteroid."

"Maybe we don't have to."

*   *   *

We went back to the Maui Museum and made ourselves visible for two days, looking through every section of the place, asking questions of the tour guides, spending substantial time in the gift shop, and sitting out in the lobby. Alex was hoping to draw the attention of somebody from the media, but it didn't happen.

"Can't find a reporter when you need one," he said. "I guess we'll have to take a more direct approach."

"You going to call a press conference?"

"One of the reporters was a big guy named Bill Garland. Or *Phil* Garland. I forget which. But he works for the Golden Network, and he shouldn't be hard to find." He checked his link. "It's *Bill*." The link made the connection, and a half hour later, Garland walked in the door. He was one of the people who'd sat down with Alex while I'd wandered off and found the Wendell Chali collection.

"Hello, Mr. Benedict," he said. "And Ms. Kolpath. Nice to see you again."

"Good to see you, Bill," said Alex. We took seats in a corner of the lobby.

"So what's going on?"

"Well, I'm sorry to say that when you and your colleagues were here a few days ago, I wasn't entirely honest with you."

Garland was young, still on the right side of thirty. But the enthusiasm that usually goes with the age wasn't there. The guy was good, controlled, ready to listen, but not overwhelmed by the reputation of his source. "Mr. Benedict," he said, "it was obvious you had something you didn't want to share. I understand that. It happens all the time. But I'm delighted to see you back here. This time, I assume you'll tell me what it's about."

"I'm *Alex*, Bill. And you know what the Apollo artifacts are?"

"Enlighten me."

"They're from the Golden Age, from the early spaceflights. From the first few centuries."

"Okay. What kind of artifacts are we talking about? Can you specify?"

"I can't be sure. But I suspect we'd find parts of the ships that made the first Moon flights. Maybe some personal items that belonged to the astronauts."

"Wait a minute. What's an astronaut?"

"Sorry. That's what they called the people who went into space. When we were first getting off Earth."

He smiled. "All right."

"The artifacts might include a radio from the Mars colony. Or a coffee cup belonging to Neil Armstrong."

"He was one of the early astronauts, right?"

"First person to set foot on another world."

"Oh. I guess I should have known that. I'm not strong on ancient history."

"That's okay. There might be a pen that belonged to Regina Markovy. She was captain of the first Mars flight. What I'm trying to say is, there might be *anything*."

"All right. That all sounds pretty valuable. Are you going to buy these things?"

"No, Bill. We're trying to find them. They disappeared eight thousand years ago."

"Oh."

"But I may know where they are."

"Really?" His eyes widened. "Good. But you say you *may* know."

"I can't be certain. I'm going to need some help finding them."

Bill nodded. "What can I do?"

"If you run this part of the story, somebody out there might have information that would be helpful. I'm only missing a couple of pieces. The person who can help might not be aware of it. With a little luck, someone will read your report and get in touch with me. I'm going to set up headquarters at the Majestic Hotel."

"All right," he said. "I don't see a problem there. But if this thing works out, and you actually find this stuff, I'll want an exclusive."

"Bill, if we find ourselves in a position to start selling Golden Age artifacts, we'll want all the publicity we can get. But yes, you'd get the lead story. Okay?"

"These artifacts, I assume, are seriously valuable?"

Alex met his eyes. "They're priceless. But you know, of course, there's always a chance this will come to nothing."

"Of course." Bill was writing in his notebook. "Let's hope not."

"So what's the point of all this?" I asked him when we were alone again.

"We're going to put some pressure on Southwick. He'll find out from Tokata what I'm threatening to do. And I think—I *hope*—they'll get in touch with us to talk things out."

"Or maybe the bomb will be real this time."

"Chase, I don't think these people are psychopaths. If they were, we'd know by now."

We went back to the hotel and wandered into the bar. "So what exactly *are* you threatening to do?"

"I thought it was plain enough. Or it will be to them. What Tokata should get from this is that, in a few days, I'm going to state publicly what I know, that the Prairie House artifacts were taken to an asteroid, that the asteroid was known as Larissa, and that meant it was pretty big. That there's a good chance they are still out there. The probable result of that will be that everyone who has access to a yacht will head out and look. Ultimately, somebody will stumble across it."

"Are you actually planning to do it?"

"Good question," Alex said. "I don't know. If we don't make this work, I might have to resort to something like that."

"Alex, I don't see how this *can* work. Tokata's in the British Isles, and we're sitting here in Hawaii. She won't even *see* Garland's report."

"You're underestimating her, Chase. She knew we were onto her and came up with a number on the spot to send us off on a wild-goose chase. You don't think she's been doing searches since then, trying to keep an eye on us? She knows we wouldn't have gone quietly into the sunset. She's probably waiting for us to call again."

"Instead of doing all this roundabout stuff with Garland, why don't we just do that?"

"I can't see how it would do any good. I don't think we can buy her cooperation."

"Okay," I said. "But I can't believe this will work."

Alex managed a smile. "It depends on what they're hiding."

It took two and a half days, approximately as long as it required a hypercomm message to reach Rimway and draw a response. *"Alex,"* it said, *"please don't do anything rash until we've had a chance to talk. I'm on my way."* It was from Southwick.

"I guess you were right," I said.

FORTY-SIX

Make some day a decent end,
Shrewder fellows than your friend.
Fare you well, for ill fare I:
Live, lads, and I will die.

—A. E. Housman, "The Carpenter's Son," 1896 C.E.

A second message arrived in the morning. *"Alex, I'll be on the Vistula. In port on the eleventh your time. Will contact you then."*

That was five days away. "I'm going to charge him," Alex said. "If he'd been up front with us from the beginning, we could have avoided all this."

"You want to tell me what it's all about?"

"I don't know yet, Chase. To be honest, I haven't even been able to come up with a decent theory."

"I think he'd like you to meet him at the space station."

"I don't think there's any question about that. But we'll let him come to us. How about heading for Barkova? We could do some sight-seeing."

I don't know why Alex decided out of nowhere that he wanted to go halfway around the planet. If he'd left the call to me, we'd have stayed on the beaches. But I said sure, and did a search on the place.

Barkova had been, for two thousand years, one of the major cultural centers of northern Europe. Alex, it turned out, was interested in it, though, because it's located less than a hundred miles south of the group of islands that are all that remains of Moscow. That ancient city, shaken for centuries by earthquakes, had been all but swallowed by its overflowing rivers. Consequently, we spent most of our time there in a rented skimmer surveying the ruins. The only visual evidence of the former capital consists of a few wrecked buildings jutting out of the water. The onion domes of St. Basil's Cathedral are still visible, glittering in the sunlight. As is the magnificent turret of the Valkan, which was the seat of government for almost three thousand years.

Today, the islands are home to an army of tourists. We wandered along an elevated walkway, rode a roller coaster, played some games in a casino, and ate dinner at Sergev's, a pricey restaurant overlooking Lake Kaczinski. Sergev's had pictures of the old days on the walls, of giant snowstorms and people wandering city streets wrapped in heavy overcoats and wearing fur hats. Hard to believe it was the same place.

We took one of the sub tours. I'd hoped to get a good look at the ancient buildings and streets, but most of what had been Moscow was buried in mud. We did get to see the Bolshoi Theater and the Kremlin Armory, more or less.

On the third afternoon, our hotel was hosting a wedding in its ballroom. I'm no longer clear on how it happened, but we became involved in the celebration. I always enjoy celebrating and will take any excuse to jump in. Alex, on the other hand, is not normally drawn to social events. He's an effective speaker, but take his audience away, and he seems to become almost shy. On that afternoon, though, he wandered away for a few minutes and returned with a woman who would become a lifelong friend, Galina Mozheika. She had bright amber eyes and long dark hair that fell below her shoulders. A cousin of the bride, she worked as one of the tour conductors. "It doesn't pay much," she told me, "but I love what I do."

I needed about three minutes to grasp what Alex saw in her: She had a taste for history. Her prime interest seemed to be ancient Russian literature. She knew all the stories, and on that night was talking with him about the accidental discovery of Dostoevsky's long-lost *Brothers Karamazov* during the Seventh Millennium. A three-hundred-year-old hardcover edition had been found in the library of a deceased book collector who apparently never realized what he had. And she knew about the trunkful of Third Millennium Russian novels found in a Greek attic and placed on board an interstellar that subsequently vanished. It sounded like another of the Sanusar vehicles.

He spent the rest of the evening with her. In years to come, they communicated back and forth. She made it to Rimway on a few occasions, and I never knew him to go back to Earth without visiting the Moscow Islands. But as far as I could tell, nothing romantic ever came of it. They were friends.

Maybe it was enough.

On one occasion, when we were alone together, Galina told me that Earth and Rimway were too far from each other. "And I'm not just talking about kilometers." By which I concluded that she wasn't ready to leave family and friends, and she assumed the same to be true of Alex.

It was an enjoyable party. People asked about my accent. Where was I from? Off-world? Really?

That night, somewhere around 3:00 A.M., my link sounded. It was Khaled. I reached over and took it from the bedside table. "Hello," I said.

His image appeared over by one of the windows. *"Chase. Ah, so you are still here."*

"More or less, Khaled."

"I can't see you."

"I'm in bed."

"Oh. At this hour?"

"It's the middle of the night here."

"Where are you?"

"I'm in Barkova."

"I didn't realize. I'm sorry."

"It's okay. Do you need something?"

"I just wanted to hear your voice again."

Alex hadn't released me from his directive that I not say anything to him. But it was hard to see that it would matter any longer. "Why?"

"Why would I want to hear your voice again? Chase, you sound annoyed."

"No, I'm not annoyed. I was just wondering whether you were looking for somebody to drop into the Atlantic."

"Oh." His shoulders tightened. "What do you mean?"

"You can stop the lies, Khaled."

He paused. Scrunched his shoulders and straightened. "I'm sorry about that, Chase. I'll regret that the rest of my life. But so you know, I didn't mean to cause a problem for you. You were never at risk."

"Yeah, you said something like that before."

"I was hoping it wouldn't—You wouldn't find out."

"I'm not surprised. Now if you don't mind, I'd like to get back to sleep."

"Chase, I'm sorry. I wish I had it to do over."

"You don't get do-overs, Khaled." I broke the connection, and his image blinked off.

I settled back down under the sheet and started rehearsing the things I should have said. *Hero of the hour: What a fake. You sold us out. Could have gotten us killed. And then you think you can make everything okay? I'm just going to forget it?*

The link sounded again. The few familiar notes, drifting through the dark.

I let it go for a while. I thought about shutting it off, but finally I opened the channel. "Chase," he said, "please listen to me. Look, I'm sorry. I'll do anything to make it up to you. When it happened, it just seemed harmless enough. And to be honest, I thought it was a chance to impress you. I had that wrong, and I know that. But all I'm asking is a second chance. Do that for me, and I promise you'll never regret it."

"Khaled," I said, "there's nothing you can do. No way you could ever fix things so I could trust you. Just go away and leave me alone."

"Chase, I—"

"Good-bye, Khaled." I disconnected again. He didn't call back. And I tossed and turned the rest of the night.

On the eleventh, I checked with operations. The *Vistula* had arrived in the solar system, but it was out near the orbit of Mars. *"Figure two days,"* they said. We took advantage of the time we had to travel to Egypt. Alex could never get enough of the pyramids. We landed at Balakat, a few kilometers from the Great Pyramid of Giza, climbed into a bus with forty other tourists, and headed out.

As customary, Alex had done his homework. "I cannot imagine how a primitive society could have put this thing together," he said, as we stood gaping at it. "Some of the individual blocks weigh up to eighty tons and were brought in from Aswan, which was more than eight hundred kilometers away.

"The thing consists of five and a half million tons of limestone, as well as some granite. The slaves were working in a desert. How could they possibly, with no technology, have hauled even *one* eighty-ton block of limestone across eight hundred kilometers under a blazing sun?"

"What are you suggesting?"

"I don't know. One fairly common theory is that it was done by aliens."

"The Mutes?"

"Who else is there?" He laughed. "But I can't imagine Selotta or Kassel hauling those things around. Can you?"

They'd ridden with us a few years earlier on a tour of Atlantis. "They *have* antigravity," I said.

"Let me put it a different way: Can you imagine either of them showing any interest in arranging blocks of limestone on a desert floor?"

We also visited the Palawi Temple, on the edge of the Libyan Desert. It's six thousand years old, and the civilization that built it is long gone. But its most fascinating aspect is that tourists who went there three thousand years ago inscribed their names and dates on its walls. The practice was stopped in the last millennium, but the names are still there, now carefully preserved and part of the history of the place.

We had just come out and were climbing back into the tour bus, grateful to be in the cool air again, when we got word that the *Vistula* had docked. "Do you want to call him?" I asked.

"No," he said. "Let's let him take the initiative."

Fifteen minutes later, the bus lifted off and started back toward Almahdi. The call came in midway during the flight. *"Alex? This is Lawrence."*

"Hello, Lawrence. How was your ride in?"

"Long. You haven't talked to any more reporters, I hope?"

"No. You asked me to hold off, so I did."

"Good. We need to get together."

"Okay. We're in Almahdi."

"Where?"

"Egypt."

"You have Chase with you?"

"Yes, she's right here."

"Okay. I was going to suggest you come up here. And please bring her with you."

"Are you on Galileo?"

"Yes. That way we can go directly to Larissa."

"You know where it is, Lawrence?"

"Not exactly. But I have its number."

"From Tokata?"

"Yes."

"KL-4561?"

"No. I got the real one. And I want to apologize for that. Heli was just trying to protect Garnett."

"Protect him from what?"

"I'd rather not discuss this over the link. Why don't you come up here, so we can talk it over and get everything settled?"

"Lawrence, so we're clear: We've been running around working on this matter for the better part of three months. We got dumped into the Atlantic and were led to believe our lives were in danger. Your associate sent us on a bogus run to the asteroid belt. And now you want us to go up to the space station and you'll explain everything. Is that right?"

"*I understand you're not happy, Alex. And believe me, I'm sorry about how this has played out. I'll make it up to you if you'll allow me.*"

"Why don't you start by giving me the Larissa designator? Then we'll pick you up, and we can talk on the way."

Southwick hesitated. "*No,*" he said. "*I can't do that.*"

"Why not?"

"*I'll explain to you when you get here. But first I have to have your word that you'll never say a word about this. Nor will Chase.*"

Alex looked at me. Glanced down at the desert moving slowly past. "I can't do that," he said. "I'm not good at conspiracies."

"*This is not a conspiracy, Alex.*"

"I wouldn't know what else to call it."

"*Nevertheless, I must have your word.*"

"You want me to promise to say nothing before you reveal what you're hiding?"

"*That's correct. I'm sorry, but I have to insist.*"

"Then you might as well get on the next flight, Lawrence, and ride back to Rimway."

"*Alex, I have no choice.*"

"Neither do I."

We could hear him breathing on the other end. "*I'll tell you this much,*" he said. "*Your plan to make public what you know, and unleash a bunch of treasure hunters will gain absolutely nothing. The odds of their finding anything are virtually nonexistent—*"

"I wouldn't agree with that."

"*No. You probably wouldn't. But there are a lot of asteroids out there.*"

"Not that many big ones."

"*Okay. Let me take it a step further. If you do succeed in getting a swarm of people to go out and do the search for you, and if one of them is able to find Larissa, I can assure you it will do nobody any good.*" He hesitated. "*Look. Don't do this. If, when you find out what has happened, you can conclude that no crime has been committed, and no one has been injured, all I'm asking is that you will agree to say nothing.*"

"Why don't you just tell me what you have, and we can go from there?"

"I can't do that, Alex. Not like this."

"Then I'm sorry. I guess we're just going to have to stay at odds. Lawrence, I think you made the flight for nothing." Alex clicked off, and he sat staring out the window.

It took maybe twenty minutes before the link sounded again. *"All right,"* he said. *"I've checked into the Galileo Hotel. When you get here, we'll talk it out."*

FORTY-SEVEN

Truth lacks the privilege of being employed at all times and under every circumstance. As noble as it is, it has its limits.

—Michel de Montaigne, *Essays*, 1588 C.E.

Southwick came down and met us in the bar. The relaxed, no-problem manner was gone. There was tension in his eyes, and his face was pale. "Glad to see you, Alex," he said, barely able to get the words out. He eased himself into a chair and sent a weak smile across the table. "Hello, Chase. I guess this has been a long haul for you guys."

"You could say that," said Alex.

Piano music drifted through the room. A lazy, quiet rhythm from another era. "I'm sorry. I wish there'd been another way."

Alex lifted his glass, tasted the drink, and put it back down. "Why don't you tell us what's going on?"

Southwick's eyes closed briefly. A waiter arrived, and he ordered something. I don't recall what it was, except that he asked for it *straight*. Then he glanced around to see if anyone was close enough to overhear us. "I'm sorry about the problems. I'd have avoided it all if I could have."

"I'm sure you would," said Alex, with a level tone.

"I met Garnett a long time ago. More than half a century. He was one of the finest people I've ever known. Totally honest. You could always count on him if you needed anything. I loved the guy. He saved my life once, and it killed me when we lost him."

Alex's eyes caught mine. We both wanted Southwick to get to the point, but the message for me was to be patient. Southwick continued for several minutes about Baylee's virtues. The ultimate stand-up guy. Eventually, his drink arrived. He literally snatched it from the waiter, but he set it down on the table without trying it. "Nothing in his life mattered as much as the Golden Age. And the Apollo artifacts. They represented who we were. Not only the beginning of the space age, but he saw them as symbolic of the beginning of the human family. It was ultimately, he used to say, those early years, when science was on the march, and a world culture was developing as a result of the rise of global communications, that imposed a sense of empathy on us. That drew us together. Showed us who we were. During the early years of the scientific renaissance, people did not believe that the human race would ever come together. Science just provided bigger bombs. But Baylee always said it was the development of new forms of communication that gave everyone a voice and that, after a rocky start, provided us with the kind of world we have now.

"It wasn't a straight line, of course. Sometimes things went badly. Dictators continued to show up. Civilization came close to collapse on several occasions and finally went under. They got through the Dark Age, only to have some of the colony worlds get into wars with each other. But Baylee maintained that once we were seriously able to talk to each other, a reasonable existence for everyone was inevitable. Which is why he so desperately wanted to find the Apollo artifacts. They marked, in his view, the launch point." Finally, he picked up his drink, tossed it down his throat, and smiled. "I know you're wondering why I'm going on like this. But you need to understand the man to understand what happened."

Alex sat unmoving.

"He was hunting for them when I first met him. But people had been looking for them for thousands of years. The assumption was that they were simply gone. I don't know how many times I told him it was all a waste. But then he came across the Marco Collins histories at Bantwell University. I don't know whether you saw them. But there it was: He'd given the artifacts to Larissa.

"I guess there was a problem in translation there, but he recognized the name. He knew that Zorbas was originally from that area in Greece, of course. But he couldn't believe there'd be any point in hiding the artifacts there. As far as we knew, it was just as unstable as the Dakotas. But a lot of people in that era, those who could, were establishing themselves on asteroids. Getting away from the civil conflicts. And he *knew* about the Larissa asteroid. Knew that one of Zorbas's friends, Quincy Abbott, was supposed to have had a retreat there. It would have been the perfect place."

"How did he find that out?"

"In Russell Brenkov's *It Never Happened*. Brenkov was, I think, a late-Fourth-Millennium historian, somewhere in there, who specialized in discounting historical myths. Abbott led the fight in the Dakotas against the thieves and rebels during the Dark Age. He was believed to have returned from an asteroid home on Larissa when everything started to break down. Brenkov argued that the story was untrue, that Abbott had never lived on an asteroid. But it didn't matter to Garnett, of course. What mattered was that the story established the existence of Larissa."

I remembered the book from the Albertson Museum. In fact, I'd held it in my hands.

Southwick took a deep breath. "I'll never forget the night he showed up at the dig site."

"What dig site is that?" Alex asked.

"We were working in the London area. And suddenly he was there, out of nowhere, telling me he was pretty sure he knew where the Apollo cache was."

"Wait a minute," I said, "assuming he suspected everything was hidden on Larissa, how did he know which asteroid that was?"

"He spent almost twenty years tracking that down. He eventually came across a two-thousand-year-old fragment of Les Carmichael's *Last of the Giants*, which was a substantive scientific history of the first two centuries of the Third Millennium. Unfortunately, most of it was illegible. But it included a list of the asteroids as they were originally known, matching them with their modern designators. Larissa was among them." He finished his drink. Our glasses were all empty by then. Alex ordered another round, but I passed for the obvious reason that I would probably be on the bridge of the *Belle-Marie* before the night ended.

"*Last of the Giants*," said Alex. "I never saw anything like that among his papers. Or in his library."

"I'm not sure where he found it. Or what happened to it. But once he knew where it was, he came to me at the London site. I'll never forget the way he looked that day. I've never seen *anyone* so happy and so excited. I suggested we get Heli to take us there."

"Why Heli?"

"We could trust her to keep her mouth shut. We didn't want to invite any scavengers."

The music stopped. And started again.

Alex examined his glass. "Whose idea was it to sink the boat?"

Southwick made a noise deep in his throat. "Heli suggested it. But I was responsible for the decision."

"We could have been killed."

"Heli assured me they could work everything out. That they wouldn't do it if there was any danger."

That got a growl from me. "I wish you'd been there," I said.

"I know. It was stupid. At the time, it seemed like a good idea. We hoped it would scare you off. I guess we should have known better. I think about it now, and I don't know where my head was. Anyway, I apologize."

"Did you have to buy them a new boat?"

"No." He smiled. "Insurance covered it. They never really asked any questions."

"Okay." Alex glanced at me. Keep cool. "So the three of you went to Larissa."

"Yes."

"And did you find the artifacts?"

Southwick swallowed. Tried his drink again. "Yes."

"And what happened?"

"The Zorbas family, or somebody, had built a house out there. A nice place, three stories, a mansion, really. They moved the smaller artifacts to the asteroid. They made no effort to take the shuttles or anything like that. Probably didn't have that capability. But the small stuff tends to be what's really valuable. Personal items, plaques, cups with mission names emblazoned on them, uniforms, helmets, journals. It was an ideal place because the vacuum inhibited decay. The objects would damned near last forever. It was a brilliant idea.

"We needed almost four days to get there. I think it was the longest four days of my life, Alex. But we *did* get there, and when we did—" He stopped, looking past me at whatever it was he'd seen that night. "Garnie was so excited he could barely contain himself.

"Then Heli told us there was a building. It was a dome, with a house inside. *Somebody* had lived on the asteroid. Maybe Abbott, maybe not. I don't know whether I've ever seen anyone as ecstatic as Garnie was. He pounded his chair and shook my hand and tried to kiss the top of Heli's head, but she told him to stay clear as long as the engines were running.

"I'd never seen him so ecstatic. And when I told him that it might be a good idea not to get too excited until we saw what we actually had, he laughed and said he knew it was still a long shot but how he was by God going to enjoy the moment anyhow. And if it really turned out just to be an old house in a strange place, then so be it.

"Heli brought us down onto the asteroid, about fifty meters from the dome, off to one side of the house. Garnett and I were both in our pressure suits by then. Heli wished us luck and said how she hoped we'd find what we were looking for. And then we went outside.

"I'd never been on an asteroid before. It was all crags and craters and broken rock. Garnett led the way. We went over to the dome, found a hatch, and pushed the entry pad. The pad glowed a little bit, but nothing else happened. He produced a cutter and told me to stand back.

"I told him it wasn't a good idea. That ancient power systems tend to get unstable when they're not shut down.

"He said not to worry. That he'd gone through a lot of old airlocks and never had a problem. 'It's a myth,' he said. He told me if I wanted to, we could go back to Galileo and see if we could hire a good electrician. Then he went on about how I shouldn't worry and aimed his cutter at the hatch. I backed off.

"I just stood and watched while he cut a hole in the thing, tried again to open it, gave up, and enlarged the hole until it was big enough for us to get inside the airlock. Then he did the same thing with the inner hatch, and that got us into the dome.

"There'd been a garden at one time. The trees were still there. Frozen, of course. And a bench. A walkway led up to the house.

"We pointed our lamps at it. The windows, except for one, were still intact. The place had a porch. We climbed up onto it and looked through the windows into an ordinary living room, with a sofa, a coffee table, and a couple of chairs. There were pictures on the walls of people posing and waving. And another of a young couple standing in front of a house surrounded by trees.

"We walked over to the front door. Garnie pushed the pad that should have opened it but nothing happened. So he aimed the cutter at it. The beam touched the door, and lights came on both inside and out. They flickered a couple of times and went off again. Then electricity rippled across everything, and the place ignited. We both jumped away from it and landed on the ground probably fifteen meters away. We were lying there trying to decide what was happening when something exploded inside. The house literally erupted. We were on the ground below the level of the deck, which is the only reason we survived. Pieces blew past us. Some hit the dome and ricocheted around.

"When it was over, everything went completely dark. Heli was screaming at us over the radio asking whether we were still alive, telling us to hold on, she was coming, and Garnett was lying on his back asking God what he had done." He fell silent.

"The artifacts were inside the house?"

"Yes. Everything was wrecked. They'd put the artifacts into a couple of storage rooms in back. Both were blown out and flattened. The contents were scattered around inside the dome. If it hadn't been there, most of the material would probably have been blasted into space. Garnett staggered around in the wreckage, trying to find something, *any*thing, screaming curses, and finally collapsing in tears. 'My God,' he said again and again, 'I can't believe I did this.' He got onto his knees and began sweeping up charred metal and plastics. At one point he lifted a blackened helmet like the ones they'd worn on the Apollo missions. We found frames, but there was no way to know what they'd held. The only thing we came across that was reasonably intact was the transmitter. Ironically, it was in a closet on the far side of the house. Everything around it was scorched and burned, but the transmitter looked okay." His eyes were closed. "He told me he wished he hadn't survived."

Alex looked pale. "You were lucky to walk away from it."

"Yes. We looked through the wreckage, hoping to salvage something, but Garnett was hurt. He was limping from the blast, and I wasn't in very good shape either."

"Why did you keep it quiet?" Alex asked. "To protect Baylee's reputation?"

"And mine. Yes. I didn't really have a reputation to protect, I guess. But Garnie did. He pleaded with me not to say anything."

"And that's what this was all about?"

"He was a friend, Alex. I gave him my word. And now I have to ask you again: Are you willing to keep this quiet? It will cost you nothing, and it will preserve the reputation of a good man."

Alex looked in my direction. He knew I'd been keeping notes and planning another memoir. "I can't do that," he said.

"Why not?" Southwick's tone took on a sharp edge. "Is it because you want some publicity? Son of a bitch, Alex, how can you be so selfish?"

"It's all right, Alex," I said. "Whatever you want to do is okay with me."

That earned me a glare from Southwick. "Do you have a veto?" he asked.

"She's not involved," said Alex.

Southwick took a deep breath. "Alex," he said, "do you still want to go out to look at the asteroid?"

"Yes."

"I'll take you there, on condition that you and Chase agree to say nothing."

"Look, Baylee's reputation won't suffer. He did exactly what every other archeologist I've ever known would have done. If anything, he'll become an icon. They'll make a movie about him. But that's not the point."

"What *is*?"

"People have been looking for these artifacts for eight thousand years. If we keep this quiet, they'll continue to look. With no chance of ever finding anything. I can understand your wanting to protect him, but you have an obligation to the truth as well."

He stared at Alex. "I have an obligation to *him*."

"And I have one to his granddaughter."

Southwick hesitated. Finally, he nodded. "Okay."

"Lawrence, did you ever go back? To the asteroid?"

He shook his head. "It would have been too painful."

"And nobody else knows about this except you and Tokata."

"That's correct. I've told no one. And I don't believe anyone could have gotten it out of Heli. She's a good woman."

"My perspective," I said, "might be a bit different."

Alex looked my way. *Don't start anything.*

FORTY-EIGHT

In the end, we retain nothing. Every act of fidelity, of courage, of sheer self-lessness, is forgotten. Even the few that make it into the history books lose much in the translation, and ultimately disappear into a quiet library. In time, the libraries themselves go away. Who can name any of the Saxon women who faced down the barbarians during the reign of Probus? Who even knows they existed?

—Alexander Meyers, *The Human Condition*, 10,122 C.E.

We saw no lights as we approached Larissa. And we were greeted by no voices.

I overheard Southwick, sitting back in the passenger cabin with Alex, say that when he'd left here, he'd sworn he would never come back.

The scopes revealed nothing until we were virtually on top of the place. Then, gradually, I caught reflections off the dome. And, finally, I could make out the skeletal remains of the house.

I brought us down about fifty meters away. We'd brought an extra pressure suit for Southwick. But he shook his head. "I have no interest in going back out there," he said.

Alex nodded. "I understand how you feel, Lawrence. But I'd prefer having you with me."

Southwick's eyes narrowed. "You don't trust me."

"You dumped us into the Atlantic."

"I explained about that."

"I know. Just call it an abundance of caution."

"I'm not a pilot. I couldn't make off with this thing."

"I know. But I'd feel better if you were with us."

"All right. Whatever you want."

We switched on our lights. I'd wondered whether some parts of the house, and possibly the artifacts, had torn through the dome and left the asteroid altogether. But no holes were visible, save the one at the entry hatch that had been cut by Baylee. That was where we entered, and made our way past the frozen trees.

"I don't think," said Southwick, "there's much chance that anything survived."

We went around to the rear of the house. That was where the debris was thickest. Alex had brought a staff, which he used to poke at it. We saw parts of a lamp and a computer and a showerhead. A broken door had been thrown against the side of the dome. Support beams, plumbing fixtures, scorched furniture were piled high. Southwick found an electrical device in the wreckage. We didn't know what it might have been, but VOYAGER 8 was engraved on its base. Another black box read MOONBASE. "Pity," Alex said, "Baylee didn't show a little patience."

Southwick agreed. "I know. I feared for a while that he'd become suicidal. He was never the same after this."

We moved carefully, trying not to walk on anything. One side of the house was still standing, more or less. We crossed onto the area that had constituted the storage rooms. It wasn't as dangerous as it might sound because gravity was almost nonexistent, so we didn't need to worry about falling through damaged flooring or having what remained of the house collapse on us. "Look at this," Southwick said. He'd found something inside some plastic packaging.

Alex shined his lamp at it. "It's a game, I think." The packaging was mostly intact. The lettering was ancient English, but there was a picture of a ringed planet and a primitive spaceship. We opened it and found model rockets and astronauts and a set of dice. He produced a plastene bag and placed the pieces inside. Then he held the box to give us a better look. There was an inscription, most of it not legible, but I could make out a date: 2203.

"Coincides within a few years," Alex said, "with the first manned flight to Uranus. This would have been worth a small fortune." He put the box into the bag with the pieces.

We found a few more objects, all damaged, plaques with names and dates, more toy space vehicles, shredded uniforms, magnets with images of stars and planets, framed photographs of planetary land-scapes, and a handheld computer. There was an intact package of arm patches, depicting a rocket liftoff. Alex examined one. "First manned Mars flight, maybe," he said. Later, we came across a couple of scorched shirts commemorating a mission somewhere.

And there were pieces of equipment. One was obviously an imager designed, it looked like, to be placed on a hull. And an early version of a scanner, which would also have been outside the ship. Most of the gear, though, was unidentifiable. If there'd been placards or anything indicating what they'd been, they were gone.

Alex switched over to a private channel so we wouldn't be over-heard by Southwick. "I just can't believe it. Baylee was in a hurry, so we lost all of this? No wonder the guy started having bouts of depression."

"You telling me *you'd* have been willing to go back and chase down an expert you could bring out here? Wait all that time?"

"Oh, Chase, I feel sorry for him. But we've lost so much." He switched back to the general channel as he lifted something else out of a pile of rocks. A framed picture. The glass was broken, but we could make out the picture. It was a woman, and she was in uniform. Her identity, which had been engraved at the base of the frame, was no longer legible. He showed it to Southwick. "Any idea who she might have been?"

"None whatever, Alex," he said.

"Here's another one." This time most of the photo was burned. "Wait," he said, "here's something else." A plastic container. The con-tainer carried a description of the contents, and had pictures of rock-ets and a comet. There were two disks inside. He held it in front of his imager, which was clipped to the suit just below his shoulder. "Belle," he said, "can you translate?"

"*Alex, it says:* Centaurus: Flight to the Stars. *And below that:* 'Join Adam Bergen for a virtual reconstruction of the first interstellar flight.'"

Alex looked at the two disks. "The *Centaurus* flight. I don't believe it."

"You know there won't be anything left on the disks," I said.

"Yeah." He sounded as discouraged as I've ever heard him. "I know."

We're pretty sure people knew extraterrestrial life existed as far back as the twenty-first century because they were able to do spectrographic analysis. But the first encounter with actual life-forms came on Europa when we cut through the ice, and the automated submarine *Diver* slipped into that world's tempestuous currents. The *Diver* had a distinctive sensor array mounted on its forward deck. We found a broken model of it. I had no idea what it was, but Alex recognized it immediately.

Eventually, we returned to the *Belle-Marie* and ate a quiet dinner. "This is exactly," said Southwick, "what happened to us. Going through that pile of junk and not finding anything intact. Garnett was hurting, physically and otherwise. We tried. But, finally, he gave up, and we just cleared out."

"I can understand it," said Alex.

I refilled the air tanks, and we slept for an hour. Then we started again. Southwick found the charred cover of a children's coloring book displaying vistas from other star systems. And Alex came up with a coffee cup marked GUMDROP. We showed it to Belle.

"*Gumdrop,*" she said, "*was the name given the command module for Apollo 9. It was the third manned mission in the Apollo program. And it was the first—*"

"Good enough." Alex wrapped it and slipped it into his bag.

I found another electronic device that I could hold in my hand. But again I had no idea what it was.

"Probably," said Alex, "an early version of a link."

"*It was called a cell phone,*" Belle said.

I opened the lid. It had a tiny screen and some buttons. "Where's the projector?" I asked.

"*The pictures appeared on the screen,*" said Belle. "*They did not do projections.*"

"It was a primitive time," said Southwick. "I don't know how they ever managed to get to the Moon, considering the kind of technology they had."

I know it doesn't seem as if moving broken furniture and electronic equipment and parts of walls around should have been difficult in low gravity. But it was a struggle. There was no easy method for getting the junk out of the way. I found bits and pieces that none of us could identify that might have come out of the cache, or might have simply been part of the house. It didn't really matter since they were thoroughly hammered.

There were more frames, but usually their contents were burned beyond recognition. I stopped periodically to watch the lights that marked the progress of Alex and Lawrence. They both grumbled and sighed and occasionally kicked something.

Then I heard Alex get excited: "Oh, God, Chase, look at this." His imager was on, and I could see what he'd found: Burned hardcover books scattered through a lower deck area on the side of the house that had escaped the worst of the blast. He was pulling a burst tank of some sort out of the way. Lawrence knelt beside him and turned his lamp on them. He began lifting the books from the rubble, one by one, opening them, and looking inside at scorched pages. I could make out only two titles: *Space Chronicles: Facing the Ultimate Frontier*, by Neil deGrasse Tyson, and *NASA's First Fifty Years: Historical Perspectives*, edited by Steven J. Dick.

They were looking frantically for surviving text. There was some, but not much. "You know," said Alex on our private channel, "I am having seriously dark thoughts about Baylee."

Lawrence realized what was happening and guessed why it was being kept from him. "Nobody got hit harder than he did, Alex."

"I know."

"Okay. We need to have a team come up here and take a serious look around. There might still be something that can be salvaged."

"You've spent a lot of time on the home world, Lawrence. You have people here you can trust?"

"Yes," he said. "I'd start with Heli."

"When we put it together, Alex," Lawrence asked, as we lifted away from Larissa, "do you want to be part of it?"

"No," he said. "I'd like to be informed what you find. Other than that, it's your project."

"All right. Thank you. I appreciate it." He was silent for a minute. Then: "I have one more question. When you get back to Rimway, what will you be saying about this find?"

"What do you want me to say?"

"I'd prefer you say nothing."

"We've already been through that."

"I know. Can I ask you to leave Garnett out of it? Just say you discovered the wreckage here and that you don't know how it happened?"

Alex looked straight ahead. "No," he said. "I'm not comfortable lying. I understand you want to protect him, but you've done all you can. It's out of your hands now."

Lawrence took a deep breath. He looked resigned. "All right," he said.

"What about Bill Garland?" I asked.

"Who's he?" asked Southwick.

Alex responded: "A reporter who was helpful. I promised I'd let him know if we found the artifacts. I should be able to manage that without going into too much detail. I'll go this far, Lawrence. I won't mention Baylee's name if I can avoid it. But we'll have to inform his family. Marissa is the one who came to us. She deserves to know what happened. But if the word gets out, and I don't see how that could not happen, I'll have to tell what I know."

"All right."

Alex turned toward me. "Is that okay with you?"

I doubt that I looked very happy. "I can live with it."

"Were you planning on doing another memoir, Chase?"

"Of this incident? Sure."

Lawrence's bewilderment was obvious. "Chase has written several memoirs of our efforts to locate lost artifacts," Alex said.

They both looked at me. "All right," I said. "I won't release anything until it becomes public knowledge. Okay?"

Lawrence nodded.

Alex was still watching me. We both had a pretty good idea how long that would take.

FORTY-NINE

Life is what happens to us while we're busy making other plans.

—Attributed to twentieth-century singer John Lennon

So it was over. We took Lawrence back to Galileo Station, had dinner there, and wished him well. Then Alex called Bill Garland, gave him an account of what we'd found and left him with the impression that no one knew precisely how it had happened. Then we started for Rimway. We kept the coffee cup from the *Gumdrop*. Lawrence had everything else. It had been a remarkably unsatisfying conclusion.

"Well," Alex said, "sometimes things just don't work out real well."

"Yeah."

"When do you expect to publish the memoir?"

"What memoir?" I said. "This thing didn't go anywhere. After all this running around, we needed to find something. All we have is a coffee cup."

He was obviously thinking that I'd been as upset by the outcome as he was. To a degree, I suppose he was right. But I shrugged it off. It wasn't the first time I'd lost a narrative that had started out with an intriguing setup. There had been, for example, the discovery of the lost tomb of Michael Truscott, the bloody-minded Director of the Lenola colony. Truscott's remains, when examined, turned out to be female. All kinds of theories had come out of the woodwork, including a faked death to mislead his numerous enemies after several assassination attempts. In reality,

Truscott *had been* a woman. The truth was revealed by the discovery of a diary while Alex was looking in a different direction.

Then there were the Lima Pearls, which had belonged to the beautiful theater star of the last century, Mora Volanda. She had been wearing them on the night she vanished, and there was some hope their discovery would lead to information on what had happened. But the investigation went nowhere. Mora's fate remains unknown.

And Allen Penrose, a beloved fourteenth-century physician, had gone with his wife and another couple to a resort in the Achean Isles, where all four had vanished. His personal belongings had become collectors' items, and Alex had gotten involved when several reports surfaced that the doctor had been seen at the annual Spook Fest celebration in Malachia.

So we relaxed and talked about other things en route back to Rimway. I was still in a kind of trance, and I remember telling Alex that I was going to use my next vacation to go back to Earth and spend more time. Just hang out in the place where it had all begun.

I wondered what Yuri Gagarin would have given for a ride in the *Belle-Marie*?

Alex never really talked a great deal, but he was unusually withdrawn on the way home. He expressed concern about neglecting his clients and that a substantial amount of work was waiting for us. But it was more than that. I couldn't decide whether it was Baylee's unhappy end or the loss of the Apollo artifacts that hung over his head. Or possibly Gabe.

He admitted he'd be glad to get back to the country house. "I'm going to bring Woody in to do some restoration work on the place," he said. "I've kind of let it go a bit. I wouldn't want Gabe noticing that when he walks in." Then he waved it away. "I'm fine. Just tired."

We came out of jump a quarter million kilometers from Skydeck and checked in. The comm op was Josette St. Pierre, with whom I'd shared a few lunches. *"Chase,"* she said, *"where've you guys been? They've been trying to reach you."*

"Who has, Josette?"

"John Kraus. The Capella's *back."*

She passed me to her supervisor. *"We don't have much in the way of details,"* he said. *"They got hypercomm signals yesterday from her. Confirmed. So yes, it is back. Last I heard, we had no explanation, and no idea whether the situation would remain stable. But the big news is that after nineteen hours, it's still on the surface. We've scrambled everything in sight. There must have been sixty ships left here in the last ten hours."*

Hypercomm signals. That indicated, at least, that they were still alive. "Where are they?"

"It's a little farther out than last time. Do you want me to forward the data to you?"

"Please."

There was a brief pause. Then: *"Done."*

"Thank you," I said. "Where's John?"

"On the Isabella Heyman. *It's a yacht. He grabbed the first thing available."*

"Roger that. And you have no idea how long it will stay up?"

"They're hopeful."

"Why?"

"The last line in the message. It said: 'Robert asked us to say hello.'" He paused. *"They're talking about Dyke. I assume you're going, too?"*

"Yes," I said. "Changing course now."

"Good luck, Chase. Skydeck out."

Actually, I hadn't reacted yet. I opened the allcomm: "Alex? You there?"

"More or less. What's going on?"

"Tie yourself in. The *Capella*'s back."

"Marvelous! Everything okay?"

"Yes. There was a message from Robert Dyke. Apparently he came through."

"Beautiful."

"I guess we didn't hear how long they might stay afloat?"

"Negative."

Another ship, the *McAdams*, was just departing Skydeck on the same mission. We wished each other luck. I knew the pilot, Sally Turner.

Not well, but enough to say hello whenever we met. She was serious and reserved, not given to getting carried away by any momentary emotions. But on that occasion, she sounded deliriously happy. *Let's go get them, baby.*

Optimism comes easily, I guess. It felt as if, during that first hour under way, we had it right this time. Everything would be okay. Time to raise a glass. Alex gave way to near jubilation. Maybe because it had all come out of the blue. Maybe because of that one line. *Hello from Robert.*

We slipped into transdimensional space, which cut us off from the rest of the universe. We spent time entertaining ourselves as best we could. Alex buried himself in his books while I watched comedies and played chess with Belle. As we drew closer to our destination, I realized there was a good chance we'd be met by the news that the *Capella* had been swept under again. Alex was obviously weighed down by the same concern. But we both remained optimistic.

As we approached the end of our jump, I started a mental countdown. Couldn't help myself. Two hours until we arrive.

One hour.

Alex kept checking the time, too, although he tried to hide what he was doing. He liked to think of himself as a rationalist, always in control, not given to emotions. But it was all a show.

He was back and forth on the bridge. He'd come up, sit down, say something of no consequence, get back on his feet, and disappear. I'd hear voices in the passenger cabin, somebody doing a historical analysis of the City on the Crag or the Maven War, then it would cut off and be replaced by soft music, then it would go silent. A few minutes later he'd be back on the bridge. When finally I told him to relax, he got annoyed. "I'm fine," he said.

Eventually, Belle spoke: *"Four minutes to end of jump."* It was almost a whisper. She understood the mood.

Alex, who was beside me, didn't move except to activate his harness.

Standard procedure when you complete a jump is first to determine where you are in relation to your destination. Not this time. "Find out if they're still there," Alex said.

I sent out a broadcast signal: "This is the *Belle-Marie*. To anyone who can hear me: What is the status of the *Capella*?"

Alex straightened his harness.

Belle said, *"I am trying to establish our position, but I will need more time."*

"It's okay, Belle," I said. "Let us know when you have it."

I listened to the air moving through the life-support system. And to the hum of the drive unit. And to the silence roaring out of the speaker. "It'll probably take a while," I said.

I couldn't make out Alex's answer.

Then, finally: "Belle-Marie, *this is the* Falcon."

"Hello, *Falcon*. What's the situation?"

"The Capella's *still up."* We both raised a fist. Clasped hands. If I could have reached Alex, I'd have kissed him. *"They're transmitting. I don't think anybody's actually reached them yet, though."*

"That's okay. As long as they're still on the surface."

"Welcome to the party."

"Chase," said Belle, *"we're getting something from them now. From the* Capella. *Sounds like Captain Schultz."*

It was, indeed: *"To anyone arriving in the area: We are awaiting assistance. Robert tells me he believes we have stabilized. But we cannot be certain. McAdams, we are glad to see you. First boats have launched."*

"Chase," said Belle, *"I've located the source of the transmission. I'm putting it together with information from the* Falcon. *You will be happy to hear we are only eight hours out."*

"Okay," I said. "Let's move."

We listened while the *Dorothy Viscidi* picked up seventeen people and pulled away. The *McAdams* was closing. We caught a glimpse of two lifeboats through its scopes. The cabin lights in one were still on, but we couldn't see whether anyone remained inside. The *Akim Pasha* was coming in behind the *McAdams*. An hour later, the *Vertigo* arrived and pulled alongside to take people directly out of the airlock. We heard Captain Schultz's voice, assuring someone that everything was proceeding quite well. *"The* Bangor," she said, *"the* Carol Rose, *and the* Zephyr *are all less than a few hours out."*

The *Bangor* was a cargo vessel that should be able to take off close to three hundred. The others were all yachts. Like us.

Alex was having a difficult time. I knew he wanted to talk with Gabe. Ideally, he'd have liked to pick Gabe up and take him home in the *Belle-Marie.* "It would be a nice ending," I said.

"Yeah, it would, Chase. But stuff like that only happens on HV." He collected a cup of coffee, asked if I wanted some, and came back and sat down. "When you write this, you could arrange to have it happen."

"Nobody would believe it, Alex. Even if we did run into the lifeboat carrying him, I wouldn't be able to write it that way."

We were getting pictures from everyone who was close to the *Capella.* We watched the *Vertigo* pull away. The *Capella*'s cargo deck opened, and another lifeboat escaped. Ninety minutes later, the *Rose* moved into position to take people directly out of the airlock. They were still at it when the *Zephyr* rendezvoused with one of the lifeboats. Then, after another hour, it was *Bangor*'s turn.

Captain Schultz returned to the radio: *"When the* Bangor *leaves, we will be down to 2106 passengers and crew. I'm happy to report we still have stability."*

"That doesn't mean much," I told Alex. "When it comes time to get swallowed, there's not much warning. Not from what I've seen."

The rescue units continued to arrive, one or two every hour. Then, suddenly, there were six, including a fleet cruiser, which took off another three hundred.

There were no Mutes this time. And nobody coming from a distant port. There'd been no time for anyone much farther away than Skydeck to arrive on the scene.

Eventually, we got close enough to think about contacting Gabe on his link. Alex tried, waited, and shook his head. Still out of range.

And then, finally, it was our turn: "Belle-Marie, *you're next. We'll be launching another boat in about thirty minutes. They will provide a signal. Just follow it in and take as many off as you can. What is your capacity, please?"*

"Ten," I said.

"Very good. Take on ten, then depart immediately. And thank you for your assistance."

FIFTY

Do not remain long from home.

—Homer, *The Odyssey*, c. 800 B.C.E.

"Hello, Belle-Marie. *This is Case Harley on Lifeboat 11. We're glad to see you."* It was a happy voice. The lifeboat was only a dim blinker on the navigation display. *"We'll be ready to go when you get here."*

"We're about forty minutes out," I told them. "How many of you are there?"

"Nineteen."

"We can only take ten."

"We know *that. They told us. There's somebody else coming in behind you."*

By then we'd heard that another forty people had been rescued from the *Capella.* And that the *Silverton* was approaching it, as well as another yacht. The *Silverton* was a transport and would be able to accommodate almost two hundred passengers. Of course, the critical news was that the *Capella,* then nearing the end of her fifth day, was still on the surface.

I couldn't resist trying for Gabe. "You don't by any chance have anyone named Benedict on board, do you?"

I heard Harley asking, heard the silence.

"Negative," he said. *"Sorry."*

"That's okay. It was a long shot."

We also received an update from John Kraus: *"So you're aware: Robert Dyke managed the fix. He describes it as temporary but says it will probably hold. There's no way to be certain, though. So time is still of the essence. We have a sufficient number of vehicles coming in, but we'll need at least another two days to get everyone off. We appreciate the efforts of everybody who has helped. If you need to reach me, I'm on the* Heyman.*"*

Lifeboat 11 gradually brightened. It took shape, and we could make out individual lights, some on the hull, others in the cabin. *"Can we do anything to help?"* asked Harley.

"Just sit tight. We'll take care of everything."

They were coming in our general direction, and we'd been braking for almost two hours. *"Chase,"* said Belle, *"I see the backup yacht."*

"When will they be here?"

"In another hour."

And Harley again: *"Do you guys know what happened? Is it really 1435?"*

"Yes, Case. The *Capella* got caught in a time warp."

"But we've only been on board a few days."

"Sit tight, Case," I said. "We'll have you guys off in ten minutes."

We drew alongside. When we were in position, Belle signaled the lifeboat, and the connecting tube activated. It expanded across the approximately forty meters separating us and used its magnets to secure itself to our airlock. *"Everything's in place,"* Belle said.

I opened both hatches. The tube was flexible, so I couldn't see all the way across. "Okay, Case," I said. "You can send your people through the airlock. Ten of them. If you can, try to keep families together."

"Of course," he said. *"They'll be right over."*

They came into the passenger cabin, looking tired and frightened. There were three elderly couples, one with two kids, a boy and a girl, both about twelve or thirteen. They told us they'd decided to take the grandchildren for a "space ride." "Bob and Mary must be frantic," they said. The parents, I assumed.

The other two passengers were both women, traveling alone. One, whose name was Sally, had been headed to the City on the Crag to join her journalist husband, who'd been working on a documentary. "I haven't been able to reach him," she told us. "I've no idea even how to begin."

The other, Juanita, had been on a business trip and appeared to be in a state of near shock. "I can't believe I've lost eleven years," she said.

We got everybody situated as soon as they were on board. I told them we'd be belting down shortly and that we'd stay that way for about forty minutes. Alex played the engaging host while I went onto the bridge and got us disconnected, talked briefly with the incoming yacht that would take off the rest of the people on the lifeboat, and said good-bye to Case Harley, who'd stayed behind. Then, finally, we were ready to move. Alex gave his cabin over to the two kids though one of them came up to sit with me on the bridge. When everyone was settled, we pulled away and began to accelerate.

I overheard some of the conversation as we moved out of the area, how glad they were to be off the lifeboat, while one of the women mentioned it was the same thing they'd said as they left the *Capella*.

"I'll sue their pants off," said one of the men in an angry voice.

"Well, I'll tell you one thing," said another male, "I'm never getting on one of those damned things again."

It didn't much matter who was speaking; the comments were all the same, how their children were now in their forties or fifties, whether Aunt Lucy was still alive, what had happened to their homes, how hard it was to believe that Janet would now be fourteen, for heaven's sake.

One of them, a tall, worried-looking male, demanded assurances that when we made our jump, we wouldn't get stuck again. When I told him it would be okay, he asked how I could be certain.

"We have a different kind of drive," I said. "Besides, we're nowhere near the time/space area that's damaged."

He stared at me. "Don't get me wrong," he said, "but I wish I could believe you."

Finally, we made our descent into transdimensional space, and they were all free to walk around again. That was when we started hearing more details of their experience. "You don't want to be out here and get told you need to be rescued," said one of the older women. "They kept telling us everything would be okay, that there was no reason to worry, and that just scared me to death."

The girl, whose name was Rinnie, told me, under her breath, that the woman scared pretty easily.

Mostly what I picked up was simply disbelief that eleven years had passed since they boarded. Sally looked terrified. "My husband thinks I've been dead for eleven years," she said. "He's probably married again."

"There's just no way to know for sure," said Alex, in his most soothing tone. "But we've been aware of what happened for several years, and that the passengers figured to be okay." He looked around at the others. "If you want to send transmissions, let everybody at home know you're all right, you can do that, and we'll send them onto the station as soon as we get back into linear space."

In the end, everybody prepared at least one message. Even the kids, who recorded comments and assurances to friends and relatives and, in one case, a teacher.

We got to know each other pretty well on the way home. We exchanged contact information, talked about getting together, watched while a grandmother tried to explain to the kids that their friends were all now adults. "That doesn't mean they won't still be your friends," she said. "But things will be different."

Both children said no, they couldn't believe it. "Mike will always be there."

I felt sorry for them. I tried to imagine how I'd have felt to lose all my friends when I was twelve. To know they were still around but not really.

Rinnie spent a lot of time with me on the bridge. She was struck by how dark it was outside and that there were no stars. She talked with Belle, who blinked and booped for her, making her laugh. "One day," she said, "I'd like to be a pilot. Like you, Chase."

"You'd enjoy it," I said.

Her brother eventually joined her and told me the same thing. Their grandfather followed him through the hatch and wanted to move him away. "You're bothering the pilot, kids," he said. "Leave her alone." Of course, the truth was that the only reason I was even sitting on the bridge was that there was no room in the passenger cabin.

Of the other two couples, one was on their first off-world vacation, which they assured me, despite everything, they would try again as soon as they could get their lives back together. The other pair were returning home to Sanusar after a tour that had taken them to Earth. "Always wanted to see it," they said.

"Was it worth it?" I asked.

"Oh, yes," the woman said. Her name was Myra. "It was an extraordinary experience, seeing all those places I'd read about. It's a beautiful place."

We ran some shows from Belle's library, a couple of musicals and some comedies. And we did some game-playing. We rescued a stranded team from a space station that had been hit by a comet and was sinking toward the atmosphere, fought off some evil aliens, and beat some bad guys into the Pyramid of Ulsa, where we salvaged the Golden Pearl.

Somehow, the games became the reality, and going home to a world that had aged eleven years receded into fantasy.

When we made our jump back into linear space, we found ourselves about thirty hours out from Rimway, which floated serenely in the sky ahead, with the Moon off to one side. I let Skydeck know we'd arrived and sent all the messages.

"Great, Chase," said the comm op. "Good to hear your voice. Please send us a list of the people on board with their home addresses and birth dates."

We collected the information and forwarded it. Then I asked the station whether anyone had brought Gabe in yet.

"Let me check."

James was sitting beside me. "Who is that?" the boy asked.

"Alex's uncle," I said.

"Was he on the *Capella*, too?"

"Yes."

He smiled. "He'll be glad to get home."

And, after a few more minutes, the response came: *"Sorry, Chase. We don't have anything yet. But we only have a few of the names. Give it some time."*

I said thanks and signed off.

"Why," said James, "don't you ask her to let you know if he shows up?"

"She's probably buried with requests like that," I said. "I didn't want to give her anything else to keep track of."

The thirty hours stretched out. Everybody was desperate to get to the station. Skydeck contacted us again. *"Chase, your passengers will be taken down to Markala City. We know that's not convenient for them, but we'll arrange additional transportation as necessary. We'll be giving their names and itinerary to the media unless they object. Please check with them."*

Nobody objected. Within the hour, transmissions began arriving. Relatives saying hello and how good it was to know they were safe, friends welcoming them back, asking whether they could help, could maybe meet them at the terminal. Sally received a message from her husband. She didn't tell us what he'd said, but she wore a happy smile for the rest of the flight.

There weren't enough bunks, so they'd been switching off. I stayed on the bridge for the most part and gave my cabin to the two unaccompanied women. The games gradually stopped, except for the kids, and mostly everybody talked about what it would be like to get home. A lot of questions were directed at us. Had anything changed? Who was president of the Confederacy now? They'd heard that the Mutes had actually become friendly. How had that happened? Had they really come a few days ago to participate in the rescue? (They were still counting time by their own calendar.)

There was talk of legal action against Orion. Did Alex think they'd been culpable in any way?

"I doubt it," he said. "Nobody saw anything like this coming."

"Is Uncle Marvie still on HV?" asked James. Uncle Marvie had been enormously popular a decade before, but comedy tends to change between generations. He'd lost his audience and dropped out of sight.

"Do you know how the Phantoms have been doing?" asked one of the guys.

The Phantoms represented Corbin City in the National Wallball League. I don't stay up with it, but I knew they were famous for an inability to handle the ball. "I don't think much has changed," I said.

And so it went.

Eventually, I turned the vehicle over to Skydeck. They brought us in smoothly, told us they were glad to have us back, and eased us into Dock 4.

The concourse was empty when we arrived except for some medical staff and a few station personnel. We said good-bye to our passengers as their names got checked against a list. Then they were turned over to the medics. No one had any medical complaints, so they simply asked a few questions and gave the passengers some forms to sign. Then one of the staff members pointed toward the terminal area. "Shuttle's waiting," she said.

I'd never seen the station so empty.

Alex nodded. "They cleared it. Last thing they'd need would be an army of reporters and relatives."

I looked back at the staff person. "Do you need us to go out again?" I asked. "Back to the *Capella*?"

"No, we're fine," she said. "Thanks for helping."

Alex asked the one with the list if he knew whether Gabriel Benedict had arrived yet.

"Don't know, sir," he said. "I'm sure they can tell you at the terminal."

Nobody at the terminal had any idea. We climbed into the shuttle, which also carried some of the passengers who'd come in on the *Ban-*

gor. I sat beside Juanita, one of the two lone women. On the way down, she told me that an old boyfriend would be waiting for her.

"That's pretty good of an old boyfriend to wait all these years."

"Well, I suppose," she said. "Of course, he wasn't an old boyfriend last time I saw him."

Three-quarters of an hour later, we got instructions about connecting flights and descended into Markala City. Everybody said good-bye as they got out of their seats, and thanked us. A swarm of reporters were waiting, including a couple who apparently knew the family with the kids. A guy came over to Juanita, and they fell into each other's arms. He looked too old for her, and I guess I finally got the joke.

Alex and I arrived in Andiquar shortly after sunset and grabbed a taxi. "First thing we should do tomorrow," he said, "is get in touch with Marissa."

"I'll set it up," I said.

"No hurry," Alex said. "Let's take care of it in the morning."

We watched the gathering darkness settle over the western half of the city. Then we picked up the Melony, and, within a few minutes, we were starting down toward the country house. "I'll be getting off here," Alex told the autopilot. "Take Chase to 451 Khyber Lane."

"Yes, sir," said the AI.

"But," I added, "you'll have to wait a few minutes for me. Okay?"

"I'll put it on the clock."

"Why?" asked Alex. "Did you forget something?"

The country house had once been an inn, providing services for hunters and travelers. But the surrounding forest had been substantially replaced by crystal houses and carefully manicured lawns. "Look." I pointed down at it.

The lights were on in Gabe's office.

FIFTY-ONE

O fortunate, O happy day,
When a new household finds its place
Among the myriad homes of earth
Like a new star just sprung to birth.

—Henry Wadsworth Longfellow, *The Hanging of the Crane*, 1875 C.E.

He came out onto the front porch as we descended onto the pad and waved at us. Alex was out of his belt and opening the door while we were still a few meters off the ground. *"Premature,"* said the taxi in a stern voice. *"A penalty will be assigned."*

"Whatever," said Alex. We touched down, and he climbed out. Gabe broke into a huge smile, came down the steps, and hurried across the cobblestones. They both stopped, stared at each other for a moment, and, without a word, fell into each other's arms.

"Gabe," Alex said, "I never expected to see you again."

"I don't feel as if I've been gone."

They both laughed. "We thought you were dead."

"That's what I heard, Alex. I couldn't believe it when they first told us what was happening. I'm glad you didn't change the locks."

Alex nodded, and Gabe looked my way. "Doesn't show on you at all, Chase. You're as beautiful as ever."

I moved in and hugged him. "Welcome back, Boss."

The taxi informed us of the amount of the penalty. Alex paid and told the taxi good-bye. It rose into the soft moonlight.

"It's great to have you back," said Alex.

"Do they know how it happened?"

"The physicists do. It had something to do with damaged space and the Armstrong drive."

"Well, I'm grateful it turned out okay." He released me, and we stood there looking at one another and shaking our heads. And, finally, we started back toward the house. "It's strange," he continued. "I don't feel as if I've been away at all. I mean, I just packed my bags the other day. But this place is sure changed. The offices have been overhauled, and the bathrooms are different. The rear deck's been rebuilt." He looked down at the cobblestones. "Even the walkway. *Everything's* different. And I see the property is home to your company. Rainbow Enterprises, is it?"

"Yes, Gabe."

"Well, congratulations. I hope it's doing well."

"It is." Alex sounded a bit tentative. He didn't expect his uncle's approval.

Gabe caught the reaction and laughed. "I see he was smart enough to hire *you*, Chase."

"How'd you know?" I asked.

"The picture of your mom is still on your desk." He took my bags, and we went inside. "Good move, Alex."

"Chase isn't bad." He grinned at me. "She tends to be a little standoffish sometimes. But she's a good accountant."

We dropped the luggage just inside the front door, walked past Gabe's renovated office, which was located opposite the conference room, and went into the study at the rear of the building. Shelves of hardbound books lined the dark-paneled walls. It was my favorite room. Gabe's framed photos were still there: an abandoned temple with an ugly idol overwhelmed by forest, a broken column lying in a bleak stretch of desert, one of his excavation teams gathered in front of a pyramid beneath twin moons. A reproduction of Marcross's portrait of Christopher Sim's *Corsarius* hung beside the door. There were individual sketches of Gabe's colleagues, and one of a four-year-old Alex.

Gabe produced a bottle of Saraglian wine and filled three glasses. We drank a toast to ourselves, another to Robert Dyke, and a third to JoAnn and Nick. Then we finished off the bottle, and Alex lifted his glass one more time. "To *you*, Gabe. For all the good years."

"Thank you," said his uncle. "I can't imagine them without you, Alex." He finished his drink. Then: "I'll need you to bring me up to date. I'm glad, by the way, you didn't get rid of the property."

Alex looked surprised. "I always loved this place. I grew up here. No way I'd have sold it."

"But you were living on Rambuckle. I'm surprised you came back."

"You left it to me, Gabe. What did you expect?"

"To be honest, I never much thought about it."

"The only reason I went to Rambuckle was that I needed to get closer to the area I was researching."

"Okay. I thought you were upset with me. But it's over, Alex. Let's not revisit all that. Whatever you're doing is your affair. It's okay."

"Thank you, Gabe." Alex sighed. "I missed *you*. We both did."

Gabe's eyes locked on me. "How's your mom, Chase?"

"She's good. She'd want me to say hello."

"I'll call her myself in the morning." He turned back to Alex. "You *do* live here now, right?"

"Yes. But I've been looking around. There's a nice place over near the lake. I'll be out of your way shortly, in a few weeks, if that's okay."

Gabe wrapped an arm around him. "You don't have to go anywhere. For one thing, I'm not sure about the legalities here, but I think you own this property. I'm the one who should be looking—"

"No. I'm pretty sure there's a legal provision for something like this. If there isn't, I'll turn it back to you as soon as Chase can put the paperwork together."

"Thank you, Alex. That's good of you. But this place is certainly big enough to hold all three of us. Chase, do you live here, too?"

"No," I said. "I have a place up on the hillside."

"All right. Anyhow, I appreciate your willingness to change the arrangement. If it's okay, I'll stay. But I don't want *you* to leave."

Alex hesitated. "Gabe, we run an antiquities business. I need some space for that—"

"It's all right. I'm surprised you decided to continue the operation here." He was referring to the fact that there was a lot more paperwork involved in dealing artifacts on Rimway than there had been on Rambuckle.

"I like the location. And Chase takes care of the details."

"Well, good. Then you'll stay, all right?"

"Yes. Of course. If you're certain."

"Absolutely." He took a deep breath. "Wouldn't have it any other way. Have you guys had dinner? No? Then why don't we go celebrate? And maybe you can tell me what happened with the *Tenandrome*."

I suspect anyone who's reading this remembers the worldwide celebration that broke out two nights later. The rescued passengers, their families, and everyone connected with the operation got together in thirty-some sites around the planet and on the space station, using omnicron technology to shake hands, share drinks, and say hello to people thousands of kilometers away. It was unforgettable. Not only for the participants but for the millions who watched and celebrated with us. The Andiquar group assembled at the Miranda Hotel. President Davis said a few words but kept his remarks short. The families of JoAnn and Nick were in attendance, including JoAnn's husband, Jerry, though they were on Sympatico Island. And Robert Dyke, the hero of the hour, who was *actually* in the building.

Gabe introduced me to people he'd met on the ship. They in turn introduced me to family members who teared up while talking about how it felt to have sons and daughters back, wives and friends, people they'd thought lost forever. The vast numbers who watched from home shared a similar sentiment. For the moment, at least, we had all become part of a single family. It was the event we would always remember. Not so much the rescue as the celebration. Nothing, they agreed, would ever seem the same again.

EPILOGUE

The *Capella* was declared stable within a few days. Its Armstrong drive unit was replaced, and it was brought home. As I write this, Orion has announced that it will relaunch the *Capella* in midsummer. When I told Alex that nobody would want to ride on it, he laughed and said how I didn't understand human nature very well. He was right. They haven't been able to print enough tickets.

We do not expect any more problems with time/space warps. There are, of course, other lost ships, and the recovery effort has been expanded.

The big party was followed by a more formal awards ceremony, which recognized the efforts of Captain Schultz and numerous members of her crew and the rescue teams. And, of course, Robert Dyke. And John Kraus, who told me later that, if they'd listened to him, the ship would still be adrift. But even in hindsight, he admitted, if he had it to do again, he'd make the same call. Take no chances.

Alex, Gabe, and I attended the soiree on Momma that Linda arranged for her husband. So we were present when Linda opened a door and showed him the Weinstein chair. It was the first time I'd heard a grown man actually *yip*.

*   *   *

Marissa was delighted to hear about her grandfather's discovery. Alex did not lie about anything, but he was able to tell Baylee's story in a way that emphasized his contributions. The explosion became a piece of terrible luck. But a mystery eight thousand years old had been solved. And without him, it would never have happened.

Gabe's arrival did not change life at the country house as much as we'd expected. Alex again offered to move Rainbow Enterprises, and his home, to another location, but Gabe wouldn't hear of it. My job expanded to include transporting my old boss to various dig sites across, and beyond, the Confederacy. He spent most of his first few months back simply catching up. One former planetary president had been indicted for corruption, and another was caught in a sex scandal. The Temple of Muntra had been destroyed in an earthquake. Robert Blandon's grave had been found. The Selian Pearls, which Gabe had been trying to track down for years, had been recovered. He was of mixed emotions about that. His suspicions about the fate of Christopher Sim and the *Tenandrome* were confirmed.

And then there were the contributions of his nephew: Largely due to Alex's efforts, the mystery of the lost *Seeker* had been resolved, and relations with the Ashiyyur had greatly improved. He congratulated Alex, and we spent the better part of a week celebrating.

Eventually, everything went back to the old normal. Gabe began rolling his eyes at Alex's activities, but he was no longer saying anything. In response, Alex usually just smiled tolerantly. So, okay, you have to recognize that some things never really change.

A few weeks after we'd returned, Alex took off halfway around the world for an antiquities conference, and Gabe joined an archeological team which had discovered a four-thousand-year-old space platform. I was alone in my office, holding the fort. I was happiest when one or the other was out of the building. Or preferably both. It made for a quiet, relaxed atmosphere.

I'd taken eight or nine calls that morning when Jacob announced one that surprised me. Lawrence Southwick, wearing a happy smile, was on the circuit. *"Chase,"* he said, *"it's good to see you again. How are you doing?"*

"I'm fine, thank you, Lawrence. How's the Larissa effort making out?"

"That's why I called. Is Alex available?"

"He'll be out of town for a few days. Can I help you?"

"You going to be in this afternoon?"

"Yes. After two o'clock."

"All right. I'll come by about three if that's okay."

"He's carrying a package," said Jacob. "And he has someone with him. A woman."

"Do we know her?"

"I do not recognize her."

I met them at the door, and my jaw dropped. Madeleine O'Rourke. She smiled defensively. "Hello, Chase," she said. "I hope you'll let me in."

"Chase," said Lawrence, "you know Heli, of course." The package was tucked under one arm.

"Of course." I kept my voice as level as I could. "You'll be happy to hear, Heli, that we didn't get eaten by sharks."

She nodded. "I'd like to apologize. I guess we went a little bit overboard."

"You did?"

"Chase," said Lawrence, "Heli has felt badly about what happened. What she did was at my direction. So it's really *my* fault. We needed something that would—"

I was staring at Tokata. "How did you know where to find us?"

She squirmed while Southwick responded: "I have to take responsibility for that, too, I guess. I stayed in touch with Luciana. She mentioned that you'd indicated you would go to Eisa at some point. So Heli simply called Khaled. I *am* sorry. We meant no harm."

"Let's let it go, Lawrence, okay?" I turned away and led them into my office. "What do you need?"

"Some coffee would be good," said Tokata.

I got it for them. And poured myself a cup, though at that moment I could have used something stronger. "Have you been back to Larissa yet?"

They looked at each other and smiled. "We have. We thought you would be interested in seeing this." He laid the package on my desk.

"You found something."

"Actually, we found a few things. But we especially wanted to show this to you and Alex." I looked at it. "Go ahead," he said. "Unwrap it."

I peeled off the packaging and revealed a curved, stainless-steel plaque. It was rectangular, roughly nine by eight inches, with two globes representing the Earth. And the inscription:

> HERE MEN FROM THE PLANET EARTH
> FIRST SET FOOT UPON THE MOON
> JULY 1969, A. D.
> WE CAME IN PEACE FOR ALL MANKIND

At bottom were the signatures of the three astronauts, Neil A. Armstrong, Michael Collins, and Edwin E. Aldrin, Jr. And, of course, Richard Nixon, identified as president of the United States.

"We found a few other items, as well." He handed me a sheet of paper listing them. A display screen from an early starship, a radio from the Mars colony, spectacles from an unknown source. (It's hard to believe people once ran around wearing those things.) Several other items. But they were all insignificant in comparison to the plaque.

"We're donating everything to the Winnipeg Science Museum. In Garnett's name."

"You could never have kept it secret."

"I guess not," he said. "I don't know what we were thinking. Anyhow, we're making sure that Alex gets some credit, too. Both of you."

"I just do the paperwork," I said.

Heli got out of her chair and extended her hand. "Congratulations, Chase."